ADAM HAMDY

Black 13

MACMILLAN

First published in 2020 by Macmillan
an imprint of Pan Macmillan
The Smithson, 6 Briset Street, London EC1M 5NR
Associated companies throughout the world
www.panmacmillan.com

ISBN 978-1-5098-9912-8

9 8 7 6 5 4 3 2 1

A CIP catalogue record for this book is available from the British Library.

Typeset in Scala by Jouve (UK), Milton Keynes
Printed and bound by CPI Group (UK) Ltd, Croydon, CR0 4YY

Visit **www.panmacmillan.com** to read more about all our books
and to buy them. You will also find features, author interviews and
news of any author events, and you can sign up for e-newsletters
so that you're always first to hear about our new releases.

For all those who've suffered the
terrible consequences of hate

In memory of Kyle Wollerton

Prologue

Nathan Foster had put plenty of bodies in the ground. A tally was tattooed on his forearm in pompadour blue. Whenever he was asked its meaning, he'd lie and say it represented the year of his birth: 87. His beginning, rather than the end of so many souls. He'd marked himself with the digits to commemorate his service because he'd thought his reaping days were over. That was before he'd met the lawyer and been reeled in by her silky words.

The lawyer had found Foster in the grey, shrinking life he'd fallen into. Civilian. It was a word he always wanted to punctuate with a gob of spit. He'd throttled brave men, drilled bullets into women, and guided bombs towards children so civilians could drift through life, swilling cheap booze and gorging themselves on even cheaper food. In truth, he despised the men and women he'd been paid to defend. Their easy days and trivial worries were no more than imitations of life. A battery farm existence: being fed and fattened until clogged arteries or black cancer took hold. Real life was to be found chasing the thrill of adventure, a razor's edge from death. Not dwelling in the ever-dwindling grey space that now confined him.

His poky office had only seen the mundane: a suspicious wife in need of proof of her husband's infidelity or an employer who wanted a background check on a job applicant. Poky jobs for his poky new life. And then the lawyer had swept in like the blazing afternoon sun banishing morning drizzle. She'd known more about him than she should: units, deployments, operations, all of which made him ponder her connections. She'd capped her smooth patter with the offer of enough money to keep him in cigarettes and vodka for years to come. All he had to do was look into a bank.

And look he had. And found he had. And now he was scared. This wasn't the vibrant thrill of adventure that had so often brought him to life. It was a numbing terror he hadn't felt since childhood, the ancient dread of creatures lurking in the shadows. He'd found things that made him, a man marked with a record of 87 kills, tremble, and now he was getting the proof. In a little over a month, the world would be changed forever. Until he had proof, he couldn't bring himself to believe the looming horror and had simply told the lawyer he was on to something big. The people he was investigating had real reach, making it impossible to go to the police. The lawyer had assured him that once he had the evidence, her anonymous client would know what to do. She must have sensed his fear, because she'd offered to double his fee and had told Foster that her client had sufficient power to protect him from the consequences of whatever he'd found.

The client, the client, the client, he thought as he crept along the corridor in his dark green overalls. He should have done some digging. He should have followed the lawyer, bugged her, tried to find out who she was working for, but he'd been so seduced by her promises of danger and glory that he'd ignored the niggle, which had become a nag and was now a mantra. *The client, the client, the client.* They say knowledge is power, but the knowledge he was about to steal was death, and he didn't have the slightest hint of the identity of the person he'd be giving it to. Foster resolved to hold onto the evidence, to use it to bargain for two things: more money and the identity of the lawyer's, and ultimately his, client.

The black boots he'd bought from a discount shoe warehouse clumped along the polished floor, but there was no one else in the building to hear. The cleaning shift had ended at 3 a.m. and he'd hidden in a store cupboard while the rest of the crew had filed out of the bank, signing their names on the security sheet next to their inbound scrawls. He'd faked writing his name when he'd come into the building so that if the security guards checked, they'd find a perfect match between those coming in and those going out. A simple and effective ploy that gave him the freedom to roam the building for a few hours until the first of the square-jawed, perfectly coiffed wannabe Rockefellers strode into the bank to begin another twelve-hour shift of real-world Monopoly.

A wall of glass lay to his left, displaying the deserted, brightly lit interior of the neighbouring skyscraper, the Leadenhall Building, which loomed over Number 1 Undershaft, the headquarters of Bayard Madison Bank. Foster was twenty-seven storeys up, but that was no longer high enough to see clear sky in London, and the stars that hung above the jagged skyline were only visible in a small space to the north of the wedge-shaped tower.

Like a trapeze artist caught in that moment of perfect inertia at the apex of a jump, neither rising nor falling, an impossibly still London was about to tumble into new day. In the quiet streets and empty offices lay the promise of things to come, the thrill of the possible imbuing those now-lifeless spaces with ripe potential. Foster had always preferred the dead of night to the tumultuous day. In the stillness lay hope, the prospect that one day everything might go just right. Bustling daylight only illuminated how wrong everything was. And there weren't many things more rotten than what lay in the server room at the heart of the twenty-seventh floor.

Foster hadn't told the lawyer what he'd found, but he had finally answered her questions about his old comrade. She'd kept pressing for details on Pearce, and the excitement she'd exhibited when he'd pointed her towards Thailand led Foster to suspect that he hadn't been top of the lawyer's list of investigators. He didn't take the slight personally. Even among the select group of people with Foster's experience, Scott Pearce was a legend. He hoped his brother-in-arms would forgive the betrayal, and if things got as ugly as he feared, there was no one Foster would rather have standing by his side.

Foster continued along the glass-walled corridor until he came to a heavy door. Two nights ago, he'd lifted the wallet of one of the bank's directors in a nearby bar, colliding with the unsteady man who'd been headed to the toilets to relieve himself of the best part of a £500 bottle of champagne.

Foster had left the bar, found the nearest storm drain and tossed the wallet and everything in it, apart from the key card, which he now swiped over a reader. Three thick deadlocks snapped back in sequence, and he pulled the handle, slowly opening the heavy door to expose the temperature-controlled corridor that lay beyond.

The huge windows were replaced by solid grey walls on either side. Foster continued along the corridor a short way until he came to a wide space that lay at the heart of the building. A few feet away stood row after row of black servers, housed in racks that stretched from floor to ceiling, their red operating lights solid and unblinking like the eyes of so many devils. The powerful machines were inside a huge glass sarcophagus that could only be breached through the single door that lay round the corner to his right. As he approached the turn, he caught a glimpse of something through the server racks. Not something, someone. Adrenalin surged, jacking his heart from 60 to 140 in the space of a beat. He could start reaching for his gun, or he could try to brazen it out. He opted for the latter, but it wasn't until he rounded the corner that he realized his mistake.

There wasn't one person, but two, and they weren't building security, but something else entirely. Something terrifying. One of the men was about his height – six two – but he was carrying more weight than Foster, maybe another ten or twelve kilos. Black hair sprouted from his head in short ragged tufts as though he'd cut it himself. His hands were balled into fists, and there, between each knuckle, was the glint of metal. The man had implanted steel studs into his hands, enhancements that were more than cosmetic; they were permanent knuckledusters. A single word was tattooed on his forehead in ragged black cursive script. It read, 'Salvation'.

His partner was an inch shorter, but carried even more muscle. His face was concealed beneath a navy-blue hoodie. They were either C-Brigade or, worse, Black 13.

'Nathan Foster.'

Shit. They knew his real name.

'We recognized you from the meetings, brother,' the man said, the last word passing his lips like a curse. '*Mortem secreto.*'

Black 13. Foster felt his legs go weak. *They were from Black 13.*

He'd been so careful infiltrating their world. He hadn't been allowed into C-Brigade or Black 13, but he had joined their feeder network. Truth be told, he sympathized with much of what they stood for, but not this. Not this evil. What they had planned was truly horrific.

'The mistake you made was lingering,' the man continued, lowering his hood. His head was shaved, which made the ancient acid scar that covered the left side of his face seem even more angry and raw. He was possibly the ugliest human being Foster had ever seen. 'Coming to the gatherings of the brethren. Casing this place like some rookie villain,' he gestured at their surroundings. 'Ripping off the boss's card. You think we can't spot a bad 'un?' he smiled, exposing a maw of rotten stumps.

Foster eased his right hand towards the lapel of his boiler suit. Tucked in a holster beneath his left arm was his fire-breathing pistol, and with it, he would put these two down.

'Go on then,' the Scarred Man said, and Salvation sprang forward with a roar.

Foster gave up any pretence of subterfuge and thrust his hand inside the suit, his fingers coiling around the familiar grip. He never took his eyes off the monster who was surging forward, but as Foster pulled the pistol from the holster, he realized that he wasn't going to make it. The beast was fast, and all seventeen stone of him was hurtling forwards at tremendous pace. Foster ducked the first punch, his hand and pistol still trapped inside his boiler suit. He wasn't so lucky with the second and the cold steel studs cracked his cheek with the power of a mule's kick.

One punch. One punch and he was swimming. The room warped around him, as though the world lay at the bottom of a swimming pool. He tried to move, and managed to get the gun out, but he was slow, too slow. An uppercut caught him in the chest, knocking the air out of his lungs. The gun flew from his hand, and bright lights speckled his vision as the ugly faces of his two attackers loomed over him. The men grabbed him, dragging him back the way he'd come. He tried to fight, but his arms and legs were unresponsive, the sense knocked clean out of them. The monsters were taking him, and if he didn't do something quickly, they were going to kill him.

As they passed through the security door, Foster kicked the Scarred Man just below the knee, catching him cleanly with his heel. It was a blow that was designed to incapacitate, but the disfigured man simply looked at Foster, his half-melted face and one milky eye impassive.

'You think I don't know pain?' he asked.

He didn't wait for a reply, but instead followed the question with a headbutt that almost knocked Foster cold. The world swam, and shapes melted and merged, the two faces of his assailants forming a single ugly creature that dragged him across the corridor towards the huge windows.

No. No. No. Not this.

Foster cursed his weakness, but even in the face of these monsters, he still couldn't quite believe his life was in danger. This was the financial district of London, not Kabul. After eighty-seven kills in war zones that stank of misery and rotten death, he couldn't meet his end here in this safe, civilized city, investigating a bank. Foster fought, struggling with all he had, but his attackers held him fast until the last possible moment when he felt the release, first of one set of thick sinewy fingers, and then the other.

Foster tried to stop himself, but angry momentum kept him going. There was slight resistance when he hit the glass, and he thought the window might hold, but he was too heavy and had been thrown too hard. The window shattered and he fell through it.

He was an experienced skydiver with over a hundred blasts – parachute jumps – to his credit, and he knew that terminal velocity blackout was a myth designed to make high-jump suicide seem less horrific. The brain stayed functional throughout freefall, as his did now. He felt the sickening pull of gravity as he plummeted earthwards. His two attackers became tiny figures in the shattered window, their heads craned to watch him fall. Foster's legs kicked, searching for purchase, and his hands clawed at air. He screamed, and the faces of many of the men, women and children he'd killed flashed through his mind. They were ready to welcome him.

But he wasn't ready to meet them. Not yet. He hit the paving slabs with a sickening crack.

Sky.

Stars.

Broken.

Bleeding.

He had no idea how long he lay, numb with shock, but when his brain finally regained some capacity for thought, Foster realized he couldn't move. His skull was glued to the concrete. His arms and legs wouldn't respond and his breaths were shallow, rapid and faltering. He had no doubt he was bleeding profusely, both internally and externally, and was certain that without medical intervention, he'd die.

Sound. Movement nearby.

He tried to speak, but all he could manage was a nasty wet rasp that rattled around his throat.

A shadow, then a face. He tried to recoil, but there was nowhere for him to go.

The Scarred Man stood over him, and his large companion loomed the other side.

'You want me to do anything?' Salvation said, the June breeze catching his black tufts.

The Scarred Man shook his head and produced a pack of cigarettes. He lit one and dragged deeply. 'No need. He's on his way.'

Foster wanted to scream. He longed to reach up and kill these two men, but his eyes seemed to be the only parts of him still working, so all he could do was stare as they watched him die.

Finally, when the Scarred Man had finished his smoke, he tossed the butt onto the ground beside Foster's head.

'Come on,' he said. 'I've seen enough.'

The two men backed away, leaving Foster with nothing but the horrific sound of his own rasping breaths, which faltered as he was inexorably pulled into the Reaper's cold embrace.

Part One

Chapter 1

Scott Pearce leaned over the bow of the long-tailed boat and watched the water roil against the stem. Balmy air brushed his skin, clean and sweet, tinged with the scent of freshly churned sea. The rattle of the boat's engine was the only thing that disturbed the perfect quiet. The water ahead was calm and still, and the bright afternoon sun made the gentle swells shimmer like the scales of a fish. The browns and greens of distant tropical islands were blown out by the light, like faded watercolours painted on the azure sky. One shape loomed clearly, jutting out of the sea like a weathered mushroom, its base narrow, its summit bulbous and almost entirely covered in thick jungle. No more than 300 metres wide, the tiny uninhabited island of Kok Arai lay directly ahead. Pearce could see the familiar limestone scar on its north-western edge, where a column had been cleaved from the island. His eyes started picking out his route.

'Last one?' Ananada yelled from the stern.

The short, sinewy boatman had his eyes fixed on the island, his calloused leathery hands gripping the tiller.

'Yeah,' Pearce called back. 'Last one.'

Lek, Ananada's tiny son, smiled at Pearce. The black-haired boy sat beneath the purple canvas canopy that covered the middle of the boat. Lek was threading tiny stones and coral onto wire, making bracelets to be sold to the tourists who usually travelled on the twenty-five-foot craft. Both father and son were bemused by the lone foreigner who chartered their vessel every Saturday afternoon, paying them to take him out to the islands, which were almost entirely deserted. As far as Lek and Ananada were concerned, Pearce was just another eccentric who paid over the odds to have private access to some of the world's best climbs. They were oblivious to the truth that he was out here searching these islands, trying to find the next link in a long chain that had led him from the violent streets of Islamabad, through Bangladesh to Bangkok, before finally bringing him to Railay, one of the most beautiful places on earth.

Pearce's knee-length shorts were almost dry, and he could feel salt pulling his skin tight as the last of the seawater evaporated. He checked his climbing shoes, which were perched on the tiny foredeck. The La Sportiva logo had almost worn away but the rubber hadn't perished. They had a couple more months in them. Pearce slipped them on, welcoming the chill of the damp chamois leather.

'OK,' Ananada shouted as he cut the engine.

The boat slowed, bobbing gently in the deep water. They were forty feet from a rope ladder which hung six feet above the waves, dangling from a teardrop of rock.

'*Xȳā tāy*,' Lek said, as Pearce got to his feet.

Don't die.

'I won't,' Pearce assured him, cracking a smile.

Lek replied with a cheeky grin.

Pearce dived into the water and broke into a crawl when he surfaced. Within moments, he was at the frayed old ladder and he clambered up, following in the footsteps of the bird's nest harvesters who'd installed it long ago. They could never have imagined that the treacherous limestone they'd braved in pursuit of food would become such a draw for climbers.

Pearce's muscles ached as he pulled himself onto the first ledge. He turned to face the sea and stretched his arms out, grabbing the tips of his right fingers with his left and pulling them back towards him. He swapped hands and repeated the process, trying to stretch his solid flexors. Across the water, on the boat, Ananada was crouched next to Lek, the two of them working on trinkets, occasionally glancing in his direction. Lek threw him a friendly wave, and Pearce responded in kind before turning to face the rock. The ledge ran off to his right towards the easy routes, but he wasn't interested in the well-worn climbs with holds that had been polished to an icy shine by so many hands. He'd already explored that part of the island and had found nothing. He was interested in a plateau that had been cleaved from the rest of the island and could only be reached by climbing a tricky overhang and treacherous vertical face.

Pearce squeezed a tiny pinch directly above him and placed his dripping-wet right foot on a tiny nub by his left knee. It was an awkward start, and the climb didn't get any easier. Pearce didn't set much store by grades, but people said the route was rated 8B. In all the time he'd been searching the islands, he hadn't heard of anyone making it to the top. Wet shoes and no chalk were the reasons why he had never topped out. Or so he told himself. The summit wasn't visible from the sea, which was one of the reasons Pearce was so keen to reach it. If there was a cave or hollow up there, it would be the perfect hiding place for gunrunners to store their shipments, and it was those smugglers who were the next link in the chain that had led him here. His source in Bangkok had said that one of the men Pearce had killed in Islamabad, a Thai national, had previously worked with the smugglers who operated in this region, running weapons from northern Malaysia into Thailand in an attempt to foment sectarian unrest. Pearce had heard whispers of strange vessels seen around the islands at night, of a fisherman who'd disappeared a few months ago, his body never found, his boat discovered, abandoned, drifting.

Pearce had little doubt he was on the right trail and if he could find one of the smugglers' caches, he could stake it out and follow them to whoever was calling the shots. But there were dozens of islands within an hour of Railay and each was covered by thick jungle that hid a multitude of caves and crevasses. The cleaved plateau of Kok Arai was one of the few places Pearce hadn't been able to explore, and he'd decided this would be his last free attempt. If he didn't summit today, he planned to return the following week with ropes and would haul himself up. The use of ropes would raise questions with Ananada and Lek, who knew him as a free solo purist, but he would put dents in the sanctity of his cover if he had to.

Within minutes, Pearce was halfway up the route, at the top of the sheer face, about to begin his climb of the overhang. His left toe was jammed into a cubby where a bird would once have made its nest. His right foot was pushed against a thin ledge. The index and middle fingers of his left hand were inside a tiny hole, his arm almost at full stretch, forty-five degrees above his head. His right hand was free, and was reaching for the first positive hold on the overhang. If he fell from this position, he was almost certain to hit rock on his way into the sea. He glanced over his shoulder to see

Ananada's boat bobbing in the water far below and Lek's tiny face poking out from beneath the canopy. His fingers crawled across the face until they felt the opening of a deep jug. He clenched them tightly, gripping the rock, and the tension ebbed out of his left hand.

He brought it up for a positive hold slightly above the one he held in his right. Robbed of his weight, his feet swung free and for a moment he hung, suspended above the water. Even with ropes, this would be a difficult ascent. If the gunrunners were using Kok Arai to hide shipments, there would have to be at least one expert climber in their ranks. Someone who could access a jib or hoist that might be concealed on the plateau.

Pearce turned his body and his taut abdominal muscles rippled as he lifted up his feet and pushed his shoes against positive features in the rock. His arms burned, but it was a soreness he was accustomed to. He kept moving, crawling up and then along the overhang, until he was at ninety degrees, parallel to the sea, which was some fifty feet below. A breeze cooled him, carrying with it the ripe smell of the jungle, but it wasn't enough to hold back the sweat of exertion. Moisture pricked every inch of his trembling body, gathering in his close-cropped hair, and Pearce knew he didn't have long before his fingers lost their grip. He climbed on, moving without haste or panic, creeping carefully across the rock, his sinews straining, his muscles bulging, propelling his six-foot-two frame forward. He was a yard from the edge, within reach of the slab that marked the final stage of the climb. One more move and he'd be as far as he'd ever got.

He braced his feet against two half-inch protrusions and let his left arm take the load, before releasing his right and reaching carefully for the nasty crimp that marked the spot where he'd fallen last time. His fingers pinched the three-inch wide grab and he sent his left hand forward, fast and deliberately towards a cubby on the very edge of the overhang. He was off-balance and his legs didn't have positive purchase. Convinced he was about to fall, Pearce flailed for the hold and found it. His legs swung out, but the cubby turned out to be a solid jug that enabled him to take his weight on his left arm. He swung wildly, his legs flailing beneath him, but his left hand held firm and he steadied himself.

Pearce pulled himself up and peered at the vertical slab above him. There, two feet higher than the cubby, was a beautiful, wide horizontal crack. He threw his right arm up and slapped his hand into it. Finding it flat and positive, Pearce raised his right foot to a knot of rock at the bottom of the slab. He released his hold on the cubby and moved his left hand up to the crack. Three or four more moves and he could top out. After the effort of the overhang, the sun felt good against his tanned skin, drying the sweat. Clinging to the crack, Pearce took a moment to catch his breath, and immediately regretted his decision. The knot of limestone snapped off, and his foot dropped. His arms weren't tensed to take the sudden pull of gravity. His hands slipped over the cool rock inside the crack, and he fell away from the slab, tumbling through the warm air, plummeting towards the water.

He landed hard on his back, the sea slapping him with the force of an angry midwife smacking a newborn baby. He sank beneath the surface, the air bubbling from his lungs.

Pearce cursed as he kicked for the surface, rubbing his back. He burst into the world gasping, his heart pounding with the exhilaration of the fall. The rock hung high above him, the features that had supported him so small they were almost invisible.

'Maybe next time, English,' Ananada shouted, craning over the side of his boat.

'Yeah, maybe,' Pearce agreed, swimming towards the vessel.

'You didn't die,' Lek said.

'No,' Pearce concurred. 'No, I didn't die.'

Not today, he thought, hauling himself into the boat.

Chapter 2

Railay Beach was as close as most people get to paradise. The half-mile crescent of golden sand curled between
two jungle-capped limestone cliffs. The southern cliffs jutted
out further than the beach, creating a natural breaker that
kept the water in the bay as calm as a garden pond. Inland,
beyond the beach, a handful of resorts lay hidden in lush
jungle which spilled everywhere. A few tourists in shorts and
bikinis lounged on the sand, while others criss-crossed from
one bar to another. Even at its most crowded, Railay was still
a peaceful place, and Saturday afternoons were far from the
busiest this beach got.

Ananada ran the boat onto shore, and Pearce grabbed his
small backpack and jumped barefoot into the shallow water.
He slung the bag over his shoulder, took the hawser that was
coiled on the prow and hauled the boat up the sand. Ananada
and Lek both jumped down and pushed the stern, and within
moments the vessel was safely beached.

'Thanks,' Ananada said, wiping his hands on his shorts.

'No problem,' Pearce replied. 'I'll see you next week.'

'Bye, English,' Lek called after him.

'Stay well, boy,' Pearce shouted back.

He started across the beach, already thinking how he was
going to excuse the ropes he'd have to bring on their next

outing. The soft hot sand massaged his feet as he continued towards the metal arch that marked the start of Walking Street, an avenue of low huts that snaked into the jungle. He picked his way past a gathering of tourists clustered around the food stall to his right. The aroma of grilled fish and rich spices set his stomach growling, but he wanted to find out about tomorrow's shift before he got anything to eat. He'd gone unnoticed in Railay by posing as a guide, working for a degenerate but highly respected Australian climbing veteran.

'Hey, Bobby,' a voice yelled, and Pearce turned to see Nam, the gap-toothed, ever-jolly barman of the Cocoloco, the large, ramshackle hut that lay to his left.

No one here knew Pearce's real name; he was Rob or Bobby.

'How's it going, Nam?' Pearce responded.

'Busy, busy,' Nam said, gesturing at the bare-chested men and bikini-clad women who crowded his bar.

Pearce walked on, following the crooked avenue past food stalls, souvenir and climbing shops. High palms loomed above the narrow passageway, and tourists clustered around displays of hats, postcards and menus, choking traffic in the bottlenecks. Pearce pushed on to reach Top Climbing, a small shack that was nestled in the armpit of a two-storey guesthouse.

Andy, the grizzled, sixty-something owner, sat outside the shack sharing a joint with Decha, one of the whippet-thin local climbing guides.

'Good day?' Andy asked, his eyes wide and unfocused. The Australian spent life in a purple haze and Pearce had no idea how the unreformed hippy kept track of business. 'Or should I say g'day? That's more Oz, right?'

Decha grinned and handed Andy the joint.

Pearce shook his head. 'What have you got for me?'

'You've been bought and paid for, mate,' Andy replied. 'Bloody lucky bastard.'

Pearce wasn't in the mood for the old stoner's jokes.

'Some Sheila's bought two weeks of private guiding,' Andy continued. 'Says she wants you to teach her how to climb. She's waiting for you in the bar.' He nodded towards the neighbouring guesthouse.

'Give her a special service,' Decha leered.

'If he doesn't, I bloody will,' Andy laughed, and the two men continued to make lewd remarks as Pearce wandered out of earshot.

A middle-aged couple were tucked in the corner, silently nursing huge cocktails. They had the look of people who'd come to Railay by mistake, their soft pink flesh already bright red, their flabby arms and spindly legs disqualifying them from any climbing. There were a few every week: sun seekers who looked at the brochure photos of the beach without realizing that almost everyone who came to Railay was here for the rocks. Most of them ended up like these two, glued to the rattan furniture that was standard in the local bars, or stuck on sunbeds at the beach.

The only other person in the room was an auburn-haired woman who was dressed like a gap-year student. She wore loose khaki combats, white canvas trainers and a green halter-neck. Her tousled hair fell to her shoulders. It was a decent attempt, but something about her felt wrong. She wore the new and expensive clothes uncomfortably, as though she'd lifted them from someone else's wardrobe, and her meticulous make-up was at odds with the weathered, windswept ethos of Railay. She was sitting on a stool by the bar, head bowed, eyes fixed to the screen as her thumb danced across her phone.

As he wound round the empty tables towards her, Pearce became aware of a familiar sensation. He called it the Reaper's chill, but his former comrades had other names for it: spidey-sense, shitstorm stink or the FUBAR alert. It was a feeling that had kept Pearce alive countless times, and he knew better than to ignore it. He eyed the red-haired woman carefully, looking for signs of danger, but she was lost in her phone and oblivious to the world around her. The sunburned couple were in sandals, shorts and T-shirts, and had nowhere to hide any weapons. Pearce's eyes flickered to the windows, and through the stream of passing holidaymakers, he saw two Thai men across Walking Street. They were watching the guesthouse. One of the men was smoking, and the other, a sour-faced man with an all-but-shaved head, was leaning against the trunk of a tall palm tree. The skinhead had two punkish fins of purple hair above his ears. His neck and hands were covered in messy jailhouse tattoos. Both men wore loose fitting T-shirts, khaki combat trousers and boots, rather than the bare chest, shorts and flip-flops favoured by locals. Despite the dark sunglasses stuck to their faces, Pearce could tell their eyes were fixed on the redhead at the bar.

'You all right, Bobby?' a voice asked from his rear, and Pearce turned to see Lamai, the beleaguered bar manager, enter. She was carrying a case of Fanta.

'Let me help you with that, Lamai.' Pearce plucked the case from her arms and ferried it to the bar, placing it on the counter next to the redhead.

'You're a kind man,' Lamai said gratefully. 'Thank you.'

'You're welcome,' Pearce replied. 'I'll have a mango juice when you get a moment.' He turned to the redhead, who was studying him. 'The name's Bobby. I think you're waiting for me. Something about teaching you how to climb?'

Up close, Pearce could see she had bright blue eyes and alabaster skin that was only broken by a few freckles clustered at the bridge of her nose. She offered Pearce her hand.

'My name's Melody Gold,' she said. 'And yours isn't Bobby. It's Scott Pearce.'

He tensed, his senses alert, as though someone had spiked him with a dose of pure adrenalin. No one here knew his real name, which meant she'd brought the dangerous knowledge with her.

'Relax, Mr Pearce,' Melody continued. 'I am here to hire you, but not to teach me how to climb.'

But he couldn't relax. He'd taken such care to remain anonymous and undetected in the two years he'd been following the trail from Islamabad and now here was this stranger blowing his cover. Almost as worrying as her presence was the question of how she'd acquired the knowledge. There were only three people in the world who knew where he was.

'What do you want?' Pearce asked.

'I'd like you to look at this,' Melody replied, pushing her phone towards him.

On screen, he saw grainy footage of a stretch of concrete paving slabs. Near the top edge of the image, two men stood either side of a third, who was lying on his back. One of the two dropped a cigarette before they both walked away, leaving the prone figure alone.

'A little over a week ago, this man fell from the twenty-seventh floor of a bank in London,' Melody explained sombrely. 'He didn't die immediately,' she indicated the slight movement in the man's right arm. 'Those two men came and watched him for a while and he died a short time afterwards. His body was finally found forty minutes later by a passer-by who called an ambulance.'

Melody withdrew her phone. 'The police are treating it as a suicide. According to their initial investigation, the man was a private investigator who was struggling to make ends meet. They believe he was moonlighting as a cleaner and that his money woes finally got the better of him.'

'That was no suicide,' Pearce observed. 'Those two guys—'

'The police say they most definitely weren't good Samaritans,' Melody interrupted, 'but that there is no evidence linking them to the man's death.'

Pearce scoffed, and cursed the parts of his brain that had already started working on the puzzle. 'You family?' he asked.

'I'd like you to find out how he died. And why.'

Pearce stared at the woman, hating her for coming here with his real name and risking his cover and entire investigation. 'I don't know where you got your information, Miss, but I've never heard of Scott Pearce. My name's Bobby. I'm a climbing guide. Wouldn't have the first clue about something like this.'

'Don't you recognize him, Scott?'

The use of his name jarred like nails down a chalkboard. He was about to deliver an angry reply when she thrust her phone at him again and tapped the screen.

'His name's Nathan Foster,' Melody said. 'I believe you served with him.'

Pearce gazed at the screen in disbelief. The image quality was terrible, but as he watched the prone figure lie twitching on the slabs, he could almost have believed it was Fozz. He now knew how Melody Gold had found him. Fozz was one of the three people he'd trusted with his location, and if this stranger was telling the truth, he'd lost a good friend. Pearce felt a pang of grief as he recalled Nathan Foster, sometimes reckless, often brash, always bold. Pearce was saddened by the thought the man on the screen might have been his larger-than-life comrade.

Pearce swallowed his emotions and looked up to find Melody staring directly at him, almost daring him to call her a liar.

'I don't know who you are, but you've got the wrong man,' he said, backing away.

Melody stood and pressed forward. 'I've got the right man, Mr Pearce.'

Lamai flashed Pearce a concerned look. She only knew him as Bobby, a quiet man who had nothing to do with booze, drugs or women. Here was this stranger calling him by a strange name and talking about strange things. He cursed inwardly. His cover was blown. Bobby the climbing guide was of no more use. He would have to leave Railay.

'I'm going,' Pearce told Melody. 'And your goons will regret it if they try to stop me.'

Melody hesitated. 'What goons?'

Pearce glanced out of the window at the two men leaning against the palm.

'What are you talking about?' Melody asked. 'I'm alone.'

She followed his gaze and caught sight of the men watching them. The confusion on her face wasn't fake, and Pearce immediately realized they were in serious trouble.

Chapter 3

All it took was an almost imperceptible nod of the head and Pearce knew that the smoker had registered that he and his buddy had been made. Smoker nudged his tattooed companion and the two men started towards the guesthouse, pushing by the criss-crossing tourists.

'We need to get out of here,' Pearce told Melody.

'Who are they?'

'You're asking me?' Pearce took her arm.

She resisted and reached for a small rucksack that was tucked beneath her stool. She slung it over her shoulder and followed Pearce through the bar.

'You OK, Bobby?' Lamai asked from behind the counter.

'All good,' Pearce said, as he and Melody went left into a narrow corridor that ran to the rear of the building.

Somewhere on the top floor a TV blared canned laughter down the staircase behind them. A dog was barking out back, and the smell of galangal and lemongrass wafted from the kitchen. Pearce hurried towards the metal gate that stood at the end of the corridor. Beyond it lay a tiny yard and an alleyway that ran to the lot where his motorbike was parked.

Light fell through four open doorways ahead of them. The kitchen and a dirty toilet were to the right, and a staff room and store were to their left. K-pop blasted from a radio in the kitchen, and Pearce's eyes almost started watering from the pungent haze of onion, garlic and spices that drifted though the doorway. He glanced over his shoulder and saw the two men mounting the porch that ran around the building. They were almost at the front door.

Pearce sensed movement ahead and turned to see an unfamiliar man leap from the kitchen, a huge knife in his hand. He slashed at Pearce. Some skill, but not enough. Pearce confounded his assailant by stepping forward as the man's knife arm swung wide. He drove his fingers into the man's throat, striking the larynx with all the force he could muster. The knife clattered onto the tiled floor, and the man staggered back and collapsed against the wall, choking.

Pearce grabbed Melody and pulled her forward, as their two pursuers burst into the building. He could hear the men's boots thudding across the tiles as he barrelled through the metal gate, dragging Melody behind him. The warm air hit him, ripe with the putrid stench of rubbish wafting from a dumpster that stood a few feet away. A fat man with a buzzcut was milling beside it, smoking.

As Pearce and Melody tumbled down the short run of steps into the yard, Buzzcut flung an arm behind his back. Pearce was in no doubt the man was reaching for some kind of weapon and rushed to meet him. Buzzcut didn't disappoint, and, as his hand swung into view, Pearce caught a blur of black metal: a pistol. Pearce didn't break stride and delivered a punishing front kick to the man's solar plexus with the heel of his right foot. The gun flew clear, and Buzzcut groaned as he stumbled back, winded.

'Hey! Stop!'

Pearce turned to see Smoker shouting from inside the

guesthouse. He and his purple-haired buddy were a few feet from the metal gate. Pearce lunged for the fallen pistol.

'Down!' he yelled at Melody, who ducked instinctively when she saw him rising with the gun.

He fired two wild warning shots over her head, and the two men retreated. Pearce sensed movement and turned to see Buzzcut coming forward. No time for pity, he thought, delivering a roundhouse with the butt of the pistol. The heavy gun hit the foolish man in the temple, knocking him cold.

'Come on!' Pearce yelled at Melody, and he turned towards the alleyway that led to the car park.

He stopped in his tracks when he saw shadows surging along the ground, and an instant later, four men came into view. There were two more prison-tattooed gangsters in combat trousers and boots, but more worrying were the peaked caps and grey uniforms of the two police officers who ran behind them.

Pearce couldn't get to his bike.

'Stop!' one of the police officers yelled.

'This way!' Pearce said, pushing Melody in the opposite direction.

She ran ahead of him, crossing the yard and pressing through the rough undergrowth to the rear of the neighbouring shacks. Pearce heard a clang of metal and glanced over his shoulder to see the guesthouse gate rattling shut and Smoker and Purple Hair sprinting down the steps to join the pursuit.

'*Hyud!*'

There was no way he was stopping, no matter how many times the police officers commanded him to do so.

Melody collided with a startled man who'd popped his

head out of a shack, and their flight came to an abrupt halt as she tried to dance round him.

Pearce raised the pistol and fired a couple of shots above their pursuers' heads, forcing them to take cover. He pushed the startled man back into his shack and urged Melody on. They turned right, edging down a narrow rubbish-strewn gap between two huts, and moments later they burst onto Walking Street. Someone screamed, and Pearce caught wide eyes all around him as people registered the gun. Shock turned to flight, and the crowd started running in every direction in a desperate attempt to stay clear of him.

'Stop them!' a voice yelled, but none of the tourists wanted to play hero, and Pearce and Melody ran on.

They sprinted under the metal arch onto the beach, and Pearce searched for some way to escape. He wasn't about to get into a shoot-out with the Thai police. The tide was receding, stranding the long-tail boats on the hot sand. There was no way he and Melody had time to push one down to the shore.

'Over there!' Melody said breathlessly.

She pointed to a boat that was on its way in, and Pearce sprinted towards it.

'Get out!' he yelled at the boat's occupants, a trio of tourists and Niran, one of the local captains Pearce vaguely knew.

All four of them registered the gun and the pursuing men. The tourists froze in shock and only Niran had the wherewithal to act. He threw the engine into reverse and there was a moment of inertia as the propeller fought against forward momentum.

Pearce had to get that boat.

He fired a shot into the air as he splashed into the water. 'Get out!' he roared.

The gunshot snapped the tourists back to reality and they all jumped overboard, stumbling in the shallow water.

'This boat is my life,' Niran growled, taking the betrayal very personally.

'Sorry,' Pearce said as he clambered aboard. 'I'll be careful with it,' he added, as he waved Niran off.

The angry captain dropped into the surf and Pearce pulled Melody into the boat, before diving to the tiller. He threw the throttle open and the engine roared as Smoker and Purple Hair ran into the water.

Smoker produced a pistol and aimed it directly at Pearce, but one of the police officers barked something at him, and the sour-faced man didn't take the shot.

Pearce stared at Smoker, holding his gaze as the boat pulled away. When they were a hundred feet out, beyond the range of pistol fire, Pearce swung the tiller, putting the beach well behind them.

'Who the fuck are you?' Pearce demanded, bearing down on Melody.

She scrabbled away from him, along the bench seat beneath the boat's green canopy. She checked her surroundings nervously. They were in a cove to the west of Koh Ya Wa Sam Island, a tiny atoll about eight kilometres from Railay Beach. Pearce kept his eyes open for any sign of the coastguard. If they had police on their payroll, it wouldn't be beyond the reach of Smoker or whoever he worked for to send a cutter to search the islands. Thankfully, there was no one in sight.

Melody's eyes turned to the pistol that hung by his side.

'I told you,' she replied fearfully. 'My name's Melody Gold. I'm a lawyer. I work for Denton Fraser. It's a law firm.'

She took off the backpack and raised her hands to indicate she wasn't a threat. Pearce nodded and she unzipped the bag and reached inside for her purse, which she handed to him.

Pearce flipped it open, and found pockets packed with credit cards, a gym membership, a driver's licence and business cards. Her name and that of her firm matched what she'd told him. Her cream business cards were thick with gold embossing, the mark of a company with money to burn.

'Who sent you here?' Pearce asked, throwing the purse back.

'I don't know,' she replied.

'You don't know?'

'I get my instructions from one of the senior partners. He's working for a client who doesn't want to be identified.'

Pearce sat on the bench opposite Melody. 'How did you find me?'

'We've been looking for you for a while. Nathan Foster wouldn't tell me where you were . . .' she hesitated.

Pearce shrugged. 'But?'

'He found something that scared him,' Melody admitted.

'Fozz? Scared?' Pearce asked. He struggled to imagine Foster being afraid of anything. 'Scared of what?'

'We'd hired him to look into Bayard Madison. The London investment bank,' she explained. 'He found something. He wouldn't tell me what, but it shook him up.'

'And got him killed,' Pearce observed. 'He was my friend,' he added, recalling Foster's exuberance and broad smile. He sat silently for a moment, gazing beyond her. 'I can't ever go back there,' he said, gesturing north towards Railay.

'I'm sorry,' Melody said.

'No you're not,' Pearce replied. 'I've been working a lead for two years and you've just blown it. Fucking amateur.'

Melody's eyes flashed with anger.

'If Fozz was murdered it was only because his killer didn't need anything from him. Didn't need to know who he worked for, or what he was doing,' Pearce suggested. 'That means they knew he was working for you. My guess is they've been following you to try to find out who's giving you orders. They're tying up loose ends.'

Melody's anger melted into dismay.

'Yeah. And now they probably think you and I are working together,' Pearce continued. 'Like I said: fucking amateur.'

He hesitated, figuring out the implications of what had just happened. 'You need to warn your boss, the one who's been giving you orders. His life may also be in danger.'

Melody took out her phone.

'This is the last time you use that thing,' Pearce told her.

Melody nodded and dialled. There was a long pause. She mouthed 'voicemail' at Pearce. 'Gabe, you need to be careful,' she said at last. 'There were men—'

Pearce snatched the phone. 'I don't know who you are but your life is in danger. Get yourself somewhere safe and wait to hear from her.' He hung up and threw the phone overboard, noting Melody's anguished look when it hit the water.

'You're going to tell me everything. What you know about me, what you told Fozz, what you wanted him to do,' Pearce said to Melody. 'We're going to London. I'm going to find out who killed him.'

Clearly relieved, she nodded slowly.

'Don't get the wrong idea,' he cautioned her. 'I'm not doing this for you. I'm doing this for Fozz. He was my friend. Besides, there's nothing here for me now. You've seen to that.'

Chapter 4

Gabriel Walker knew he was dead the moment he opened the door.

He'd spent the past week regretting ever agreeing to help with the investigation into Bayard Madison Bank. His commute had once been a short respite from the chaos of family life and the pressure cooker of the office. In recent days it had become a source of anxiety. He believed he was safe at home, but Dulwich Station – with its hard platform edges and speeding express services – made him feel vulnerable. Then there were the crowded carriages, with bodies pressed all around him. How easy it would be for someone to slip a knife between his ribs and walk away without him ever seeing their face. Or a heavy hand on the back, pushing him head first down the escalators at Old Street. He'd thought about taking a taxi to work, but travelling alone in a confined vehicle with a driver might be more dangerous than his nerve-racking trips on public transport.

His only consolation was that the people who had killed Nathan Foster would probably want to know who he was working for. If they had connected Foster to him, they would want to go further up the chain and find out who was giving Gabriel orders.

Gabriel heard his young children playing in the garden,

and couldn't believe he'd been so reckless. He'd been sweet-talked by a modern day Sun King, an untouchable man who had more money than half the world's population combined, a man who'd sold Gabriel on the dream of making a differ-ence. Gabriel hadn't required much persuasion. Crossroads, his Santa Monica school, had imbued him with an inde-pendent streak, teaching him that one person can change the world. This activist philosophy had been nurtured by his years at Cornell University, and then indulged by his firm, Denton Fraser, who knew that high-profile pro bono work helped bolster its image. He'd met Jessica, his captivating wife, at a party following a march against global warming, and they'd raised their three children in affluent but deter-minedly activist Greenwich Village until Gabriel had been seconded to London.

He'd put it all at risk. Everything. Not only his life, but the lives of his wife and children. Ever since Foster's death just over a week ago, Gabriel had been thinking more and more about his family and had tried to spend as much time with them as possible. This was meant to be one of those occa-sions. He'd even done the unheard of and switched off his phone – no emails, voicemails or social media for the whole day – giving his family his full attention. It should have been a warm, carefree Saturday afternoon. Instead, he was stand-ing on his doorstep, looking out at the two men who heralded death.

'Mr Walker?' the shorter of the two men asked. He was about Gabriel's height, five ten or so, but about twice as wide. He had no neck – his head simply emerged from his shoulders – and Gabriel noted that he looked ill at ease in his shiny grey suit, as though his muscles were straining to break free of the constricting fabric. When the squat man rubbed his shaved head, Gabriel caught sight of the edge of an intricate tattoo on his wrist. 'Gabriel Walker?'

Gabriel nodded. The taller man had light brown hair that had been shaved at the back and sides to create a tuft at the top of his head. He was thin, almost gaunt, and had the pinched angular face of a fighter. He too looked as though he welcomed his suit about as much as a rash.

'My name's Detective Sergeant George Dawson,' the bald man said. 'I'm investigating the death of Nathan Foster. I believe he was doing some work for you.'

Acid rushed up Gabriel's throat and he thought he might be sick. This man was not George Dawson, the detective in charge of the investigation into Nathan Foster's death. Gabriel had been paying great attention to the case, and had run a background check on the real George Dawson, so he knew what the detective looked like. He was most certainly not a shaven-headed thug. More disturbing than the fact this man was impersonating a police officer was the revelation that they had connected Gabriel to Foster. That was never supposed to happen. Gabriel had told Melody to instruct Foster to keep no record of his engagement. He had taken great care to only ever exchange information with Melody verbally, never setting anything in writing, so there could be no record of his involvement. He thought of her now, another idealist, easy to win to the cause with talk of doing something good. He owed her an apology. She'd wanted out after Foster's death, but Gabriel had talked her into rolling the dice one more time, going after their first choice, Pearce. If these men had got to Gabriel, there was no doubt they'd also got to Melody. Maybe that's how they knew he was involved? A wave of nausea washed over him as he thought of Melody being tortured for what little information she had. He'd made a mess of so many lives, and if he didn't do the right thing now, he'd ruin so many more.

'You need to come with us,' the heavyset man continued, 'down to the station to answer some questions.'

Gabriel heard Samantha's laugh drift through the house. The sweet sound of his daughter counteracted the weakness in his knees. It reminded him of what he needed to do. If he fought, tried to resist, these men would rush into his home, storm through the kitchen onto the patio, where they would grab Jessica, Samantha, Ellis and little Jamie and hurt them until Gabriel told them what they wanted to know. If he ran to the police, his family, his beautiful family who now loomed so large in his thoughts, but had been inconsequential when he'd made the foolish decision to get involved in the investigation, they would be taken and killed. There was only one thing he could do to beat these men and keep his family safe.

'OK,' Gabriel said, preparing himself for the hardest thing he'd ever done. He walked through the front door and shut it behind him.

A lump formed in his throat as he realized he'd never see his family again. He'd been on marches, protests, fundraisers, signed petitions, campaigned, but nothing he'd ever done could even compare to what he was doing now. This was good, he told himself, this was real good. A sacrifice that would keep his family safe. He thought of Samantha and her passion for telling stories, Ellis's ambition to be a helicopter pilot, and Jamie, who just liked kicking footballs. He couldn't bear to think about their lives without him, but hoped they wouldn't be too damaged by the loss. And then there was Jessica: sweet, kind, engaging, everything he could have hoped. Wife. Friend. Lover. She would never want for anything, his life insurance would see to that, but he knew she'd be wounded by the bereavement and couldn't stop himself from picturing all the sadness that was about to spill from this foul moment.

The two men said nothing as they fell in beside him and walked down the stone steps, through the beautifully land-scaped garden onto the pavement. Gabriel looked at the tiny tufts of grass and moss sprouting through the cracks between the slabs. It reminded him of the Jeff Goldblum line from *Jurassic Park*: 'Life finds a way.'

Not this time, he thought bleakly. Life had no way.

'Over here,' the skinhead said, indicating a Volkswagen van with blacked-out windows that was parked to their left.

Gabriel nodded and walked towards the vehicle, his stom-ach churning. He could feel his whole body trembling, and his mind tried to trick him into a last-minute betrayal of his family by suggesting there might be some other way. But there wasn't. He'd spent the past week thinking about what he'd do in the event these men or others like them came to his door, and he knew this was the only way to keep his family safe. The price was high, but he'd done enough deals to know it was a fair one. And it came with the bonus of keep-ing his client's identity secret.

Resigned to his fate, Gabriel surprised the two men by breaking into a sprint as they neared the van. As he raced past, he caught a glimpse of a woman with albinism in the driver's seat. She jumped out and joined the two men who were now giving chase.

'Oi!' one of them yelled, but Gabriel didn't bother turning round.

He kept running, the sound of their footsteps pushing him faster. He shot across the street and turned the corner onto Melford Road. He felt a hand on his shoulder and lashed out, his fist connecting with something soft and fleshy. He heard a groan and the hand released its grip. He glanced over his shoulder to see the woman and the broad, shaven-headed man pass the younger guy, who was clutching at his face as he tried to run on. Gabriel sprinted, the wooden fence beside him becoming a blur of lines, the hedge that sprouted above it nothing more than a haze of green.

He ran down the hill, praying he could maintain the lead he'd established. He caught sight of a woman in the window of one of the low red-brick apartment blocks that flanked the end of the road. She gave the briefest puzzled look at the sight of a man being chased by three people, but then withdrew from the window. 'None of my business' was standard practice in a big city, and Gabriel wished he'd heeded the mantra. But it was too late now. He was running for his life, but not in the way his pursuers thought.

'Stop!' the woman from the van yelled, her voice coloured by a strong French accent. 'Stop right now!'

Gabriel ignored her and sprinted towards the corner with Lordship Lane, one of the busiest roads in the area. His lungs burned as he wove round a woman pushing a pram up the hill. He looked along Lordship Lane and saw what he needed. He raced past the tapas restaurant where he, Jessica and the kids had enjoyed so many fun meals, and ran across the street directly into the path of a double-decker bus.

Chapter 5

Pearce was as restless as a bull trapped in a rodeo pen. He looked out of the plane window and saw the city of Manchester far below, shining in the evening sun, a sprawl of skyscrapers, old industry, Victorian terraces and modern residential estates. The cathedral stood equidistant from City's stadium to the east and United's to the south. After a week in Bangkok, Pearce longed to be on the ground, finally free to pursue his objective. The lawyer leaned round him to see through the window. They'd hardly spoken since the attack at Railay Beach. He could tell it had shaken her, but Pearce had little sympathy. Melody Gold had barged into his world, blown his cover and, most damningly, was probably responsible for roping Fozz into an investigation that got him killed. Nathan Foster might not have been the best soldier, but he was one of the bravest. He always volunteered to be first in, last out, nearest the heart of darkness, and he did it all with a brash confidence that people mistook for arrogance. Once, when he and Pearce had been deployed in the Democratic Republic of Congo, Fozz had confided that his bullishness stemmed from a desire to confound death.

'If I'm going to meet the bony old fucker,' Fozz had said, 'I don't want him to know I'm afraid.'

Pearce wondered whether Fozz had been afraid as he lay

dying on a patch of London pavement. He pushed such bleak thoughts from his mind and instead considered what he'd learned since they'd been chased out of Railay. As they'd journeyed north, following the coastline in the boat he'd stolen from Niram, Pearce's mind had clouded with suspicion and he'd found himself wondering whether the lawyer was indeed what she seemed. There was no proof that Foster was dead. The video footage was too grainy for a positive identification. Pearce had considered the possibility that she'd been sent to disrupt his investigation and lure him into a trap. But her responses to the attack had seemed natural, and she'd sat at the bow of the boat in stunned silence, occasionally looking as though she might cry. Mastery of emotions was essential for an operative, and no matter how genuine she seemed, Pearce had reminded himself he couldn't trust her.

They'd travelled until the appearance of the first stars, when, protected by the cover of darkness, Pearce had steered the boat towards a cluster of lights that twinkled on the shore. They'd reached the Bulan Anda Baba Resort, a large hotel complex. Abandoning the boat on the beach, Pearce had led Melody inside, where they'd bought her a garish T-shirt, bright red shorts and a pair of flip-flops from the gift shop. She'd put up some resistance when he'd told her to get changed, but had buckled when he'd explained that they couldn't take the chance she had a tracking device in her clothes.

When she'd emerged from the ladies' toilets looking every inch the clueless tourist, Pearce had convinced Melody to ditch her bag and all her belongings for the same reason: they weren't sure how she'd been followed and couldn't bet against the possibility of electronic surveillance. She'd reluctantly dumped everything in a bin by the lobby phones, and

Pearce had led her out of the hotel to a dimly lit layby full of taxis and mini-buses. He'd sounded out a couple of drivers and found one, a leathery, middle-aged man with a face puckered from years of chain smoking, who'd welcomed them aboard his bus, one of a number of regular shuttles ferrying seasonal workers home to Bangkok.

When they'd arrived in the city, Pearce had left Melody in a cafe on the Silom Road. She'd been worried he was abandoning her, but he'd reassured her that he'd be back, saying that if nothing else, he needed her to tell him in detail how and why she'd hired Nathan Foster. Mollified, Melody had waited while Pearce had gone to a high-rise office block on the Charoen Krung Road where CB Lockers rented out safety deposit boxes. After confirming his identity, he'd retrieved his 'exit bag', a small backpack he'd stored there when he'd first come to Bangkok. Inside the backpack were a false passport, driver's licence and credit cards in the name of James Edgmond, along with cash and two loaded Berettas. He'd returned the guns to the safety deposit box and left the building with the rest. Years of experience had taught Pearce the wisdom of secreting an exit bag in any potentially hazardous location, and it was one of the first things he did upon arriving in a new city, paying for ten years' storage up front. Paranoid, but alive, he now had twenty-two exit bags stored around the world.

He'd returned to Melody, who made no attempt to conceal her relief. After a short detour to buy her some new clothes, they'd gone to the small apartment building on Song Wat Road, which had been his home when he'd arrived in Bangkok the previous year. The owner, a small, wilted old woman called Kannika, lived in the ground-floor flat and rented apartments to tourists. Kannika had remembered Pearce and greeted him and Melody warmly, offering them a two-bedroom flat on the top floor of the three-storey building.

They'd stayed for six days and rarely ventured out. Pearce had been into the city twice, to see an old contact, Chuan Pitsuwan, Pitsu to family, friends and the fighters he coached. Pitsu ran the Sor Vorapin Muay Thai Gym, but had a previous life as a field agent and recruiter for the Thai National Intelligence Agency. Pearce had met him while working on a joint British–Thai operation, and the two men had bonded over a shared love of martial arts. Months earlier, Pearce had taken a coaching job at the gym and Pitsu had helped him chase down the link between Islamabad and the gunrunners operating off the coast of Railay. Pearce now turned to the old agent for a false passport for Melody.

Pearce had stopped in an Internet cafe on the way back to the apartment to email a photo of Melody to an address Pitsu had given him. He'd also taken the opportunity to do some research into Nathan Foster, and had discovered that his old friend and comrade was indeed dead. His instincts had told him that Melody had been telling the truth, and external confirmation only made him numb. Sitting in the Internet cafe, Pearce had recalled the footage Melody had shown him of the two men standing over his old friend, watching him die. Pearce had made Fozz a silent promise that he'd find those men and make them answer for what they'd done.

Pearce had then turned his attention to Melody, and further online investigation revealed that she seemed to be who she said she was. She had a professional profile on the Denton Fraser website, and the social media presence of a successful singleton living in London; she'd been tagged in a few photos at a wedding, a couple of parties and a trip to Royal Ascot by a seemingly real network of friends. If it was a cover, it was a good one and to truly test it, Pearce would have to dig deeper. He would need expert help to run a thorough background check on Melody and to assist with the investigation of Bayard Madison Bank. He would also need help keeping Melody safe, so he'd used secure emails to reach out to two people he could trust, before returning to the apartment.

Over the following few days, Pearce had tried to talk to Melody about Fozz and the investigation into Bayard Madison Bank, but she'd refused, saying she'd only reveal details when she was safely in the UK. Pearce realized he'd given her the idea when he'd left her at the cafe. She now knew he wouldn't abandon her as long as he needed the information she held.

So they'd spent their days in the apartment speaking very little, trying to find meaningless ways to pass the time. They'd played a lot of cards and slept a great deal, and finally, after six days, Pearce had returned to the gym to collect the passport. He'd thanked Pitsu and had immediately taken Melody to the airport where he'd purchased two tickets on an Emirates flight with a stopover in Dubai. Their false passports had held up to scrutiny and within a few hours they'd been airborne, finally heading for Manchester.

'My boss, Gabriel Walker, asked me to find you. He'd been given instructions by a client whose identity I don't know,' Melody said as the aircraft continued its descent.

Pearce could almost sense her relief at seeing the familiar British landscape. They were as good as home.

'Gabriel had been given instructions to locate you and hire you to look into Bayard Madison. When I couldn't find you, we went to the number two choice, Nathan Foster.'

'I was first choice?' Pearce asked, wondering how he'd made it onto the radar of Melody's mysterious client.

She nodded.

'Why were you looking into the bank?' Pearce asked.

'I don't know. I'm not sure Gabriel does either. After Nathan died, he seemed genuinely shaken. He said we needed to find out what Nathan had discovered to make sure our lives weren't also in danger,' Melody replied.

'And Foster never told you what he'd found?'

Melody shook her head. 'He said it was something big, that he was going to bring me evidence. He said he wanted to make a trade. Maybe he was going to ask for more money.'

Pearce tapped the arms of his seat thoughtfully. 'You don't know anything,' he said. 'And if you weren't such an amateur, you'd have realized you're just a pawn in a very dangerous game. You're a liability and a problem and your life is almost certainly in danger.'

Melody blanched.

'You're a link to whoever instructed you,' Pearce continued. 'You're a link to me. These people have killed already. If they're so minded, they'll take you, make you tell them what little you know, and then eliminate you.'

Melody was jolted back as the wheels touched the runway. She looked as though she wanted to be sick.

She said nothing as they went through immigration and customs. When they reached the arrivals hall, Pearce tried to steer her towards the car hire desks, but she resisted.

'I need to call Gabe. I want to make sure he got the message,' she said, moving towards the payphones.

Pearce glanced around and saw no danger in the people who filled the busy arrivals hall. He followed Melody to the phones and watched her dial.

'Hello, Mrs Walker, is Gabriel home?' she asked. Her face went white as she listened to the reply. 'I'm so sorry,' she said, before hanging up. She turned to Pearce, her distress palpable. 'Gabriel Walker is dead.'

Chapter 6

Pearce had seen the reaction before. Melody was sitting beside him, hunched against the passenger door, her eyes distant, her face taut and grey with distress. She hadn't said a word since learning of Gabriel Walker's death and had simply followed Pearce to the Hertz rental desk, where he'd used his James Edgmond credentials to hire a silver BMW 325i. He'd shepherded a shocked Melody to the vehicle, helped her into her seat and set off, leaving the airport and heading west on the M56. By nine thirty, they'd reached the A41 and were driving south. Off to their right, the westering sun hung low, casting a golden glow over the green fields that lay either side of the snaking road.

Pearce noticed the black Ford Mondeo just north of Milton Green. It was a couple of vehicles behind them, and something about it didn't feel right. The right wing kept poking into the median as though the driver was looking to overtake, but despite having a clear run, the Mondeo stayed where it was, lurking behind the intervening cars. The glare of the sun against the windscreen made it difficult to see inside the car, but Pearce discerned the shapes of two occupants, both male. He waited until he was approaching a hairpin, then threw the BMW into second and accelerated past the car in front. The driver of the lorry that came round the bend was

startled to see a car on his side of the road and stepped on his
brakes, as Pearce swerved into a tiny space ahead of him. The
lorry driver signalled his disapproval by giving Pearce a prolonged blast of his horn. As Pearce turned into the bend, he
heard another horn blast and looked in the rear-view mirror
to see the lorry's brake lights flare bright red as it slowed
to avoid the Mondeo, which had copied Pearce's dangerous
manoeuvre. There was little doubt they were being followed.
Whoever it was had some training, but they weren't very
subtle.

'What's happening?' Melody asked. The terrifying manoeuvre had roused her from her dark thoughts.

'We've got a tail,' Pearce replied.

Melody looked over her shoulder.

'Two cars back. Black Mondeo. Two men,' Pearce told her.
'I can't see their faces.'

'How?' she asked.

It was a very good question. Unless there had been a bird in
the sky, a satellite tracking them, they couldn't have been followed from Railay. Once they'd ditched Melody's belongings,
any electronic devices would have been rendered useless.
There was a remote possibility Pitsu had betrayed them, but
if he had, Pearce would have expected them to be picked up in
Bangkok. Pearce had only just noticed the tail, but it seemed
likely the Mondeo had been on them since the airport, which
meant the men in the car probably had their flight information. If someone was watching for Melody, they'd be able to
use photo recognition technology to alert them when a traveller used a passport with her image, but that was high-level
systems work that required coordination between government
agencies, something that only MI5, MI6 or GCHQ would be

capable of. If the photo in Melody's false passport had flagged an alert, the fifteen-hour flight would have allowed plenty of time to arrange a tail. And if the men in the Mondeo were from the Box or Six, they'd also have tied Pearce to Melody and identified him from his photo.

'We need to find out,' Pearce told her, slowing to take the next left turn.

He steered the BMW onto a narrow country track that ran through a small wood. The high branches of the trees met far above the vehicle, casting the road in shadow. Pearce stepped on the accelerator and the car shot forward, springing from the shadow into sunlight as the trees gave way to large fields of wheat. Pearce glanced in the mirror and saw the Mondeo follow.

'They're coming,' Melody observed nervously.

Pearce shifted down a gear and the engine roared as the car surged forward. With all pretence lost, the Mondeo accelerated to keep up as Pearce pointed the BMW into a long, sweeping bend. His heart skipped when he saw a huge combine harvester looming ahead. He stamped on the brakes and swung the wheel, aiming for the driveway of a farmhouse. The car fishtailed, but Pearce countered the skid and slid into the space moments before the combine was on them. The shocked farm worker scowled at them, but his attention was immediately caught by the Mondeo, which screeched to a halt inches from the jagged teeth that hung from the huge machine.

Pearce jumped out of the car and saw the driver of the Mondeo, a broad, squat man with huge shoulders and a shaved head, try to restart the stalled vehicle. His companion was a tall, thin man, with light brown hair that had been shaved at the back and sides. He stepped from the vehicle when he caught sight of Pearce.

'What the hell are you playing at?' the ruddy-faced farm worker called down from the cabin of the combine harvester.

Pearce ignored him and vaulted the drystone wall that separated him from the Mondeo. The guy with the light brown hair adopted a fighting stance, hunching slightly, turning to one side and raising his arms into a tight guard. He clearly had some training. Pearce ran between the Mondeo and the combine, and ducked as the boxer threw a punch. He barrelled into him, putting all his weight behind his shoulder and sending the guy tumbling backwards. Pearce felt blows on his back, but Boxer was falling and couldn't muster any real power. The man collided with the road, and Pearce rolled clear and came up quickly, snapping out with a couple of punches that caught the man in the face. Boxer's eyes went wide, losing focus, and Pearce smacked him again, delivering another pair of blows that sent him sprawling. He fell onto his back and his eyes rolled up into his head.

'Don't you fucking move!' the bull-necked driver said, brandishing a pistol at Pearce from the other side of the Mondeo.

Pearce sensed movement and caught a glimpse of the combine driver tumbling out of the cabin and running away. Bullneck was also distracted and made the mistake of glancing at the fleeing man. Pearce took the opportunity to duck behind the car, moving as close to it as possible. A couple of loud reports tore the silence and bullets whipped over his head as he crawled round the vehicle. When he heard Bullneck clamber onto the bonnet, Pearce broke cover and ran for the drystone wall. Shots rang out as Pearce plucked two large stones from the top of the structure. He turned and flung one of the stones in the general direction of the gunfire.

His aim was about a foot off, but the attempt had the desired effect, causing Bullneck to duck for cover behind the Mondeo. Pearce sprinted round the car and brought the second rock crashing down on the man's head before he got the chance to get another shot away. Both Bullneck and Boxer were out cold, lying almost head to head, sprawled flat on the tarmac.

Pearce knew he didn't have long before the police arrived. The combine driver would almost certainly have called them by now. He was trying to figure out how best to transport the two unconscious men to a place where he could interrogate them, when he heard the sound of an approaching engine. Pearce turned to see a Land Rover Defender coming down the lane at speed. The driver was a woman with albinism, her shock of white hair shining in the bright sunlight. Her passenger was a man with short dark hair and the sharp features of a raptor. These were no casual country drivers. They were approaching with purpose, and there was recognition in their eyes. Raptor was readying a pistol, and Pearce glanced down to see Boxer stirring. Four against one wasn't good odds.

Pearce crouched down and rifled through Bullneck's pockets to find a wallet and phone. He pressed the phone against the man's thumb to unlock it and activated the camera. He snapped pictures of the two unconscious men and leaped through the gap between the combine harvester and the Mondeo as the Land Rover neared. Pearce found Melody standing beside the BMW, craning to see past the giant combine.

'Get in,' he yelled, as the Land Rover screeched to a halt behind him.

Pearce jumped into the driver's seat as Melody complied. He threw the BMW into first and steered it through the gap between the farmhouse wall and the combine harvester. As they re-joined the road to the rear of the abandoned vehicle, Pearce saw Raptor running round the huge machine, pistol raised. The BMW gathered speed, and Pearce saw the man take aim, but they were already out of range. The man lowered his gun and watched them with contempt before turning back the way he'd come.

Pearce followed the road east, racing along the narrow lane, finally slowing when he felt he'd put safe distance between them and their pursuers.

'Who were they?' Melody asked.

'I don't know,' Pearce replied. *But I soon will,* he thought, glancing down at Bullneck's phone between his legs.

Chapter 7

Home. Or the closest to it I'll ever know, Pearce thought as they drove into the valley. Melody was asleep beside him, her head lolling with each bump in the road, her skin silver in the moonlight. He looked down the deserted country lane towards the rough track that led to his house and felt relief. He wasn't sentimental, but there was something reassuring about the familiar view.

Pearce had been homeless since the age of six, when his mother had abandoned him to Camden Council Social Services. He'd been known by a different name then, and had bounced around the city and then the country from one foster family to another, a time he'd come to know as 'the wilding' when his behaviour had steadily deteriorated. Later in life he'd realized that he'd been reacting to the profound rejection and had become disagreeable, unruly and violent to make sure that no one would ever want him. He'd continued on this dark path until he'd ended up at St David's, a tiny state boarding school near Newtown in Wales. St David's was the last stop for twenty-four troubled children drawn from local authorities all over Britain. If St David's couldn't turn them around, chances were they'd roll on to young offenders, prison or the grave. Pearce had been nine when he'd first met Malcolm Jones, the inspirational head teacher who had transformed his life. St David's had never felt like a home – it was closer to a Spartan academy where troubled youngsters were meant to be reshaped into productive citizens, their roughest edges smoothed away by Jones and his diligent staff. Much of the foundation of his life had been laid in St David's: his love of mountains, music and martial arts, and while he could never say that his years there were happy, they were better than the three that had preceded them. Pearce, ever the keen observer, had seen older children struggle to cope with the responsibilities of life after school, and many had drifted into unemployment, drugs or wound up in prison, so he'd learned from their mistakes and traded one structured environment for another, joining the army aged eighteen.

Since then his life had been a series of postings, deployments and missions, and then, of course, Islamabad. In the months that had followed his intervention in the city, Pearce had been hailed as a hero for thwarting a catastrophic attack, but his dogged pursuit of those involved – and his persistent belief that some as-yet-unidentified perpetrators had escaped justice – had resulted in him being derided as a conspiracy nut. His character had been assassinated by Six desk jockeys, and he'd effectively been forced out of the service. Since then he'd relied on his savings and the income he'd earned from his cover jobs to pursue the leads he'd found in Pakistan. He'd posed as a climbing guide in Railay, a boxing instructor at Pitsu's gym in Bangkok and a translator in Islamabad.

Pearce turned off the country lane onto the rough track that ran beneath wild, ragged trees. He owned the track and all the land between the road and the stone cottage that stood at the bottom of the valley. Pearce had bought the place shortly after he'd been recruited into the Increment, the specialist SAS

unit that provided operational support to MI6. His decision
to acquire the cottage had been driven by a growing unease
at the nature of his work. Ostensibly stationed at the Duke
of York's Barracks in London, Pearce had been travelling the
world on missions that were usually dangerous, deniable and
on the hazy grey edges of legality. He'd realized he needed a
bolt-hole in case things ever went sour, and St David's had
instilled in him a fondness for Wales. The cottage had the
added bonus of being close to mountains and crags that
offered great climbing. Taking advice from Kyle Wollerton,
the MI6 operations specialist who'd eventually lured him
from the Increment into Six, Pearce had purchased the cottage through an international web of shell corporations that
made it impossible to link back to him personally.

Ynys Dawel, or Quiet Island, as the cottage had been named
by some long-forgotten soul, was a nineteenth-century building constructed of solid Welsh stone. It lay in the fold of two
hills, near a stream that wound through the surrounding
woodland. Five acres of the woods belonged to the cottage,
along with twelve acres of the adjoining farmland. Beyond
the seventeen acres that were his own, Ynys Dawel was surrounded by hundreds of acres of forest and pasture. The
village of Llanfrynach was two miles away and Pearce's nearest neighbours were the Driscolls, a farming family who had
a large house half a mile to the north. They knew Pearce as
Steve Anderton and thought he worked in the oil industry.
He sweetened his relationship with the Driscolls by allowing
them to graze their sheep on his land and take lumber from
his part of the forest during his long absences on the rigs.

Pearce pulled to a halt when they reached the end of the
track. His yard was as he'd left it, the wooden gate closed and

the short wheelbase Land Rover Defender parked so as to block the driveway. Melody stirred as he cut the engine.

'We're here,' Pearce told her as he stepped out of the car.

He opened the gate and held it for Melody, who stretched as she followed him. They passed the Defender. The black paintwork had picked up some new rust patches since he'd last seen it. He paused by a cluster of stones that lay near the porch. One of them was a key safe, and he picked it up, wheeled the dials round to the correct code and took his keys from inside.

The cottage was dark and musty. He moved through the rustic three-bedroom property, drawing back the curtains and opening all the downstairs windows, welcoming the breeze. It had been over two years since Pearce had last set foot in Ynys Dawel, but he was reassured to see that nothing had been disturbed. The previous owner had done an exceptionally good job of renovating the property from a derelict wreck. The interior was a mix of exposed stone, painted plaster and original wooden beams. Pearce had furnished the place with second-hand pieces acquired for cash from dealers all over Wales. Nothing matched, but it worked well enough for him and, having no family of his own, he liked to think he'd inherited some of the history and spirit of the previous owners.

'I'll show you your room,' he said, leading Melody upstairs.

He gave her the largest bedroom, which had its own bathroom and overlooked the south fields.

'There are towels in the cupboard.' Pearce gestured at the large dresser he'd bought in Welshpool. 'I'll get the boiler running in the morning.'

'Thank you,' Melody responded.

He shut the door and walked to the other side of the house, eager for sleep.

Pearce woke shortly after dawn and crept downstairs into the yard, which was cool and shaded. He went to the brick shed that adjoined the cottage and got the old boiler running again. He returned to the cottage and quietly climbed the stairs to the bathroom, where he took a hot shower. After dressing in a black T-shirt and a pair of armoured motorcycle jeans, Pearce went downstairs, where he made himself a tea. He carried the steaming mug outside and crossed the yard to the garage, which was part of a row of outbuildings that stood opposite his home. Inside, Pearce found his silver Honda CBR 1100 Super Blackbird where he'd left it, under a tarp.

He spent about an hour fitting the battery, servicing the bike, changing the oil and checking the brakes and chain set. It was shortly before seven when the garage door swung open and Melody appeared wearing a pair of jeans and a white shirt.

'Morning,' she said.

'Morning,' he replied.

He turned the ignition and pressed the starter button, and listened critically as the bike came to life. The Honda roared, and the brickwork reverberated with its rumbling power, before the engine settled to a purr as it warmed.

'Did you hear that?' Melody asked over the noise of the motorcycle. 'It sounded like a car.'

Pearce cut the engine and moved past her into the yard. She stayed closed to him as they walked towards the gate. A rusty white Ford Fiesta was parked behind the BMW, and striding towards them was an old friend.

'Scott Pearce, you invisible motherfucker,' Wayne Nelson

said, smiling broadly as he opened the gate. 'Sorry I'm late. The chariot blew up on the M40.' He scowled at the Fiesta and indicated his jogging bottoms, which were covered in oil stains.

'Nelson!' Pearce called out.

He was as imposing as ever. At six four, he dwarfed most men, but it wasn't just his height that was so intimidating; his broad frame was encased in muscles, which were on full display, rippling beneath his tight blue T-shirt like strange creatures angry at their confinement. His dark skin, inherited from his Nigerian parents, was covered in even darker, intricate tattoos. Full sleeves ran the length of his arms, the designs further embellished since Pearce had last seen him. But that wasn't the most noticeable change.

'What the hell have you got stuck to your face?' Pearce asked, indicating the thick three-inch beard that clung to his friend's chin. He glanced round to see Melody relax as she realized the newcomer wasn't a threat. 'Melody Gold, this is Wayne Nelson. We served together.'

'Before you got all high and mighty and joined the best of the best,' Wayne mocked. 'Nice to meet you, Melody,' he added, offering her his hand. 'Or do you prefer Mel?'

'Melody,' she replied, her tiny hand lost in the folds of his huge grip.

'Bring it in,' Wayne said, turning to Pearce, his arms outstretched.

Pearce gave his old friend a hug. 'Let's go inside. I'll make some coffee and bring you up to speed.'

They sat around the farmhouse table with their mugs of sweet instant coffee. Wayne had listened silently as Pearce had briefed him.

'I heard about Fozz,' Wayne said once Pearce finished. 'Saw it in the news. I was gutted.'

'Yeah,' Pearce agreed. 'I can't believe he's gone.'

The two veterans sat in silence for a moment, remembering their fallen comrade.

'Sounds like we need to get rid of the rental,' Wayne suggested.

Pearce nodded. 'Whoever they were, they'll be looking for it. Maybe running the plate. You and I should take a drive and dump it. There's an old quarry with a deep pool about ten miles from here. We can roll it into the water.'

'And then?' Wayne asked.

'Sit with Melody,' Pearce said. 'Watch her until I send word.'

'I want to help,' Melody protested. 'Gabriel was my colleague. He was my friend.'

'You need to lay low for now,' Pearce responded. 'And we need to contact anyone close to you, friends, family. We need to warn them.'

'Why?' Melody asked.

'If these people can't get to you, they'll try to apply pressure elsewhere.'

Wayne nodded sombrely.

'My mum,' she said. 'She's my only family.'

'No one else?' Pearce asked.

Melody shook her head. 'My dad died a few years ago. Drink. Both my parents came from small families. Apart from Mum, I've got some distant cousins. And my friends of course. I'll make a list.'

'Good. Wayne will show you how to get in touch with them safely,' Pearce said. 'And we need to agree terms.'

Melody looked puzzled.

'You were sent to Thailand to hire me,' Pearce explained. 'Day rates, fees. Travel expenses. That sort of thing.'

'But I don't know who the client is,' Melody protested. 'And my firm won't cover the—'

'We'll agree the maximum Gabriel Walker authorized you to offer me,' Pearce interrupted. 'I'll make sure your client honours it.'

Melody nodded. 'OK.'

'Once we've dumped the car, I'm going to hit the road. We'll use the old numbers to verify any communication,' Pearce said as he got to his feet. 'I'm going to see an old friend from Six.'

'The Syrian?' Wayne asked.

'The Syrian,' Pearce replied.

Chapter 8

Ya Rub, Ya Rub, Ya Rub, Leila thought as she shifted uncomfortably on her stool. Her knee grazed her walking stick, which had been leaning against the bar, and it clattered to the floor. *Fucking brilliant,* Leila cursed inwardly, *result.* She looked at the expensive black Derby stick with its gold, onyx and mother-of-pearl collar and considered leaving it. Stooping wasn't an option, and even though the pub wasn't crowded, she had no desire to entertain the patrons with the strange contortions that would have been required to get her to ground level.

'Let me get that?' Toffee Boy remarked, as he bent to grab the stick.

Toffee Boy was one of three men in khakis and pastel-coloured shirts who'd come in soon after Leila. She'd given him the moniker because he looked the poshest of the trio and sounded like they'd force-fed him plums at Eton.

'Thanks,' Leila responded as she took the stick and leaned it against the bar.

'You're a bit young for one of these,' Toffee Boy observed, sizing her up. He started with her legs, which were wrapped in a pair of skin-tight black jeans. They were Leila's best feature, when they worked. His eyes moved quickly over her torso, which was concealed beneath a loose-fitting light jumper. He took in her black, wavy shoulder-length hair, before finally settling on her face. She could see him studying her Mediterranean colouring, her Greek nose, dark eyebrows and wide, opal eyes, and his expression shifted from attraction to awkwardness when he noticed the scarring around her neck and the flat section of her cheek, where the bone had once been broken.

'Battle scars,' Leila smiled. 'On good days, I can walk. On bad days, I need the chair.'

'Seriously?' Toffee Boy asked. 'Battle scars?'

Leila nodded and smiled mischievously.

'I'm Roderick.' He offered her his hand. 'What's your name?'

Leila was about to politely give him the brush-off, when she saw the familiar figure of a fallen legend. Scott Pearce stepped into the open doorway, motorbike helmet concealing most of his face. His leather jacket clung to him and he looked as strong and sharp as ever. Pearce didn't come into the saloon bar, and instead stood in the doorway and nodded at Leila, signalling that it was time to leave.

'I'm sorry, my friend's here,' Leila told Roderick, taking advantage of the easy excuse Pearce's arrival gave her. 'Thanks for helping me out.'

'No problem,' he replied, failing to conceal his disappointment. 'Maybe we'll bump into each other again?'

Leila smiled and got to her feet, hoping that her legs wouldn't betray her. She steadied herself against the bar, picked up her stick and shuffled out.

'Did I interrupt something?' Pearce asked, as she drew near.

'No,' Leila replied, clasping his arms affectionately. 'It's been too long, *ya hayawaan*.'

'Do you greet all your friends by calling them an animal?' Pearce asked.

'Only my close ones,' Leila replied. 'Come on. We've got a lot to talk about.' She pushed Pearce through the open doorway. Before she shuffled on, she glanced over her shoulder and caught Roderick watching her from the bar. *Flattering*, she thought, as her treacherous legs carried her unsteadily out of the pub, *but most definitely not my type.*

Anyone else, and Pearce would have offered a steadying hand, but Leila Nahum was proud and stubborn. She was also one of the strongest people he'd ever met. Twenty-eight-years-old, Leila had been raised in Raqqa, Syria. She was the youngest of six children born to a Muslim doctor and a Christian civil servant, and when war broke out, her family suffered terribly. The four eldest children had left home many years before, but Leila and her older brother, Ibrahim, had still been living in Raqqa with their parents. Ibrahim had been a tech-head with dreams of making it to Silicon Valley, but when conflict came, he'd joined the Free Syrian Army and was assigned to their tiny digital warfare team. Ibrahim had specialized in hacking Syrian government installations. Leila, who worshipped Ibrahim, had learned everything she could from him, and was soon involved in social media campaigns and running systems operations for the FSA. Everything had changed when Raqqa had fallen to ISIS. The extremists slaughtered Leila's father, Arfan, and her mother, Iqbal, and publicly beheaded all the soldiers in Ibrahim's unit. Leila had been forced to watch her brother's murder, and then she'd been compelled to marry one of the ISIS fighters involved in the massacre, an Egyptian called Moharram. Leila had never said whether

Moharram was the man who'd killed her brother and Pearce could never bring himself to ask.

For two years Leila had lived a pious life, satisfying the needs of her heroic husband. At least that's how ISIS propaganda presented it. In truth, Leila had been forced beneath the burka, into a harsh existence with a pitiless man, an existence that denied her true nature: she was, as she'd once drunkenly revealed to Pearce, gay. Pearce wasn't sure whether it was a legacy of his childhood, but he hated the thought of anyone, particularly women, forced to endure suffering alone. He'd often wondered whether his mother would have given him up if someone had been there to help her.

Leila had experienced nothing but horror at the hands of her husband and had been raped almost daily. In the beginning, when she'd resisted, she'd been brutally beaten, but she'd stopped fighting after she'd become pregnant. The hideous source of the child hadn't tempered the sense of responsibility she'd felt for its life. Moharram had died in a suicide attack two months before the child was due, and thirty days after his death, Leila had been married to another fighter, Raouf, a cruel man from Iraq. He had an ugly temper and fast, heavy hands. He'd beaten her every single day, and eventually the brutality had proved too much. Leila had gone into labour two weeks early and the child had been delivered stillborn. Leila never said whether it had been a boy or a girl.

She had almost lost her life during the horrific birth and came away with injuries that left her disabled. On good days, she could walk with the aid of a stick, but when the pain became intolerable, she needed a wheelchair.

Few people knew what had happened next. Once she'd recovered, Leila had returned home and played the dutiful wife. Raouf's temper hadn't changed and she'd accepted his brutal sexual and physical assaults without complaint. But each day, she'd prepared, and those preparations made his greasy, sweaty, stinking presence just about bearable. Then one night, when she'd made all the necessary arrangements, Leila had taken a sharp knife from the kitchen, slit Raouf's throat as he lay sleeping, and watched with satisfaction as he'd woken and clutched at the gaping wound, choking on his own blood. Leila's eyes had been full of tears when she'd recounted the tale, and Pearce had known that she hadn't been thinking about the man's death but rather the loss of the child who'd inspired such vengeance.

Leila had escaped the miserable apartment, fleeing into the night with a taxi driver who'd agreed to take her and two other women over the border into Turkey. From there, she'd travelled across Europe, doing whatever had been necessary to secure passage. She hadn't told Pearce much about the journey, but her eyes had become even more haunted as she'd glossed over the four-month ordeal in a few sentences. Along the way, she'd learned that her three eldest brothers had been killed, and that her only surviving sibling, her older sister, was missing. Her family was gone, destroyed by the war.

When she'd arrived in Dover, smuggled in the back of a lorry, Leila had claimed asylum. Her unique skills with computers, her fluency in English, French and Arabic, and her experiences in Syria brought her to the attention of the security services, and after a prolonged probationary period, she'd eventually been hired as a contractor for MI6, which is how she and Pearce had met. Neither of them fitted the common media portrayal of spies: the well-spoken, suave, public-school educated, middle-class graduate typically associated with Six. They were rough and rugged and had been through fire and pain to escape misery, dragging themselves up from nothing, creating such lives as they had through sheer invention and willpower. They recognized in each other the inner strength such journeys required and that mutual respect was the first step towards what had become a friendship. Their bond had been forged into something unbreakable when Pearce had saved her life during an operation. Leila had been running surveillance on a possible Russian spy ring and had been compromised. She'd been kidnapped by two Chechen loyalists who'd been planning to torture and murder her, but Pearce had found and killed the men before they could harm her, earning Leila's undying gratitude.

'I wondered if I'd ever see you again,' she observed as they walked slowly through the pub's small beer garden. The weathered tables were all occupied by people enjoying the warm evening.

'Sorry it's been so long,' Pearce replied. 'Where's your car?'

'The Peugeot.' She gestured towards a 3008 parked in the layby opposite, a few cars along from his bike. 'It's not sexy, but it takes the chair.'

'I'll follow you,' Pearce suggested.

He'd been to her house once before, shortly after he'd left Six. Leila had been a welcome confidant, believing in him when everyone else had turned their backs. The way Pearce had been treated had a profound effect on Leila, and she'd resigned soon afterwards. She was one of the few people in the world he could trust, but even she wasn't above his suspicion. The best operatives could be compromised or followed, which is why he'd suggested meeting in the pub so he could be sure she was alone. Before setting foot in the bar, he'd motored past the place four times and had then parked and spent five minutes just sitting on his bike, watching to ensure the pub wasn't the subject of surveillance.

Leila limped across the road, leaning heavily on her walking stick. Pearce mounted his Honda as she eased herself into the driver's seat of the Peugeot, grimacing as she finally swung into position. She took a moment to catch her breath before shutting the door, and Pearce felt nothing but admiration for this woman for whom such simple things were a painful ordeal. She rarely complained and pressed on with life as best she could.

Leila pulled out, heading west, and Pearce brought the bike to life and followed. A hundred yards up, Leila turned right onto a tree-lined residential street that wound into open countryside. Half a mile further, the road forked and she took the right branch, heading down a narrow private track that ran under the shadows of densely packed trees. They passed a couple of driveways, and continued on until the track came to an end by a set of black gates. They swung open and Leila drove through, onto the gravel driveway that led to her large Edwardian house. The elegant red-brick structure stood at the head of a semi-circular drive. In all, Leila had about three acres of Berkshire countryside, which was mainly given over to lawn and old woodland. Large oaks, elms and firs mingled in copses around the house, their fluttering leaves dappling the last of the sunlight, throwing red gold on the short grass. Leila had made her home in a picturesque, secluded part of England that was only an hour's drive from London. Another drunken revelation to Pearce was that she'd bought the place with the proceeds of an early investment in Bitcoin.

*

If the interior of Leila's home was a reflection of her soul, she was truly beautiful. The walls were painted seashell white, the floors were hardwood, the furniture warm and comfortable, and everywhere there were fine touches of her Middle Eastern heritage. Pearce could see a four-piece *mashrabiya* screen standing in one corner of the large hall, atop an ornate rug. Leila was a passionate if anonymous patron of the arts and framed contemporary pieces hung everywhere, each beautifully lit by its own lamp. She was fastidious and she and Pearce shared a common belief that it wasn't enough to do something; one needed to do it well. Pearce wondered whether her quest for perfection was born out of compulsion, or whether she'd surrounded herself with beauty to keep the ugliness of the past at bay.

'Have you eaten?' Leila asked as she put her cane in a stand near the front door. 'You look like a mangy alley cat.'

'Don't hold back,' Pearce scoffed.

'I won't. When was the last time you ate?' She moved down the hall, leaning against a long low wooden rail for support.

'I've been climbing. Weight is the enemy of height.'

'Climbing!' she snorted derisively.

'I could eat something.' Pearce admitted. 'Let me make it,' he offered, following her into the kitchen.

Leila threw him a deep frown, and he replied with a smile at her stubborn refusal to accept help.

Minutes later, the small radio on the windowsill was on and he was seated on a stool beside a marble counter, watching her propel herself around her kitchen, making chicken escalopes. She'd rejected a second offer of help and insisted he sit as she prepared a mix of crushed oats, matzo crackers, flour and spices, which she used to coat chicken breasts before browning them in oil and finishing in the oven. While they were baking, she shuffled over to the counter and took the stool next to him.

'Who got you the woman's passport?' she asked, referring to Melody.

'Are we safe?' Pearce replied, looking around the airy room.

'I sweep the place every couple of weeks,' Leila told him. 'Most recently this morning, in honour of your visit. So we only have to worry about directionals,' she continued, gesturing towards the garden which was now in shadow, 'but the radio should take care of that.'

She was right, of course. If someone was lurking in her garden with a directional microphone, the noise of the radio would be almost impossible to filter out, but Pearce still kept his voice low. 'Pitsu,' he replied. Leila was aware of the old Thai agent through her time with Six.

'I'm sorry about Foster,' she said.

'It was a bad way to go.'

'So this is personal?'

'Yeah,' Pearce conceded. 'They watched him suffer.'

'You're going to be taking on some real power,' Leila warned.

'What kind of power?'

'After we eat,' Leila said. 'I'll show you everything after we eat.'

Chapter 9

The chicken was delicious. Leila served it with fat-toush, and Pearce ate quickly, the first mouthful of food awakening his hunger. Leila talked of her time since she'd stopped working for Six. As far as the outside world was concerned, she'd embarked on a new career as an artist and had recently started to show locally. She confided she was also keeping her tech expertise current by taking on the occasional contract, specializing in the programming of artificial intelligence systems, a field that offered some of the most demanding challenges.

When the meal was finished, Leila led Pearce through the quiet house, past a large library, to a boot room and utility area. She grabbed a thick bamboo cane from beside the back door, and leaned on it as she went outside. They walked through the garden up a small incline, weaving around a cluster of old trees, until they came to a clearing. In the middle of the lawn stood a thirty feet by ten feet wooden studio. Pearce sensed movement as they neared the dark cabin and looked up to see bats darting around the sky. Leila punched a code into an electronic combination lock and opened the door.

'This is where I get to play artist,' she announced, switching on the lights as they stepped inside.

A three by two, partially completed painting rested on an

easel. Pearce recognized the image instantly: it was Leila's house, seen from a distance. In the middle ground, a solitary female figure stood, her head bowed, her back to the viewer. The branches of a circle of ancient oaks arched above the woman, their leaves breaking the soft sunlight, speckling her surroundings with shadow. Pearce examined the painting closely. The brushwork was precise, the oil paint delicately manipulated to create the illusion of depth and dimension. This was painstakingly fine art.

'I had no idea,' Pearce said at last, turning to Leila, who looked away bashfully. 'This is beautiful.'

'Come on,' she said, moving towards the other end of the room, 'we're not here to stroke my ego.'

Pearce followed her, carefully threading his way past a drawing board covered with preliminary sketches of the painting, tables laden with paints and blank canvases. Leila went to the far corner of the room and put her hand against a particular patch of the wall. A moment later, a section of the wall clicked open to reveal a concealed door.

'OLED palm reader,' she said as she limped through the opening.

Pearce followed, stepping inside a small room. Leila shut the door, plunging them into total darkness. He heard her shuffle further inside, and she switched on the lights to illuminate a ten feet by four feet computer room. A long bench lined the back wall, and on it stood five screens. The wall behind them was made up of large LCD panels, put together to form a single screen. Beneath the bench lay racks of servers and ancillary gear.

'It'd take a good eye to notice the interior and exterior dimensions of the studio don't match,' Pearce observed. He instantly noted the way his voice died against the walls of the small room and realized they were encased in black acoustic foam.

'Yeah,' Leila agreed proudly. 'I made the modifications myself. Pull up a seat.'

She gestured at three chairs that stood against the interior wall. She took the furthest and pulled it towards the bench. Pearce immediately tried to help, but was treated to a hostile scowl.

'*Ya ghabi!*' she told him. '*Balash.*'

You idiot, don't bother. Pearce's Arabic was as good as her English and she knew it.

She settled in front of the middle screen and switched on the server beneath it. Pearce took a seat next to her.

'I spliced into the cable box at the top of my road. The line runs through the woods, buried in about six inches of soil. Took a while, but it means that even if my counter-surveillance measures are defeated, any hostile will only ever trace the signal back to a line that doesn't exist.'

She typed a series of commands and the big screen came to life, filling with windows that displayed information about Nathan Foster, Melody Gold, Gabriel Walker and Bayard Madison Bank. As she spoke, Leila moved the pointer around the screen, highlighting relevant pieces of information.

'It looks like your lawyer is who she says she is,' Leila remarked. 'Her boss was a man called Gabriel Walker. Dead under a bus. An accident,' she observed sceptically. 'He may have been being chased. Witnesses aren't clear. He was Cornell alumni, ten years practising in New York before he moved to London. Wife and three kids. If he was a Company man, it's as clean a cover as I've seen. I can't find anything that points towards Agency recruitment or training, no breaks in his education or career, and his social media profiles tally perfectly with his official records. The CIA has got better at this sort of thing, but it's still not that good,' Leila said. 'So what the lawyer told you about him is probably also true: he was being directed by someone else.'

'Anything on who that might be?' Pearce asked.

Leila shook her head. 'Not yet. I'll need to access his phone and computer records.'

'And the bank?'

Leila brought up a selection of windows that displayed information on Bayard Madison. 'It's a private investment bank, similar to Rothschild's. It manages money for thousands of extremely wealthy people from all over the world. The client list is a who's who of power,' she revealed. 'We're talking serious connections. It's run by Lancelot Oxnard-Clarke.' Leila moved the cursor over a photograph of a slim, middle-aged man.

'Lancelot?' Pearce interjected.

'Lancelot Bayard Oxnard-Clarke, eighteenth Viscount Purbeck,' Leila responded theatrically. 'Old money, old power, a legacy of entitlement the English like to kid themselves doesn't exist any more,' she continued. 'His family has deep links to the Conservative Party. He's a major donor and he founded Lexicon, a right-wing think tank.'

'You find anything that might have got Foster killed?'

Leila shrugged. 'It's a bank with clients and investments all over the world. It would take years to examine everything it does.'

'See what you can do. Concentrate on any big changes in

the last couple of years,' Pearce said. 'I'll give you a percentage of my—'

'Do I look like I need the money?' Leila interrupted. 'I'm doing this for you.'

'If you want to volunteer, go to the local food bank. If you're working, you're getting paid,' Pearce countered. 'Give it to charity, or go to Vegas, I don't care.'

Leila shrugged. '*Tayeb, ya ragul,*' she conceded. 'I'll see what I can find.'

'I also need you to run a couple of IDs,' Pearce said, producing Bullneck's stolen phone from his jacket pocket. 'It belongs to one of the guys who attacked us on the way from the airport. I took some photos of the two of them. They'll be the most recent in the library. I removed the SIM, to make a trace more difficult.' He delved into his pocket and retrieved a tiny SIM card, which he handed to Leila.

'I'll crack it and run a search on the PNC for starters,' she responded, referring to the Police National Computer. She took the phone. 'I'll also do a full diagnostic. Pull any emails, call data, that sort of thing. Might be able to get some fingerprints, if you haven't mauled it too badly.'

'Good,' Pearce replied. 'Can you delve into the Box or Six and find a safe house somewhere near London?' MI5 and MI6 had a portfolio of empty flats and houses around the country, places where operatives could lie low, or sources could be debriefed.

'Sure.'

'Send Wayne the details. I want the lawyer close in case we need to put her in play.'

'I'll find somewhere tonight,' she replied. 'Do you want to stay here in the meantime? The spare room's made up.'

Pearce shook his head. 'Thanks, but I need to get some gear.'

Leila nodded and struggled to stand.

'Let me help,' Pearce said, hurrying over.

'*Ya walad!*' Leila brushed him away.

She reached beneath the bench and pulled out a small backpack. 'Here,' she said, handing it over. 'I've created a legend. Your name's David Rowland. You work for Albion Mutual, Foster's life insurer. And I've given you a little something I designed myself, a way for us to communicate.'

Pearce reached into the bag and pulled out a radio handset with an alphanumeric keypad. He frowned. 'A walkie-talkie?'

'No,' Leila replied irritably. 'It's a satellite communicator. A special one. It's unhackable. It doesn't use GPS and only transmits a signal when it sends or receives a message. A few years ago, Anonymous claimed it had developed an encrypted radio that used the old UHF ham packet frequencies. It gave me an idea – using the same principle, I've modified satellite phone circuit boards to act as transceivers, creating a secure link between two or more devices. The signal piggybacks on commercial satellites, and the data packets are so small no one will even notice them. Even if they do, they'll never be able to trace the origin or hack the encryption. I call it Ghostlink.'

Pearce looked at her blankly, 'So it's a walkie-talkie?'

Leila scoffed and elbowed him. 'A very good one. With global range, and it's totally secure . . . Frankly, it's amazing,' she added in exasperation.

'So you won't take help, but you want compliments?' Pearce smiled. 'It looks amazing. I wouldn't have expected any less.'

'The encryption code is already set, so just hit transmit if you want to talk,' Leila told him.

'Got it,' he assured her, putting the communicator in the backpack.

'Let me get the door,' Leila responded.

Pearce shook his head in disbelief. He knew why she went to such efforts to maintain her independence. People often thought she was being stubborn, trying to prove to them that she didn't need help. In truth, she was trying to prove it to herself. She limped over to the concealed door and flipped a hidden latch.

Pearce sighed. 'You're so stubborn, sometimes I think I'm looking in the mirror,' he said, leaning in to plant a kiss on her cheek. 'Thanks, Lyly,' he said fondly, using her childhood nickname.

'Be careful,' she cautioned.

'I will,' he assured her before leaving.

Chapter 10

The rumours about Scott Pearce were all true. The man was exceptional. He could handle himself in combat, that much was obvious, but it wasn't just his military skills that made him so formidable – there was a clarity about him, a simplicity that made Melody feel safe. He didn't seem a man of shade and shadow who would shift his objectives for the sake of expediency. This was someone who'd stuck to the trail of his own truth for two years, despite the fact it had cost him his career. He'd risked his life to help Melody escape and had kept his word, bringing her safely back to the UK. She felt she could trust him and for the first time in nearly six months she thought there might be a way to escape the dangerous situation she'd blundered into.

Like a naughty child encouraging a friend to mischief, Gabriel Walker, her American boss, had played up the cloak-and-dagger assignment, talking about the associated danger as though it was a roller coaster ride or skydive. Risky, but ultimately manageable. Melody had lured Nathan Foster with the same conspiratorial encouragement, and when she'd sensed that the former soldier turned private detective was desperate for excitement to return to his life, she'd exaggerated the threat of danger, but she hadn't truly believed they were taking any real risks. Bayard Madison was a bank, and white-collar criminals weren't noted for their high body count. So, for a while, Melody had relished the play-pretend thrill of the investigation. Until Foster had died.

She didn't care what the police said. It was no suicide. Foster was onto something and he'd been silenced. The childish thrill evaporated the moment she'd heard about his death and as a sickening fear had hollowed her out, she'd realized that the danger was far more real than she could possibly have imagined. She'd gone to Gabriel and told him she wanted out. She had watched the surveillance footage enough times to know that the two men who had stood over Foster's twitching body had something to do with his death and she never wanted to look up and find them standing over her. But Gabriel had convinced her that until they knew how and why Foster had died, they'd never truly be safe. Melody didn't know whether Gabriel had reached that conclusion on his own or whether the mysterious client had helped him towards it, but even though she hadn't entirely agreed, she'd seen the sense in seeking protection from Scott Pearce. But now Gabriel was also dead, and there was no one left to protect but her.

Sitting curled up in an armchair in the living room of Pearce's remote country cottage, Melody re-examined all the precautions she'd taken. The chartered private jet from London, the anonymous, paid-in-cash taxi from Bangkok to Railay, the dirty no-questions-asked lodgings. She doubted her senses and wondered at the lack of awareness that had enabled a group of men and a cadre of Thai police officers to follow her. Who were the men that had chased them out of Railay? How were they connected to events in London? And what had Foster found? Why had he been murdered? What kind of people could co-opt the Thai police?

It was no surprise that Melody couldn't answer any of the questions. She wasn't a spy. She wasn't even a cop. She was an eight-year qualified corporate lawyer, who specialized in financial services regulation and didn't have the first idea about espionage or combat. She was way out of her depth, which was why she was now stuck in the Welsh hills, holed up with a bodyguard.

Wayne Nelson was a huge man. He was in great physical shape, and had the kind of welcoming face and warm smile that would normally have drawn Melody across a bar to talk to him. But they weren't singletons in a crowded bar, they were bodyguard and victim. No, not victim – Melody hated thinking of herself in those terms – principal. They'd been thrown together in a confined space, and life was difficult enough without the added complication of physical attraction.

Straight after their acrid instant coffees, Wayne and Pearce had taken Melody to an old quarry, where they'd dumped the BMW in the pool. Wayne had driven them back to the cottage in his old Fiesta and shortly after their return, Pearce had roared out of the yard on his Honda, heading for some unknown destination on a huge motorbike that did nothing for Melody. Life was dangerous enough without jumping on a two-wheeled rocket.

Wayne had retrieved his bag from his car and set up his laptop in the kitchen. He'd accessed one of his anonymous email accounts and had given it to Melody to enable her to contact her loved ones. Wayne had told her to communicate in code, in case the emails were intercepted. She'd emailed her mum first, warning her and suggesting she visit an old friend on the island for a while. Melody knew that her mum would understand that she meant Joan, her mum's cousin, who had a tiny cottage near Burwen on Anglesey. Melody then sent messages to her friends and colleagues telling them she was OK and advising them to be vigilant about their personal safety. She'd missed the degree module on what to do if you find yourself at the heart of an espionage plot and didn't really know what else to say. *Run for the hills, best wishes, Melody,* she'd thought bleakly.

One painful aspect of the process was that it made Melody realize she didn't have that many close friends. She'd been a reclusive academic at university, otherwise known as a geek, and had thrown herself into her training and job wholeheartedly. She'd devoted more than a decade to her career. Billable hours. The magic words that governed the lives of lawyers all over the world. Melody's billable hours were among the highest in the firm, which left her with little time for living. As she sat back from Wayne's laptop, she felt very alone.

Wayne had been milling around the cottage while Melody had sent her emails, but when she'd finished, he packed away the computer and suggested they went on a supply run. They'd driven into the tiny village of Llanfrynach to pick up fresh provisions from the local shop.

After they'd returned to Pearce's cottage, Melody had spent ages in the living room, taking books off the shelves, absently scanning the first few pages before putting them back. Wayne had gone for a run and she'd watched him through the window, doing sprints up a steep hill to the west of the cottage. He would run up at full pelt and then jog down, and for almost two hours he repeated the routine until it started getting dark. Melody had switched on the living room lights by the time Wayne had finally returned to the cottage, drenched in sweat.

Melody had settled with a well-thumbed book called *Remember Me*. She'd heard Wayne go upstairs and shower. A short time later, he came downstairs and went into the kitchen. Soon, there was the clatter of dishes.

'Do you want something to eat?' he said. 'I'm making my speciality.'

His speciality turned out to be cheese on toast. But it wasn't any old cheese on toast. Wayne had grated cheese, whipped it with egg and sprinkled in some pieces of grilled bacon, before spreading the mixture on a slice of bread and popping it in the oven. It was good honest comfort food and it was delicious.

'You're a man of many talents,' Melody said.

'Not really,' Wayne replied. 'This is about as far as I go.'

'Somehow I don't think that's true.'

Wayne smiled and they sat in silence for a while, crunching their way through the meal.

'How long have you known Pearce?' Melody asked.

'Seven years.'

'When he was in E Squadron?'

Wayne frowned.

'I was given a file on him,' Melody explained.

'By who?'

Melody shrugged. 'My boss. But I don't know who gave it to him.' She hesitated. 'I can't believe he's dead.'

'I'm sorry,' Wayne said. 'It's never easy.'

They lapsed back into silence. Outside, leaves rustled in the wind and an owl hooted a warning to all the small creatures hiding in the darkest corners of the wood.

'What else did Pearce's file say?' Wayne asked.

'It gave details of his schooling, his enlistment, everything up to E Squadron,' Melody replied. 'There was nothing about his time with MI6.'

'You shouldn't have had anything.' Wayne said. 'His background is classified. Just like mine.'

'What happened in Islamabad?' Melody asked.

Wayne smiled wryly. 'Everyone always wants to know what happened in Islamabad. Even me. Pearce is a straight shooter. He swore an oath and takes the Official Secrets Act very seriously. He hasn't even told me. You know the official story?'

Melody nodded. Someone, most likely Pearce, had thwarted a serious terror attack that had involved some rogue elements of Pakistan's government. No one had wanted to talk about it, not the Pakistani government, not the British, but one thing had been clear: whoever had stopped the attack was a real hero.

'The guy's become a legend. I've heard whispers about what he did out there, but it's not my story to tell,' Wayne replied. 'What is mine is the time a few of us were sent to rescue a pilot who'd been shot down over Iraq. Didn't make the news. ISIS had him and they were planning to execute him live on Facebook. Pearce was leading the unit. We ran into some real trouble. Three of us got taken down. Me included.' He lifted his T-shirt to reveal his scar. A slug had torn through his right side, opening him up pretty badly. Wayne had made the scar part of a large tattoo of the Grim Reaper, which sat atop his rippling six-pack. The old bullet wound was the jewel in a ring that adorned the bony fist which gripped Death's scythe. 'Pearce got us out. All of us. And he rescued the pilot. I've served with a lot of great men and women, but Scott Pearce is special.'

Wayne's laptop sounded a tone, and he checked his secure email account.

'Come on,' he said to Melody as he got to his feet. 'We're going to London.'

Chapter 11

Pearce woke in the basement bedroom of a small two-bedroom maisonette in Archway. The flat was council-owned and he'd bought it for key money five years ago, when he'd been working an operation in London. The council's tenant was a man called Colin Hemmie. Pearce had heard about him from a scrawny crook who hung out at a pub in Dalston. Pearce had been posing as a painter and decorator who specialized in funeral homes, and the boozer had been one of the places where he'd augmented his legend. The painting and decorating got Pearce into specific funeral homes which acted as transport hubs for MI6 informants, who needed to be retrieved for debriefing. The informants would be brought in as bodies during the night and would leave as one of Pearce's assistants, dressed in paint-covered overalls, and when they'd been debriefed, the process would be reversed. It had been a vanilla assignment, and the flat was the only notable thing to have come from it.

The real Colin Hemmie had needed to leave London in a rush and had been willing to sell the keys to his flat for twenty grand. Pearce had seized the opportunity for an illicit safe house, and had not only taken Colin's flat but also his name. Colin Hemmie was one of his aliases, and he'd had a passport, driving licence and birth certificate created to enable him to open a bank account. The rent and bills were paid automatically and as far as Islington Council was concerned, Colin Hemmie was still living in his two-up two-down flat.

Pearce pulled back the curtains to reveal the dirty window, steel bars and, beyond them, the concrete well that was filled with litter and long-dead leaves. Pearce hadn't bothered redecorating and everything in the place was grimy and worn. A bit of dirt and age didn't bother him – it felt authentic for a single man struggling in London.

He stretched, working the tightness out of his arms, and then stepped out of his boxer shorts, grabbed a towel and hurried upstairs to the bathroom. Pearce got the shower going, and as he waited for the water to warm up, he checked his reflection in the rust-mottled mirror. He could only just remember his mother, an Englishwoman called Kelly. She'd given him her angular cheeks and small nose. He guessed he must have inherited his wide eyes and full lips from his father, a half Sudanese, half Egyptian man called Adel, but he couldn't remember him at all. The man had abandoned them when Pearce was three. As a child, Pearce had struggled to understand what he had done to make both his parents leave and he'd been full of guilt, confusion and anger. Now he knew it was just life. He'd been dealt a raw hand: a wastrel father who'd seeded a child without thought of consequence, a man who hadn't been able to handle the hard reality of being tied down; a frayed mother who couldn't cope with being a single parent; a system that didn't know how to treat a sensitive, intelligent, angry child. He'd been lucky to get Malcolm Jones, his old headmaster, on the flop. That had been the one card that had saved his life from being a complete bust.

Over the years, Pearce's anger at his parents had faded and he now felt nothing towards them but disinterest. He could have made efforts to find them, but he had no reason to look. He'd heard about other people who'd been put up for adoption being desperate to understand where they'd come from, but Pearce had no desire to build a connection to a man and woman who'd been callous enough to abandon a young kid. The only good thing his parents had left him was his mixed heritage, which had proved particularly useful in his professional career. When he caught the sun, as now, his skin turned a light brown that enabled him to pass as a native of any Mediterranean or Middle Eastern country. The melanin boost that had earned him so much racist abuse in childhood had become a real asset. Over the years, he'd been mistaken for an Egyptian, Israeli, Italian, Spaniard, Frenchman, Greek, Indian – so many nationalities that he'd lost track. After spending his childhood years hating himself for being different, Pearce was grateful for whatever alcohol-infused cross-cultural encounter had led to his creation.

After he'd showered, Pearce put on a suit, shirt, tie and black leather shoes, and, looking every inch the claims adjuster, he grabbed the backpack Leila had given him, left the dilapidated flat and made for the tube station. The Northern Line was crowded and stuffy, but Pearce managed to find himself a few inches of space and took out one of the folders Leila had put in the backpack. It contained documents relating to the police investigation into Foster's death. Pearce had glanced at them the previous night, but he read them closely now. The officer in charge of the investigation was Detective Sergeant George Dawson, who worked out of Bishopsgate Police Station. Leila had included Dawson's personnel file. He was an experienced cop with over fifteen years on the force, an exemplary record and a couple of high-profile busts to his name. He had a wife and two kids who lived with him in Ruislip. Not the profile of someone on the take, or an incompetent fool, so why had he ignored the two men who'd stood over Fozz as he lay dying? Why hadn't he flagged them as material witnesses and sought to establish their identities?

Bishopsgate Police Station was a five-storey grey stone pill-box located opposite Liverpool Street Station. Travelling with the tide of commuters, Pearce picked his way across the busy road and ducked inside the austere building. He presented himself to the receptionist and was asked to wait. He took a seat in a small area near the door and watched the comings and goings of the station for a little over an hour before a grey man with grey hair and a crumpled grey suit approached. He looked as though someone had wrung the life out of him.

'Mr Rowland?' he asked. 'I'm DS Dawson.'

'Thanks for seeing me, Sergeant,' Pearce replied, getting to his feet and shaking the man's hand.

'You said it's about the death of Nathan Foster?' Dawson moved towards the door. 'Do you mind if we walk and talk? I'm dying for a coffee.'

You need something, Pearce thought, *but it's probably not coffee*. The deep bags beneath Dawson's eyes and the translucent grey of his skin spoke of a troubled man. 'No problem.'

They left the station and started south along Bishopsgate, navigating the crowded pavement. The morning was already warming with the promise of a sweltering day, and Pearce couldn't wait to get out of the stifling suit.

'You work for Mr Foster's insurers?' Dawson asked.

Pearce nodded. 'We just need to check a few things. Obviously suicide might have implications for his policy.'

'I didn't say it was suicide,' Dawson remarked. 'Just that there was no further reason to investigate. The coroner will make the final determination.'

'Of course,' Pearce acknowledged. 'We'd just like to understand why you felt there was no need for further inquiry.'

'Mr Foster was having financial problems. His detective practice hadn't taken off the way he'd hoped—'

'Did you speak to his clients?' Pearce interrupted.

'A couple. We went through his financial records. He was borrowing heavily. His landlady said he was a drinker, often depressed. No family, virtually no friends. His military records showed he'd been prescribed antidepressants after an incident in Afghanistan,' Dawson said. 'He'd had to take a second job as a cleaner. He used a fake name to get it. He was probably ashamed. Civilian life wasn't working for him. It's quite common with ex-military types.'

Pearce's fists balled up as he heard his former comrade's death being dismissed so casually, but he reminded himself he was playing the role of a pencil pusher. 'Were there any witnesses?' he asked blandly.

'Just the man who found him,' Dawson replied.

They turned left onto New Street, a narrow alleyway flanked by high buildings. Pearce studied the detective and wondered why he'd lied. Did he want to keep things simple and bring their encounter to an end? Or was there a more sinister reason for the deception?

'Oh,' Pearce remarked. 'I'd been led to understand that there were at least two witnesses.'

Dawson stopped suddenly and looked at Pearce with fierce suspicion.

'No,' he said coldly. 'There was no one else there.'

They stood silently studying each other. Dawson had no idea that Pearce had seen the surveillance video and had pressed on with a lie that meant he was either dirty or afraid. Judging by the man's beleaguered appearance, Pearce suspected the latter.

'You know, I once worked a case that was supposed to have been a suicide,' Pearce lied. 'But it turned out a local gang had pressured the detective in charge, threatening him and his family to make him back off from a murder investigation.'

'Where's your office?' Dawson asked, his eyes narrowing.

'Milton Keynes,' Pearce replied.

'Who do you sit next to?'

'Bob Richards and Tina Collins,' Pearce said.

Dawson produced his phone. 'So if I call Albion Mutual right now and ask to be put through to Bob Richards or Tina Collins, the operator will know who I'm talking about?'

'Of course,' Pearce scoffed. He wasn't concerned. He'd studied the file Leila had given him, and Bob Richards and Tina Collins both existed and did indeed sit by the real David Rowland. 'I don't know what's going on here, Detective Sergeant, but I can assure you I'm on the level.'

Dawson slipped his phone back into his pocket. 'That other case you worked. Did the gang send people round to test the detective in charge? Check he wasn't going to talk?'

And there was the answer. Dawson had been pressured into tossing the investigation and he suspected Pearce represented those who'd intimidated him. In his mind, this was a test to see whether he'd stick to his official report. As far as he was concerned, Pearce was a potential threat, which meant the detective would offer up nothing truthful or useful.

'No, Sergeant Dawson,' Pearce replied. 'And I'd feel sorry for any detective that ever happened to. It would be impossible to know who to trust.'

Dawson held Pearce's gaze for a moment. 'Yes, it would.' He looked in the direction of a small coffee shop. 'Well, unless there's anything else, Mr Rowland . . .' he tailed off.

'No,' Pearce replied. 'Thanks for your time, Sergeant.'

Dawson nodded and backed towards the coffee shop. Pearce watched him for a moment before heading for Bishopsgate. It was hard to intimidate experienced police officers like Dawson, which meant whoever had threatened him was someone to be taken very seriously indeed.

Chapter 12

Nathan Foster had rooms on Southwick Street. His landlady, an octogenarian called Mickey, brimming with the hostility of someone who'd spent a lifetime at war with the world, scowled at Pearce when she answered the front door. She wore a loose, shapeless floral dress and a bright auburn wig, and looked old enough to have been the building's original owner. It was a grand brown-brick Georgian terrace that lay between Star Street and Sussex Gardens.

'I'm watching my programme,' she muttered after Pearce explained that he was from Foster's insurance company. 'That man ain't been nothing but trouble.'

'I was wondering if I might take a look around,' Pearce suggested sweetly. 'You'd be doing me a real favour.'

'What do I give a toss about you for?' she snapped, but then she softened. 'Mind you, there might be something you can make yourself useful with. If you're handy.'

Pearce could only guess at what the old woman had in mind as she allowed him into the building. He followed her along a narrow, dark hallway before turning right into her flat.

'This is my place,' she said. 'The whole building's mine, but this is where I live. With my husband, until he decided to run off with the devil a few years ago.' Mickey caught Pearce's puzzled expression. 'It's a joke. He's dead,' she exclaimed loudly. 'Dead. I tell people he's gone to live with the devil because he was such a mean bastard. I hope they've got him on gas mark seven.'

Pearce had no idea what he was supposed to say to that, so he kept quiet.

'Right,' she said. 'Let's put you to work.'

'Work' turned out to be fixing her cistern, which was leaking a constant stream of water into the toilet. She provided Pearce with her husband's tools, which, like everything else in the flat, were relics from another era. The leak was caused by a loose washer, and once Pearce had tightened it and Mickey was satisfied with his work, she gave him his reward, leading him back into the hallway and up a steep staircase to Foster's place.

A sign on the door at the top of the stairs read 'International Investigative Solutions'.

'I've got to get that removed,' Mickey told Pearce, 'but it's going to leave a bloomin' mark on the door, ain't it?'

'Did Mr Foster also live here?' Pearce asked as they stepped onto a tiny landing.

'Course. He didn't have no blinkin' money,' she replied. 'I was friends with his aunt. That's why I let him have the place so cheap. He couldn't afford it otherwise. Not with all the Arabs and Chinese circling. That's what I'm going to do when it's time for me to retire. Sell the place to one of them foreign fellows.'

Pearce longed to ask what she would be retiring from, but he resisted the urge and nodded blankly.

'The fuzz left the place in a terrible state, so don't make it any bloody worse.' Mickey led him into an office at the front of the building. She was right: the place looked like it had been ransacked, but not by the police. The desk had been turned over and the contents of the drawers spread everywhere. Books had been pulled off shelves and scattered, and files had been torn from metal cabinets and tossed around the room. Even at their most zealous, cops were usually more considerate and systematic.

'How many times have the police been here?' Pearce asked.

'How the hell am I supposed to know?' Mickey replied angrily. 'I'm not a bloody diary service. Four or five times maybe.'

'Was it the same officers each time?' Pearce asked.

Mickey leaned towards him and pointed at her eyes, which were milky and styed. 'You're all just voices and shapes to me, mate,' she said. 'Office, kitchen and toilet on this floor. Bedroom and living room are upstairs.'

Pearce glanced around. 'Did he have a computer?'

'Didn't trust them any more than I do,' Mickey replied. 'Old-school like me. Said he only used paper.' She shuffled towards the stairs. 'Get back to my show. Probably missed it now, though. Bloody pain,' she muttered to herself and then, as if suddenly remembering Pearce was in the room, she turned to him and said, 'And if you feel like tidying up, you won't find me complaining.'

She left the door open and Pearce heard her groan and mumble her way downstairs. Minutes later, the sound of a blaring television rose through the floor. Satisfied that he wouldn't be disturbed, Pearce put down his backpack and surveyed the mess, wondering where to begin.

The office really had been well and truly turned over. Pearce had little doubt someone other than the police had been here. If he was right and DS Dawson had been threatened, he would have had the place searched once, maybe twice for the sake of appearances. Four or five visits meant someone else had been back multiple times. That suggested they were searching for something specific or were paranoid about what information Foster might have had in his possession.

Nathan Foster. The man had been so brash and loud, it was hard to believe he'd been forever silenced. Pearce had been through his handwritten files, which were little more than a collection of sad stories: the wife whose husband was cheating; the insurer who wanted proof that an injury claimant was spending his days doing cash-in-hand labouring; the businessman who'd finally got the evidence he needed that his partner was cooking the books. It was all so small. Pearce had found a couple of half-empty vodka bottles and could picture Fozz sitting in the little office, staring at his filing cabinet, feeling constrained by his cases, getting drunk and dreaming of bygone days when he'd been part of events that had shaped the world. No wonder he'd jumped at Melody's assignment, doubtless rushing into it with the balls-to-the-wall enthusiasm he'd been known for on the battlefield. The one thing absent from any of the strewn documents was a single reference to Bayard Madison. The investigation into the bank had no file, which meant it was either missing, or Foster had never created one.

Pearce moved out of the office and quickly searched the ransacked kitchen and tiny bathroom. Finding nothing of interest on the lower floor, he went upstairs. There was another landing and two doors leading off. The first opened into a tatty living room. The windows were grimy and the wallpaper yellowed by decades of cigarette smoke. A solitary frayed sofa stood against the north wall and an ancient television rested on the floor opposite. Cushions were scattered in the middle of the room, their covers removed. The base and back of the sofa had been cut open, increasing the sense of squalor. Whoever had been here had searched the place thoroughly.

Pearce looked around in frustration and then recalled an old story Foster used to tell when he was drunk. He'd been in the ACF – the cadets – at school and had once driven the detachment lieutenant wild during a week's exercise. Fozz had bragged about taking a bag of grass with him and how he'd shared it with the other cadets each night, but despite the pungent smell wafting from their barracks, whenever the lieutenant had searched their quarters, he'd found nothing. Pearce hurried from the room as he recalled Foster's drunken pride at his hiding place. He'd discovered that the legs of his bunk were hollow and had stuffed the drugs inside.

Foster's bedroom was as depressing as the rest of the flat. Thin grey curtains covered the window, and in the gloomy light Pearce saw that the old double mattress had been tossed off the bed and sliced open, its innards spilled all over the floor. The wooden frame was on its side by the wall. Constructed of cheap pine soft enough to push a fingernail into, the rickety old skeleton wobbled violently as Pearce unscrewed the nearest leg. It came away to reveal nothing but solid wood, from which there protruded a three-inch heavy bolt. Pearce crouched and repeated the process with the next leg and found it was the same. He moved to the top of the bed and unscrewed the leg that was at head height. As it came away, he felt the bolt moving more freely than the other two, and he discovered that a small hollow had been carved in the wood. To his disappointment, he saw that it was empty.

He was about to toss it when he caught sight of the edge of something pressed against the side of the little hollow. Pearce reached in and felt a smooth surface. He pulled out a glossy five- by three-inch card. It looked like a flyer. On the front, outlined in gold, was the symbol of a many-pointed star. In its centre were the Roman numerals 'XIII'. Black against a black background, it looked like something that might have been carved on a pagan shrine. On the back there was nothing but a mobile phone number scrawled in biro. Pearce studied it for a moment, wondering what it signified and why Foster had hidden it.

Pearce didn't get the chance to study it more closely. He was startled by a commotion downstairs. There was a loud bang, a crack and then a woman's scream. Pearce pocketed the strange card, ran to the living room and looked through the dirty window at the street below. A silver Volkswagen Transporter van with tinted windows was parked outside the building, it's side door open. Crouched on the flatbed, looking up at Foster's flat, was someone Pearce recognized: the woman with albinism who'd driven the Land Rover down the country road after the fight by the combine harvester. Pearce would never forget her face: it was the colour of paper, her eyes were an electric blue, her lips pale, her eyebrows and hair a vibrant white. She caught Pearce's gaze and held it with a faint smile. He grabbed his backpack and slung it over his shoulders as he ran from the room. He was acutely aware of thundering footsteps getting closer and his mind raced. Had Mickey called them? Had Detective Sergeant Dawson told these people there was a guy poking around? Had they been watching the place?

Pearce burst onto the small landing and heard steps one floor below. They started up the stairs and Pearce glanced over the rail to see three familiar faces racing up – Raptor, Bullneck and Boxer, the men he and Melody had encountered on the journey from Manchester.

'Come here!' Bullneck snarled, his face marred by an ugly bruise where Pearce had hit him with the stone.

Pearce sprinted into Foster's bedroom and ran to the window. He pulled back the curtains to reveal a filthy pane of glass. It overlooked an oblong courtyard whose uniform shape was broken by the jagged lines of extensions that had been added to the surrounding buildings over the years. Pearce saw that Mickey's building had a ground-floor extension. A two-storey jump? He'd done worse.

Pearce flipped the latch and yanked the sash window open. He was about to climb out when he realized he wouldn't have time. The footsteps were on the landing, and an instant later Bullneck and Boxer burst into the room. Bullneck wore a T-shirt, exposing his tattooed arms. The one on his right forearm left Pearce in no doubt the guy was ex-forces. It was an image of a skeleton in a First World War Tommy's uniform, standing over the skulls of many fallen.

Bullneck rushed forward, snapping his right hand to extend a police baton. Pearce ducked the first swing of the heavy metal stick, grateful that the confined space meant Boxer had to hang a couple of paces behind. Pearce surprised Bullneck by rushing him and the man lashed out ineffectually as he was propelled back. He lost his footing against the mattress and tumbled over, hitting the bed frame, which fell onto Boxer. Raptor, the flinty-eyed man who'd been in the Land Rover with the white-haired woman, entered, his path to Pearce blocked by his two companions, who were struggling to their feet.

'Oi!' Raptor shouted at Pearce, brandishing a wooden club.

Pearce didn't wait to hear what else the man had to say and instead hurled himself through the open window, praying he'd judged the distance correctly. He hit the tarpaper roof with a thud, and looked back over his shoulder. To his dismay, Boxer was at the window gauging the jump. Pearce moved to the edge of the little extension and leaped off as his pursuer took flight. Pearce hit the concrete courtyard moments before Boxer landed on the extension roof. His hawkish associate, Raptor, was in the window, ready to make the jump as Pearce started running. He raced across the courtyard, sprinting past a large extension. Pearce could smell fragrant aromas that reminded him of the food stalls in Railay and when he looked through the window of the brick structure, he saw a commercial kitchen. He recalled a Malaysian restaurant a few doors down from Mickey's building, and instantly thought of all the knives such a place might contain. He made for the white metal door and barged into it with his shoulder, but it didn't give. Pearce glanced back to see Boxer closing, with Raptor a few paces behind, talking into a phone. Pearce didn't have time to tackle a secure door and took to his heels again, sprinting towards a high fence on the other side of the courtyard.

He scrambled up and over the fence and found himself in a tiny gravel-covered garden. He raced round the potted plants and headed for a passageway that ran beside the four-storey building. Six feet wide, the passageway was bounded by brick walls on either side. Pearce saw a window ahead of him, and realized that someone had built an extension in what was formerly a pathway used to access the communal gardens. He heard his pursuers running across the gravel behind him and picked up his pace as he sprinted towards the single-storey structure. Pearce planted a foot against the right wall and leaped towards the extension, grabbing the roof with his fingertips and scrambling up. He ran across the roof and came to the edge of Star Street, finding himself in a narrow gap between two neighbouring buildings. Two storeys beneath him was a concrete basement well, ten feet long and three wide. Star Street was only one storey down, but it was on the other side of the spiked metal railings that marked the well's perimeter. Pearce heard movement behind him and saw a hand grab the flat roof as one of the chasing men tried to pull himself up.

Pearce took a few paces run-up and jumped, leaping through the air, clearing the well and landing on the pavement heavily. He rolled and, as he got to his feet, he heard steps behind him. Bullneck rounded the corner of Southwick Street and charged Pearce, his baton swinging. The bulbous metal tip caught Pearce on the shoulder and the glancing blow sent waves of pain through his body. Pearce ducked inside the big man's reach and delivered a rapid series of uppercuts, his fists thumping like a rabbit's feet. He saw Bullneck's eyes roll back, but didn't stop until the heavy man fell. Pearce snatched the baton from the man's limp hand. He glanced up at the first-floor roof and saw Boxer and Raptor glowering at him from the edge.

'You're fucking dead!' Raptor yelled.

Pearce heard a screech of rubber and saw the Volkswagen bounce to a sudden halt a few feet away at the junction with Southwick Street. The striking woman sat in the driver's seat, her shocked eyes on Bullneck's prone figure. She raised them to meet Pearce's gaze and they stared at each other for a moment before he rushed towards her. Rather than throw the vehicle into gear and accelerate away, the woman calmly got out of the van and faced him.

It wasn't until Pearce was almost upon her that he noticed she had something in her hand. He stopped just in time. She lunged for him with a Glauca B1, a tactical knife that had a razor-sharp black switchblade. It was standard issue for French counterterrorism units and was rarely seen in civilian hands. Pearce sidestepped and brought the baton up towards her chin, but the woman threw her forearms together, absorbing the blow. She thrust at his chest, but he blocked the knife with the baton and rolled past her, rising quickly. As she turned to face him, he brought the baton whipping round, and it caught her on the temple. She toppled like a felled tree. Pearce was about to search her when he noticed Bullneck stirring. Finally plucking up the courage to make the leap, Boxer sailed over the well and landed near the big man.

Realizing he couldn't afford to hang around, Pearce threw his backpack into the Volkswagen, jumped inside, put the van into gear and drove off, racing west along Star Street.

Chapter 13

Fuck, fuck, fuck, Pearce thought as he steered the van around Gloucester Square. He'd blundered into a situation with no idea what or who he was facing and so far he'd survived thanks to a couple of lucky breaks.

He pulled into a space halfway along the tree-lined street. In the square, he could see a couple of chubby toddlers, grinning as they tottered over the grass, running from a young woman – their mother? A nanny? – and he envied them for not having to contend with the world's ugliness.

Every challenge has dark moments, Pearce told himself. Patience and perseverance overcome them. If he'd misjudged the situation, he would change his approach. If he didn't know what he was up against, he'd find out. He reached into his backpack for Leila's Ghostlink and pressed the transmit button. After a moment's silence, he heard a short tritone.

'*Go ahead,*' Leila said.

'I ran into four friends. Same ones who crashed the party on the way from the airport,' Pearce told her. He didn't care how encrypted the system was, speaking in partial code would make life difficult in the unlikely event Leila's tech could be hacked.

'*Are you OK?*'

'Yeah. We need to meet,' he said.

'*Agreed,*' Leila responded. '*I've found some interesting nuggets. The kid is being moved to a new home.*' She gave him the address of a place in West London, which he committed to memory. The kid was Melody, the new home a safe house.

'I need to find an old friend. I only have his number,' Pearce said.

'*Land or cell?*' Leila asked.

Pearce checked the number on the back of the card he'd taken from the compartment concealed in Foster's bed. 'Mobile.'

'*OK. Give it to me,*' she said.

Pearce read out the digits. 'Is there any way I can call it without being traced?'

'*Yes,*' she replied. '*Actually you'd be doing me a favour. I can find your friend more easily if the phone is in use. I'm going to give you a proxy number, call it from any payphone and it will give you instructions on how to dial the end user you want to reach.*'

Leila gave Pearce what seemed like an ordinary London landline number. '*Give me twenty minutes to get set,*' she told him.

'One last thing,' Pearce said. 'The four friends lent me their van. It's a Volkswagen Transporter. Pricey. I need to know where to return it.'

'*No problem. Give me the registration,*' Leila responded, and Pearce obliged, recalling it instantly.

'I'll see you soon,' he said.

The line went dead and Pearce put the communicator in his backpack and stepped out of the van, walking west towards Paddington Station.

*

Pearce leaned against the payphone, watching passers-by weave around the main concourse. The PA system announced the departure of a train to Reading, and a swarm of travellers broke from the main crowd and buzzed towards the platform. The clock beneath the departures board told Pearce that twenty minutes had passed so he picked up the receiver, inserted coins into the slot and dialled the number Leila had given him. There was no ringing tone, the line simply clicked and Pearce heard a mechanical voice.

'*Please dial your number now.*'

Pearce keyed in the digits from the back of the card. There was a short silence, followed by a ringing tone. As he waited, Pearce studied the gold embossing that outlined the black star on the front of the card and wondered what the image symbolized. He noticed that in addition to the 'XIII' in the centre, the star had thirteen points.

'*Hello?*' a man's voice came on the line. English. Northern, with the hint of a Yorkshire accent.

'Yeah,' Pearce said. 'I was given this number by a friend.'

Silence.

'He said I should call,' Pearce continued.

Silence.

'*This friend have a name?*' the man said finally.

'Dave,' Pearce said, choosing something common.

'*Where you based?*' the man asked.

'Reading,' Pearce lied. It was accessible to much of the country.

'*Blackbird Leys Community Centre,*' the man said. '*Thursday, eight o'clock.*'

The line went dead, leaving Pearce puzzling about exactly what he'd just made an appointment for. He pulled the

Ghostlink communicator from his backpack and leaned against the payphone's metal divider, pretending to make another call. He pressed the transmit button.

'You there?' he asked.

'*Yes,*' Leila replied. '*It seems like your friend doesn't want to be found. The number bounces to a relay, a server located in Connecticut. Your friend is doing the same thing I did for you, running calls through a proxy. I'll keep working at it, but . . .*'

'My friend is a professional,' Pearce suggested.

'*Seems so,*' Leila agreed. '*I'll see you soon.*'

'I'm on my way,' Pearce said, before slipping the Ghostlink into his bag.

He glanced around, checked he wasn't the subject of undue attention, slung the backpack over his shoulder and headed for the Underground.

Chapter 14

Leila arrived at the house on Vyner Road shortly after six. The drab, functional dormitory community of East Acton was sandwiched between city and suburb, being neither one nor the other. Rush hour clogged the nearby Western Avenue, infusing the air with acrid fumes that gave the sunlight an ugly grey tint. Leila grabbed her satchel and cane and hauled herself out of the Peugeot, which was parked outside the Six safe house. The building was one of a number of 1930s semi-detached houses that stood in a proud line. Unlike its neighbours, with their tile-clad bay windows, tidy front gardens and neatly kept drives, the safe house was a shambles. Weeds were rampant in the overgrown garden, the brickwork was cracked like old parchment and if there had ever been a drive, it was now lost to moss and ragged tufts of grass. She'd used an old back door into Six's network to check the place was vacant and wasn't scheduled to be used for any upcoming operations. They'd only be disturbed in the unlikely event an operative needed emergency access.

Leila caught sight of a figure she recognized in the upstairs window. The woman looked far less glamorous than she did in her social media photos. Greyed by a grimy pane of glass, Melody Gold stood staring, not at Leila, but at the high spire of the modern church opposite. She looked pale, troubled and drawn. Leila wondered whether the lawyer was religious and wished her luck with whatever silent hope she might be casting at the holy building. Leila knew from bitter experience that even the most heartfelt prayers went unanswered. Her cautious shuffle caught Melody's attention and the two women locked eyes for a moment, before Melody withdrew from sight.

The property was accessed by means of a numeric key lock, and Leila tapped in the code and pushed the front door open. She was glad to see Wayne Nelson emerge from a doorway to check the new arrival. They'd met only once, about three years ago at a pub in Highgate. Pearce had invited her to drinks with some of his former comrades and Wayne and Nathan Foster had been there.

'Leila, right?' Wayne said.

'Good to see you again, Wayne,' she responded, briefly clasping his outstretched hand.

Melody Gold came downstairs, fragile, beautiful with the stunned expression of a rabbit who's found itself in a cave full of jackals.

'Ms Gold, my name is Leila Nahum.'

'Where's Scott?'

'On his way,' Leila replied. 'Is there somewhere I can plug my laptop in?'

'There's a table in the kitchen,' Wayne said, indicating a yellowed door that lay directly ahead.

Leila followed the huge man through the tatty hallway, labouring against her cane. There was a yeasty smell about the place, as though it had been empty for a long time and some spore had taken root in a secret space.

'Do you think my mum will be OK?' Melody asked Wayne as she trailed Leila into the kitchen.

'Hopefully,' Wayne replied. 'I can check the email. See if she's replied.'

Leila put her satchel on the table and eased herself into a rickety chair. She unpacked her laptop and used a 4G dongle to connect to a secure private network that kept cycling through various proxy servers to keep the machine's identity and location secret. She offered the keyboard to Wayne, who crouched over it and logged into a secure email account.

Leila peered over his shoulder to see an email from Melody's mother, Bella Adler. She'd reverted to her maiden name after divorcing Melody's father.

'She's done what you suggested. She says she's gone to stay with Teddy's mum,' Wayne said.

'That's her cousin Joan,' Melody replied, relieved.

'She's worried about you,' Wayne added.

'Can we let her know I'm OK?' Melody asked.

Wayne looked at Leila, who nodded. 'Sure. Just type whatever you want here,' he said, indicating a window. He moved aside to give Melody space.

As she was typing her message, they heard the front door open, and Wayne went to investigate. After a brief, indistinct exchange, he returned with Pearce in tow.

'Everyone OK?' Pearce asked.

Leila nodded and Melody and Wayne did likewise.

'We need to talk,' Pearce told Leila.

'Here's what we know,' Pearce began. 'Ms Gold works for a law firm called Denton Fraser. A few months ago an unidentified person contacted one of the partners, Gabriel Walker, and asked him to hire someone to investigate Bayard Madison—'

'Not someone, you,' Melody corrected. 'Gabe was given a list. Your name was at the top. We were told to hire you.'

They were arranged around the kitchen table like the points of a compass. Pearce was north, Leila was east, Melody south and Wayne west.

'Yes,' Pearce acknowledged. 'The client provided Gabriel Walker with a list of operatives he or she wanted to engage. My name was top, Nathan Foster was next. Gabriel Walker asked Ms Gold to do the legwork.'

'I didn't know it was going to be this dangerous,' she said regretfully. 'When I couldn't find you, I engaged Mr Foster. He discovered something, I don't know what, he wouldn't say until he had proof. But he died . . .' She trailed off.

'He fell through a reinforced window on the twenty-seventh floor,' Pearce said. 'Two unidentified men watched him die. He was found forty-five minutes later by a third man who called an ambulance. The police believe it was suicide, but I spoke to the detective running the investigation and he's been leaned on. Someone's scared him into backing off.'

'Shit,' Wayne sighed. 'You got proof?'

Pearce shook his head. 'He as good as admitted it, though. Fozz gave Ms Gold my location, so I suspect he wanted backup.'

'But not me,' Wayne observed sourly.

'You weren't on the list the client gave us,' Melody replied.

'Try not to let it bruise your ego,' Leila teased.

'When Ms Gold found me, I spotted the guys tailing her and we escaped,' Pearce continued. 'There were at least four chasing us alongside local police.'

Wayne whistled. 'Overseas?' he asked.

'Yeah,' Pearce replied.

'So we're talking about a coordinated international operation? Feels like a tussle,' Wayne said, sitting back and
shaking his head slowly.

'A tussle?' Melody asked.

'It's slang for *tusovka*. Russian for party,' Pearce replied.
'An operation run by the SVR. *Sluzhba Vneshney Razvedki*,
Russian Foreign Intelligence.'

'Fuck,' Wayne remarked.

'If they were running an operation, Six would likely know
something about it,' Leila observed.

'Unless Six was compromised,' Wayne responded grimly.

'It'd have to be high up,' Pearce noted. 'Whoever is behind
this, they're organized and well-funded. They came at us
again on our way from the airport and they took another crack
when I went to Fozz's place. This is heavy stuff and I can't
offer you any money just yet. There are no guarantees you'll
ever see any cash, which means I've got to remind you where
the door is. You're free to walk away. No hard feelings.'

Wayne and Leila exchanged glances.

'I'm here for Fozz,' Wayne said. 'If it comes, the payday
will be a bonus.'

'Old age is for those with nothing better to do,' Leila
announced. 'Of course I'm in,' she added.

'OK,' Pearce said. 'I want us to find out who instructed
Gabriel Walker. Would you feel comfortable going back into
your old life?' he asked Melody.

She didn't reply and suddenly found the cracked tabletop
fascinating.

'You'll be safe,' Pearce assured her. 'I think Gabriel ran in
front of that bus to protect his family. My guess is he knew
that if he was taken, they'd use his family as leverage, he'd

give up the name of his client and he and his wife and kids would be killed. That means there is probably some direct link between him and his client. Some form of communication or record.'

'The others will be looking for it,' Leila observed.

'Right,' Pearce agreed. 'Which is probably why they turned over Fozz's place and are so eager to get their hands on Ms Gold. You're part of Mr Walker's life,' he said to Melody. 'You can get into Denton Fraser, you can talk to his wife, you can find out who was giving him orders. We'll keep you safe and if there's any trouble, this time we'll be ready for a snatch and grab.'

'Snatch and grab?' Melody asked.

Leila frowned. 'You've got to tell her what you're really doing.'

Pearce gave Leila a dirty look.

'She isn't a toy,' the dark-haired woman observed.

Pearce sighed. Melody was a civilian and he didn't want to overwhelm her, but, irritatingly, Leila was right. It was the lawyer's life and he had no right to gamble it without her consent. 'There's a good chance they'll be watching your home and office,' he admitted at last. 'We'll be ready to grab one of the bad guys if they make another attempt to get you.'

'You're using me as bait?' she asked incredulously.

'Yes,' Pearce admitted. 'If we get the opportunity to take one of these people, we will.' He watched Melody look at each of them in turn, her sunken, shadowed eyes wide with fear. 'We will keep you safe,' he assured her.

'It's worth the risk,' Leila told her. 'We'll get valuable intel.'

'Where are you on ID-ing the two I got on camera?' Pearce asked.

'I'm running an image search,' Leila replied. 'Could be a couple of days.'

'Do you promise?' Melody asked. 'Do you promise I'll be OK?'

'No one can make that promise, Ms Gold,' Pearce replied. 'But I'll do everything in my power to keep you safe.'

Melody sighed and nodded slowly. 'OK,' she said. 'I'll do what I can.'

'Thanks.' Pearce turned to Leila. 'You said you found something.'

The tough Syrian pulled a file from her satchel and handed it to Pearce. She leaned forward as he opened it. 'Just over a year ago, Constellation Holdings, a company domiciled in Monaco, took a minority stake in Bayard Madison. I tracked the ultimate owner of Constellation through a chain of fronts and shell corporations. He's a man called Artem Vasylyk. Billionaire with interests in Ukraine's chemical and mining industries, now based in London. Vasylyk doesn't smell good to me. Lot of shady connections.'

'I found this hidden in Fozz's flat.' Pearce produced the card he'd discovered in Foster's bed: the golden outline of a black star. 'I'd like you to run an image search. See if this means anything. Keep digging into the bank, but I'd also like you to look at any foreign ops running in London. When I met our new friends at Foster's place, the woman was carrying a Glauca B1, a specialized blade that's issued to French counterterrorism units. See what you can find out from Six, the Box, DGSE, CIA, SVR and all the other usual suspects. If this is an intelligence operation, there will be a file on it somewhere.'

Leila nodded and took the card.

'I'll check out Artem Vasylyk,' Pearce said. 'I've also been invited to a meeting on Thursday night by the person whose number was on the back of that card. There's something happening at the Blackbird Leys Community Centre in Oxfordshire.'

'You want any backup?' Wayne asked.

'Maybe,' Pearce replied. 'You got any more of those walkie-talkies?' he asked Leila.

'You mean my state-of-the-art satellite communicators?' Her voice dripped acid.

'Yeah, if you want to be flash,' he responded with a smile.

'Yes,' Leila said coldly. 'I have some more of those walkie-talkies.' The last word was spat out like poison. '*Ya ebn sharmouta.*'

Son of a prostitute. It was a commonplace insult in Syria and one of Leila's favourites. She elbowed Pearce, who feigned injury and the two of them smiled.

'OK,' he said. 'Leila will issue communications gear. Let's get some rest.'

'Rest be damned,' Leila responded quickly. 'I need a drink.'

Chapter 15

The night started well enough. Wayne went out for fifteen minutes and returned with an assortment of bottles. There was red wine, beer, vodka and gin, all arranged on a low table in the grotty living room.

Pearce sat in an armchair and nursed a single beer. The others weren't so circumspect and hit the bottles with enthusiasm. Melody went for the red wine and her cheeks soon brightened with a warm glow as she relaxed on the sofa. Propped on one of the kitchen chairs, Wayne drank vodka and lemonade. Sitting next to Melody on the stained sofa, Leila was making a solo assault on the gin. After a few drinks, she staggered over to a small radio and put on a late-night dance show. She might have struggled to walk, but Leila could still move her hips freely and wiggled them like a professional folk dancer. She tried to drag Pearce up, but he stayed glued to his chair. She turned to Wayne, who got into the spirit of things by dancing with her.

Melody downed the last of the wine and got to her feet. 'How do you do that?' she asked, her words loud and slurred. She pointed towards Leila's hips, which popped from side to side.

'It's all in your core,' Leila replied. 'You snap your abs one way then another.'

Leila staggered over to Melody and put her hands on

Melody's hips, trying to demonstrate the movement. After a few attempts, Melody managed a poor approximation.

'That's it.' Leila laughed. 'Now if we could just get Captain Sober to join in, we'd have a party,' she teased Pearce.

'Dancing this good needs an audience,' Pearce responded, raising his glass in salute.

He watched the three of them drinking, dancing and laughing the night away, until Leila's legs gave up on her and she had to sit down. Then, as though fatigue had brought with it darker emotions, Leila's mood changed.

'My mother taught me how to dance,' she brooded.

The remark was the wellspring of stories about Syria. Pearce had heard many of them before and they always pained him. Her sadness overflowed, steeping the room in melancholy, and Wayne and Melody returned to their seats and refilled their glasses. Most of the people Leila had ever known were dead and each of the tales was an impromptu obituary. Wayne stood and swayed his way to the radio to turn it off, and Leila carried on drinking and telling stories, her voice swelling with emotion as the tales grew more and more personal. She was partway through telling them about her older brother, Ibrahim, when she stopped abruptly. They sat in silence for a moment, before Leila started chanting. She began softly, her voice hardly travelling, a deep sense of tragedy in the words.

'*Sabihuu alraba alh alalihat li'an 'iilaa al'abad rahmatah,
Alleluia.
Sabihuu raba al'arbaba. li'an 'iilaa al'abad rahmatah,
Alleluia.
Aladhi wahdah yaemal eajayib eazimatan: li'an rahmatah
tadawm 'iilaa al'abd.*

Alleluia.'

'It's a lament,' Pearce whispered to Melody. 'She's singing for her family.'

They sat listening to Leila's song, each of them cast into sombre reflection as her beautiful voice permeated the room with the kind of solemnity only found in the highest of holy places. Tears glistened in Leila's eyes and, finally unable to cope with the potent blend of alcohol and grief, she started weeping. Ashamed, she tried to stand, but her legs failed her and she fell back onto the sofa. She cried even more, and Pearce's heart broke for her.

He went over to help. She tried to brush him away, but there was no conviction in the gesture and she allowed herself to be lifted. Wayne also moved, but Melody beat him to it and positioned herself beneath Leila's right arm. They carried her up the stairs and helped her onto the bed in the back bedroom. Melody sat beside the prone woman and stroked her hair. Pearce wished he could take Leila's pain away. She had suffered more heartache than anyone should ever have to bear. After a few minutes, her tears were replaced by the deep rhythmic breath of sleep.

Melody turned to Pearce, her eyes still brimming. 'What happened to her?'

When Pearce tried to speak, the words choked in his throat. He took a moment to compose himself. 'It's not my story to tell,' he said. 'You take the other bedroom. Wayne and I will sleep downstairs.'

Pearce returned to the living room, where Wayne was refilling his glass. He looked up, but couldn't quite focus.

'You OK?' Pearce asked.

'Fuck,' Wayne replied. 'Better than her. She's had it rough.'

Pearce nodded. 'Doesn't mean you can't talk.'

'I'm all right. Just need to get my shit together. Figure out this thing called life,' Wayne slurred. 'Like you did.'

'Like I did?' Pearce smiled. 'I haven't got anything figured out. I've spent the past two years chasing shadows.'

'But you could afford to do that because you were smart.' Wayne's index finger tapped the side of his head a little too hard. 'I pissed my money away on cars, holidays . . . bullshit. Now what? I'm thirty-three, ain't got shit, don't know what to do to get it, or what I want.' He hesitated. 'But like I said, I'm doing better than the Syrian. So I'm not going to sit here and bitch about life.'

'I'm going to take the sofa in the front room.' Pearce got to his feet. 'Don't stay up too late.'

'I won't,' Wayne replied, draining his glass and reaching for the vodka.

Chapter 16

Pearce woke at five. He dressed quietly before going into the living room, where he found Wayne passed out on the sofa, his fingers still curled round his glass, a stain beside it where the contents had spilled onto the frayed cloth. Pearce shook the snoring man, and he came round in sudden confusion. He rubbed his face, stretched and groaned.

'Why did you let me do that?' Wayne asked, his ripe breath filling the room.

'You're big enough and ugly enough to make your own decisions,' Pearce said.

'Even if they're always terrible?' Wayne fell back onto the sofa. 'I think I'm still drunk.'

'Probably. Sleep it off,' Pearce advised. 'When you're up to it, take Melody to her office. See what you can dig up on Gabriel Walker and the client.'

Wayne nodded. 'Sorry, boss.'

'What for?'

'For being a degenerate fuck-up.'

'As long as it doesn't affect your performance, I don't give a shit how you R and R,' Pearce assured Wayne. 'You see any sign of trouble, you call immediately.'

'Will do,' Wayne responded.

'We'll do an airport run,' Pearce said. 'Heathrow.'

'Got it.'

Pearce left his friend to sleep off the rest of his hangover in his fetid nest and went into the hallway, where he picked up his helmet and the Knox all-weather backpack which contained the gear he'd collected from his flat in Archway the previous afternoon.

He went outside and shut the front door quietly. It was going to be another hot day and the cloudless sky was already brightening. Pearce's motorbike was parked behind Leila's Peugeot. His early departure would spare Leila any embarrassment she might feel about what had happened the previous night. He knew her well enough to be sure she'd hate the thought she'd shown them any weaknesses. Pearce looked back at the house as he mounted his motorbike and hoped that Leila would one day find some peace.

London was the city of his birth, but he couldn't remember his early years there and had never felt entirely at home in the vast metropolis. The first experience he could recall was when Malcolm Jones had treated Pearce and three other St David's pupils to a day out in the Big Smoke, as he'd called it. Mr Jones had taken them to the Victoria and Albert Museum on the day of a hoax terror attack. Someone had phoned in a bomb threat and the museum had been evacuated. As he'd stood outside the grand old building, watching the swarming police and milling crowds, Pearce had been struck by how vulnerable everyone was. This was the perfect place for an attack: cause an evacuation and create hundreds of easy targets. His sudden realization had made him feel anxious and afraid, and ever since that moment, London had been synonymous with danger.

His military and intelligence service postings in the city had been under the constant cloud of peril, but even when he was off-barracks, there was a lingering sense of menace. Crime seemed to be getting out of hand, and if the media was to be believed, the city had reached a point where the wrong bus or tube journey could end in a random knife attack. Pearce preferred the solitude of his Welsh hideaway or the calm paradise of Railay. He couldn't understand the millions who congregated in the crowded, polluted city, spending their days as tiny anonymous cogs in this huge, dangerous machine. It didn't seem a particularly pleasant existence. Unless, like the man he was going to investigate, one had money. People like Artem Vasylyk were Olympians who could buy their way out of the filth. They lived in a parallel universe and it didn't matter whether they were in London, Paris or New York, their experience would be almost identical. For them, a big city was simply a view from the back of a limousine, or high in a helicopter as their riches literally and figuratively enabled them to rise above the masses. To them, a city's people were functionaries who sold luxury watches, tailored bespoke suits or served Michelin-starred meals. The rich mixed with their own, putting down no real roots. Instead, like a travelling circus, they moved from place to place as a troop, wintering in the Caribbean to ensure they didn't cross the UK's residency threshold for tax purposes, skiing in the spring, before heading to the Côte d'Azur for the Cannes Film Festival and the Grand Prix. Summer would be spent in London, which was a short hop by private jet for any European or Middle Eastern social events.

Pearce didn't believe in the self-regulating power of the market. In his experience, too often it wasn't the most industrious who accumulated wealth, but the most deceptive, dishonest or ruthless. Sometimes the rich were none of those things and had simply inherited their money from a parent or ancestor who'd successfully exploited such traits. According to the file Leila had given him, Vasylyk had done his own dirty work. He was a criminal kingpin who had strong-armed his way into the heavy industrial interests that had made his fortune. Vasylyk had since spent millions trying to buy respectability. He'd purchased stakes in a number of art galleries, was a patron of the opera, and had minority share-holdings in a number of high-profile companies, including tech giants and a football club. Despite his efforts to civilize himself, every photograph of Vasylyk showed a man who had cruelty imprinted on his soul. His narrow eyes had the dead stare of a shark and the smile that was customarily fixed to his face was thin and false. He had a heavy brow, a thick crop of short grey hair, and terrible acne scars that pocked his whole face. Built like a wrestler, the tall, barrel-chested man dwarfed the petite women who were often pictured on his arm. Pearce struggled to imagine Vasylyk sitting in the boardroom of a British institution such as Bayard Madison. But then it was unlikely his investment had bought him a seat. Vasylyk's money had been funnelled through a complex web of fronts, suggesting his participation was secret. Any influence he had on the bank would come from the shadows.

Pearce steered the Honda down Edgware Road and along the outer edge of Hyde Park, which was already full of early morning runners wilting in the rising heat. Avoiding the swelling traffic, he navigated the back streets around Knightsbridge to take him into Kensington. Artem Vasylyk had a home on Phillimore Gardens, a street whose residents probably had more combined wealth than some of the poorest countries in the world. Pearce arrived on the corner of Phillimore Gardens and Stafford Terrace shortly before seven and cased the neighbourhood. Vasylyk's house was a huge, perfectly appointed villa that sat behind high black railings. Directly beyond the railings was an immaculately trimmed hedge that ran the full width of the front garden. The building itself was a three-storey brown brick Edwardian structure, with large bay windows and a basement. There was no driveway or garage, which meant Vasylyk's car would be one of the luxury vehicles parked in the nearby residents' bays. The brown brickwork was broken up by painted white stonework and decorative features. The two grand porches that jutted out from either wing suggested the building might have once been two homes, or even a block of flats. None of the surrounding houses were quite as grand, and directly opposite stood a similar structure that had been split into flats, the roof of which might provide a perfect vantage point for a camera. Pearce studied the exterior of the block of flats, making a note of its ledges and contours. It would be an easy climb, even at night.

Pearce loitered on the corner of Stafford Terrace. He took off his helmet and pretended to be fixing a mechanical fault on his bike. He waited with the patience of a buzzard hovering over a rabbit hole, and after more than ninety minutes, shortly before eight thirty, Artem Vasylyk emerged from his home. He was even more imposing in person – his sour, cruel face sitting atop a body that was so broad it strained the seams of his expensive blazer. Two men in dark suits came with him, one in front, one alongside. Close protection. The lead guy looked like a prop forward – tall, muscular and fit. His sharp eyes, broken nose and scarred chin spoke of a man who'd seen combat. The second bodyguard was a huge ball, at least six foot seven, and almost as wide. He had a bulbous nose and a round shaved head. Pearce wasn't close enough to be sure, but he suspected the man was getting out of breath just walking down the paved path. This guy was a showman, a huge bodyguard designed to intimidate anyone who might be thinking of taking an opportunist crack at a principal. Despite the guy's size, Pearce knew he'd be less dangerous than the prop forward who was climbing into the driver's seat of a brand-new black Overfinch. The giant opened the rear door and Vasylyk slid onto the back seat of the modified Range Rover. The car dropped an inch when the giant laboured into the front passenger seat.

Pearce put on his helmet as the car passed, speeding south on Phillimore Gardens. He took a small circular tracking device from his backpack. It was about the diameter and thickness of a penny. Pearce jumped on his bike and set off after the Overfinch. He caught up with Vasylyk at the junction with Kensington High Street. As he pulled to a stop just behind the SUV, Pearce leaned over and attached the tracking device inside the rear wheel arch. He felt a satisfying click as a tiny but powerful magnet snapped the disc into place. The tracker was one of a number of useful devices Pearce had accumulated during his time at Six. It could provide a subject's location almost anywhere in the world.

Rather than turning right and heading for the less crowded streets of West London, Vasylyk went left and soon hit rush-hour traffic heading into the capital. With an average speed of under seven miles per hour, Pearce could have kept up on foot. On the Honda, he needed to slow and stop every now and then as Vasylyk made his way across the busy city.

Pearce tailed the Overfinch through town until they reached the financial district. He followed them onto Leadenhall Street and as he turned left onto St Mary Axe, Pearce realized he was passing the plaza where Nathan Foster had died. He looked at the broad square, which was covered with people crossing from one side to the another, and wondered if any of them knew that a man had perished on the stones beneath their feet.

The Overfinch turned left onto Undershaft, a narrow street that wound behind the City's high towers. Pearce followed it and passed the back of 1 Undershaft, the building in which Bayard Madison was located, and for a moment Pearce thought Vasylyk was going to the bank, but the modified Range Rover carried on until it reached the end of the street, pulling to a halt by a pair of glass-fronted vehicle elevators that were located at the foot of the Leadenhall Building, the towering skyscraper that stood beside Bayard Madison's headquarters.

Pearce watched the Overfinch roll slowly into one of the elevators and descend beneath the ground. He looked around and caught sight of a motorbike bay in Great St Helen's, a short street that lay beyond a narrow walkway. He rode the bike across the pavement and parked it in the bay. After he'd removed his helmet, he pulled the Ghostlink from his backpack and pressed the transmit button.

'*Go ahead,*' Leila said moments later. She sounded throaty and subdued.

'You OK?' Pearce asked.

'*Just feeling fragile,*' she replied. '*You left early.*'

'I'm on our new friend,' Pearce said. 'Can you see if he has any ties to the Leadenhall Building?'

'*Will do*,' Leila assured him. She hesitated and, in the silence, Pearce could feel mounting pressure as she steeled herself.

'It's OK,' he said. 'You don't need to say anything.'

'*Who said I was going to?*' she challenged.

'Then I take it back,' Pearce smiled.

'*You do that*,' she replied, her tone lighter. '*I'll see you later,* ya hayawaan,' she said, goading him with the Arabic for animal.

Pearce slipped the satellite communicator into his backpack and scanned his surroundings, looking for somewhere inconspicuous to settle. The sheer glass-and-steel buildings and bare concrete pavements offered little in the way of concealment, but he spied a trio of benches on a wide pavement opposite the Leadenhall Building. Standing next to an old stone church, two of the benches were empty, but there were a pair of homeless men on the third. Pearce made for one of the vacant benches. For the next few hours, he was just a London motorcycle courier on a protracted break.

Chapter 17

Leila settled in her made-to-measure RGK Octane, feeling slightly better for having spoken to Pearce. Her hangover had left her wrung out, and her legs had given up on her, so it was a chair day. She'd woken up in a strange bed shortly after dawn and had staggered to her feet unsteadily. She'd shuffled across the landing to the front bedroom, where she'd discovered Melody fast asleep. The redhead's skin was almost translucent and looked so soft and smooth. Her eyelids flickered to the rhythm of a dream. Through a gap in the curtains, Leila saw Pearce mounting his huge motorcycle, but she had no desire to speak to him. She wished she could blame the alcohol for the depressing display of the previous night, but the truth was she would never be free of the wounds the war had inflicted – they'd fester, opening at the slightest touch for the rest of her life. Her people were gone, taken from her in the most hideous ways imaginable, and now she was alone.

Leila had slipped out of the safe house without waking Wayne or Melody and had driven home. She was now in the concealed room at the back of her studio, digging into a server located in a secure vault in the Vauxhall headquarters of Six, checking details of current operations. She'd built the back door into the network soon after Pearce's departure. A virtual private link, it was a discreet way inside Six's system without leaving it vulnerable to cyberattack by its enemies. She'd found service alerts noting eight possible foreign intelligence operations in London, but none that fit the profile of whatever was happening at Bayard Madison. Certainly nothing that suggested Six was aware that Nathan Foster had been murdered as part of a coordinated plot.

The next machine along was piggybacking a Police National Computer terminal in the Isle of Man, running an image search for the two men who had tailed Pearce and Melody from Manchester Airport. Leila had dusted the phone Pearce had given her but she hadn't managed to recover any useable prints. An image search took longer and she watched the machine cycling through thousands of pictures, trying to find matches to the photos of the two unconscious men lying on the road.

Leila's mind was foggy and she knew she had to sharpen up. Six would have put an entire analytical team on an operation like this; there were already so many threads to pull at. Instead of five or six backroom experts, Pearce just had her, so she needed to be at her best. *Probably not a good idea to get blind drunk then*, she admonished herself. As she struggled with the grimy residue of alcohol polluting her body, Leila turned her mind to the question of why Artem Vasylyk had gone to such lengths to conceal his investment in Bayard Madison. Billionaires from all over the world, some completely legitimate, others less so, had invested in British companies. Like the ancient empires of Persia, Greece and Rome in their decline, Britain had become far less picky about the sources of its capital as its own reserves had fallen. Within the intelligence community and beyond, London was known as a hub for those who wished to launder funds of questionable provenance. Someone like Vasylyk didn't need to conceal a legitimate investment, which meant his money was most likely being used for illegal purposes. What was the bank doing with it? She pondered the question as she turned to a thick printout of the bank's latest transaction settlement report. She started leafing through the pages, wishing once again that she hadn't drunk quite so much the previous night.

Wayne's head throbbed as he walked Melody to the car. She looked untroubled by any after-effects of the previous night.

'I feel terrible,' she said, as they reached the end of the garden and crossed the pavement towards his old Fiesta. 'I haven't drunk that much in years.'

'You're kidding. You look fresher than a baker's loaf,' Wayne replied.

It was true. Her eyes gleamed and her hair was glossy. He'd heard her shower while he made the two cups of instant coffee that had passed for breakfast. She wore a figure-hugging T-shirt and a pair of tight navy jeans and trainers; an outfit she'd found in one of the supply cupboards in the safe house. Wayne caught himself admiring her, and made a point of focusing on the car. The central locking was broken, so he opened the passenger door for her before folding his huge frame into the tiny vehicle.

After an hour spent battling London's rush hour, Wayne pulled into a parking bay on Finsbury Street, and he and Melody got out and headed south. There were six cars parked in bays ahead of the Fiesta, and then in the final bay, near the corner of Ropemaker Street, Wayne saw something that jolted him out of his stupefying hangover. A lone biker astride a red Suzuki Hayabusa. The man had a distinctive close-crop bowl haircut and sharp features that matched the description of one of the men who'd attacked Pearce at Nathan Foster's flat. Pearce had given him the moniker 'Raptor'. The man's helmet rested on the bike's fuel tank and he was studying a dog-eared A to Z. Wayne thought that was a tell; no one used maps in the age of the smartphone.

He took hold of Melody's arm and led her across the street.

'I think we've got company,' he said, and her eyes immediately darted towards the biker.

They were on the same side of Finsbury Street as Melody's office, which was located in 25 Ropemaker Street, a shining skyscraper that had a decorative fascia of horizontal glass slats. Raptor caught sight of them as they neared the entrance, and even though the man tried to downplay it, Wayne saw a flash of recognition in his eyes.

Inside, Wayne hovered by the reception desk, keeping an eye on the biker, while Melody signed him in as a visitor. Outside, Raptor watched the building as he made a phone call. When they were waved through the lobby security gates, Wayne followed Melody into a lift, and reached into his trouser pocket for the satellite field radio Leila had given him the previous night. He pressed the transmit button.

'*Go ahead.*' Leila's voice came through the speaker.

'We're at the kid's office,' Wayne replied. 'You'd better tell the boss we've got company.'

Pearce sat on the bench, the shade of the tall buildings protecting him from the worst of the heat. From his vantage point, he had a view of the building's main entrance. It opened onto the plaza where Fozz had died, and Pearce couldn't believe that Vasylyk's proximity to Bayard Madison was simple coincidence.

The two old homeless guys on the other bench had tried to scrounge cigarettes from Pearce, but once they'd worked out he had nothing worth having, they left him alone. He'd taken what looked like a pair of shabby old NHS glasses from his backpack and put them on. No one gave him a second glance. Most of the polished City workers were too busy trying to avoid making eye contact with the two guys on the next bench – as they passed, they suddenly found themselves interested in clouds or the church's brickwork, paving slabs or their phones.

Pearce listened to the two old men on the other bench trading horror stories of life on the street. Both were hooked on spice, a cheap, previously legal high, which they despised with almost as much passion as they desired it. They traded tales of their hard lives, lingering on the memories of friends who'd fallen over the years, killed in fights, drug overdoses, suicides or simply dying in sleeping bags as crowds of people passed them.

Pearce pitied the two men – he understood the path that had led them to that bench. He was closer to them than he was to the wealthy gods and goddesses who worked in the gleaming towers that loomed all around him. If it hadn't been for St David's, his name might have been spoken by one of these two in their list of the dead. Fortune had put him on a very different path. The ambitious, self-assured workers who passed them would probably believe otherwise, but in all his experience and study, Pearce had come to the conclusion that luck, fate, fortune, whatever one called it, was the deciding factor in all human existence. Good fortune might come at birth, being born into a nurturing, well-off family, or it could intervene later, as it had in his case, landing him in St David's.

Partly driven by the desire to understand why his father had abandoned them and why his mother had given him up, Pearce had completed a distance learning degree in Philosophy. Initially unsure what to expect, Pearce had been taken on a journey through time, studying some of the most influential thinkers in history, analysing their understanding of everything, from the fundamental structure of the universe to the inner workings of the human mind. After four years of fitting study around deployments and taking leave to complete exams, Pearce graduated, armed with a new perspective on the world. He'd read hundreds of books, thousands of pages, millions of words, tested his mind with some of the most rigorous logic, explored outlandish creative thinking about plural worlds, time and dimensions, but at the end of it all, he walked away with the simple belief that fate did more than anything else to shape life.

It was a humbling perspective and one that demanded empathy as its logical consequence. The two men on the next bench weren't stupid or lazy or villainous. Fate had dealt them a hard hand, and faced with what it had thrown at them, any one of the passing upright citizens could have found him or herself hunched and humbled on that self-same bench. Fate, not hard work, not talent, not skill, was what created the gulf that separated them.

Pearce's reflections came to an end when Prop Forward, Vasylyk's bodyguard, emerged from the main entrance of the Leadenhall Building and walked in the direction of the church. Pearce reached up and swiped a concealed switch on the right arm of the glasses. A souvenir from his time with Six, the glasses had supposedly been damaged beyond repair during a mission and were meant to have been destroyed by the quartermaster, but Pearce had pilfered them and given them to Leila, who'd been able to bring them back to life. A sophisticated recording system, the lenses were purely cosmetic, and within the frames were concealed two high-powered 4K video cameras and a stereo microphone. The system would currently be writing huge quantities of data to cards concealed in the arms, capturing every moment of whatever Pearce was looking at.

When Prop Forward reached the semi-circle of potted topiary that lined the bend in the road between the two neighbouring skyscrapers, he stopped and loitered beside one of the plants. Moments later, Pearce saw a woman in her twenties leave Number 1 Undershaft. She had a deep tan, black hair that reached the middle of her back, and wore a white shift dress that was covered in thickly scrawled black script. She tried to look nonchalant, vaping as she crossed the pavement, but Pearce could see her eyes glancing at Prop Forward. She made some casual remark as she approached, and the big man laughed and touched her shoulder. But Pearce's eyes were on his other hand, which slipped something into hers. With the delivery complete, Prop Forward ambled back to his building. The woman smoked for a minute or so and then did likewise, returning to 1 Undershaft. Pearce watched her closely, and when she'd gone inside, he deactivated the glasses, wondering what the footage would reveal about the object concealed in her left hand.

He heard the soft tone of the Ghostlink coming from inside his backpack and reached in and answered.

'Go ahead.'

'*The kid's uncle says they've got company,*' Leila responded.

'Where are they?' Pearce asked.

'*At her office.*'

'I'm on my way.'

Chapter 18

Melody stood in the lift, her stomach churning. Wayne checked his reflection and ran his hand over his head. His old jeans were stained and torn at the hems, and his T-shirt had seen too many washes, its original dark blue leached a dirty grey. Skulls and stars mingled with angels in the complicated sleeve tattoos that ran down both arms to his wrists. They made him seem dangerous, but his broad smile and open face did the opposite, inspiring nothing but trust. It was an attractive mix and he carried himself with a confidence that suggested he knew his allure. Melody examined herself in the full-length mirror and felt anything but confident. Her skin was pale and dark circles shadowed her eyes. Her hair needed a good brush and the sour taste in her mouth reminded her she needed to get a toothbrush. The overall vibe she projected was hungover student.

'Should I be worried?' she asked, referring to the biker who was watching the building.

Wayne threw her a disarming smile and shook his head. 'You just do your thing and let us do ours.'

Denton Fraser had the sixteenth, seventeenth and eighteenth floors of the building. As the lift doors opened and she and Wayne stepped into the firm's lobby, the knots in Melody's stomach tightened. She wished she could have gone straight to her office on the seventeenth floor, but Pearce had binned her key card after they'd fled Railay.

'Hey, Mel!'

It was Linda, one of two receptionists whose sparkly smiles and geniality belied their clockwork efficiency.

'Melody,' Karen, the other receptionist, said with a smile. 'We've missed you.'

These two women probably knew more about the firm and its day-to-day operations than the managing partner.

'I got caught up in something,' Melody said sheepishly.

'Isn't it terrible about Mr Walker?' Karen remarked.

'Awful,' Linda agreed.

Melody nodded. 'I can't believe it. It was such a shock. This is Mr Teller,' she said, giving Wayne a false name. 'He's a client. Is Mr Norton in today?'

'Yes,' Linda replied. 'He'll be glad to see you.'

Melody felt a stab of panic. If Michael Norton was aware of her absence, it probably wasn't for good reasons. She led Wayne through the lobby to the security doors. A handful of immaculately dressed men and women sat in the waiting area, and Melody could feel their eyes on her and tried to carry herself with as much confidence as she could muster. She felt so out of place and unprepared for a return to the firm. She'd escaped death at least twice, the people who wanted to kill her were still out there, and here she was touching her old life, engaging with colleagues who couldn't possibly understand what had happened.

'Would you mind, Karen?' Melody called back. 'I forgot my card.'

'Sure,' Karen responded, slipping her hand beneath the large reception desk.

The glass doors clicked off their magnets and Melody pulled one open. She took Wayne through and led him onto the sweeping staircase that wound its way up the large atrium that connected the three floors. The view from the huge window was stunning, the bright summer sun helping London look beautiful. Melody nodded greetings at one or two puzzled colleagues who caught her eye from a distance. No one came close. Office politics meant she probably had to be sanitized by one of the higher-ups before she was considered safe.

There was no one higher than Michael Norton. He was king of the London office and had cultivated a reputation for excellence. He was methodical, bordering on slow, dedicated to the point of obsession, and possessed a mind capable of outstanding logical reasoning. Melody could imagine him as the sort of child who'd spend hours building Airfix models, but she knew that young Norton would never have indulged in such a populist pursuit. He was from an old English family and his childhood had been spent at Winchester School, where he'd been moulded into a strange Edwardian throwback. He'd once told Melody that as a teenager he enjoyed spending time at his father's London club, because it was close to the Royal Opera House. He sometimes spoke of his other childhood hobbies – grouse shooting and hunting rabbits with his two lurchers.

Melody's heart pounded as she climbed the final few steps, crossed the landing and went through the door that led to the senior partners' offices. Gabriel's was located halfway along the corridor, and Melody noticed that his assistant, Bethany, wasn't at her desk. When she and Wayne passed Gabe's open door, Melody saw that the office had been stripped bare; his things were gone. All that remained was a desk and his high-backed leather chair.

'This was Gabriel's office,' she said, indicating an open door.

Wayne peered in and frowned when he saw how empty it was.

Norton's office was located at the very end of the corridor; a vast corner suite that had views to the west and south. His two preppy assistants, Nick and Jason, were both hard at work, hunched over their computers at desks situated by Norton's open door. Jason looked up when Melody was a few feet away and dismay flickered across his face before he replaced it with a snake oil salesman's smile.

'Ms Gold,' he said. 'Michael's . . .'

'Is he in?' Melody asked, not bothering to slow as she approached the open door.

Jason stood and Nick looked up, but they were too slow to stop her and she caught sight of Michael Norton sitting in an armchair, studying some papers.

'Mr Norton,' Melody called, aware that Jason was now hovering at her shoulder. She glanced round to see an apologetic look on his face. 'I'd like to talk to you if you've got a few minutes.'

'Ms Gold, we've been deeply concerned about you.' Norton replied, his accent polished, his words clipped. 'Please do come in. Perhaps you could fetch some tea, Jason.'

'I'm OK, thanks,' Melody replied, leading Wayne into the room.

'Where have you been? Are you all right?'

Norton's eyes lingered on Wayne.

'This is—' Melody began.

'An associate,' Wayne interrupted.

'An associate?' Norton remarked. 'Well, any associate of Ms Gold's is welcome here. Shut the door please, Jason.'

Norton's young assistant looked sheepish as he withdrew, closing the door behind him.

'Please do sit,' Norton said, gesturing at the long leather couch that lay opposite two wingbacks.

The influence of his father's club could be seen in the décor of his office, which was furnished like the library of a country house. The two interior walls were covered in books, ranged on floor-to-ceiling cases. The leather seating area was surrounded by large plants in brass pots and in the corner, near where the windows met, was a huge antique desk.

Melody sat and Wayne leaned against the arm of the couch, keeping an eye on the door. Norton looked at the man and briefly grimaced. Knowing that the misuse of his furniture would trouble Norton deeply, Melody wanted to drag Wayne down next to her, but when he looked down at her and gave a cheeky wink, she wondered whether her bodyguard knew exactly what he was doing.

'What can I do for you, Ms Gold?' Norton asked. 'And your associate, of course.'

Melody wasn't sure what to say or why she was being put on the spot. A senior partner had asked her to do some work for a client. She wasn't to know what it would lead to. *Give him nothing*, she told herself, recalling the advice Gabe had once given her on negotiating strategy. 'Where do you think I've been?'

'According to your billing records, Mr Walker had you working on a research project,' Norton replied. 'No one really seemed to know. And then you vanished. As you can imagine, it's been a difficult time for the firm, what with Mr Walker's untimely passing. After so long, well, we were wondering whether you were coming back.'

And there it was. It was subtle, but with that simple statement, the buttoned-up patriarch of the firm had shared his desire. He wanted her gone. Gabe's death had been difficult for the firm, and Norton knew as well as Melody did that 'research' could cover a wide range of questionable activities.

'We discovered some irregularities in Mr Walker's affairs and were forced to report them to the SRA,' Norton said, referring to the Solicitors Regulation Authority. 'They've opened an investigation into what you and Mr Walker were doing.'

Melody's heart sank. Even if she could extricate herself from this dangerous situation, her career was now on the line. The SRA could sanction her if it found she'd breached the code of conduct.

'Mr Norton, Michael, I think it's important you know what's really been going on,' Melody said.

Norton raised his hand. 'You need to think carefully about whether the firm will be damaged by the information you're about to share.'

The firm? You mean you, Melody thought, but she didn't voice her low opinion of the egotistical selfishness that made Norton synonymous with the firm in his own mind. Instead, she told him about the mystery client who'd instructed Gabe, her involvement in the investigation, Foster's death and the attack in Railay. She made no mention of Pearce, Leila or anything that might jeopardize the ongoing investigation. After talking for a little over ten minutes, Melody sat back, aware that Norton's wide eyes were looking from her to Wayne, his mouth open, searching for words.

'Are you sure of all this?' he asked at last.

It was his polite way of calling her a liar.

'She's telling the truth,' Wayne interjected, staring Norton down.

'And you are?'

'Better you don't know my name. I served in special forces and I'm here to protect Ms Gold.'

Norton shifted awkwardly, casting his eyes around the room as if searching for a lifeline. 'Taking instructions from a client without proper vetting is a serious breach of the SRA Code of Conduct, and, well, you seem to be suggesting that Gabriel killed himself because of this.'

'I'm not suggesting,' Melody said. 'I'm telling you we think he did it to protect his family.'

'And you knew he hadn't been properly instructed?' Norton asked.

Melody could have tried to lie, but it wasn't in her blood. Her training had instilled a habit of scrupulous honesty. 'Yes,' she admitted.

Norton took a deep breath and brushed an imaginary speck of dust from the lapel of his suit. 'Well, it's clear what we must do. I need to share this new information with the SRA. You must take a leave of absence until we know the outcome of their investigation.'

Melody frowned.

'For the good of the firm,' Norton said, getting to his feet. 'As I'm sure you're aware, the SRA Code of Conduct is incumbent not only on the firm, but the individual solicitors operating within the firm.' He crossed the office and opened the door. 'I think it's only fair to warn you that the SRA takes a very dim view of improper instruction these days, what with money laundering and terrorism. I'm afraid there's a good chance you'll be struck off.'

As he spoke, he opened the office door. 'And even if you're not, we need to satisfy ourselves that you've done nothing that would bring the firm into disrepute.'

Melody had come here in need, trying to do the right thing. Instead of offering her a helping hand, the firm she'd devoted her life to was cutting her loose. Norton's meaning was clear – even if the SRA didn't find against her, the chances were she didn't have a future with Denton Fraser.

Seething, Melody got to her feet. She caught Wayne shaking his head at her glumly.

'I'll go,' Melody said when she was at the door, inches away from Norton, 'but before I do, I want to know what happened to Gabriel's things. His office is empty.'

Norton shrugged, but Jason, who was hovering just beyond the doorway, said, 'The police came and took everything that wasn't client privileged. Said it was part of the investigation into his death. Mr Walker's client work has been assigned to other lawyers.'

His professional life picked bare in mere days, Melody thought sadly.

'They leave a crime reference number?' Wayne asked.

'I wouldn't know. Facilities would have handled that,' Jason replied.

'Well, if you'll excuse me. Jason, don't I have . . .' Norton said.

'Yes, Mr Norton,' Jason chimed in, his face momentarily

blank before the lie injected some conviction into it. 'You have the partners' meeting.'

'Of course he does,' Melody said. 'I look forward to hearing the outcome of the investigation, Mr Norton. I hope I'll be able to come back to the firm soon.'

'So do I, Ms Gold.' Norton's broad smile was almost large enough to conceal his dishonesty. 'So do I.'

Wayne said nothing as they walked back along the corridor, past offices where quiet, studious lawyers were paid fortunes for their advice. He remained silent as they descended the sweeping staircase and crossed the lobby. It wasn't until they got inside the otherwise deserted lift that he finally spoke.

'Your boss is a real tosser,' he said, before reaching into his pocket for the Ghostlink. 'The kid's done,' he said, after pressing the transmit button.

'*Copy*,' Leila replied. '*You're good to go for the airport run.*'

'Copy that,' Wayne responded, before returning the communicator to his pocket.

'An airport run?' Melody asked.

'Yeah.' Wayne smiled. 'We're going to take a ride out west.'

Chapter 19

Pearce had spied their enemies. London, with all her crooked streets and tight turns, had revealed them. He'd parked at the end of Ropemaker Street and watched Wayne bring the rattling old Fiesta to the junction with Finsbury Street and point it west. As the rusty car had moved off, it had been followed by a man on a red Hayabusa, one of only a handful of road bikes in the world faster than Pearce's Honda. But Pearce didn't need speed, he needed discretion, and for the next forty minutes, he followed the Hayabusa at a distance, tracking it as it tailed Wayne on a meandering route across town.

Soon, the Hayabusa was joined by a silver VW Golf GTI and a blue Mondeo. Pearce didn't need to rely on the almost imperceptible nods the motorcyclist gave the car drivers as they rotated the pursuit; he recognized the occupants of the cars immediately. The woman with albinism was in the Golf and Boxer and Bullneck were in the Mondeo. Pearce's visor, which was reactive to light, had been rendered jet black by the blazing sun, and his identity was well concealed as he followed the trio of vehicles. They were cycling through a standard surveillance pattern, each taking turns to tail the Fiesta for a few minutes, while the other vehicles peeled off down side streets. These people had received police or intelligence training, but they didn't realize that multiple vehicles made Pearce's job easy. He was able to hang back, well beyond their field of awareness, and head in the general direction of Heathrow. Even if he lost them for a while, sooner or later he'd pick up one of the trailing vehicles. His job wasn't to tail them, it was to make sure he identified everyone involved in the pursuit of Wayne and Melody as they headed for the pre-arranged destination: Heathrow Airport.

By the time they reached the M4, Pearce was confident there were no other vehicles involved. His targets were the Hayabusa, Golf and Mondeo, and he was going to get at least one of the occupants to talk to him. The number of them and the probability they were armed stacked the odds against Pearce, but he had learned long ago to use an enemy's perceived strengths to his advantage.

Pearce slowed as he came down the ramp of the M4 flyover. He saw the Fiesta a few hundred feet ahead, followed by the three tailing vehicles. As the flyover ended and he reached level ground, Pearce lost sight of his targets and pulled onto the hard shoulder. He kicked down through the gears, stepped on the brake and killed the engine. He removed his helmet, swung the backpack off his shoulders, produced a phone and made a call.

'*Emergency. Which service?*' the operator said.

'Police,' Pearce replied.

There was the slightest pause.

'*Hello,*' a second voice said. '*Police emergency.*'

'I've just seen two cars and a motorcycle stopped on the hard shoulder of the M4,' Pearce responded. 'I can't be sure, but I think one of the occupants had a gun. They drove west towards Heathrow, but I got their plates.'

Pearce gave the operator the registrations, and then, ignoring requests for further information, hung up and tossed the phone into the bushes on the other side of the roadside barrier.

The Honda's engine hummed rhythmically as Pearce throttled down and joined the slow-moving queue of vehicles heading for the short-stay lanes outside Terminal 3. He could see the biker on the Hayabusa in the very first bay of the lane nearest the glass terminal building. The Mondeo was in the same lane, a few cars to the bike's rear, and the Golf lay to the Mondeo's right in the next lane across, four vehicles behind Wayne's Fiesta.

Pearce had hammered it along the M4 and through the Heathrow Airside Road Tunnel, and guessed Wayne and Melody had only been waiting a minute or so, sitting quietly in the Fiesta. Already, Pearce could see early signs that his plan would work. The single mention of Heathrow in his emergency call would have been sufficient to put armed response on alert, and he spotted officers in body armour running through the terminal. No one else had noticed yet, not the men and woman he'd been following, nor the dozens of travellers who were being dropped off at the airport.

Pearce wove around the cars in front and pulled into the same lane as the biker. He moved into a space on the other side of the lane, six bays behind and opposite the Hayabusa, where he'd have a great view of what came next.

As he switched off his engine, Pearce spotted an armed response vehicle stop on the link road beside the short-stay lanes. Another two unmarked vehicles pulled up behind it. Armed officers spilled from the cars, assault rifles raised, and people started running and shouting.

'Stay in your vehicles!' one of the officers yelled as he sprinted to the Mondeo.

Pearce turned to see a pair of armed officers emerge from a Mercedes that had been parked two cars behind the VW. Both men wore protective vests that were emblazoned with the word 'Police'. They ran forward, their Glocks trained on the woman in the driver's seat.

The sight of weapons sparked panic, and people ran for the terminal, past the squad of uniformed police who came racing out, their Heckler & Koch MP5s trained on the Mondeo. Within moments, the two men in the Mondeo and the woman in the VW were surrounded by police officers yelling instructions.

Pearce was dismayed that no one had tackled the biker, who kicked the Hayabusa into gear and shot forward, unchallenged in the pandemonium. Pearce's plan had been to draw their four pursuers to the airport, where people were arrested for simply breathing the wrong way. Even if they weren't armed, the merest report of a gun would see them taken into custody while their vehicles were properly searched and background checks were carried out. Custody would mean identification, and Leila would be able to pull their arrest records and find out who they were, and then, however long they were held for, Pearce and Wayne would be there when they were released and would pick them off one by one, taking them to a secure location he had in mind for a long and undisturbed interrogation.

However, the armed response unit's oversight in allowing the motorcyclist to escape presented Pearce with an opportunity. If he could catch the man, he might be able to begin the interrogation process sooner. He thumbed the ignition, kicked into first and raced after the Hayabusa, which had pulled out of the short-stay lanes and was speeding around the link road. As he gave chase, Pearce saw the two men being pulled from the Mondeo.

'Gun! Gun! Gun!' one of the armed officers yelled, snatching a pistol from the waistband of the larger of the two men.

Already in cuffs, the white-haired woman was being frog-marched towards the terminal. One of the police officers guarding her was placing a tactical knife and a pistol into separate evidence bags.

Pearce knew possession of firearms would mean at least forty-eight hours in custody. He signalled Wayne as he shot past the Fiesta, and, when he glanced in his wing mirrors, he saw the little car start to follow.

He soon lost sight of it as he moved up through the gears. With the police distracted by the incident outside Terminal 3, he wasn't worried about drawing attention to himself, so he opened up the throttle and rolled and curled his way round the slower-moving traffic, speeding past startled drivers. The other biker must have caught sight of him in his mirrors, because as it approached the Airside Tunnel, the Hayabusa suddenly shot forward, accelerating between the two lanes of traffic.

Pearce raced on, matching the blistering pace his target set. He shot into the tunnel between two lines of vehicles that were never more than a few inches either side of him. Fumes filled his nose, and the Honda's growling engine echoed off the tunnel walls as the bike touched 110. The yellow tunnel lights flashed by faster and faster until he popped out and was greeted by open sky. The Hayabusa swung right, heading for the Bath Road. As Pearce passed the scale model Emirates A380 that stood in the central reservation just beyond the tunnel mouth, a BMW changed lanes in front of him. He pulled the front brake lever and stamped on the rear brake pedal to prevent the bike flipping, and then swerved past the offending vehicle.

Pearce shot by on the inside of the BMW, riding the tight space between the car and the verge. When he got in front of the oblivious driver, Pearce accelerated, racing beneath the A4 bridge. Emerging on the other side, he banked right, sped past the line of traffic, jumped the lights, wove between the vehicles filtering from the left – to the consternation of the nearest drivers – and raced up the A4 slip road with the sound of car horns blaring in his ears.

At over a quarter of a ton, the Honda wasn't easy to get off the ground, but Pearce caught some air as the slip road levelled out. He shot through another set of red lights, narrowly avoiding a collision with a white Mazda, and sped onto the A4. The encounter with the BMW had cost him valuable time, and he could see the Hayabusa about a quarter of a mile ahead. It was the kind of gap that required mortal risks to close, and Pearce wasn't going to gamble. He'd wait until Bullneck, Boxer or the white-haired woman were released.

Pearce slowed and glanced up at the sky to see a fat jumbo jet descending. When he looked back at the road, a sudden movement caught his eye. For a moment, time stood still, and Pearce saw the Hayabusa in an impossible position, high in the air, its front wheel pointing straight down, three feet from the road, its rear wheel facing the bright sky, the biker thrown clear, his back contorted into a dreadful arch. The moment seemed to last an age, but reality finally came rushing in and the bike flipped and spun as the rider was tossed like a doll before slamming to an abrupt halt when he hit a Transit van.

Pearce didn't know whether the biker had clipped another a vehicle or if he'd simply been going too fast to keep control, but he'd seen enough battlefield trauma to know the man was dead.

A tailback built quickly, but Pearce filtered his way through the stationary traffic and was soon level with the scene. People were out of their cars, crowding round the motionless biker. Someone had lifted the man's visor, revealing a face Pearce recognized. It was the man he'd named Raptor. A woman in a suit was performing CPR, but the wicked angle of the Raptor's neck and the growing pool of blood oozing from an unseen wound told Pearce that the man's lifeless eyes would never see again.

Pearce didn't stop. He wove through the wreckage of the crash, past the last parked cars and opened up the throttle when he reached the empty stretch of road that lay ahead.

Chapter 20

'One of our friends made a mess on the A4,' Pearce said. He'd pulled into the car park of the McDonald's on Henlys roundabout and was looking at the converted pub, absently watching hungry people tapping away on the self-service screens as he used the Ghostlink to talk to Leila. 'Raptor won't be coming to any more parties.'

'*I'll keep watch,*' Leila replied. '*See if the police name him. What about the rest of our friends?*'

'They got picked up.'

'*I'll keep an eye on them too,*' Leila said.

'You got a read on the Ukrainian?' Pearce asked, referring to the tracker he'd planted on Artem Vasylyk's car.

'*Give me a moment.*'

'I need to see you,' Pearce said, while Leila was occupied. 'My glasses need fixing,' he added, referring to the footage he'd captured earlier. He wanted to know what Vasylyk's bodyguard had handed to the woman who'd emerged from the Bayard Madison building.

'*I'll come by later,*' Leila replied. '*Our friend is in Golden Square. He's been there for over an hour.*'

'Thanks,' Pearce responded, before disconnecting. He put the Ghostlink in his backpack and was soon racing east along the A4.

*

It was a little after six when Pearce rode into Golden Square. He parked his bike in a bay in the north-east corner and removed his helmet as he dismounted. He could see Vasylyk's Range Rover on the other side of the square. Prop Forward was in the driver's seat, watching something on the TV in the central console. Pearce walked into the square, grateful for the cover provided by the scores of people clustered in the small green space, soaking up the evening sun. Even if Prop Forward noticed him, he was just another face in the crowd.

Pearce sat on the grass and scanned the surrounding build- ings, wondering where Vasylyk might be. The square was overlooked by four- and five-storey buildings, terraced in tight rows. Mostly office blocks, there were a few bars, restaurants and boutiques set in the ground floors of the buildings. The bars were filling up, and people spilled onto the pavements, puffing cigarettes or vaping as they chatted and drank.

Pearce's gaze lingered on a five-storey brown-brick build- ing in the south-west corner. The simple Georgian structure would have been unremarkable but for its opaque black win- dows and the two lean men in suits who stood either side of a large glossy door. Pearce watched a Mercedes pull up and disgorge two men who looked like they'd just walked off an Armani catwalk. Tanned, stubbled and oozing easy confi- dence, the new arrivals were greeted with nods, and one of the suited doormen swiped a key card and opened the large door. Pearce took the Ghostlink from his backpack and called Leila.

'*Go ahead,*' she said.

'I need you to run an address. Find out what it is,' Pearce responded. He guessed the building number from the digits on the doors of its neighbours and gave it to Leila. While he was giving Leila the details, a navy blue Rolls-Royce pulled up outside.

'*Give me a few minutes,*' Leila told him.

'As quick as you can,' Pearce told her, getting to his feet so he had a better view of the man exiting the Rolls. He'd seen him once before, on screen in the secret room hidden in Leila's studio. One of the doormen nodded as Lancelot Bayard Oxnard-Clarke, the eighteenth Viscount Purbeck, glided into the mysterious building.

Pearce returned to his bike and chained his helmet to the rear wheel. He crossed the square, heading straight for the south-west corner. When he reached the junction with Lower John Street, Pearce was no more than twenty feet from the two security guards who manned the door, but he knew that even if he could bluff his way past them, there was likely to be another layer of security inside. Getting in would require more than simply waltzing through the front door.

He continued down Lower John Street, reaching into his backpack when he heard the soft tone of the Ghostlink.

'Go ahead,' he told Leila.

'*Looks like a private members' club,*' she responded. '*It's owned by Nine Holdings Limited, which is itself owned by a company domiciled in the Cayman Islands. I'm following the chain, trying to find the ultimate owner, but it will take a while.*'

'Thanks,' Pearce responded as he continued south, scanning the unbroken line of Georgian buildings.

He was looking for an alleyway or service entrance that ran to a rear courtyard, but there was none. Pearce turned right onto Brewer Street and was considering picking the lock of one of the buildings on the block, until he reached the corner of Warwick Street. A few feet along from the junction a building was undergoing major renovation. Scaffolding covered the upper floors and the pavement had been shielded by a protective plywood tunnel. Pearce scanned the street. Plenty of pedestrians, but most crossed to the other side to avoid the tunnel. It was an awkward, confined space that required people to stand aside if they met someone coming the other way. Pearce made straight for the structure. When he was halfway along the narrow wooden tunnel, he found what he was looking for: a sill that led to a two- by one-foot duct which ran up from the right wall. He glanced in both directions to check he couldn't be seen and tossed his backpack into the duct. Then, with his back to the wall, he jumped to grab the lip of the sill. In one fluid movement, he brought his legs over his head and sent them up into the duct. As his body curled, he pushed against the lip of the wall and momentum carried him through the narrow space onto a wooden walkway on the first floor of the scaffolding. Shielded from the street by the opaque dust protection sheets that encased the structure, Pearce picked up his pack and started climbing. Once he reached the roof, he pulled himself over the balustrade, took off his jacket and stashed it behind a skylight next to his bag. He grabbed the surveillance glasses from the backpack and set off.

He dusted off his black T-shirt and motorcycle jeans and picked his way across the rooftops, heading north-east, trying to gauge exactly where the club was. After a couple of minutes, he realized he wouldn't have to rely on his memory of the block layout; he could hear a hubbub of voices. As he rounded a stairwell, Pearce caught sight of a roof terrace three buildings along. A wooden canopy covered one half of the terrace and huge plants and abstract sculptures were laid around the space asymmetrically, making it seem more spacious than it really was. Attentive staff in red waistcoats swept around the chattering clientele, serving drinks and snacks. There were tables and chairs under the canopy, all of which were occupied. The exposed space was standing room only and small groups of people gathered beneath the shade of the potted trees and bushes.

Pearce inwardly cursed his bad luck. There was no cover on the two adjacent roofs, so he wouldn't be able to mask his approach. He could go back the way he came, but there was no guarantee he'd be able to find a better way in. There was nothing for it. Pearce walked forward, his brown Arma boots clomping on the rooftop as he made no attempt to conceal himself. He pinned a smile to his face when he noticed some of the patrons eyeing him and gesturing to their companions. Pearce spotted a waiter on an intercept course and quickly scanned the faces of the people nearest the southern balustrade. He spied a group of three women in colourful summer dresses, standing with a guy in a blue linen suit. Pearce hopped over the balustrade and headed straight for them.

'That's the last time I do anything like that for a dare,' he said, his voice plum posh and jovial. 'Bloody scary high, 'specially at the edges.'

The women smiled politely, but the man wasn't so easily won over. 'Sorry, but do I know you?' he asked.

'Not yet,' Pearce smiled, glancing sideways at the approaching waiter, who hesitated, eyeing the group with suspicion. 'But we can work on that.'

'Sir?' the waiter asked. 'May I ask what you were doing?'

'Winning a bet,' Pearce replied confidently. 'Viscount Purbeck wagered me my soul that I couldn't walk the perimeter of the roof.' He looked round quizzically. 'Don't tell me the old duffer wasn't even here to see it. Blast! I'm not doing it again.'

The waiter smiled indulgently. 'I'd advise against it, sir,' he said, backing away.

Relieved, Pearce gave the puzzled man next to him a chummy pat on the arm and smiled at the ladies. 'I'll buy you a drink later,' he told them as he withdrew.

He crossed the terrace, heading for the glass doors that led into the building. The sensation of his arrival had passed. He'd been dismissed as yet another rich, reckless eccentric, and hardly drew a second glance as he picked his way round the assembled groups. Once inside, he followed a landing to a hardwood staircase and casually skipped down the stairs.

When he came to the next landing, a sign on a door to his right told Pearce that a private cinema lay beyond. To his left another flight of stairs ran down to the floor below, and when he peered over the bannister, Pearce saw a large, crowded dining room. A queue of people gathered by a counter, waiting to be seated. Pearce heard laughter behind him, coming through a set of glass doors the colour of thick smoke. Each door had a handle that was illuminated by a crimson neon strip. He crossed the landing and pushed one of the doors open to reveal a dimly lit cocktail bar.

Decorated in the style of a futuristic speakeasy, it had semi-circular booths lining three walls of the room. The bench seats were trimmed with red and orange light strips. The fourth wall was taken up by a long bar that stood behind low-backed stools that had red neon strips running up their stems. The bar itself was covered in LED lights that were set beneath a glass counter. There were dozens of lights hanging from the high ceiling, their neon orange filaments glowing like fireflies. Colours moved everywhere, and Pearce realized customers and serving staff were using glasses that had LED lights built into their bases. Like stars drifting around a tiny galaxy, the lights created a beautiful, trippy environment.

Pearce eased his way into the room, heading for the bar. As he reached it and pressed up to the counter, he spied Artem Vasylyk sitting in a booth in the right-hand corner of the room. There were two women seated either side of him: one Japanese, one black and two white. Although they were different ethnicities, the women shared certain common characteristics. They were all stunningly beautiful, young, slim and clad in very short summer dresses. Vasylyk's huge bodyguard leaned against the corner of the bar opposite the booth, keeping a watchful eye on his principal.

Pearce thought he was simply watching a billionaire at play until he spotted who was in the adjacent booth. Seated with a mixed group of gorgeous young men and women was Lancelot Bayard Oxnard-Clarke, the eighteenth Viscount Purbeck.

Oxnard-Clarke had a gaunt, puritanical face. His tailored navy blue suit clung to his rangy frame perfectly. There wasn't a single crease out of place and his crisp white shirt was bisected by a woven silk tie. According to Leila's briefing, Lancelot was fifty-six, but Pearce would have guessed he was younger. Thick black hair sprouted above a remarkably fresh face, and only his temples were flecked with grey. It was either an exceptionally good dye job or middle-age hadn't yet taken a proper hold. The intense eyes of an eagle lay either side of a patrician's nose. Pearce couldn't help feeling he was looking at a tamed predator.

'What can I get you?' one of the bartenders asked.

'Rum and dry,' he replied, and the man moved along the bar to make the drink.

Pearce turned and settled against the counter, putting the surveillance glasses on and activating the recording system. He scanned Vasylyk's and Lancelot's booths, settling on each of their companions for a moment, hoping that the system would capture sufficiently high-quality images to enable identification.

'Here you go, sir,' the bartender said, placing a rum and ginger ale on the counter. It was served in a black glass that had a pulsing red LED in its base. The rhythm of the light was mesmerizing.

Pearce reached for his wallet, but the bartender shook his head.

'There's no money in here,' he said. 'Your host should have told you that.'

'Yes, sorry,' Pearce said. 'It's just habit.' Of course the rich wouldn't sully themselves with actual money.

'Who should I bill this to?' the bartender asked.

'The Viscount Purbeck,' Pearce replied. He doubted Oxnard-Clarke would settle his own bill and even if he did, a single drink was unlikely to be noticed, given the size of his entourage.

'Thank you, sir.'

The bartender moved on to his next customer and Pearce turned to study the two booths in the corner of the room. He nursed his drink and watched the two seemingly unconnected groups. Finally, after a few minutes, Pearce realized that these weren't two separate conversations. He was watching a relay that followed a particular pattern. Vasylyk would say something to one of his companions, who would repeat it to her neighbour. The neighbour would then lean over to one of the people in Oxnard-Clarke's booth and relay what had been said. The message would move along the chain until it reached Oxnard-Clarke, who would then reply in similar fashion. The two men could sit holding a conversation for hours without anyone but the closest observer having any clue that they were talking to each other.

Pearce eyed the booth on the other side of Vasylyk's, wondering whether he could get close enough to hear what was being said, but it was occupied by an animated group of young men and women. Pearce was considering whether he could return with a directional mic when the blonde who sat to the left of Vasylyk, and had been whispering in his ear, eased herself past her companion and slid out of the booth. About five foot seven, the blonde had wavy shoulder-length hair that fell about her unblemished face. Her bright blue eyes met Pearce's as she walked towards the bar. She looked ill at ease and Pearce immediately found himself wondering what troubled her. She wore a white and red dress that was patterned with kisses and her feet were bound in lace-up red high heels. She paused by Vasylyk's huge bodyguard, touched his arm and said something to him before heading in Pearce's direction.

The blonde edged her way into the tiny gap to Pearce's right and pressed against him. He could smell subtle floral notes of an expensive perfume.

'This place seems to get busier and busier,' the blonde observed. 'I couldn't help notice you watching us.'

'Sorry,' Pearce said, kicking himself for being careless enough to get spotted. 'So many beautiful women. It's hard not to look.'

'Honest, but not very politically correct,' the woman smiled. 'I haven't seen you here before.' Her eyes travelled the length of his body, taking in his casual clothes, which were out of place in a room full of designer labels and couture.

'It's my first time,' Pearce replied. 'I'm thinking of joining.'

She frowned. 'I suppose some people must be into this sort of thing,' she remarked. 'I'm Alexis.' She smiled and offered her hand.

'David,' Pearce replied.

'Nice to meet you, David.'

'So you wouldn't recommend it?' Pearce asked. 'Joining, I mean?'

'I wouldn't come here by choice,' she said seriously. 'Sometimes you do things because you have to.'

'It can't be that bad,' Pearce joked, but his words didn't even raise a smile.

'Even the most beautiful illusion is built on a lie,' Alexis said. Then, after a moment's hesitation, she added, 'Have you ever needed help, David? But just didn't know who to ask?'

Pearce was about to reply when he sensed movement.

'Everything OK?' Vasylyk's huge bodyguard loomed up behind them. He had a thick Ukrainian accent.

'I'm just getting a drink,' Alexis replied. Her eyes fell to the floor. She was clearly afraid to meet the man's gaze.

'Table service,' the bull-necked man said, nodding towards a passing waiter.

Alexis glanced at Pearce before backing away. 'Nice speaking to you.'

Pearce watched her return to the table, wondering whether he'd just found a way to get into Vasylyk's inner circle.

Chapter 21

Pearce watched the big bodyguard steer Alexis back to the booth. As he looked at the three other women sitting with Vasylyk, Pearce saw them in a new light. Their smiles seemed forced, their faces strained. Were Alexis's words more than a casual remark? *I wouldn't come here by choice. Have you ever needed help?* Were these women Vasylyk's willing companions? As she slid along the bench, Alexis kept her eyes on Pearce. The sadness in them made him want to reach out to her. He'd seen the look before, on the faces of Leila, Melody, Wayne and the countless other people he'd helped over the years. It made him think of his mother, struggling alone as her life fell apart around her.

When Alexis had been returned to her position at Vasylyk's side, the giant bodyguard glared at Pearce, who knew he'd drawn far too much attention to himself. He stepped away from the bar and pushed his way across the crowded room. He left through the smoked doors, hurrying down the winding stairs until he reached the ground-floor reception area. He crossed a tiled mosaic floor and the front door was held open by a uniformed doorman. Nodding to the security guards, Pearce made a right and walked to Brewer Street. Once he'd turned the corner, he started running and returned to the wooden tunnel beneath the scaffolding on Warwick Street.

He repeated the manoeuvre that got him inside the structure, flipping himself up through the drainage duct. He climbed to the roof where he retrieved his backpack and jacket, before returning down the scaffolding and dropping through the duct.

Within minutes, Pearce was back in Golden Square, sitting on a bench next to a couple of young shirt-and-tie office workers who were sharing a joint. People came and went while Pearce watched and waited.

It was approaching ten thirty when Pearce finally saw Alexis leave the club. She was accompanied by the giant bodyguard, who led her to Vasylyk's Overfinch. The lumbering man opened the rear passenger door and ushered her inside. Pearce got to his feet and headed for his bike, watching as the giant returned to the club and the Overfinch drove away. Reaching the edge of the square, Pearce unlocked his helmet, jumped on the Honda and followed.

He hung back, keeping just in sight of the Range Rover as it sped along the back streets of Soho. He almost lost the big car when it turned right onto Regent Street just as the lights changed, but he jumped the red, ignored the angry horn blast of a cabbie and re-established contact when the Range Rover was forced to stop at the junction with New Cavendish Street. He tailed it into Regent's Park, along the Outer Circle past London Zoo and onto Avenue Road, over the bridge that crossed the Regent's Canal. The Range Rover made an illegal right onto Prince Albert Road and Pearce followed, shooting through the lights as they changed. Shortly after the junction with Titchfield Road, the large car slowed and turned left into the driveway of an apartment complex. Pearce turned into

Titchfield Road, dropped the bike onto its kickstand and hurried across Prince Albert Road, taking shelter in the shadow of a tall beech tree. From his vantage point, he saw the Range Rover stop outside the first block in the apartment complex, a six-storey red-brick art deco structure that overlooked the park.

Alexis got out of the car and walked into the building. She left the back door open, a minor act of rebellion, and Pearce could feel Prop Forward's annoyance when he got out and jogged round to shut it. By the time he'd driven away, Alexis was nowhere to be seen, but Pearce was patient. He removed his helmet and stood in the gloom, the leaves rustling high above him, cars speeding by on the busy road.

After a few minutes, Pearce saw Alexis step onto a broad balcony that overlooked the park. She leaned against the railing and peered beyond the treetops. Even from a distance, Pearce could feel the same melancholy he'd sensed in the club. This was someone in trouble.

The sound of the Ghostlink interrupted Pearce's thoughts and he pulled it from his backpack.

'*I have news on our friends,*' Leila said when he answered.

Pearce looked up at the sad figure on the balcony, reluctant to leave someone in need.

'I'm on my way,' he replied.

Pearce arrived at the safe house on Vyner Road after eleven, and Wayne nodded a greeting when he opened the door.

'I hear we lost one,' he said, referring to the death of Raptor.

'He took a tumble,' Pearce replied, following him into the kitchen.

Leila and Melody were sitting at the kitchen table with three cups of tea.

'You want one?' Wayne indicated the brews.

Pearce shook his head, put his helmet on the worktop and slung the backpack off his shoulder, before taking a seat.

'Everyone OK?' he asked.

Leila and Wayne nodded, but Melody gave him a troubled look. 'Did one of the men die?'

'Yes,' Pearce replied. 'He lost control of his bike. There was nothing I could do.'

Melody didn't look convinced, but kept any worries to herself.

'What have you got?' Pearce asked Leila.

She pulled a laptop from her satchel. Within moments she had it set up on the table and was cycling through a series of arrest records, personnel files and photographs.

'I checked the booking system and custody reports,' Leila said. 'Three suspects arrested outside Terminal 3 on charges of illegal possession of firearms and preparing an act of terrorism. One woman, Brigitte Attali, a French national, and two men, Robert Kemp and Steve Dunbar, both British. They've been taken to New Scotland Yard. I checked the Police National Computer, but these three don't have criminal records. However, two of them, Kemp and Dunbar, are on there, listed as exclusions. I'm still running background, but they were *askari*.'

Wayne exhaled loudly. 'Fuck.'

'Are you sure?' Pearce asked.

'What's *askari*?' Melody asked.

'*Askari* is the Arabic word for police,' Leila explained. 'Exclusions are fingerprints held on file to enable crime scene technicians to rule officers out of investigations in the event they contaminate a scene. Kemp and Dunbar were cops.' She pointed at two photographs on her screen and Pearce recognized the two men who stared back at him.

To avoid any doubt, Leila opened one of the images Pearce had taken of the two men he'd knocked unconscious in the country lane. Kemp and Dunbar were the men he'd called Bullneck and Boxer.

'Keep track of Scotland Yard's booking system,' Pearce told Leila. He looked at Wayne. 'I want us there if and when they get released. We should be able to grab at least one of them.'

Wayne nodded.

'We've got time. They'll be held for at least forty-eight hours. More likely seventy-two,' he said, before turning to Leila. 'Can you get files on them? Personnel records, high-profile cases they worked, anything like that.'

'Yes,' Leila sighed.

'Problem?' Pearce responded.

Leila looked around the room. 'We're running thin, Scott. This sort of operation would normally have a team four or five times this size. We don't have the resources.'

'What are you saying?' Pearce asked.

'That you shouldn't expect miracles.'

'You've been doing a great job,' Pearce assured her. 'I'm not expecting miracles and I know that we've got to take a lot of rough to get to the smooth. It's the nature of this gig.'

Leila was right, though. An operation like this would have had an entire Six team on it, maybe a dozen people, perhaps more.

'I want out,' Melody said to the surprise of the other three. 'I want to see my mum,' she continued, her voice cracking. 'I'm not like the rest of you. I can't take living like this. People are dying.'

'You're the only one who absolutely can't go home,' Pearce replied as gently as possible. 'You leave and you'll be in immediate danger. If the people behind this get hold of you, they will torture you and anyone you love to find out who your client is.'

'But I don't know,' Melody protested.

'You can try to convince them of that,' Pearce said coolly, 'while they hurt you. And when they can't break you, because you don't have the information you need to be broken, they'll wheel your mum in strapped to a car battery, or maybe they'll use a blowtorch to burn her inch by inch.'

Melody shuddered.

'I'm sorry to be so blunt,' Pearce said. 'But that's the reality of this world. You can't leave until it's over. It's too dangerous.'

'It's going to be OK,' Wayne said. 'Things always get ugly before they get better.'

'Vasylyk has an office in the building next to Bayard Madison,' Pearce told them, producing the surveillance glasses from his jacket pocket. 'I caught his bodyguard handing something to a woman who came out of the Bayard Madison building. My guess is it's a USB drive.'

'I'll have a look,' Leila said, taking the glasses.

'After the airport run, I picked Vasylyk up at a private members' club on Golden Square,' Pearce continued. 'Lancelot Oxnard-Clarke, Viscount Purbeck, was there at the next table. They were running messages through a human chain. Probably coded so none of the links know what the messages mean. It's old-school tradecraft, but it's effective. The light was poor, but you might be able to get some IDs. There was one woman, she made me . . .'

Leila shook her head in dismay.·

'Not like that,' Pearce said. 'I don't think she's a threat. She suggested she was under duress. She might be a way in. I followed her to a flat on Prince Albert Road. I'm going to need a file on her. I'll give you the address.'

'OK,' Leila responded.

'Thanks,' Pearce remarked. 'I know it's a lot, but we couldn't do this without you.'

'What next?' Wayne asked.

'Even a state intelligence agency will struggle to get another surveillance team up and running by tomorrow,' Pearce said. 'So I'd like you to go to Gabriel Walker's house and talk to his wife. See if you can find anything that links him to the client.' He looked at Melody. 'Do you think you can do that?'

Melody stared back and for a moment he thought she might start crying. Her gaze shifted to Leila and Wayne, and in the end he sensed weary resignation. Finally, she nodded.

'And you?' Wayne asked.

'I'm going to work the woman who made me,' Pearce replied. 'See if she can be turned.'

Chapter 22

Pearce lay in the front room staring at the walls. The lime green wallpaper had been turned a sickly colour by the orange light that bled through the tissue-thin curtains. He squirmed restlessly on the sofa, which was lumpy and sagged in the centre, but his inability to sleep was nothing to do with his uncomfortable surroundings. He was replaying everything in his mind, going over every moment since Melody had torpedoed his investigation in Railay. He was trying to understand the link between a Ukrainian mobster, a British viscount and Nathan Foster's death. Kemp and Dunbar were former cops, and they, the white-haired woman, Brigitte Attali, and their as-yet-unidentified dead comrade known only as Raptor, all seemed to have at least some rudimentary training in tradecraft. It felt like a foreign intelligence operation in so many ways, but according to Leila's research, neither the Box nor Six were aware of it. •

It was that dark time of night when ugly thoughts took hold, and Pearce reflected on Leila's remarks. They didn't have the people, resources or array of skills to tackle an operation of this scale. Maybe he should go to Six, share what little they knew? But he'd left under a cloud, after trying to get the organization to see that the men he'd killed in Islamabad weren't the end of the story. They refused to listen when he suggested the attack had been planned overseas, the strings pulled by as-yet-unseen hands. His reputation had been trashed by his old boss, the Director of Intelligence, Dominic McClusky, and Pearce had let rip, giving the soulless careerist the full force of his anger during a department meeting. Pearce had been placed on immediate leave, before being shown the exit after a cursory internal investigation. He'd crashed from hero of Islamabad to insubordinate conspiracy nut in a matter of months. No, he couldn't go back to Six, not until he had evidence and knew much more about who and what they were up against.

There was a knock at the door, which opened an instant later.

'I'm coming in,' Leila said, shuffling inside. She leaned against the sofa for support.

Pearce knew something was wrong.

'They've been sprung,' Leila revealed. 'Kemp and Dunbar are already out. The woman hasn't been released yet. Her nationality is causing a delay. They've got someone from the French embassy with her now.'

Pearce was reeling. Carrying guns at an airport, being charged with preparing an act of terrorism – these weren't things that just disappeared. He'd been cautious in his assessment of a forty-eight-hour hold, even secretly worried they might not have been released at all, an outcome that would have robbed him of the opportunity to pick one up for interrogation. A release this swiftly meant they were either working for the government in some capacity or for someone else who had significant pull.

'How?' he asked.

'I don't know,' Leila replied. 'My legs were doing their bit to make sure I couldn't sleep, so I started working on files for the three of them. I was checking their arrest reports for addresses, dates of birth, and that's when I saw they'd been released.'

This was the worst possible result. They'd have to act fast if they were to have any hope of salvaging something positive from the situation.

'Wake Wayne up,' he said. 'Have him meet me at Victoria Embankment with his car. You stay here with Melody.'

'What are you going to do?' Leila asked.

'I'm going get there before the Frenchwoman is released.'

Pearce shot into Central London on the Honda, arriving at New Scotland Yard soon after 3.30 a.m. As he rode along Victoria Embankment, the overripe fruit and faint sewage smell of the River Thames filled his helmet, the lingering aroma of another sweltering day. Pearce followed a couple of black cabs and a delivery truck past the modern concrete building that was Metropolitan Police Headquarters. He slowed as he came to the gated access road that led into the secure complex. He needed to know whether the Frenchwoman, Brigitte Attali, was still inside and had thought about posing as her boyfriend or lawyer and approaching the receptionist. The risks involved in claiming to be associated with her were huge. Someone had arranged for her accomplices to be sprung and there was no telling whether they or their liberator were still around. Pearce had decided on a simpler, less risky approach. A representative from the French Embassy would probably have diplomatic plates. Pearce glanced along the access road, beyond the high black gates, and scanned the parking bays. As his bike growled slowly past, he saw what he was looking for: a silver Renault in one of the spaces. The central 'D' in its plate signified the driver was to be accorded diplomatic privileges.

Pearce rode along the quiet road until he reached the traffic lights by Horse Guards Avenue. He did a U-turn and rode back towards New Scotland Yard. When he was fifty feet from the building, Pearce slowed and hopped the kerb. He steered across a cycle lane and brought his motorbike to a halt on the broad promenade beside the river. He was next to a long, low monument that commemorated the Battle of Britain. He killed the engine and lights and wheeled the Honda round to face the police station. There was no law preventing motorcycles stopping on pavements, but he was in the heart of the government district and didn't want to risk unwanted attention by staying put for too long.

He needn't have worried. Minutes later, he saw the Renault with the diplomatic plates reverse out of the parking space and drive through the security gates. The driver – a thin, dark-haired young man – slowed as he approached the junction with Victoria Embankment, and turned left, heading east towards Waterloo Bridge. Pearce looked at the police station as Brigitte Attali, the striking woman he'd disarmed and incapacitated in the street outside Nathan Foster's flat, walked through the main doors. She scanned her surroundings with the air of a wild predator checking to see if there were any other beasts around.

Pearce sat absolutely still, but the woman had keen eyes and spotted him. He expected Attali to run and was trying to figure out how best to capture and hold her until Wayne arrived with his car, but she did something very surprising. She started down the station steps and crossed the wide pavement, heading straight for him. When she reached the road, she ran across the three empty lanes. Pearce dismounted and removed his helmet. Held by its strap, it was a potent weapon. The woman showed no emotion as she recognized him, not even the slightest sign of fear.

'*Qu'est-ce que tu fous là?*' she said angrily. She had a thick Parisian accent. 'What the hell are you doing here? Who are you?'

'Who are *you*?' Pearce countered. He hadn't been expecting this.

'You're not British Intelligence, that much is clear,' she continued as though he hadn't spoken. 'And you don't work for them.' The way she said 'them' suggested she was talking about an unidentified enemy. 'Whoever you are, you're in danger of fucking up everything! So get lost and stay lost.'

She turned to walk away, but Pearce grabbed her by the arm. The reaction was instantaneous: she wheeled round and threw a punch, which he ducked. She tried a knee to the side, but he stepped away from it. She knew how to fight, but when he backed off, so did she.

'Why were you following us?' Pearce asked.

Brigitte shook her head. 'You still don't get it.'

Pearce hesitated. 'The knife,' he remarked, with a sudden moment of realization. 'DGSE, anti-terrorism. You're undercover. The embassy guy who just left wasn't helping you with an immigration snafu. He's your handler. You used your arrest as an opportunity to debrief.'

Brigitte watched him impassively, her white hair and sparkling blue eyes almost shining in the darkness.

'You're undercover,' Pearce repeated.

'I don't know you,' Brigitte said, 'but if I'd wanted to, I could have stuck that knife in your heart. You owe me your life.'

Her mood had softened, so Pearce resisted the urge to correct her misunderstanding of what had happened when they'd faced each other outside Foster's flat.

'I'm asking you to back off,' she continued. 'You keep playing this game, you're going to jeopardize everything.'

'Tell me what the game is,' Pearce responded.

'If you don't know, it's because you aren't qualified to play,' Brigitte said, moving off. 'Just stay away.'

Pearce made to follow, but she raised her hands menacingly.

'Really?' she asked. 'Here?' She looked across at New Scotland Yard. 'I can afford to get arrested again. Can you?'

She smiled darkly when she saw Pearce stop in his tracks. He watched as she turned and ran across the street. She dodged a passing taxi and kept running north until she'd disappeared along Richmond Terrace, a narrow passageway that ran alongside New Scotland Yard and led to Whitehall.

Pearce climbed on his bike, rested his helmet on the fuel tank and switched on the Ghostlink.

'*Go ahead,*' Leila's voice filled his ear.

'Let Fiesta know he can stand down,' Pearce said. 'I'm on my way home.'

'*You sure?*' Leila asked, obviously perplexed.

'Yeah,' he replied.

He pocketed the communicator and put on his helmet. As the bike roared to life, he consoled himself with the thought that his journey had not been entirely wasted. He now knew that whatever was going on was of sufficient importance to have attracted the attention of French Intelligence.

Chapter 23

Leila was feeling the grimy effects of fatigue by the time Pearce returned to the safe house. Wayne had arrived twenty minutes before him, and Leila could tell he was confused and somewhat disappointed not to have been part of the action. Leila leaned against the kitchen counter for support. Melody, who had woken when Leila roused Wayne, offered her a chair, but Leila's legs had reached the stage where they were painful whether she was standing or sitting. At least remaining upright would help keep the pain out of her back.

Pearce was telling them about his encounter with Brigitte Attali. Wayne was listening intently. Melody seemed exhausted, her eyelids parting like reluctant lovers whenever she blinked. She was seated by the kitchen table, her heavy head propped up by her hands.

'You think she was telling the truth?' Wayne asked, when Pearce finished.

'Yeah,' Pearce replied. 'She seemed to have a problem with Six, which suggests the French have made efforts to conceal the operation from both Six and the Box.'

'The Box?' Melody asked.

'MI5,' Pearce responded. 'Domestic Intelligence.'

'Attali won't be her real name,' Leila observed.

Pearce nodded.

'But it gives us a definite starting point. DGSE will have an ops file. Someone will be running this from Mortier,' Leila said, referring to DGSE headquarters. 'I'll do some digging.'

'Thanks,' Pearce responded, checking the time. It was 5.03 a.m. 'We should get some rest.'

'And tomorrow?' Wayne asked.

'We proceed as planned. I'll see what this Alexis—'

'Alexis Tippett-Jones,' Leila interrupted. She was gratified by Pearce's surprise. 'I couldn't sit around and do nothing while you were out on a date with a French girl.' She smiled. 'The flat is registered to Constellation, the Monaco company Vasylyk owns through a chain of fronts and shells. Constellation pays all the utility bills. But I did a reverse look-up on bank accounts and credit cards and found a couple in Alexis's name registered to that address. Her mother is Willow Tippett-Jones, a British socialite who now lives in France. Willow is married to Philippe Durand, a French multimillionaire. According to Alexis's birth certificate, she was born before Willow and Durand met. Her biological father is listed as unknown on the birth certificate. She did a masters in Comparative Politics at LSE. Constellation clears her credit card balance every month.'

'OK, so we have a link to Vasylyk,' Pearce said. 'I'll check out Alexis tomorrow, and you –' he signalled Wayne – 'and Melody go to Gabriel Walker's house, but be careful. Our friends got sprung early, so we can't be sure there won't be surveillance. If you see them again, you call me.'

'Got it.' Wayne replied. 'Any idea how they got sprung?'

'Not yet,' Pearce said, 'but I'm going to find out.'

Leila woke with the sound of a scream ringing around her head. She couldn't be certain she hadn't given voice to her nightmare, but as she lay on the mattress in the back bedroom, she heard nothing to suggest she'd disturbed the peace of the house. Her nightmares were one reason she slept so little. Whenever she closed her eyes, she was assailed by memories of lost loved ones, and if she was particularly unlucky, by horrifying recollections of the evil men who'd called themselves her husband, their foul faces returning from the dead, tormenting her.

Light defeated the curtains, illuminating the room with the glow of morning. The faint hum of traffic came through the windows and she could hear the clatter of plates and clang of pans coming from downstairs as someone moved around the kitchen. She rolled out of bed and looked at herself in the old mirror that hung beside the door. Her reflection was mottled with dark patches where the glass had come away from its backing, adding to the general sense of dishevelment she exuded. She'd slept in her clothes, which were crumpled, but she didn't care. Living with creases was a great deal easier than trying to contort her way out of her clothes without the supports she had at home.

Leila went to the toilet, splashed some water on her face and then headed downstairs. She found Melody alone in the kitchen. The redhead was leaning over the stove, watching four eggs cook in a pan of boiling water.

'Morning,' Melody said. 'You want one?'

Leila nodded. 'Where are the others?'

'Scott has gone. Wayne's working on his car.'

Leila shuffled to the table and lowered herself onto one of the seats. She opened her laptop and brought it to life. She could feel Melody watching her.

'How did you learn about computers?'

'My brother taught me,' Leila replied, trying not to think about the way he'd smile at her when she finally understood some new aspect of coding.

'Is he—' Melody began.

'Dead? Yes,' Leila cut her off.

'I'm sorry.'

'It's OK. War is like that. It turns even the most innocent question into a potential source of pain,' Leila said.

They waited in silence, listening to the eggs boiling.

'What was it like?' Melody asked. 'Syria, I mean.'

Leila hesitated and her eyes drifted towards the floor. 'My mother's favourite thing was to sit on the balcony of our apartment, knitting. She'd make jumpers, scarves, baby clothes, anything for winter. It never gets as cold as here, but Syrians are terrified of catching a chill. My grandmother would always tell me to wrap up warm, even on a sunny day. So that's what my mother would do in the evening, sit on the balcony, her needles clicking over the sounds of the city. It was a peaceful place. Noisy, yes, and always bustling, but there was no trouble. People just went about their lives. My cousin on my mother's side, Tawfik, he was gay. The whole family knew, so did his friends. The Western media likes to portray the Arab world as backward and extreme, but there was as much diversity in Syria as there is in London, all happening quietly, without fuss. I watched American TV shows, learned English and French in school. Religion was just one part of life, much like it is here. There were a few who were observant, but most sprinkled faith on their lives like a spice, adding flavour when they needed to. When the war started and the mujahedeen came to Raqqa, Islam became everything. There could be no other thought in a person's mind.

They killed so many. That's how a place becomes backward and extreme. Violence, murder and intimidation. But if a man only claims to love God because he fears what you will do to him, because you will kill him or slaughter his family, how can you not see you have won an empty victory for your Almighty?

'Some pious person –' she spat the words with derision – 'informed on my cousin, told the mujahedeen he was a sinner. There was no trial. They just executed Tawfik. Pushed him from the roof of his own building in the name of a god that sees such evil, but does nothing.'

Leila's eyes glistened, and Melody put a soothing hand on her shoulder.

'I don't like to think of that. I prefer to remember my mother sitting on her balcony. She had planted jasmine all around it and the smell of the flowers mingled with the flavours coming from our neighbour's kitchens. Sumac, cinnamon, cloves, garlic, meats roasting, rose water cakes, the most fragrant coffee you've ever encountered, all rising to her. She said that balcony reminded her who she was and where she came from.'

Leila wrestled with the painful memories.

'My home was a country much like this. Then anger came and created the space for hate to thrive and within months Raqqa had become a hell on earth. I lost everyone I ever loved.' Tears rolled down Leila's right cheek, but she quickly wiped them away.

Melody looked down at her with eyes that shimmered with sadness. 'I'm so sorry. I shouldn't have asked.'

'It's OK,' Leila said. 'I need to remember them. I'm the only one who can.' She broke the awkward stillness that followed by pushing herself to her feet and shuffling to the stove. 'I don't like mine too hard,' she said, picking up the pan and moving awkwardly to the sink. She ran cold water over the eggs and then returned the pan to the stove, before reaching in to take one.

'Let me help.' Melody stepped forward to take a second egg from the pan.

The two of them stood side by side, shelling the eggs. Once done, Leila put her eggs on a plate that had been prepared with buttered toast. Melody did likewise and followed her to the small table where they sat and ate. Leila's reminiscences had taken the edge off her hunger, but Melody wolfed her food. She'd just eaten the last corner of toast when Wayne entered, his hands covered in grime.

'I've got her running,' he said, going to the sink. He glanced at Melody. 'You ready to go?'

Melody looked at Leila, her eyes seemingly searching for something. Forgiveness perhaps, or maybe reassurance. Maybe she was drawing strength from Leila's hardship. Leila nodded at the fearful lawyer, who smiled back.

'You're going to be OK,' Leila told her.

'I'm ready,' Melody said, getting to her feet.

Chapter 24

The Walkers lived on a quiet suburban street in Dulwich. The front garden was beautifully landscaped and well-tended. A horseshoe of low shrubs hugged the bay window of the yellow-brick Victorian house, and a narrow bed lay before it filled with summer wildflowers and lavender. A perfectly trimmed box hedge ran alongside the path that led to the front door, separating the property from its equally well-groomed neighbour. Melody gave Wayne a nervous glance as they neared the front door.

'You OK?' he asked.

Melody nodded, but she didn't look OK. She seemed terribly nervous. 'I don't know what I'm going to say to her. How am I going to explain what we were doing?'

'Just tell the truth,' Wayne suggested.

Melody smiled and Wayne couldn't help but be impressed by her pluck. It took heart to face the things she was facing and style to handle them gracefully. She'd been cool and calm during her encounter with her boss, and had remained so throughout their journey across London. Her resolve had faltered when she'd learned of the biker's death, but that was only to be expected. She was a civilian. She lacked their experience of blood and death.

Melody hesitated on the tiled doorstep before pressing

the bell. Inside, a buzzer sounded and moments later a voice came through an intercom. Wayne noticed a tiny video camera beneath the doorbell.

'Hello?' a woman said.

Melody took a deep breath. 'Mrs Walker, Jessica, it's Melody Gold. I wonder if I could talk to you.'

'Melody?' Jessica's voice was flat and lacklustre. 'I didn't recognize you. Just give me a minute.'

Wayne scanned the street for signs of danger, but all he saw were a couple of birds flitting from one tree to another.

The door opened and Jessica Walker peered through the narrow gap. She looked like someone who'd gone twelve rounds with a monster. Her hair was unkempt, her eyes sunken and haunted, her skin pale. She wore a simple olive green knee-length dress, but it was stained and creased. Her feet were grimy and her bare legs were covered in tiny sprouts of dark hair. She looked at Melody and Wayne, but said nothing.

'I'm very sorry for your loss,' Melody said, but that was all she managed before she choked up.

'We'd like to talk to you about your husband,' Wayne said. 'We might be able to tell you why he was killed.'

He'd dealt with his fair share of death and knew that people often like straight, clear talk when in the shadow of bereavement. Jessica swung the door wide.

'Come in,' she said.

'I've been waiting for someone to help me make sense of it all,' Jessica said. 'The police have come and gone. Accident!' She spat the word like the punchline to a sick joke. 'Accident,' she added quietly as though to herself. 'It wasn't an accident.'

'How many times have the police been here?' Wayne asked.

Jessica stared at him and for a moment the only sounds were the distant hum of traffic on the South Circular and the tick of the mantel clock on the marble shelf above the fireplace. High bookcases lined two walls and the third was given over to a gallery of family photographs. Wayne saw a history that could never be recreated, one of its key components forever gone. Gabriel Walker with Jessica, the two of them alone in various picturesque environments, then in other photos with their children, grandparents, friends and relatives, here in the UK and back in America.

'Who are you?' Jessica asked Wayne, not taking her eyes off him.

'My name's Wayne Nelson,' he replied. 'I work in close protection and am currently looking after Ms Gold.'

'And why do you need protection?' Jessica's New York accent gained a sharp edge.

Melody sucked in a deep breath and started talking. She told Jessica about the first time Gabe had asked her to assist him, how they'd gone looking for someone with the right skills to investigate the bank. She kept Pearce's name out of her tale, but did recount what had happened to Nathan Foster. Jessica's face reddened as Melody spoke, and as she was nearing the end of her tale, the widow's cheeks were glowing like coals in a blazing fire. Her fingers were balled into fists, her face was taut and her eyes were shining.

'That stupid, stupid man,' Jessica erupted when Melody finished. 'How could he!'

'We didn't know. When we signed up for this, neither of us had any idea how dangerous it would be,' Melody said.

'And when you did?' Jessica challenged.

'By then it was too late.'

'It's never too late! He should have gone to the police or the government. We could have left the country. Gabe was an activist for the Democrats. Any one of his political friends could have helped get him protection back home. We might have been safe in America. We could have had a life there. We could have been safe. Him, me and the children. What a fool! What a damn fool! We should have . . .' Jessica's fury, which had been building throughout her tirade, vanished suddenly, and the abated storm of anger was replaced with a swelling sadness. 'He did it for us,' she sobbed. 'He did it for us. It wasn't an accident. He knew what he was doing and he did it to protect us.'

'That's what we think,' Wayne agreed. 'It was the only way he could be sure they wouldn't threaten you.'

Jessica wept and Melody rose to comfort her. She wrapped her arms around the grieving woman's shoulders and held her.

'How many times have the police been here?' Wayne asked again.

Jessica took a moment to compose herself, wiped the tears from her eyes and replied. 'A few.'

'The same officers?'

'No,' Jessica said. 'There was the original detective who came with a colleague and then a few days later, another cop came alone.'

'I'd like to show you some photos,' Wayne said, reaching into his pocket to produce a phone. He presented Jessica with Kemp and Dunbar's police identification photos. 'You recognize either of these men?'

Jessica nodded at the image of the bull-necked Kemp. 'The first one. He was the detective who came alone.'

'Robert Kemp. We don't know much about him, except that he used to be a police officer,' Wayne told her. 'We think he's involved in whatever got your husband killed.'

'And he came here? To my house?' Jessica's anger returned, and she shrugged Melody off. 'To my house!'

'I'm afraid so,' Wayne replied. 'He's looking for the identity of the client who instructed your husband.'

Melody returned to the sofa, and Jessica seethed.

'Did he take anything when he left?' Wayne pressed.

'Not that I saw.' Jessica responded.

'We'd like to search your husband's things, if that's OK,' Wayne said. 'We have to identify his client.'

When Jessica looked at Wayne, her entire being seemed charged with such powerful, ferocious energy he was worried she might lash out. Her eyes blazed with anger. 'Do whatever you have to. Find the people who did this to my family.'

Melody and Wayne stood in Gabriel's home office, surveying the room they'd just searched. Jessica had accompanied them through the house, leading them to all the nooks that contained anything relevant to his work. They'd checked drawers in the kitchen, shelves in the dining room, his wardrobe, a chest in the attic, but Jessica had left them alone when they'd come to the office. There was, she'd told them, nothing that belonged to the family in the room, so they could search it unsupervised. They'd taken her at her word and had spent two hours going through the office carefully. Wayne could tell they weren't the first ones to have done so. Everything was out of place. Books and papers were askew, strewn across Walker's

Detective Sergeant? You didn't look away from anything because you felt the wrong kind of pressure?'

'Who are you? What do you want?' Dawson asked, his eyes flashing anger as he freed himself from Pearce's grip.

'I can't tell you who I am or who I work for,' Pearce said. 'But I don't work for the people you're afraid of. I think they're the ones I'm after.'

Dawson said nothing, but he didn't move away.

'Yesterday, three suspects were picked up outside Heathrow. All three were carrying unlicensed firearms. They were taken to New Scotland Yard, and then late last night they were sprung. I want you to find out who the order came from.'

'Takes a big wheel to turn that kind of charge.' The jaded detective shook his head slowly and Pearce thought he was going to refuse, but the man surprised him. 'I'll see what I can find out. How do I contact you?'

'Email me here,' Pearce said, handing him a scrap of paper with a secure, anonymous email address on it.

Dawson looked as though he was going to say something, but his lips kept the thought prisoner, and Pearce turned and started up the busy road towards Middlesex Street, where his bike was parked.

Pearce rode to the Archway flat, where he showered and changed into a black suit and a white shirt. He walked to Highgate Hill and caught a taxi to St John's Wood. He had the driver drop him off on the corner of Wells Rise and St Edmund's Terrace, and walked south towards Prince Albert Road, checking for any sign of Artem Vasylyk's men. He walked up the driveway of Alexis's building and went to the main entrance. He peered through the glass door into a lobby that was deserted save for a liveried porter. The grey-haired man sat behind a marble counter, his wrinkled face directed at a screen. Pearce grabbed the brass door handle and pinned a confident smile to his face.

'Bob, is it?' he asked as he crossed the grand reception hall. His heels made no sound on the deep, ornately patterned carpet.

'John,' the porter replied uncertainly as he looked away from his computer and sized up Pearce. 'Do I know you, sir?'

'John! Of course! My apologies. Ms Tippett-Jones did tell me your name. Is she in? She said I should wait in the apartment if not. I have a key.'

John frowned, but he said nothing. 'I believe Ms Tippett-Jones is home. May I have your name?'

'David Rowland,' Pearce replied. 'I'm a friend from the club.'

'If you'll take a seat.' John indicated a waiting area near the front door.

Pearce sauntered over as John picked up a phone. The old man spoke for less than a minute before he signalled to Pearce.

'Ms Tippett-Jones will see you now,' he said.

The third-floor corridor was swathed in beige and cream wallpaper and the same plush carpet that had cushioned Pearce's steps in the lobby. Four flats led off the corridor, and it took Pearce an instant to work out which door he needed. He rang the bell and, after a moment, the peephole darkened and the door opened to reveal Alexis Tippett-Jones. She was barefoot and wore a pair of tatty jeans and a green T-shirt. She wasn't wearing any make-up and her hair was tied in a scrappy bun. She looked younger than Pearce remembered.

'What are you doing here?' she hissed.

'You said you needed help,' Pearce replied. 'At least it sounded that way to me.'

'I was drunk. I had no idea what I was saying.'

'I don't believe you,' Pearce countered. 'I think you're in some kind of trouble.'

A door slammed somewhere above them, startling Alexis. She glanced along the corridor nervously. 'You'd better come in.'

There was no enthusiasm in the invitation, but Pearce took advantage of it anyway. He stepped into a whitewashed hallway dominated by a huge potted plant – some kind of fern with arched leaves that spread in front of the walls like angry brushstrokes.

'Who are you?' Alexis asked.

'Just a guy who saw a woman in distress. Someone who wants to help.'

'You're an idiot,' she responded, striding ahead of him into a large living room. 'And you're risking more than you could ever know.'

The white room was coloured by even more plants and abstract paintings, most of which were shades of green. A single large couch faced the glass doors that opened onto the balcony. Beyond it lay the tops of the trees, stretching out into Regent's Park.

'I'm not one of those people who can stand by when they see something wrong,' Pearce said truthfully. 'I got the sense you didn't want to be with those people.'

'And you thought you'd save me?' Alexis asked. 'You have no idea who those people are.'

'Why don't you tell me?'

'I can't.'

'Why not?'

She hesitated.

'What are you hiding?' Pearce asked. 'What are you afraid of?'

'I don't owe you any answers,' Alexis snapped suddenly. 'I'd like you to leave.'

'Tell me about the messages being run between Artem Vasylyk and Viscount Purbeck,' Pearce challenged, and Alexis looked as though she'd been stung.

'How do you know their names?' she asked.

'All I can tell you is that I'm here to help,' Pearce replied.

'Let me show you something,' Alexis said with bitter resignation.

She went through a doorway that led to the innards of the flat. Pearce glanced around the living space again, and was struck by just how devoid of any real personality it was. It was more like an extremely expensive hotel room with a view that was worth millions. Alexis soon returned, carrying photographs, which she presented to Pearce.

He was shocked to see a series of images of a battered woman tied to a chair, blood streaming down her face onto the cloth that gagged her.

'That's my mother,' Alexis said sadly. 'These photographs were taken in her kitchen. They did it to prove they could get to her whenever they want,' she continued, her voice taking on a hollow quality. 'If I ever speak of what happens, they'll kill her. And then they'll kill me.'

'What?' he asked. 'What can't you talk about?'

Alexis held Pearce's gaze for a moment and then looked

away, ashamed, and he knew. She was talking about sexual exploitation.

She sighed. 'I was out with a few friends, celebrating handing in my thesis. We were in a club. I don't remember what happened. I think my drink was spiked. I woke up in bed with a man. In this apartment. I was told that if I ever left, I'd die. I didn't believe it at first, but there were other men . . . they . . . they beat me up. I tried to escape,' tears sprang to her eyes, 'but they kept me here. A few days later, when they showed me these pictures, I stopped fighting.'

She was weeping now and Pearce marvelled at her strength. She was sacrificing herself for her mother, an act of courage that reminded Pearce of Leila. She too had endured such horror and was possessed of a similar dignity and a core of steel.

'I'm sorry,' Pearce said quietly.

'It's not just me. There are others.'

'How many?'

'At least a dozen,' she replied. 'Maybe more. In flats around London. I personally know of nine women and three men.'

Pearce recalled the mixed group of men and women he saw sitting with Oxnard-Clarke in the private club. Did the Viscount know they were unwilling victims? Or was he only aware of the veneer?

'They keep us for Artem and his associates,' Alexis continued. 'People see us in the clubs, but they don't see the chains that bind us. They look at us in these homes, and don't realize that they're prisons. They envy my life, but I don't want it,' she choked up and began weeping again. 'I don't want it.'

As Pearce watched this stranger weep, he felt his fury build. Crooked rich men like Vasylyk believed the world had been created to bring them nothing but pleasure, and if their whim involved the capture and enslavement of others, so be it. They would exploit, pillage and rape as the want took them, carefree in the belief that their wealth and criminal connections put them above the law. Was this what Foster had found? Sex slavery? Was this why he'd been killed? Despite how appalling it was, Pearce felt sure there had to be more to it.

'What about the police?' he asked, but he knew the answer the moment he posed the question. Dawson had been intimidated out of a murder inquiry. What salaried cop was going to risk violence and death in order to investigate a sex trafficking ring?

Alexis simply stared at Pearce with tears in her eyes, not even bothering to answer him. He wanted to reach out to comfort her, but he hardly knew her and had no idea how she felt about physical contact given her experiences, so he stood silently as she hugged herself and wept.

The sound of the phone shocked them both and Alexis looked at Pearce awkwardly before straightening herself out. She wiped her eyes, patted her hair and took a deep breath, fixing her mask before she answered the call. She listened for a moment, her eyes widening.

'OK,' she said. 'Of course I'm ready.'

She hung up and turned to Pearce. 'Artem's here. You have to leave,' she said quickly. 'Get out. He'll kill us both. And my mother.'

A large part of Pearce wanted to stay and confront the Ukrainian, to introduce him to a world of suffering, but that would put Alexis, her mother and many others at risk.

'Please go,' Alexis implored. 'Hurry.'

Pearce nodded and ran for the door. He went into the

corridor and headed for the stairs, slipping through the stair-well door as the elevator chimed. As Pearce scurried down, feelings of shame started to cloud his mind. He wondered whether fleeing made him a coward. *There's a difference between cowardice and intelligence,* he told himself as he opened the door to the lobby and checked that it was clear. John the concierge gave him a bemused look as he rushed out. Pearce saw Vasylyk's Overfinch parked in a space near the entrance and as he walked towards Prince Albert Road, he made himself a promise that Alexis would not spend much longer in lavish enslavement.

Chapter 26

By the time they met back at the safe house, Leila was too exhausted to care about pride and was sitting in her wheelchair in the small living room. She didn't like people seeing her in it, because she was worried they might think her weak and incapable, when nothing could be further from the truth. When the pain got too much, the chair made life easier, allowing her to focus more attention on the tasks at hand. For a while, she'd tried the numbing painkillers her GP had prescribed, but hated the way they fogged her mind. She needed to be able to think straight. And in certain circumstances, on flat surfaces, the chair enabled her to move faster than most people could run. But tonight wasn't about mental or physical agility, it was about comfort. The pain in her legs and abdomen always seemed to be worse when she was tired, and she hadn't been this fatigued for years.

After Melody and Wayne had left the East Acton safe house, Leila had returned home to Upper Bucklebury and had spent the day pulling at the handful of threads Pearce had given her. Going through Bayard Madison's business affairs should have been the job of an entire team, and she had so much more to follow up than simply examining what the bank was doing. There was the Frenchwoman Pearce believed was DGSE, the two former police officers who'd been arrested with her at Heathrow, Artem Vasylyk and his operations, Alexis Tippett-Jones, the video Pearce had taken of Vasylyk's bodyguard handing something to the woman outside the bank, the faces of the people with Vasylyk in the private club on Golden Square – there were so many threads and each of them led her to many others. It would have kept a team busy for months, and Leila had concerns that the sheer volume was fazing her. She was adept at seeing patterns, but she couldn't get this straight in her head. There wasn't an obvious connection or agenda.

Pearce had shared the information about the suspected sex trafficking ring, which had transformed Leila's opinion of Tippett-Jones. Based on what she'd discovered about Alexis, she'd thought the privileged woman to be a vacuous socialite, but Pearce's revelation had touched upon her own experiences. She knew what it was like to be living a different truth to the one people perceived. In Raqqa, most had thought Leila to be the pious, dutiful wife of a *mujahid*. Few knew that she was utterly unwilling, that she was subjected to daily violence, threats of death and sexual assault. And here, in Central London, was a woman who seemed to be enduring similar suffering. *And there could be more of them . . .* Leila bristled with anger.

But something about it didn't feel right. Her grandmother, a tiny woman who had seemed to spend her life frozen at the age of fifty and had been known as something of a sage in Raqqa for her ability to read coffee grounds, always said, '*Alshueur bishay' ma hu hqyqt al'amr. 'Iidha lm yakun al'amr shyhana, fahi laysat alhaqiqat.*'

The feel of something was the truth of it. If it didn't feel right, it wasn't the truth.

Would Foster have risked his life to break a sex trafficking ring? Was it something people would kill for? And why would it involve a British banker and a Ukrainian gangster? Would French Intelligence be so interested in a London sex ring? Leila was convinced there was more to it, but as she rubbed her tired eyes, she only felt frustration that she couldn't see the truth.

'I think she was honest. She seemed scared and desperate,' Pearce said, wrapping up the account of his encounter with Alexis, and bringing Wayne and Melody up to speed. 'But I can't figure out why French Intelligence would be tangled up in a London sex slavery ring.'

The four of them were ranged around the living room. Melody was on a kitchen chair, her back hunched, her elbows on her knees. She looked shattered. Wayne was sprawled on the sofa and Pearce leaned against the arm. The two men looked tired, Pearce particularly so. Leila was convinced he'd lost weight and wondered if he was eating properly.

'I think you're right, but it's all we've got to go on right now,' Leila told him. 'Constellation, the Monaco corporation that pays for Alexis's flat, has leases on another twenty.' She tossed a manila folder onto the coffee table. 'All in upmarket neighbourhoods, all one or two bedrooms. I checked some of the addresses against bank and credit card records and, just like Alexis, these flats seem to occupied by single young men and women.'

'I want you to go to Port Quin,' Pearce said. Wayne and Melody had recounted their fruitless search in Dulwich and their conversation with Jessica Walker. 'See if you can find anything in the Walkers' cottage that clues us in to the client's identity.'

Wayne nodded. 'What about you?'

'I'm going to check out some of these addresses,' Pearce replied, picking up the envelope. 'See if Leila's right and there are more like Alexis. Then I'm going to Blackbird Leys.'

'You want backup?' Wayne asked.

'I couldn't get anything on that black star symbol you found, but I checked out the community centre,' Leila cut in. 'It's hosting a meeting of Progress Britain tomorrow night.'

Pearce and Wayne looked blank, but Melody sat up. 'Progress Britain? Those crazies? It's a right-wing political group. Very vocal about Europe, immigration, free speech. You see them all over Twitter, usually at the receiving end of tirades from people I follow.'

'There are three speakers: a Brit, some guy from the Czech Republic and a French poet. I printed the flyer, it's in the folder,' Leila said.

Pearce leafed through the folder until he found a sheet that was dominated by an image of a Union flag. Beneath it were photos of three men and their bios. Dominic Strathairn, Professor of Modern History at Leeds University and Deputy Chairman of Progress Britain; Markus Kral, Emeritus Professor of Geostrategy at Charles University in Prague; and Bastien Collet, a poet and philosopher from Marseilles.

Leila thought it an unremarkable trio, another group of middle-aged armchair pundits who hectored those with real power. A brief examination of the three men found nothing that linked them to Bayard Madison or Vasylyk. All she'd discovered were books and articles espousing their ideologies, which were firmly to the right.

'It's a public meeting,' Pearce told Wayne. 'I'll be OK.

We're going to want to capture faces at the event, so Ley will have eyes on me, right?'

Leila nodded, trying to conceal her disappointment. The surveillance glasses Pearce had liberated from Six had a broken transmitter, which was part of the reason they were supposed to be decommissioned. Leila had fixed the record and playback functions but had never got round to repairing the transmitter because it was a time-consuming job. But if Pearce wanted live eyes on him tomorrow night, she'd do the repair. Who needed sleep anyway? She owed him her life and would do whatever it took to help keep him safe.

Chapter 27

Early morning sunlight was blowing the colour out of the city, turning the jagged, distant skyline a dark grey. Even the buildings in the middle distance had been leached of any richness by the bright light and were reduced to pastel shades. Pearce rode down Highgate Hill, Leila's list in his backpack, along with a change of clothes, a camera and other gear he'd packed on his return from West London. He'd come back to the Archway flat the previous night, soon after Leila had left the safe house. She'd said she wanted to get home to sleep in her own bed, but Pearce knew her sufficiently well to recognize a lie. She'd been planning to work the case, and, knowing there was little he could do to dissuade her, Pearce had shrugged and said farewell.

He'd hit the road soon afterwards and had spent a fitful night chewing over the investigation. He needed to get a better picture of the whole, but the few pieces they had so far had been hard won. They knew so little about what they were up against and his reflection had yielded no further insight.

Pearce selected half a dozen addresses from the list Leila had provided. All six were in luxury blocks in St John's Wood and Primrose Hill. After spending the day staking out the apartments, he discovered five were occupied by beautiful young women and the last was home to an equally attractive man in his early twenties. Pearce recognized the guy and two of the women from the club. All three had been sitting with Oxnard-Clarke. Was the peer involved in a sex ring? Is that why Fozz had been killed?

Pearce photographed the man in his home. He took pictures of three of the women in their apartments, one with an unidentified middle-aged male who walked her to his chauffeur-driven car, and another as she was going for a run. All six seemed to be living unremarkable lives of privilege, but if they, like Alexis, had been threatened, their families terrorized, then what he was seeing was a clever and dangerous illusion. It was mid-afternoon by the time Pearce had taken his last photo. He had sufficient evidence to establish a pattern and enough pictures for Leila to run image searches that might help identify each individual.

He was about to mount his bike when the Ghostlink rang. He pulled the communicator from his backpack.

'Go ahead.'

'*I've got the glasses ready,*' Leila said. She sounded fatigued. '*And we've had an email. Looks like it's from your flat-footed friend.*'

'Got it,' Pearce said, recognizing the slang for police. 'I'm on my way.'

He arrived at Leila's house soon after six thirty, taking a circuitous route across London to ensure he wasn't followed. She was waiting for him on her porch, sitting on a collapsible camping chair like a tiny sentinel. He couldn't be sure, but he thought she might have been asleep when he first started up the drive, and that the sound of his bike's rumbling engine

woke her. She forced herself to her feet, picked up her walking stick and shuffled to the edge of the porch.

'Mark Sutton,' she announced.

Pearce looked at her incredulously.

She nodded. 'The cop's email said the order to release
them came from Mark Sutton.'

'Sutton?' Pearce asked.

'Mark Sutton, Parliamentary Undersecretary of State for
Crime, Safeguarding and Vulnerability,' Leila said. 'A junior
government minister. This one goes deep, Scott.'

Pearce ran his hand through his hair and rubbed the back
of his neck. He hadn't dealt with Sutton directly, but was
aware of his reputation as a political high-flyer. This was a
huge piece of the puzzle, but he wasn't sure how it connected
to the others. All he knew was that he felt the familiar surge
of adrenalin that came when he caught a scent of prey.

'I need to talk to Detective Sergeant Dawson, make sure
he's got this right,' Pearce observed.

'If he has, we've got a minister of state using his influence to free three criminals,' Leila remarked. 'We need to
find out why.'

'Can you start a file on Sutton? Find out who he's connected to?' Pearce said.

'Already on it,' Leila responded. 'Here,' she said, producing
the surveillance glasses. 'I cleared the drive and got the transmitter working. I'll be able to see and hear everything that's
happening in real time.' She put her hand into the pocket of
her black trousers and pulled out a small plastic case, which
Pearce recognized as an in-ear comms unit.

'I really appreciate everything you're doing.'

'What can I say? You inspire loyalty.' She flashed a cheeky

smile. 'You'd better go. It starts at eight and I want you to get me as many faces as possible.'

'Thanks, Lyly,' he said, before returning to his bike.

Wayne stood at the bedroom window and watched Melody. She was outside, at the very edge of the garden, watching the waves churning against the immoveable cliffs. The Walkers' holiday home was neither a hut nor a cottage, but was in fact a four-bedroom Victorian stone and slate house that overlooked Port Quin Beach, a small strip of shale that lay at the end of a narrow inlet. The beach was only visible at low tide and although it lacked the golden sand of other Cornish beaches, the rock pools that were being revealed by the retreating tide looked like a child's dream. The Atlantic was a deep blue, black in places, and the crests of the waves sparkled in the lowering sun. The air was cooler by the coast than it had been inland, and their journey, which had been prolonged by a terrible accident on the M5 south of Weston-super-Mare, had taken most of the day. Wayne's Fiesta had no air conditioning and they'd spent the seven-hour trip in the sweltering heat, windows down, which had limited conversation.

After taking a long, winding route from the motorway, they'd pulled off a narrow coastal lane that followed the contours of the nearby cliffs, and climbed a steep driveway to the imposing house which sat in a plot that overlooked the ocean. The beach and the small cluster of houses that passed for the village of Port Quin were located a couple of hundred feet east and a few hundred feet below the Walkers' home. It was idyllic.

They'd found the combination key safe and let themselves in. Melody had left the front door open in an attempt to cool the stuffy house. The giant angular bay windows acted as lenses and trapped the sun's heat in the high-ceilinged rooms, making the entire place feel like a tropical glasshouse.

They'd split up and each taken a couple of rooms. They'd regrouped moments later when they'd discovered that someone had beaten them to it. The house had already been turned over and all the rooms were a mess. Wayne had quickly checked the house to make sure the intruders weren't still there. Satisfied there was no one else around, they'd split up and resumed their search. Melody had looked upstairs, while Wayne had examined Gabriel's second home office. The room was decorated in a more contemporary style than the office in Dulwich, and was furnished in a nautical motif. Wayne found nothing of any use, just books, documents, and another basket stuffed to the brim with a collection of old newspapers similar to the one in the family home in Dulwich. The search of the rest of the house proved equally fruitless and they'd discovered nothing that gave even the slightest hint of the client's identity. Any clues had either been found by the people who'd been there before them, or simply didn't exist.

Frustrated by their long, wasted journey, Wayne turned away from the window and went downstairs to join Melody outside.

'Anything?' she asked, as he approached.

Wayne shook his head. 'You?'

'Nothing,' she said.

'I'd like to get a look at the stuff that was taken from his office at Denton Fraser,' Wayne responded. 'I'd lay money that it wasn't taken by the police.'

Melody sighed.

'It's OK,' Wayne told her. 'We'll get there.'

But in truth, he wasn't so sure.

Chapter 28

Pearce had been concerned that his presence at the meeting would be noted, but as he rode towards the Blackbird Leys Community Centre, he realized that he needn't have worried. A huge crowd was gathered outside the two-storey building. He was about a quarter of a mile away and couldn't pick out the details, but he could already sense mayhem in the air. There were a handful of faces pressed against the windows of the tower block across the street from the centre, people watching the action, which was obviously offering better entertainment than whatever was on TV. Opposite the block was a chain of high-vis jackets – police officers struggling to contain a portion of the crowd which was spilling into the road.

Pearce pulled into a parking bay on Blackbird Leys Road, a couple of hundred yards from the centre, and, when he killed the engine and removed his helmet, he could hear the angry calls of a hostile mob. As he started along the road, the situation became clearer. A hundred or so protesters were gathered outside the community centre. Many were carrying banners decrying Progress Britain and its racism and Islamophobia. Nearly all were hectoring the people going into the building and some, wearing balaclavas and masks, were making real efforts to breach the police line. A two-man camera team was filming from just behind the struggling officers, and there were quite a few other individuals who had their phones out to capture the action. Across the road, standing in the shadow of the tower block, were a group of locals, streetwise kids and their families, some of whom were yelling abuse at anyone and everyone.

Pearce took a baseball cap from his back pocket and pulled it low over his head. As he approached the building, he tried to keep track of anyone with a camera. He had no desire for his face to be plastered all over someone's social media feed.

The Blackbird Leys Community Centre reminded Pearce of a 1980s police station. Large windows lined the ground floor, but the second floor above them was nothing but yellow brick, making the centre seem bleak and unforgiving. An access road ran down the west side of the building, and a small paved area lay in front of it. The forecourt was separated from the access road by bushes and a run of bollards. Thirty or so police officers were keeping the protesters to the east of the bollards and had them clustered on a small green beneath some low trees. Those attending the meeting were encouraged by a couple of community support officers to reach the main entrance via the access road, to keep some distance from the mob.

'You getting this?' Pearce asked, touching the surveillance glasses.

'Yes,' Leila replied, her voice loud in his ear. '*You're walking into a madhouse.*'

'Let's hope I'm not too brown to get in,' Pearce responded dryly.

He needn't have worried. Progress Britain had attracted

people of all races. Ahead of him, he saw a middle-aged Sikh hurry into the building under a hail of abuse. When he crossed a short mews called Moorbank and started past an austere, modern pub, the storm of hostility became decipherable and Pearce could pick out distinct phrases.

'*Fucking Nazis!*'

'*Don't touch me, you fucking pig!*'

'*Remember Grenfell!*'

'*Nazis, Nazis, Nazis, out, out, out!*'

This last phrase was taken up by the crowd and soon dozens of protesters were yelling it like a battle cry. The air was charged with trouble and as Pearce got within a few yards of the building, he could feel the anger of the crowd bearing down on him like a storm. He was just there as an observer, and couldn't begin to imagine the effect such condemnation would have on people who were attending the meeting in support of Progress Britain. What made them angry or desperate enough to brave such derision? Or were they simply lost-cause extremists?

'Racist!'

A black man who'd been heading into the building stopped in his tracks. He locked onto a face in the crowd and hurried across the forecourt towards a ginger-haired man. The protesters surged at the black man's approach, and the police countered, gathering to prevent the crowd breaking the line.

'Get back, sir,' one of the uniforms yelled at the approaching man.

'Did you just call me a racist?' the black man shouted at the ginger-haired guy.

'*That's Owen Lucas,*' Leila said.

'Who?' Pearce asked, stopping on the forecourt beside a

silver sculpture of a tree, whose bare branches reached up to the cloudless sky.

'*You really have been living in a cave,*' Leila replied. '*Owen Lucas is one of the most well-known social campaigners around. He's rumoured to have links to the left's more radical factions.*'

Lucas's scraggly ginger hair touched the shoulders of his black bomber jacket. His face was red and twisted with anger, but he looked a little surprised to have been challenged.

'Did you call me a racist?' the black man repeated.

'Racist fuck!' came a voice from the middle of the crowd.

'They're using you!'

'Nazis out!' said another.

'You people make me laugh,' the man scoffed. His cockney accent and don't-give-a-fuck demeanour gave him a rough charm. 'I've been called a lot of ugly things, but this is the first time I've ever been called a racist.'

Lucas recovered from his surprise and shouted over the strained arms of the police officers holding the crowd back. 'You're being radicalized, you idiot.'

'And you're not?' the man countered. 'Look at you in your stormtrooper gear,' he gestured at the crowd. 'We're all being radicalized. The only real choice we've got is which side we're on.'

'Fuck off!' someone yelled.

'Have you got anything useful to say?' the man challenged over the sound of boos and catcalls. 'I'm here to listen to people speak. What do you know about me or my life that gives you the right to judge me? You want to talk to me about the problems this country faces, then let's talk. But it's much easier to label people and hurl abuse than it is to try to win an argument.'

'There is no argument. We just have to get the Nazis out,' Lucas yelled. 'Nazis, Nazis, Nazis, out, out, out!'

The cry was taken up by the crowd and delivered with such passion that Pearce was worried the police line might be breached.

'There's a war coming!' the black man shouted, but his voice was lost beneath the chant. He shrugged and went into the building, and Pearce followed him inside.

Progress Britain was running a slick operation. Everyone coming into the building was searched by one of four suited security guards. It wasn't a cursory check; this was a proper fingertip pat-down. The guards all shared the same hard look, close-cut hair and lean, muscular physique. They were ex-cops or military, of that Pearce had no doubt, but he couldn't tell whether they were members of Progress Britain or if they'd simply been contracted to provide security for the event. Pearce's motorcycle helmet was confiscated and he was told it would be kept safe for him until after the meeting. Pearce wasn't questioned about his reasons for coming, and as he listened to the noisy crowd outside, he considered how easy it would be for a few of them to infiltrate the building.

When Pearce was cleared by security, he started across the lobby, but he didn't get far before he was intercepted by one of half a dozen ushers. Like the other five, the man who approached Pearce was middle-aged and wore a dark suit.

'I'm Keith,' the man said, offering his hand. 'And you are?'

Keith was ruddy and jowly, with the crooked nose of a boxer, but there was nothing belligerent about him and he spoke with gentle confidence.

'David Rowland,' Pearce said, taking the man's hand. He

glanced over and saw another usher talking to the black man who'd entered the building ahead of him. Behind him, yet another usher had approached a middle-aged white woman. They were all being vetted.

'Is this your first meeting?' Keith asked.

Pearce nodded.

'How did you hear about it?'

'A friend,' Pearce replied. 'He said you speak a lot of sense.'

'Not me.' Keith smiled. 'But we have some members who really know what they're talking about. As I'm sure you've noticed, there are some people who have a problem with confronting difficult questions. We take steps to ensure such people are excluded from our events, but sometimes they slip through and it becomes necessary to forcibly remove them if they threaten to disrupt our meetings. I just want to warn you in case we need to take such steps. I wouldn't want you to be caught by surprise.'

Pearce read the true meaning of the warning loud and clear. As a first-timer with no history, he'd be watched carefully and ejected at the first sign of trouble.

'Welcome, David,' Keith continued. 'Find yourself a seat inside.'

Pearce went through a set of solid double doors into a large hall full of chairs that faced a small stage. At the centre of the stage stood a lectern emblazoned with the Union flag-inspired Progress Britain logo. Most of the seats were occupied, and, as he scanned the room, Pearce saw that although the people in the room tended to skew older than the protesters outside, there was a representative mix of genders and ethnic backgrounds. It wasn't what he'd expected. He slid onto a seat in the back row. Ahead of him most people sat in silence, although here and there some exchanged quiet words with their neighbours. The large room was warm and the air thick and still. The noise of the crowd was now an indistinct rumble and Pearce couldn't help but feel as though he was in the eye of a storm.

The black cockney who'd exchanged words with Lucas came in and sat near the front. According to the large clock that hung above the stage, it was approaching eight. A few more people arrived and then there was a lull, and the security guards who'd been searching attendees entered and took up evenly spaced positions around the room. There was somewhere in the region of 150 people in the hall, and almost all of them were now silent, the sense of expectation heightened by the indistinct chanting that penetrated the building. Someone coughed. A phone rang and was quickly silenced.

Then a woman with long dark hair, a zealot's eyes and a humourless face emerged from the wings and crossed the stage. She wore a dark blue skirt suit and sensible shoes with block heels. She looked like an accountant or mid-level civil servant, but a faction of the assembled crowd broke into spontaneous applause and cheered as though she was a celebrity.

'Good evening,' the woman said when the clapping died down. 'Thank you for the warm welcome and thank you for coming. For those of you who don't know, my name is Annabelle Crawford. I'm head of policy for Progress Britain and it's my distinct pleasure to host this evening's event.'

'*She used to be in UKIP,*' Leila said, and Pearce could hear her tapping on a keyboard. '*Left the party after falling out with the executive.*'

'You're all here because you know Britain is broken. There are so many things wrong with the country and none of them are the fault of hard-working people like you. We've been let down by our political class, who have transformed our legal system without our consent, changed the social fabric of the country without any mandate and neglected all the important issues that we, the British people, hold dear. Those angry people out there,' she gestured vaguely, 'they say we're extremists, but the truth is we represent the views of the average person. The truth is that the extreme left has seized control of the mainstream and if you question its dogma, you're branded a racist or a bigot. They won't debate us, they won't argue with us, because they're on a mission to promote a globalist agenda and left-wing orthodoxy at all costs and they know that such things don't hold up to rational scrutiny, so instead, they shout and scream insults, using emotion rather than logic to try to defeat us.

'But the truth cannot be silenced and more and more people are waking up to the honest logic of Progress Britain . . .' A small cheer interrupted her, and for the first time a smile softened her hard features. 'We have three speakers tonight. Dominic Strathairn, Professor of Modern History at Leeds University and Deputy Chairman of Progress Britain, Markus Kral, Emeritus Professor of Geostrategy at Charles University in Prague, and Bastien Collet, one of France's most enlightened and visionary thinkers. These men are vilified by the left for daring to challenge the assumptions that have caused society so much damage. I hope you'll listen to what they have to say and hear the good sense of their words. Once you have, it's hard to remain silent while our politicians continue to steer us towards disaster and I hope you'll channel your frustration and political energy into an organization that will represent you. An organization that cares about all Britons regardless of colour, race or creed. Progress Britain wants to change things for the better and we want you to be part of that change.'

'You go, Annabelle!' someone near the front yelled.

She laughed. 'I do have a tendency to get carried away, but that's because I care. We all do. That's why we're here. But that's enough from me. It's my pleasure to introduce our first speaker, a man who's been hailed as one of the leading lights of true liberal thinking, Dominic Strathairn.'

Chapter 29

'*This is so dangerous,*' Leila's voice came through the earpiece. '*It's so cunning.*'

Straitharn made Pearce think of everyone's favourite grandfather. He had an almost square, honest face, thick grey hair that was styled in a classic short back and sides. He wore a pair of brown cords, woollen waistcoat, a shirt, tie and a tweed jacket. The hall was getting hotter by the minute, but Straitharn showed no signs of discomfort and Pearce suspected that the old man knew that his costume was part of his allure and would have fainted in the heat rather than shed a single item of clothing.

He'd started with Magna Carta, the most potent early example of people holding those in power to account. He'd examined the conditions that led the barons to bring King John to heel, and drawn parallels with contemporary challenges facing the British people. Who, he'd asked, had authorized the government to spend hundreds of billions bailing out the banks? Who had endorsed the Bank of England's policy of quantitative easing, which had enriched the wealthy? Who had voted to give the government a mandate to surrender more and more sovereign powers to the EU? As he looked around the room at the rapt faces, Pearce could see that Straitharn was asking exactly the sort of questions that many had posed in the pub or around the dinner table. This wasn't what he'd been expecting. There had been no mention of nationalism or immigration or any of the subjects typically associated with the far right. Straitharn was using the themes and language of the left and appealing to people's sense of social justice.

He went on from Magna Carta to trawl British history for examples of what happens when governments diverge too far from public opinion. When he used the abolitionist, suffragette and anti-apartheid movements to illustrate how the people can force progressive change, Pearce realized just how right Leila's assessment had been. It was impossible to argue against the rightness of the anti-slavery movement or the idea that women should have the vote or the prospect of a free and equal South Africa. He was tying himself to causes that were widely recognized to have been on the right side of history. It *was* cunning.

Then, at last, he came to recent history and the subject of immigration.

'There are those, some of whom are gathered outside, who would have you believe that British culture is a bust, that we have given nothing to the world but war and suffering. They forget our rich and generous history as a progressive nation, championing some of the causes I've mentioned, pushing for the abolition of slavery even as other nations embraced it, campaigning for equal rights for women when other countries continued to deny them suffrage. Britain has been a beacon of liberal ideas, exporting progress and helping shape the world for the better. But now we are told to be ashamed. If I, a white man, stand up and say I am proud of my country and my culture, I am decried as a racist. But this isn't about race. A Scot or Welshman can be proud of their nation. A Somali is encouraged to celebrate his culture, a Frenchman is invited to mark Bastille Day. We now live in an anything-other-than culture. Anything other than British, anything other than English. Do not be proud, do not be vocal. Be ashamed, be quiet, behave.'

Straitharn took a breath, and in the silence, Pearce could hear the crowd outside, still chanting, shouts rising above the commands of the police.

'But I will not behave. I see many races and religions represented here tonight and want to tell you that this has nothing to do with the colour of a person's skin. It is about values. Do you share the values of tolerance, liberalism and free speech that have made this country so great? Yes? Then welcome. But how can we be sure of a person's values if we allow them to settle without vetting? And how can we vet people properly when we have migration running into hundreds of thousands every year?'

So this was the ruse. They would justify discriminatory immigration controls by claiming they protected a set of values. And Pearce guessed the fact that certain races or religions would be found wanting by this test of values would be dismissed by Progress Britain as pure coincidence.

Straitharn's voice was alive with emotion and Pearce wondered how much of it was genuine and how much was performance. 'What is the magic number that transforms immigration into invasion? We have already seen people come in such numbers that they have formed enclaves. They aren't integrating, they aren't assimilating. Instead, they are spreading their culture, forcing it on their hosts and when we, the people, object, we're told by the powers that be that we're racist and intolerant. Even as these new cultures engage in practices that are contrary to the law of the land, our authorities look away, telling us not to judge. But someone must judge. The laws of Britain must apply to one and all and they must be upheld universally. It is not enough to say it's their culture. This is Britain, this is British culture, these are British laws and if we cannot defend them, then this country is lost forever.'

The applause shocked Pearce. He'd been lost in Straitharn's powerful oration and felt almost as though he'd awakened from hypnosis when the clapping of dozens of pairs of hands echoed around the room.

Leila whistled. '*Bloody hell*,' she said. '*So dangerous.*'

This is how it always begins, Pearce thought. Arguments everyone could understand made by seemingly reasonable people. But no one could ever tell what lay in their hearts. He was sure that the men who'd terrorized Raqqa might have been eloquent and reasonable to begin with, until they felt secure of their positions and turned the city into a medieval hellhole. In truth, neither Straitharn nor the ginger-haired man outside, Owen Lucas, represented the vast majority of people in Britain. They were two sides of the same extremist coin, and under normal circumstances the easy-going, comfortable mainstream would have nothing to do with them. But these weren't normal times. People were furious with the established order and this made them ripe for radicalization by both the left and right.

Straitharn said a short thanks and bowed before leaving the stage. As the applause died away, Bastien Collet came to the lectern. He was a walking contradiction. According to the background briefing Leila had provided, Collet, like Pearce, was mixed race, the child of an Algerian philosopher and a French university professor. Despite his background, he had a long history of flirting with the far right and had endorsed the Front Nationale for years. Collet had warm, friendly eyes, a broad nose, long dreadlocked hair and sported a moustache and goatee that helped him look much younger than his fifty-three years. He wore tight black trousers and a black T-shirt that clung to his toned body and accentuated his youthfulness.

He stood watching the audience silently for a moment.

'They scream but they don't listen,' he said, gesturing towards the crowd outside. His voice was deep, his accent broad. 'You are here to listen, but most of you already understand more than those out there. The greatest crime ever perpetrated in this country was the abandoning of tens of thousands of young girls to the hands of what they call grooming gangs. These are rapists, and were the girls any colour other than white, there would have been outcry. Instead, the authorities not only abandoned the girls, they refused to investigate and to prosecute when the scale of the abuse finally became clear. Why? Because they were afraid of being labelled racist. Those people out there know the power of that word and they use it to silence dissent. Will they call me a racist? My father was an Algerian Muslim. A man with dangerous and backward views. They celebrate him and his culture without knowing anything about it. I have lived it and I'm here to tell you that the war of cultures is not a zero-sum game. I'm not afraid to say that I value Western liberalism. The freedoms we have are worth far more than the misguided superstitions of any backward religion. But I will not stand here and appeal to your emotions, I will tell you exactly why.'

For a man who didn't want to appeal to people's emotions,

Collet had started with one of the most contentious subjects in recent British history: the failure of authorities to protect vulnerable girls and young women from grooming gangs. It was emotive stuff designed to stir up hatred against the perpetrators and by extension the communities from which they came. Purely a legitimate grievance aired, Progress Britain would say, nothing to do with race or creed, but Pearce knew better. This was an initiation, a meeting designed to prime the pump and draw people into an organization that had dangerous racial politics at the heart of its agenda.

In a speech which asserted that the only role of government was to guarantee individual liberty and protect fundamental freedoms, Collet argued that the British and other governments throughout Europe were failing miserably to discharge what should be their only true function. Young women were being menaced, people were being slaughtered by terrorism, philosophers were being no-platformed and denied their right to free speech, and entire communities were being silenced, their concerns decried as the rantings of a few extreme racists. Freedom was in retreat and as a consequence, liberty was under threat. There was just enough truth in Collet's words for him to be credible. And someone with a shred of credibility was a far greater threat than the wildest raving lunatic.

Collet received a rapturous response and kissed his hands before holding them up for the crowd, who were on their feet applauding. So far, Pearce had heard a mishmash of conservative, liberal and radical thinking, bundled in a populist package that clearly had racist undertones, but there had been nothing to tie this organization to Nathan Foster or his investigation. Why had Fozz hidden the symbol of the black star in his bed? Pearce hadn't seen it in evidence anywhere in the meeting and couldn't understand what linked it to Progress Britain. What did a few angry philosophers, academics and failed politicians have to do with Bayard Madison? And if there was a link, what could possibly be worth protecting with murder?

Most of the people in the hall stayed on their feet after Collet retreated from the stage. They stood silently, and Pearce felt a growing sense of anticipation.

'It's like they're waiting for the Pope,' Pearce whispered.

'*Markus Kral is an enigma,*' Leila told him. '*Beyond his books, papers and university bio, there's very little on the guy.*'

Pearce was startled by the reception given to the little man who took the stage. The crowd applauded and cheered as Markus Kral ambled to the lectern. He was walking with the ease of a king about to bless his subjects. He wore a light blue suit, a sky blue shirt that was unbuttoned at the collar, and a pair of brilliantly shined formal black shoes. Everything about him oozed refinement, except the beard that reached halfway down his throat. Like his hair, it was black with broad streaks of grey, but unlike his hair, it was curly and unkempt, giving the man a slightly wild, dangerous air. His eyes were bright blue, and their keenness was evident even at a distance. He smiled while he waited for the acclaim to die down, but it seemed an expression of patient indulgence rather than joy.

'Friends,' he began. His accent was most definitely Czech, but there was a hint of upper-class English refinement, as though he'd learned the language at an elocution school. 'I see that some of you have already heard of me.'

There were a few laughs.

'And those of you who don't yet know me have been most

welcoming. I welcome you in turn and I thank you for coming. It is no small thing to stand against prevailing opinion and give voice to the truth when everyone else is still pretending that the emperor is fully clothed. Those of you who have read my work will know that I always begin with the assertion that I know nothing. I have no answers, but I am prepared to ask questions, no matter how difficult they may be, and together we can find the truth. Any man who claims he knows more than his brother is a fool. Any woman who says she knows how another should live is an idiot. We have no right to govern each other's lives, and no one man has the answer to how the best life is lived. That's why I believe in collective wisdom, the wisdom of the crowd and why I, unlike many others, respect populism. The ruling class has always looked down on the people, they will dismiss us as ill-informed and unintelligent, and for centuries that approach worked because they were able to maintain the illusion that they were superior. But the death of mass media and the rise of the Internet has exposed them. We can see the mistakes of the ruling class, one after the other, after the other, after the other. They are as fallible as the rest of us, if not more. None of us is so confident in his or her own judgment that we would presume to shape the destiny of nations, but these rulers, the elite, are so puffed up with their own sense of righteousness and inflated egos that they think they can tell the rest of us how we should live. But we have seen them exposed as failures and we talk and we remember. The Internet means we never forget. All their lies, their errors, are recorded forever. They are not better than us, they simply have more power, more money and less shame. Do not let them call us racist or ignorant. Do not let them police your thoughts. Go wherever the truth beckons you, and address such problems as you find. The price of not doing so, the price . . .'

Kral hesitated, distracted by the sound of a commotion outside. Pearce heard raised voices, the crash of breaking glass, pounding feet, whistles, a voice broadcasting through a loudhailer, sirens and screams, and he knew that the police had lost control of the crowd. He got to his feet as the first masked men burst through the double doors.

'Kill the Nazis!' one of them yelled.

Somewhere across the room, a woman screamed, her shrill voice acting as a starter's pistol, marking the moment the mayhem truly began.

Chapter 30

Masked protesters streamed into the hall, lashing out at everyone in their path. The suited stewards tried to engage them and Pearce caught sight of Keith, the man who'd questioned him, fighting with one of the invaders. The bodyguards who'd searched Pearce pushed through the fleeing, turbulent crowd and rushed onto the stage, bundling Markus Kral away. Everyone else was trying to escape through one of two fire exits that stood either side of the hall. The large room was alive with panic and violence, the cries of those fighting, the screams of the fearful, and from outside came the sound of police cracking down on anyone causing trouble.

Pearce felt hands on him and turned to see a man in a ski mask trying to pull him down. He jerked free and his assailant threw a punch. The guy was shorter and skinnier than Pearce and had no clue about the fundamentals of fighting. Pearce stepped back, dodging the blow and then leaned into the gap the wild swing had created. He delivered two sharp jabs before putting all his weight behind a cross. There was a crunch of bone beneath the balaclava and the man crumpled. Pearce glanced around and saw yet more protesters streaming into the hall, their faces concealed by masks and bandanas.

'Fuck 'em up!' a new arrival yelled, and Pearce turned to

see a scrawny man in a black hoodie push his way inside. A black bandana with a skull and crossbones motif concealed his face, but the strands of scraggly ginger hair that escaped the confines of his hood left Pearce in no doubt about his identity: it was Owen Lucas.

At his instruction, the protesters set about their attack with renewed vigour, engaging with anyone they could lay their hands on. Scuffles were now happening throughout the room, and when he saw the first police officers pressing through one of the emergency exits, fighting the fleeing crowd, Pearce knew it was well past time to leave. The police, in helmets and body armour, weren't messing around and were cracking heads, their batons raining down indiscriminately. People were crying, yelling, pleading, fighting, fleeing, and Pearce pushed his way through it all. He avoided either fire exit and forced his way down the central aisle.

When he reached the space in front of the stage, a couple of black-clad protesters were there to meet him. One was holding a metal chair leg and lunged with it. Pearce ducked and replied with a kick to the man's kneecap that sent him tumbling down. He cried out, dropped the length of metal and clutched his injured knee. As Pearce grabbed the makeshift weapon, the second guy jumped him, trying to get him into a chokehold. Mistake. Pearce brought the chair leg up and planted it in the man's face. His hold evaporated as he fell back unconscious.

Pearce leaped on stage and followed the route Markus Kral had taken when he'd been bundled away by the security guards. Behind a small curtained section, he found a door that led to a narrow corridor which wound through the rear of the building.

Sunlight shone against a wall ahead, falling through a re-inforced picture window set in the back door. Pearce burst out and found himself in a small car park. A gold Mercedes E-Class was parked at the mouth of the narrow driveway that ran alongside the community centre, and three of the security guards were fussing around it. Pearce could see Markus Kral and Dominic Strathairn in the back. Bastien Collet was in the front passenger seat and Annabelle Crawford was driving.

'Let's clear a path,' one of the security guards said to the others, and the three men started running down the narrow driveway towards the road.

The car followed, and Pearce ran after it. Movement to his rear caught his attention and, he saw people spill through the back door, a mix of protesters and those who'd been at the meeting, still brawling as they tumbled into the fading sunlight.

Pearce ran along the narrow driveway. A high wooden fence lined one side, and the community centre lay on the other. Violence filled the air and, rising above it, sirens, as ambulances and police vehicles raced to the scene. Somewhere out front, an officer used a bullhorn to issue instructions, but his words were indistinct beneath the sound of the brawl. Ahead, the security guards were bundling people out of the way of the Mercedes, pushing them back through the fire exit or forcing them against the fence. Pearce caught an acrid scent, and the people by the road were suddenly enveloped in grey smoke. Someone had tossed smoke bombs. The Mercedes drove past the security guards into the thickening cloud.

'*Get out of there, Scott,*' Leila urged.

'I'm on it,' he assured her.

With mayhem in every direction, Pearce couldn't risk

getting caught in a fight, or being arrested, so he ran to the high fence and pulled himself over. He landed in the beer garden of the neighbouring pub and saw a handful of patrons peering through the windows, searching out violent entertainment. Two men, one protester and one attendee, were obliging, slugging it out to Pearce's right. He ignored them and ran round the pub to join Moorbank, the short mews he'd passed on his way in. Slowing to a fast walk, Pearce hurried along the residential street. Police cars and vans whizzed past the junction ahead, and as he looked to his left, beyond the pub's patio, Pearce saw that the brawl had become a full-blown riot. Shield-toting officers in helmets and body armour were spilling from vans to engage the crowd, which was lost in swirls of smoke and turmoil.

Pearce cursed the confiscation of his helmet, but the police were too busy to worry about a lone motorcyclist riding without proper gear. As he reached the corner of Blackbird Leys Road, he saw his bike still in its space. A few locals had emerged from their homes and were peering past him, towards the rapidly deteriorating situation.

He heard the sound of a vehicle coming along the road behind him, but turned too late. A rusty old white Renault van mounted the pavement and drove directly at him. The driver was a large guy with black hair which sprouted from his head in short, ragged tufts. He had a word tattooed on his forehead, but Pearce couldn't make it out. The man gripped the steering wheel and sunlight glinted between each knuckle where it hit the steel studs implanted into his hands. His companion in the passenger seat was shorter, but looked broader. His head was covered by a grey hoodie, but Pearce caught a glimpse of the terribly scarred face that lay beneath. Had he looked sooner, Pearce might have been able to avoid the van, but all he could do in the split second he had was limit the damage. He jumped back and turned as the van struck him. The impact threw him into the main road and his head cracked against the tarmac. The world became a nightmarish kaleidoscope and Pearce could feel the dread pull of unconsciousness reaching up for him. Trying to fight it, he forced himself to his feet as the two men jumped out of the van.

'*Shit, Scott,*' Leila exclaimed. '*Are you OK? I'm alerting the police.*'

'Scott Pearce,' the Scarred Man said as he approached. Both he and his companion were clad in the black garb of the protesters. 'It's time we got to know each other.'

Fuck! My name, Pearce thought. *They have my name.* The implications of that simple fact cascaded through his mind.

'*How do they know you?*' Leila asked.

'You've got to get out,' Pearce replied. 'Find the grey wolf. Go to him.'

'*Scott,*' Leila pleaded, '*run!*'

He removed the glasses and slid the earpiece out.

'*No, don't,*' he heard Leila say, but her voice faded to nothing as he dropped both items onto the road. With a tremendous effort, he lifted his foot and crushed the earpiece and glasses beneath his boot. Destroyed, the signal would be impossible to track.

Pearce raised his fists, but his arms felt weak and unsteady, and his feet seemed a million miles away. The Scarred Man scoffed and nodded at his companion. The tall, lumbering giant with knuckledusters implanted in his fists came at

Pearce. As Pearce's eyes focused, he could make out the word tattooed on the man's head: 'Salvation'.

Pearce tried to move, but he was simply too battered and dazed to do anything other than take the punches the man threw, and as he tumbled into darkness, he cursed himself for being so weak.

Chapter 31

Leila was breathing rapidly, struggling to come to terms with what she'd just witnessed. She knew people died playing the game, but she'd always assumed Pearce was one of the few who'd make it to gold watch retirement. The footage left her in little doubt. The shocking moment of impact, the picture becoming a jumble before settling on the clear blue evening sky. Pearce's horrific groans as he slowly got to his feet. She could tell he'd been badly hurt. When she'd seen the faces of the two men who'd knocked him down, she knew the collision was no accident. They were killers. Killers who knew Pearce's name.

Leila had called the police the moment she'd seen the men's faces, stifling her rising grief to give the operator the information he needed. She had to do something, no matter how futile, but she knew that even if the police could pull officers out of the riot, by the time they got down the road, those men would have finished whatever they had planned.

Find the grey wolf. Go to him. Pearce's last words before he'd destroyed the surveillance gear. He'd done it to protect her. If they'd moved on him, it was entirely possible that they'd picked up the signal coming off the ear transceiver and surveillance glasses.

An alarm sounded, and Leila's grief was lost to fear. She

clicked a tab, which opened a window on the monitor. The window was divided into four panels, each of which showed an image from a surveillance camera positioned around her house. She could see two masked men, dressed in grey and black urban camouflage gear, creeping through the grounds.

Khara! Leila thought.

She leaned beneath the counter and located the keypad that controlled a tiny safe. She punched in the numbers and the steel door popped open to reveal a pistol and two clips of ammunition. She slid them down the side of her wheelchair and returned to the computer, which was now displaying footage of the two masked men breaking into her beautiful house.

'*Ya ebna sharmouta,*' Leila cursed as she watched one of the men smash her kitchen window.

She opened a command prompt and quickly typed a short script that would corrupt every digital device in the room. Although it pained her to fry the machines beyond retrieval, she consoled herself with the knowledge that the backup RAID drive she pulled from a rack contained a copy of all the data on every computer in the room.

Leila put the drive on her lap and manoeuvred to the door. She switched off the lights before she opened it, and slid out of the concealed room at the back of her studio. She moved quickly, but cautiously, keeping an eye on the house, where she saw the occasional flash of black and grey as the intruders worked their way through her home. To her dismay, one of the figures moved outside, and even though the man briefly disappeared behind a copse of trees, she could tell he was headed for the studio. She opened the door and rolled down the ramp, into the garden, grateful for the heatwave that had baked the lawn dry.

She moved round the studio, glancing over her shoulder to keep track of the shadow she could see through the trees. Leila gripped the rims and pushed her wheels with all her strength. As she cleared the corner, she glanced back one last time to see the man in a ski mask emerge from the copse. He hadn't seen her.

Keeping the studio between her and the approaching intruder, Leila rolled down the sloping lawn towards a path that ran along the western edge of her garden. She pushed her way through the undergrowth, grateful when she felt the soft black tarmac beneath her. She'd had it laid for just such an eventuality. She moved quickly north, towards a garage and yard that were concealed behind a thicket of Leylandii.

As she rolled past gaps in the shrubbery, Leila caught glimpses of the man searching her studio. He hadn't found the secret room yet, but she had no doubt he would. She ducked to pass beneath a low archway she'd cut into the Leylandii, and reached the yard. A double garage stood to the left and ahead was her escape pod – a Golf R, a tiny rocket of a car that was loaded with clothes, money and equipment. She moved to the driver's side, found the key taped to the front bumper and opened the car. She hauled herself behind the wheel and pushed her chair away, before slamming the door shut. She started the engine and when she pressed the accelerator, the car shot along the narrow driveway connecting the yard to the road beyond her property.

On one side, the setting sun burst through the trees in blinding flashes, on the other, Leila saw shadowy figures sprinting towards her through the garden. But they wouldn't reach her. They were too slow and, as she glanced at their receding, hateful forms, she promised to make sure they all paid for whatever happened to Scott Pearce.

A hard slap brought Pearce back. He opened his eyes to find himself in a small, dark room. The high windows suggested it was some kind of basement. It was dark outside, but the pale yellow light of a distant street lamp offered some illumination. Pearce was strapped to a chair, bound by his torso, arms pulled tight behind his back. Cool hard metal around his wrists suggested handcuffs, and he reached out with his fingers to feel solid plastic between his hands. Police issue. His ankles were tied to the legs of the chair. He'd been trussed up by a professional, and he guessed it was the same man who was craning over him. Pearce felt panic rise and forced it back.

'Scott Pearce,' the Scarred Man said, his breath hot and fetid against Pearce's face. 'Hero of Islamabad. It's too bad they didn't believe you.'

Pearce glared at him. As his eyes focused in the darkness, he made out the larger, dark-haired man, lurking in the shadows.

'We know all about you,' the Scarred Man said. 'But you have more to tell. The lawyer. We're going to talk to her. Maybe the people close to her. We need the name of her client.'

'She doesn't know,' Pearce said.

'Maybe that's what she's told you. But people aren't always honest.' The Scarred Man stood and gestured to his companion, who stepped into the narrow well of pale light and handed over something small. 'SP-117 can help with that,' the Scarred Man said, revealing a syringe.

SP-117 was a truth serum developed by the Russians. It had a fearsome reputation.

'We've made our own modifications to improve it.' The Scarred Man leaned over Pearce. 'Haloperidol, midazolam. It feels like your blood turns to acid.'

Pearce tried to show no fear, but inside he was reeling. He'd been trained to withstand torture, but not anything like this. Haloperidol induced psychosis, tremors and Parkinson's-like symptoms. Midazolam was an anaesthetic, but the incorrect dose caused terrible pain. Pearce fought against his restraints as the Scarred Man found a vein and injected pure torment. As his body began to burn from the inside out, Pearce was grateful for one thing: he'd sent Leila to a man he could trust, but whose location he didn't know. Even if these men got him to talk, there were some things he simply couldn't reveal and his ignorance of Kyle Wollerton's location would hopefully keep Leila and the others safe.

The Scarred Man reached out and touched Pearce's forehead, which was beaded with sweat. 'Let's begin,' he said.

Pearce did the only thing he could.

He screamed.

Chapter 32

Leila had grown up with a sun that set at more or less the same time throughout the year. True, Britain's winter days were miserably short, but the summers were magical. It was almost 10 p.m. and the sun still cast warm, hazy light on the tops of distant trees. She'd been travelling all day, but as she gazed beyond the woodland that flanked the road, over the fields towards the forest on the horizon, she could almost believe she was on holiday, that Pearce had not been missing for over twenty-four hours, and that she would soon see him again.

She'd spent most of the night trying to locate the man Pearce had called the grey wolf. His real name was Kyle Wollerton, and he had once been one of Six's most effective assets. His path had been similar to Pearce's, rising through special forces, proving himself in operational support before being recruited by the service. And like Pearce, he'd departed under a cloud, when an operation in Iraq had gone wrong and two locals had been killed. The head of the special forces team providing Wollerton support had blamed him for outdated, archaic practices that had directly resulted in the two deaths. Wollerton, then forty-eight, had been suspended and, following an investigation, was quietly eased out of the service.

After escaping her home, Leila had checked into a B & B

on the outskirts of Aylesbury and used the custom-built Chillblast laptop she kept in the Golf to access Six's payroll systems. She'd been trembling as she'd searched for the man, her imagination churning up terrible pictures of what had happened to Pearce. Eventually, she'd grown angry with herself. She was no use to anyone, least of all Pearce, if she couldn't control her emotions. She'd focused on the task at hand: finding Wollerton.

She knew he would probably have assumed a new identity, but one way or another, he'd be getting the pension he'd been given to convince him to go quietly. Leila discovered an address: Overlook, a house on the Moray Firth that lay between Nairn and Elgin. Once she'd found it, Leila had searched for news of Pearce, checking the emergency call logs and local police follow-up for any developments. There was nothing. No word of the accident and no sign of the missing man.

Leila had finally fallen asleep for a couple of hours before being woken by sunlight streaming through the window. She'd contacted Wayne, who was still in Cornwall with Melody, and had told him what had happened to Pearce. Shocked and bewildered, he'd asked what they should do, and Leila had told him to head north, assuring him she'd be in touch as soon as she'd confirmed she'd found somewhere safe for them to regroup.

Knowing the men who'd invaded her house might be looking for it, Leila had left the Golf on a side street and had grabbed a holdall of clothes, a flight case full of computer equipment and a spare cane from the boot. She transferred it all to a waiting cab and instructed the driver to take her to Milton Keynes Central, where she'd caught the train north. She'd dozed fitfully for the entire journey, her waking moments plagued by memories of Pearce being run over, her nightmares troubled by imaginings of what had happened to him. Ten hours and three changes later, Leila had finally arrived in Elgin.

'This is the place,' said the driver, a bearded old man in a tatty jumper. He turned off the main road onto a lane that cut across an open field.

Overlook was an isolated double-fronted whitewashed house that lay beyond a large, square courtyard. High, sloping roofs capped each wing and large windows overlooked the field, lane and countryside beyond. As they drew closer, Leila saw that the forest on the other side of the house had thinned to little more than a single line of trees, and through their weather-swept branches she saw the white caps of rolling waves. The air took on a briny tang, and even above the sound of the engine, Leila could hear the crash of the sea, and the drawl of retreating water clawing against the shore.

A figure emerged from the house: a tall, lean man, his face half hidden in the glare of the westering sun. He wore pale, frayed jeans, weathered brown boots and a white shirt with the sleeves rolled up and, most noticeably, he sported a shotgun.

'I dinna want ony trouble,' the driver said nervously.

'It'll be fine,' Leila assured him.

'Drive on,' Wollerton said the moment they stopped. He crossed the courtyard menacingly. 'You're not welcome here.'

He had the wrinkled, tanned face of a man who'd spent a lifetime outdoors. Grey stubble clung to his pinched cheeks and a shock of unkempt grey hair was tousled by the wind. His narrow eyes were unforgiving and cold.

Leila ignored his instruction and opened the door. He levelled the shotgun almost immediately.

'Go away,' he said. 'You're trespassing.'

'Sir,' Leila responded, leaning on her cane as she pulled herself out of the car. 'I was sent here by someone you worked with. Scott Pearce.'

Wollerton hesitated.

'He's in trouble,' Leila added.

'What kind of trouble?'

'The worst,' Leila said. 'And I've got nowhere else to go.'

The dark, hollow barrels of the gun didn't move. Then they slowly started to drop. Wollerton turned towards the house and, without saying another word, strode inside.

'I'll be OK,' Leila said to the shaken driver. 'If you could just leave my things by the front door.' She handed him twenty pounds, more than double the fare. 'Keep the change,' she told him, before following Wollerton into the house.

'Prop him up,' a voice said, cutting through the dark fog.

Pearce opened an eye. He was in an alleyway, sitting on cold pavement, his back against rough brick. His body was tender and sore, but the pain was distant, as though his nerves had been rewired. Everything felt strange, unreal. He'd lost track of time in that dark room, and could only recall flashes of the torment he'd endured. He couldn't remember what he'd told the two men, the strangers who'd tortured him, but it didn't matter. He knew what was coming. He could see them preparing the way.

The steel glinted in the light cast by the shop sign. The man with the hideous, raggedy face brandished the razor as he approached. The other one, the dark-haired monster with 'Salvation' tattooed on his head, loomed a couple of paces back. They'd taken off Pearce's jacket and top. He was bare-chested, his arms exposed and vulnerable. Pearce tried to move, but his body was unresponsive. A lingering effect of the anaesthetic, perhaps?

These men now had total control over him. He was their puppet and they could do whatever they wanted. Nothing would ever be as bad as what he'd experienced in that room, so Pearce was quite sanguine about the journey they were about to send him on. No more pain. No more suffering. Blessed release.

The Scarred Man looked down at his arm and sliced diagonally, cutting the flesh and releasing the rich liquid within.

'He's awake,' Pearce heard the voice drift out of the shadows and realized it had come from the bigger man. Salvation.

The scarred face leered at him, but Pearce's eyes weren't on it. He was watching the pool of blood growing around his left wrist. He felt a sharp pinch on his right forearm as the razor was drawn across it, the wound deep and long. Blood sprang forth immediately.

The Scarred Man placed the razor in Pearce's right hand and then leaned close. 'And so it ends,' he said, and his words seemed to echo around Pearce's head.

The Scarred Man stood, and he and his companion watched Pearce for a moment before they turned and walked away, their footsteps like thunderclaps in the deserted alley.

Pearce screamed inwardly, but he couldn't move his mouth to give voice to his terror. He now knew what Fozz had felt lying in the plaza in front of the Bayard Madison building: failure.

The word was Pearce's last thought as his mind shut down and darkness took him.

Part Two

Chapter 33

Leila had struggled to bring her things into the house and had deposited them in the hall before propping herself against a bench seat that was built into an ornate mirror. A beaten face looked back at her and she'd been glad of the twilight, which had thrown most of the house into shadow and concealed the worst of her fatigue and shock. She'd sat there for some time, expecting Wollerton to reappear, but he never came. Eventually, after what had seemed like an age, she'd leaned heavily on her cane and shuffled through the hall into a living room that contained a few pieces of decrepit furniture.

She'd walked on to find Wollerton sitting in another room at the back of the house. A dark varnished table and twelve gothic chairs were arranged to her left and two tatty corduroy armchairs faced the chipped French doors, which were open, filling the air with the smell of the sea and the rhythmic crash of the Moray Firth. Beyond the ragged line of trees, the water sparkled in the moonlight, shimmering and dancing before Leila's eyes. Without asking, she'd taken the chair next to Wollerton, who hadn't raised any objections.

The two of them had sat there in silence, watching the waves roll in, listening to the music of forest and sea. As time drifted on, Leila's thoughts had turned to Pearce and through him to her family. She'd had too much grief for one lifetime and as the smiling, happy faces of the dead came alive in her mind she'd felt tears well in her eyes.

'Don't you want to know what happened?' she asked eventually.

'It's written on your face. If he needed saving, you would have told me by now,' Wollerton said. 'He's gone the way of many good soldiers.' Leila couldn't help feel that Wollerton's words were tinged with envy. 'I've been here too many times. Too much sadness. Too much loss. All for nothing.' His voice had a slight Highland lilt. 'What do you want from me?'

'We just need somewhere to stay while we figure out what to do,' Leila replied quietly. 'Scott told me to find you. I'm not sure why.'

'I recruited him,' Wollerton explained. 'But when they kicked me out, I wanted nothing to do with anyone from my old life, so we lost touch. He trusts me but he doesn't know where I am, which means he can't give you up. Someone he can trust, somewhere safe. This is where I would have sent you. How did you find me?'

'Pension records.'

'Bureaucracy,' he smiled wryly, 'the enemy of national security.' He hesitated. 'You said "we". . .'

'There's a lawyer, and she's got a close protection officer.'

The sound of the waves filled the ensuing silence.

'Pearce,' he sighed. 'I think about all the good friends I've lost and I wonder what they died for. I sit here listening for the answer in the tide and the birds and the whisper of the wind. And do you know what they all say?'

Leila didn't rise to the question and simply watched the man, whose mood was growing maudlin.

'They say, "We're here and we'll be here, unchanged, long after you're gone."' Wollerton rose and walked to the open doorway. He leaned against the frame and gazed over the moonlit water. 'Six said I was a throwback, an anachronism. That what I knew wasn't any use any more. The training they'd given me, the knowledge they'd put in my head. Useless. But I'm not useless.' He turned to Leila. 'See, I've been watching and listening and I know that it's them that are useless. They're fighting the same old wars, but the old enemies are dead. They're trying to play the game, but the rules have changed.'

'And how do you know this?' Leila asked.

'The waves, the birds, the wind, they all tell me,' he answered dreamily, before fixing Leila with an intense stare. 'And if you can't speak their language, just watch the news. It's all there. That feeling that nothing is what it seems, that things don't make sense, the dread that something ominous is about to happen. That's no accident. That's someone playing a new game.'

'What game?'

Wollerton scoffed. 'If I knew that, I'd probably be dead.' His expression softened. 'I'm sorry. That was in poor taste. This "we", are they going to get me killed?' he asked.

Leila shook her head. 'No. It will just be for a couple of days. Until we find out what happened to Scott and work out what to do next.'

'*Inti Suriun, mish keda?*' Wollerton asked, surprising Leila with the fluency of his pronunciation.

'Yes, I am,' she replied. 'I'm from Raqqa.'

Wollerton gave a slow, grave nod. 'What's your name?'

'Leila.'

'*Ahlan wa sahlan, ya Leila,*' he replied, giving her a formal welcome. '*Aietaba nafsik fi baytik,*' he said, telling her to make herself at home.

'Thank you, Kyle.'

He nodded and left the room. As she heard his footsteps retreating along the hallway, Leila pushed herself to her feet. She staggered after him, and when she got to her bags, she reached into one and produced a Ghostlink, which she used to make a call.

Wayne put the communicator down on the sideboard. Leila hadn't told him the exact circumstances, but she'd been clear: Pearce was dead. Wayne was numb with shock. He couldn't believe the Reaper had got his hands on Scott Pearce. His mind filled with memories of shared moments, but Wayne told himself this wasn't the time for grief. Leila had given him an address and he had a job to do. Melody's life depended on him.

Wayne had spent the day speculating over what had happened as he'd followed Leila's instruction and headed north. Melody had known something was wrong, but Wayne wouldn't answer her repeated questions. She wasn't ready for the news. With Pearce gone, their chances of cracking the case were almost zero, and Melody's prospects of survival had plummeted.

They'd stopped on the outskirts of Blackburn and taken rooms in a grotty bed and breakfast that stood beside a dual carriageway, the building's white pebble dashing greyed by pollution. Wayne had pushed a microwave meal around a chipped plate, sitting in silence as Melody did likewise.

After dinner, Wayne had retreated to his room, fidgeting

about the place impatiently until Leila had called with instructions and details of their final destination. They were to head
for Scotland immediately.

Wayne went to the tiny, grimy bathroom and splashed
some water on his face before heading along a gloomy corridor to Melody's room. He knocked softly.

Moments later, Melody answered. She was wrapped in a
towel and her hair was coiled in another. She looked beautiful, like the only creature of light in this dark, depressing
place.

'I can't sleep. My room's baking and the windows won't
open,' she said. 'I was taking a shower.'

'Leila just called,' Wayne said. 'We've got to go.'

'Now?'

'Yeah. Get dressed and—'

'Not until you tell me what's going on,' Melody interrupted.

Wayne sighed. Was he really protecting her by keeping her
in ignorance? 'Scott was hit by a van. Two men inside the
vehicle attacked him,' he hesitated, trying to keep it together.
'No one's heard from him since.'

'Then—' she began, but he cut her off.

'That's all we know.' He wasn't even convincing himself.

'I'm so sorry,' she said, taking his hand.

Wayne hadn't felt a kindly touch for a very long time. 'Like
I said, we need to leave.' He stepped back, but she held his
hand and pulled him towards her.

'It's OK,' she said, wrapping her arms around him.

Death took people to the threshold of reality and forced
them to contemplate what lay beyond. Wayne burned with the
raw, painful energy of such contemplation, but as he looked

at Melody, it seemed to dissipate and, in her sympathetic eyes, he saw something pure and good. She stood on tiptoe, pulled his head towards hers and kissed him.

This is wrong, he thought, but he did nothing to resist as she kicked the door shut.

Chapter 34

Yellow. Hard. Pain.

Teeth.

Orange gems with black hearts.

Eyes.

Pearce inhaled a long rasping breath and the large fox that was pulling at one of his fingers retreated into the shadows of the alleyway. It stood watching, waiting to see whether the dying man would have the strength for a fight. He looked down at the cold stone beneath him and saw his life spread in a dark pool. His arms and legs were already chill with the touch of death. He could feel erratic thumping in his chest and knew that he didn't have long before he went into hypovolemic shock, his heart deprived of enough blood to continue pumping.

He tried to move his arms, which were still weeping blood. Either the anaesthetic had worn off, or it could not subdue the irresistible force that motivated him: survival. His arms shifted slightly. They felt numb, as though they belonged to someone else, but he could direct them, and he pushed himself onto his knees. He crawled through the pool of congealing blood, along the narrow alley towards the lights that lay beyond an archway. He was aware of movement behind him. The fox was following.

He kept his eyes fixed on a shape beyond the archway.

Green metal. Glass.

Bus stop.

Inch by agonizing inch he crawled through the darkness, bleeding, dying, until he cleared the archway and found himself on a broad pavement. Everywhere was eerily still, as though the rest of the world were dead and he was the only person left alive. A large church stood in a square across the road, and as he looked left and right, he recognized the centre of Oxford. He was on a parade near the High Street. His right arm gave way and he collapsed, his chin hitting the pavement heavily. He glanced behind him and saw the glint of the fox's sharp eyes. It was trying to hug the shadows, biding its time until Pearce's business with the world was done.

Noise.

Movement.

Pearce looked to his right and saw three people, a man and two women, stumble around the corner. He tried to shout, but could only muster a rasping breath. He tried to move his head, but it was stuck to the pavement. His cold arms and legs were unresponsive and he could only watch with growing despair as the trio joked and jostled their way north, taking all hope with them. They would vanish and he would die lying in his own blood.

'No!'

Pearce was surprised to hear the word spring from his mouth. The three people turned at the sound and one of the women spotted him, lying shirtless and bloody, half consumed by the dark archway. As they ran towards him, Pearce heard movement to his rear and saw that the fox was retreating, frightened by the drunk, noisy students who'd become Pearce's saviours.

Pearce said a silent prayer of thanks to the scavenger who had woken him from the last sleep, closed his eyes and dared to hope.

Fury and the doctors of the John Radcliffe Hospital kept Pearce alive. The first few hours had been a patchwork of horrific dreams of the time he'd spent being tortured and interrogated by the two men who'd tried to murder him. When he'd emerged from his awful sleep, Pearce had drifted in and out of the world, coming to his hospital ward every now and then, like an astral traveller. When he finally gained a more substantial hold on reality, his doctor, a young Mancunian called Heywood, a man with a cheeky glint and casual manner, told Pearce about the transfusion that had saved his life and the emergency surgery he'd undergone to repair the vascular and tendon damage inflicted by the razor. He looked down at his hands, which lay on the thin cotton blanket that covered him. The tips of his fingers protruded from soft casts that ran from the first knuckle to the middle of his forearm.

'Your arms should be OK and you should make a full recovery,' Heywood assured him. 'Twelve weeks to get you back to strength, six months before any lingering niggles are gone.'

Pearce sighed.

'I saw evidence of other injuries. Old ones,' Heywood hesitated. 'The scars of knife and gunshot wounds. What looked like shrapnel spray. Combat injuries.'

Pearce held his gaze, but said nothing.

'My brother was a helicopter pilot in Afghanistan. He

works in a bookshop now. I guess some find a way into civilian life more easily than others.'

Pearce understood the implication and remained silent. The doctor took him for some beaten-down veteran who'd run into trouble on the street.

Heywood nodded slowly. 'OK, well, the police will be by later,' he said. 'The ward nurse said sometime between ten and eleven.'

Pearce's face must have betrayed his dismay.

'When you were admitted, we assumed you'd, well, we thought you'd attempted to take your own life,' Heywood explained. 'But you kept talking about the two men who'd attacked you, and I found bruising on your wrists and ankles, consistent with restraints. You've been tied up, haven't you?'

Pearce cursed his delirious mind for its betrayal. What else had he told these people? Officers of the law would bring with them questions of identity, causation and motive, none of which Pearce could answer without further endangering himself. He tried to talk, but his dry throat would only emit a hoarse noise. Heywood poured him a glass of water from a jug that stood on a tray table.

'Here.'

Pearce ignored the distant burning that came from his arms as he propped himself up to take the drink. The worst of the pain was being held at bay by drugs. His wounds had much more misery to give. For now, though, the water felt like a balm on his raw insides.

'What time is it?' Pearce asked.

'Quarter past eight,' Heywood replied, glancing at his watch.

'What day?'

'It's Saturday. Saturday morning,' the doctor said.

'I need to leave.'

Heywood smiled in disbelief. 'You can't. We need to keep you in for at least—'

'If I stay, I'm a dead man,' Pearce interrupted. 'I'm leaving. One way or another.'

Heywood eyed him coolly.

'Can I call—'

Pearce shook his head. 'I need clothes. And some money.'

'I can't do that,' Heywood said, raising his hands.

'If your brother had been shot down and needed help, what would you think of a person who refused it?'

'He was at war,' Heywood objected.

'So am I,' Pearce told him. 'Just like your brother.'

Heywood frowned and his mouth guppied open a few times.

'You've seen what they've done to me. If they find me here, they'll kill me,' Pearce assured him.

The doctor looked around nervously. 'I'll see what I can do.'

An hour later, Pearce was crossing Bury Knowle Park, heading for the imposing Georgian building that stood on its northern edge. The bone-dry ground rose and fell like an ocean and the trees shim-shammed back and forth like the last drunk dancers in a nightclub. Pearce couldn't tell whether the sickening dizziness was a consequence of the horrific cocktail of drugs his tormentors had administered, the blood loss or the surgical anaesthesia. Even though it was less than a mile on foot from the hospital to the park, his progress had been slow and he'd got lost more than once. Every so often, he'd lean against a wall, prop himself by a tree or sit on a bench to take a breather. His heart was racing like a sprinter's, and sweat soaked the clothes Heywood had given him. Pearce had misjudged his condition, and in his weakened state, this short walk had become a marathon.

He sat down on the cropped grass beneath a vast cedar tree and lay back, his head still swimming even after he'd rested it against the hard ground. He watched the branches and blue morning sky roil and bubble, and felt vaguely nauseous at the tricks his mind was playing. He turned his thoughts away from disturbing reality and tried to remember what he'd told the two men who'd tortured him. Had he given up Leila? Wayne? Melody? Had he told them anything that might lead them to Wollerton?

Pearce saw haunting glimpses of agonized screams, but the words were unintelligible and when he tried to catch hold of a moment, it slipped away, leaving nothing but a sense of tremendous pain. Troubled, Pearce forced himself to his feet, stood still for a moment waiting for the unsteady world to settle, and then shuffled on towards the grey hall at the edge of the park.

Built as a country home before the surrounding fields were overrun by houses, Bury Knowle House had once been a grand residence, but was now council offices. Pearce leaned against the wrought iron railing as he climbed the curved stone staircase that led to the large front door. He stepped inside and was hit by a musty smell common to many old public buildings, a blend of boiled cauliflower and bleach. When he entered the library, all sense of commotion died away. He'd forgotten how still and peaceful they could be. The smell of old books was overpowering, as though knowledge was spilling off the shelves and filling the air. A middle-aged man with wild hair and big glasses was hunched in a chair, reading. He turned a page emphatically and gasped, lost in some other world. An elderly lady in a blue dress sat by one of three computers that stood on a counter across from the librarian's station. The librarian, a young woman in brown trousers and a white blouse, was returning books to the shelves. She glanced at Pearce and smiled hesitantly as he approached. He couldn't fault her caution. He was wearing a pair of dirty grey trainers that were a size too small, brown cargo shorts and a torn sky blue T-shirt, clothes Heywood had salvaged from lost property.

'I'm sorry to bother you,' Pearce said as politely as he could. 'But I'd like to use a computer.'

'Of course,' the librarian replied, moving towards her station. 'I'll just log you in.'

'I wondered if you might be able to help me type an email.' Pearce smiled and indicated his casts.

She looked at him sympathetically. 'Of course. Just give me a minute.'

Chapter 35

Wayne steered the Fiesta off the road onto a narrow track that ran towards an isolated house. He could smell the sea, and saw an expanse of shimmering blue water beyond the trees that stood behind the building. Melody was asleep in the seat next to him, her head lolling gently. They hadn't spoken much since leaving Blackburn. They'd shared a bed without inhibition, but as the intense passion faded, their intimacy had been replaced by awkwardness. Wayne wondered whether what had happened between them had been purely physical or whether there might be an emotional connection. For his part, Wayne thought there might be something deeper. In the brief time he'd spent with her, he'd grown to like Melody, but maybe she'd just been carried away by the same swirling emotions that had led him to abandon his better judgment. Death did strange things to people. Whatever her reasoning, they'd crossed a line that would make their future far more complicated. He'd seen bodyguards become overly familiar with their principals and soldiers fall for each other. It rarely ended well.

As they approached the house, Leila walked through the front door, leaning heavily on her cane, exhausted and pained. Wayne thought he saw a face in one of the upstairs windows, but when he looked again, there was only the bright glare of the morning sun against dark glass. Wayne pulled to a stop, and he and Melody climbed out to give Leila muted greetings. To his surprise, she was smiling.

'Pearce is alive,' Leila told them.

'Are you serious?' Wayne asked.

Leila nodded, but gave Melody a sad, sideways glance.

'Thank fuck. What happened?' Wayne asked, his relief stretching to a smile.

'He didn't go into details,' Leila said. 'It wasn't a secure email. He's stranded down south. He's got no money, no phone, nothing. And it sounds like he's in a mess.'

'You want me to—' Wayne began.

'I've said I'll get him. I need to do it,' Leila cut him off. 'For me. I need to be sure he comes back safely.' She paused. 'That thing run OK?' she asked, indicating the Fiesta.

'It's temperamental, but should get you where you want to go,' Wayne said. He understood her resolve. She and Pearce were tight. 'Key's in the ignition.'

Leila turned to Melody, her face full of sorrow. 'I . . .' she stumbled over the words and Wayne tensed. Good news was never this difficult. 'I don't know how to tell you this,' she continued. 'Your mother's been taken.'

Melody's legs failed, but Wayne moved quickly and placed a supportive arm around her.

'This morning an email was sent to the anonymous account we used to warn her. It came from your mother's email address and was written by someone who claims to have abducted her,' Leila revealed. 'If Scott was tortured, it's possible he revealed where she went.'

'No!' Melody cried.

'They say they just want to talk, that she'll be released if you agree to meet and answer questions.' Leila put a reassuring hand on Melody's arm. 'They won't hurt her until they have what they want.'

'I have to go,' Melody said, pulling away from Wayne. 'I have to get to my mum.'

'No,' Wayne responded. 'There's no guarantee they'd let her go even if you could give them what they wanted.'

'The name of the client,' Melody suggested.

Leila nodded slowly. 'So it would seem.' She took a couple of steps towards the car. 'I'll be as quick as I can. Please sit tight until I'm back. We need to talk this through with Scott before we do anything.'

Leila walked to the car, her cane dragging across the driveway.

'This a friend's place?' Wayne asked, looking at the big house.

'Yes,' Leila replied. 'You'll be OK until I get back.' She eased herself into the car, adjusted the seat and started the angry little engine.

Leila pushed herself to the limit. At times, the road south seemed unreal, like a projection, her surroundings simply details added by a Hollywood special effects house. At one point the motorway shimmered and shifted and instead of speeding through lush countryside, she found herself driving into the high desert with her father. She looked to her left and there he was, smiling, his hands on the wheel. Much as she missed his company, she realized it was an illusion brought on by exhaustion and focused hard on what she knew to be real. The greenery of England came flooding back, and she turned off at the next services and slept for an hour before filling up with fuel and resuming her journey.

It was shortly after six in the evening when Leila pulled into the car park behind Headington's Old High Street. She eased into a space at the edge of a large park and saw children laughing, running and swinging in a playground a few yards away. Their bright faces glowed with happiness and the golden sunshine only served to accentuate the perfection of the scene. The warmth that made the playground a paradise for the young had been a blight on Leila's journey and sweat pooled in the small of her back, soaking into her top. She grabbed her cane and clambered out, her legs and hips aching sourly. The pain eased after a few steps and she was grateful to be on the move after so many hours trapped in the car. The slightest breeze kissed her, but after her time in the baking oven of the little Fiesta, it felt like an Arctic wind and Leila welcomed its cooling touch. She scanned the park, her eyes falling on parents, most of whom were lost in their phones, paying no attention to their joyful children. Beyond the playground, Leila caught sight of what she was looking for – a solitary figure lying on the grass, near an outdoor fitness area. A couple of men in shorts and vests were spotting each other on the equipment, totally ignoring the prone figure. Homelessness had become so commonplace it was unremarkable, and Pearce looked utterly beaten down by life, as though he'd simply collapsed mid-step.

Leila walked over as quickly as she could and was soon standing over Pearce, who hadn't stirred. Worried, she leaned down to check his pulse. His eyes snapped open as soon as her hand came within a few inches of his neck and he sat up suddenly, startling her. His skin was grey, as though death's shadow had fallen upon him. He wore a ragged T-shirt, shorts and filthy trainers and both arms were in casts. His sunken, haunted eyes caught her looking at them.

'I was lucky,' he said. 'If it hadn't been for the fox . . .' he tailed off.

'The fox?' Leila asked.

'I think it planned to eat me,' he replied with a dark smile.

Leila's stomach turned and she frowned, wondering what horror he'd endured. Judging from his pained expression, it was not something he'd soon forget.

'Drink?' he asked, reaching beneath his leg. He'd been lying on a plastic bag full of soft drinks and sugary snacks. 'The doctor gave me twenty quid and I blew it on sweets and pop.'

Relieved, Leila laughed. 'Come on,' she said, trying to help him up.

'I'm OK,' he told her.

It was a response she'd dished out many times herself, but he wasn't OK and needed a steadying hand as he got to his feet.

'Look at the two of us,' Leila said as they shuffled towards the car park. He was walking slowly and seemed frail enough to be toppled by the breeze.

Pearce gave a thin smile, but she'd seen the expression in the mirror enough times to know he was in great pain. She ushered him through the park gates to Wayne's Fiesta and helped him settle in the passenger seat. She was full of questions, but by the time she'd rounded the car and hoisted herself behind the wheel, his head had lolled onto his shoulder and the sound of rhythmic deep breathing filled the vehicle.

Leila sighed and turned the ignition. She backed out of the space and tried to shake off her fatigue before starting the return journey north.

Pearce couldn't face what he had to tell her. He was ashamed.

He'd slept most of the way to Scotland, waking a couple of times when Leila had stopped at motorway services. He'd feigned unconsciousness because he couldn't handle telling her the truth, but he knew there was no way to avoid it forever. As they turned onto a track that led to a large isolated house, Pearce opened his eyes. He no longer felt death's cold fingers wrapped around him. His exhaustion was still profound but he was back in familiar territory and the world was no longer buckling and spinning. His wrists were throbbing painfully beneath the soft casts. He tried to flex his fingers, but couldn't manage more than microscopic movements. He hoped the doctor had been right about a full recovery.

It was dark outside and the dashboard clock read 04.06.

'Good sleep?' Leila asked.

Pearce glanced at her sheepishly. She looked terrible. A wraith in the form of the vivacious woman he'd met in the pub days before. 'Sorry,' he said.

'I underst—'

'Not just about this,' he cut her off. 'About everything. I told them things. I don't know what. Lyly, I . . . I don't even, there's nothing I can . . .' He felt the type of filthy failure that was impossible to wash away.

'I know you, Scott,' Leila replied. 'I know how strong you are. Whatever they did –' she glanced at his arms – 'you wouldn't have given us up cheaply.'

'Thanks,' he said, in awe of her grace.

Wollerton emerged from the house as they drew to a halt. He hadn't aged much, but there was a hangdog sadness about him. 'Glad to see you alive, kid,' he said as Pearce staggered out of the car. He stepped forward and hugged Pearce warmly, before putting his shoulder under his arm. 'Let's get you inside.'

Chapter 36

Pearce woke to find himself in a huge bedroom that contained no furniture beyond the mattress he lay on. He had a couple of pillows, and a sheet had been pulled over him. The two sash windows were open and heavy old curtains swayed in the breeze. Judging by the golden light that edged the curtains, he guessed it was evening. He must have slept all day. He rose slowly, shifting his weight carefully, but pain shot along his arms and set off every other nerve in his body. When he was finally on his feet, he staggered to the door, wary and disorientated. He had no recollection of coming to this room.

Through the door, he found a landing that edged a grand staircase. He heard voices drifting up and followed them downstairs. Wollerton's house was big, but it was devoid of life, and Pearce wondered where the man's family were. The only positive consequence of Wollerton's disgrace had been the prospect of spending his retirement with his wife and children, but there was no evidence of them anywhere in the huge, hollow building. No photographs, no toys or sports kit, none of the typical detritus of family life. Pearce stumbled at the bottom of the stairs and took greater care picking out his steps as he crossed the hall. He found Leila, Wayne and Melody in a room at the back of the house. Leila was seated at a long dining table, bent over a laptop. Melody was in a high-backed chair and Wayne rested against the arm.

'You shouldn't have let me sleep so long,' Pearce said as he entered.

'You needed it,' Leila replied, rising. 'But it's good to see you up and around.'

'I'm sorry,' Pearce said, turning to Melody and Wayne. 'I should have done better.'

Wayne gave him a sympathetic look, but Melody was less forgiving. 'They have my mum.'

Pearce looked at Leila, who nodded. He felt a terrible pang of guilt and tried to cast his mind back to what he'd told those evil men in that foul room, but it was no use. Whatever he'd revealed was lost behind a fog of narcotics.

'I'm so sorry,' Pearce said.

'They've offered me a deal. My life for hers,' Melody responded flatly. 'I want to take it.'

'You can't,' Wayne protested. 'There's no guarantee they'll—'

Pearce interrupted him. 'We don't have the right to tell Ms Gold what to do any more.' He turned to Melody. 'It's your call.'

She was about to speak, but a voice interrupted her.

'I don't want to wade in.'

Pearce turned to see his old mentor lurking in the doorway.

Wollerton smiled before continuing. 'But I think you and I should talk before you make any big decisions.'

Shadows danced over the face of the man who'd recruited him into MI6. The fire had burned down, but there were still small flames licking the charred driftwood. Wollerton had checked Pearce was well enough to walk and the two of them had left the house and slowly crossed the lawn to the wood that lay at the bottom of the garden. Each step had been a terrible labour and Pearce just wanted to sit, but Wollerton rarely spoke of things that weren't worth hearing.

The older man had stopped to gather fallen twigs and branches as they'd passed through the wood. Pearce's casts had prevented him from even making a feeble show of helping. By the time they'd reached the sandy beach, Wollerton had an armful of sticks, which he'd laid in a well-used fire pit. He'd placed larger pieces of bleached driftwood on top and then lit the pyre with an old Zippo. As the flames had taken hold, the two men had sat opposite each other, and Wollerton had invited Pearce to tell him exactly what had happened. There'd seemed little point in secrecy with the man who'd mentored him, so Pearce had opened up, revealing everything from the moment Melody had first arrived in Railay.

Now, over an hour later, with night truly beginning to take hold, the fire packed with the embers of yet more driftwood, and the waning sickle moon reflecting off the gently lapping water, Wollerton sat back and studied Pearce.

'Look at us,' he smiled wryly. 'A couple of rejects.'

Pearce smiled bleakly.

'I didn't cope well with rejection,' Wollerton said. 'When they bounced me out for being a dinosaur,' he looked at Pearce coldly, his eyes alive with anger, 'telling me I had nothing useful to offer, I could have skulked off and faded away.' He paused. 'But that would have been an admission they were right. As it happens, when I was around more, my wife realized she didn't actually like me, so she left and took the kids with her, and this empty place, my little family retirement hidey hole, which I've been saving for my entire life, became my fortress of solitude. A lonely fucking shell. I take rich Americans deerstalking every now and then to bring in a bit of cash, but you know what I've really been doing?'

Pearce shook his head.

'I've been up here proving the buggers wrong. When someone tells you you're worthless, you can either accept it and run away to lick your wounds,' he lingered for a moment, 'or you can swagger back stronger and prove just exactly how much you're worth.'

Wollerton looked at the sea, which was far away at the bottom of the broad beach, the waves gently receding towards low tide. 'Are you going to run away and lick your wounds?' he asked at last. 'Or are you going to swagger back? Prove what you're worth?'

'How?' Pearce asked, but his heart wasn't in it. Right now, all he wanted to do was hide.

'Conventional methods won't work,' Wollerton observed. 'You don't even know who or what you're fighting. Let alone why. You've approached this like a standard operation. Surveillance, intelligence gathering, detective work, but from what you've told me, there's nothing standard about this. It's a different beast.'

Silence descended for a moment and Pearce gazed into the fire, his mind racing to keep up with Wollerton's truths. He felt the spark of inspiration crackle somewhere deep within him.

'Why did you succeed in Islamabad?' Wollerton asked. He didn't wait for a reply. 'You were isolated. Cut off. You weren't supposed to be there, so everything you did was on instinct. You didn't have the bosses breathing down your neck so you were able to operate how you saw fit. No rules of engagement.'

'I beat them at their own game,' Pearce acknowledged.

'What happened in Islamabad?' Melody's voice surprised both, and she emerged from the shadow of the woods behind them. 'Leila's working and Wayne crashed out. I don't want to sit by and have my fate decided by others.'

'How long have you been there?' Pearce asked.

'Long enough,' she replied, taking a seat at the fire. 'What happened in Islamabad?'

Pearce looked at her, his mind already on other things. 'I might tell you one day. When we know each other better.' He turned to Wollerton. 'No rules.'

'Which is the only rule of asymmetrical warfare. Be creative, innovate and win at all costs,' Wollerton responded, tossing another piece of wood on the fire. 'From what you've told me, that's what they're doing.'

Pearce shook his head slowly, watching the flames rise up to consume new fuel. He cursed his stupidity. Ever since Melody had found him, he'd approached the investigation as a conventional assignment, following the same operational rules he might have been subject to when working for the government. Those constraints were worse in many ways, because he lacked the resources that made them tolerable. Wollerton was right.

'You can't go to the police,' Pearce told Melody, finding new resolve. 'And you can't exchange yourself for your mother.'

'I have to,' Melody responded. 'You heard what he just said. We can't beat something like this.'

'We can,' Pearce said, excitement bursting through the cloud of pain and self-pity.

'But you can hardly move,' Melody protested, indicating his arms.

'Give me a few days,' Pearce responded. 'I don't need to move much. Just enough to pull a trigger. We're not doing things the old way. We have to burn the rulebook.' He caught Wollerton nodding, a knowing smile on his face. 'And I'm going to light the fire.'

Chapter 37

Wayne woke suddenly, snapping upright with a start. It took him a moment to remember where he was. He looked around the strange, empty dining room and pushed himself out of the wingback chair that had cradled him to sleep.

He headed for a ghostly light that emanated from what passed for a living room. Leila sat hunched on the solitary sofa, which was flanked by empty bookcases. She had her headphones on and was studying something on an iPad. When she looked up, Wayne saw nothing but exhaustion writ large. The synthetic blue light of the screen accentuated the shadows and lines of her face. He wasn't sure how she kept going. The journey to collect Pearce would have wiped him out.

'You should get some rest,' he said, when she removed her headphones.

'I slept a little earlier,' she replied, but he suspected she was lying.

'Where are the others?' he asked, taking a seat next to her.

'No idea. Melody wandered into the garden,' Leila replied.

Wayne rose. 'I'll go look for her.'

He paused when the sound of voices drifted along the rear corridor. The missing trio came into the gloomy hallway and Wollerton switched on the light. The bare bulb shone brightly and Wayne saw the change in Pearce immediately. He still looked tired and his movements pained, but there was something about his eyes, a hard glint, a determination that had replaced the pitiful cloud.

'How are you feeling?' Wayne asked as the three of them entered.

'Better,' Pearce replied, sliding onto the arm of the sofa beside Leila.

'There's something you should see,' Leila said, showing Pearce her iPad. 'It's a news piece about the Progress Britain riot.' She unplugged her headphones and put the volume up before pressing play.

The BBC News logo filled the screen before being swiftly replaced by footage of an angry crowd outside the Blackbird Leys Community Centre.

'*A meeting of the far-right Progress Britain group held in Blackbird Leys turned violent on Thursday night,*' the newsreader said over the images. '*Anti-fascist protesters broke through police lines and clashed with members of the militant group.*'

The images on screen moved from angry protest to scenes of horrific violence. Men and women were fighting each other with makeshift weapons. Many of the combatants were dressed in black and wore masks.

'*Two people died at the scene,*' the newsreader continued. '*Ted Latham, a seventy-five-year-old resident of Bicester, was crushed to death by people fleeing the violence.*'

A photograph of a happy old man holding a pint of beer in some unknown garden filled the screen.

'*The second victim was Max Webb, a computer programmer from Hounslow, who was discovered in the community centre when police finally managed to restore order. Mr Webb died from multiple stab wounds,*' the newsreader said.

The graduation photo of a young black man appeared on screen.

'I saw him,' Pearce said sadly. 'He was there when I arrived. Got into some argy with the protesters. They called him a racist.'

'*Police are appealing for anyone who saw these two men on the night to come forward,*' the newsreader said. The on-screen image changed to a woman standing outside the House of Commons, looking earnest and joyless. The caption told them she was Deborah Jenkins, the Shadow Home Secretary.

'*This is just the latest in a long line of incidents that proves the government has lost control of the streets. We've got a crime epidemic in London and the far right on the march across the country. People just don't feel safe any more. The Prime Minister needs to take urgent action to reassure members of the public that they are safe with this government in charge, but instead, she's losing ministers.*'

The screen displayed stock footage of Cabinet members arriving at Downing Street, focusing on Donald Malcolmson, a porcine man with a jowly face and a ragged, thinning sweep of grey hair.

'*Donald Malcolmson, the Minister of State for Security and Economic Crime, met with the Prime Minister and offered his res-ignation,*' the newsreader said. '*The PM is said to be considering two possible replacements. Evangeline Lewis, Parliamentary Undersecretary of State for the Environment, regarded by many as a moderate centrist. However, according to Downing Street sources, the favoured candidate is Mark Sutton, the Parliamentary Undersecretary of State for Crime, Safeguarding and Vulnerability.*'

Mr Malcolmson's replacement will be responsible for overseeing the new extremism taskforce and shaping the government's response to a growing problem. Mr Sutton is known for his hard-line views on law and order and has a great deal of support from the right of the party.'

Sutton's face filled the screen. He too was being interviewed in front of the House of Commons. His sandy hair turned to grey at the sides, making him look older than his unlined face suggested. He had a small, pointed nose and thin lips, but it was his eyes that struck Wayne. They seemed full of sadness and there was a hesitancy about them that wasn't reflected in his words.

'I think the difference between me and many other politicians is that I don't vary what I say to suit the crowd. I've long spoken of the need to have tough policies to combat crime and, thanks to my experience in the Home Office, I've developed some thinking that will make a real difference. If the Prime Minister calls on me, it will be an honour, but until then, I'm going to focus on my job.'

Leila shut the window, bringing the piece to an end.

'Mark Sutton,' she said.

'The man who ordered the release of three gun-toting criminals arrested outside Heathrow,' Pearce observed. 'Connections, connections,' he muttered. He turned to Wollerton, his eyes alive. 'How would you feel about working with Leila?'

'Sure. If she doesn't mind carrying an old dinosaur.'

'We're going to need to draw them out somewhere,' Pearce said, looking at Wayne. 'Get them to believe we're going to trade Melody for her mother. Some place public with lots of security. Somewhere with armed response nearby. I think I've figured out a way to get your mum back and put you in the clear,' he told Melody, who looked uncertain.

Wayne took a moment to think of suitable locations.

'There's an England match on Saturday,' he remarked. 'It's a friendly. We're playing Nigeria at Wembley. Lots of security. You want something that public?'

'It's perfect,' Pearce said with a smile. 'It'll buy us time.'

'What for?' Wayne asked.

'For my hands to get better,' Pearce told him. 'So I can shoot.' He paused, looking round the room. 'It's going to be dangerous from here on in, but things are going to change. We'll be playing a different game, one suited to our strengths, but if anyone wants out, now is the time,' Pearce said, looking round the room.

'We're in,' Leila said, and Wayne nodded.

'What the hell,' Wollerton agreed. 'It beats getting drunk and listening to the sea.'

Chapter 38

The huge lattice arch curved through the electric blue sky, the sun reflecting in bright flashes where it caught the white metalwork. Wayne led Melody south along Olympic Way towards the giant stadium. The sound of the cheering crowd drifted along the wide avenue, and the beat of a distant drum was punctuated by the distinct cry of 'England!'

Wayne always felt a little conflicted when England played Nigeria. The land of his forefathers versus the country of his birth. He always rooted for the three lions, largely because he felt more English than anything else, but his heritage allowed him a momentary swell of pride whenever Nigeria won.

A few hawkers were milling around with bags stuffed full of flags and scarves, waiting for the game to finish and the crowds to return. A handful of local residents scurried along the avenue, taking advantage of the peaceful interlude to dart into cafes and shops while the match was on. There were police on every corner – regulars carrying Tasers and pepper spray, and community support and cordon officers to control the crowd. Wayne had no doubt there would be rapid response armed units stationed nearby, and as they passed between the concrete bollards that were covered with artificial grass, he looked along Fulton Road and saw a line of police vehicles parked in a layby.

They crossed the street and continued towards the stadium. There was a sudden moment of silence as tens of thousands held their breath, and then came an eruption, a cheer that bubbled over the lip of the massive bowl and rolled down the avenue. England must have scored. The noise startled Melody and she gave Wayne a concerned look.

'Just a goal,' he told her.

Wayne had spent the week skirting the issue, he and Melody doing a strange dance around Wollerton's sad home, not quite trying to avoid each other but never sharing any private moments. They were both awkward, doing that very British thing of refusing to address the issue, being polite and pretending their relationship hadn't changed as a result of sleeping together. But it had changed. At least for Wayne. He found himself increasingly drawn to her, fascinated by the idea there could be more between them. He wondered what she thought, but circumstances prevented him from finding out. The high stakes of their situation made indulging his emotional curiosity wildly inappropriate.

He was proud of the tough woman who walked next to him. They'd spent the week preparing for this encounter and no matter how challenging the drills got, Melody kept at it, listening to Pearce's instructions, doing what he told her over and over, until she was exhausted.

'It's going to be OK,' Wayne assured her.

She looked up and smiled, but her expression did nothing to convey a sense of ease. It was one Wayne had seen many times before, usually on the faces of young soldiers about to go into combat for the first time. They so desperately wanted to be brave, but inside, fear was chewing them up.

The worst of the day's heat had passed and a breeze blew

south towards the stadium. Wayne was glad the weather had eased, for Melody's sake. She was in jeans, black boots and a brown leather jacket, which was designed to give her some stab protection and conceal the Kevlar vest that covered her torso. Even with the relief of the slight wind, Melody looked as though she was sweltering. Beads of sweat shone on her brow and her normally pale cheeks were blushing. He'd been denied any private moments with Melody, but he'd managed some time with Pearce and had spent it going over the plan in meticulous detail. It was risky and Wayne was worried. Melody's life was on the line, and Pearce's plan didn't have any margin for error. Wayne shared his concerns subtly, avoiding anything that might lead others to believe his worries about Melody were anything other than completely professional. Pearce had been patient, going over things again and again until Wayne felt he had no choice but to accept what they were about to do.

This is why professionals don't get involved with their principals, he told himself. He'd lost sight of what was legitimate concern and what was emotional attachment. He reassured himself by patting his black bomber jacket, feeling the vest and tools he was packing underneath.

He placed a hand to his ear and spoke into the microphone concealed on his wrist. 'How's it looking?'

'*Nothing yet*,' Leila replied through his in-ear receiver.

She was parked in a black Volkswagen Caravelle on Oakington Avenue, less than half a mile away from Wembley Stadium. Wayne was in awe of Leila's stamina. She'd worked the last few days almost without rest. She was acting as both analyst and quartermaster. Each role was challenging enough on a team this small, but the combined responsibilities meant that Leila got little sleep. She'd given Wayne a list of equipment, which he procured when he wasn't rehearsing with Pearce and Melody. Top of the list was the Caravelle, an MPV that was equipped with privacy glass and had a large cabin and multiple power sources that made it perfect for customization. Then Leila had come up with a long list of electronics, cameras and screens, which enabled them to rig a couple of remote surveillance units on the approaches to the stadium and the area where the exchange was meant to take place. Four wide-angle, wireless buttonhole cameras had been concealed against structural supports and lamp posts the previous night, and were now feeding images to four monitors inside the Caravelle, giving Leila eyes on the scene.

'*I don't see anything yet,*' Pearce responded.

Of all of them, it was Pearce who'd had the most difficult week. He'd laboured against his injuries, working to restore some movement in his hands with a single-mindedness that rivalled anything Wayne had ever seen. He'd served with some nutters, proper headcases who'd done the required PT drills as a warm-up for their own punishing fitness regimes, but Pearce was on another level, chasing health like a man possessed. And in many ways, he did seem possessed. Their nights had invariably been disturbed by the sound of the man's screams bursting out of his nightmares and echoing around Wollerton's cavernous house. At least, when they moved back to the safe house on Vyner Road, Pearce's night terrors didn't have such good acoustics and died quickly in the tiny front room.

None of them had spoken to Pearce about his troubles, there was no need. He wore them on his face, which was strained with anxiety and fatigue, but there was also an unmistakeable air of detached pride about the man, and Wayne knew that if he'd tried to broach the subject, he would have hit a brick wall. His own experiences had taught Wayne that activity, distraction and time were the best treatments for trauma, and Pearce was certainly following a regime that met those requirements. He'd spent the week doing exercises to strengthen his fingers and the tendons that joined them to his forearm. He'd started with elastic bands and then moved on to grip tensioners and finally, by the end of the week, had managed to do a few pull-ups. When he hadn't been working his arms, he'd been on the beach, pounding miles into the sand, walking at first, and then jogging, returning from each excursion full of questions and ideas about the exchange. He'd obsessed over the meeting, playing each and every angle, again and again, leaving nothing to chance. It was as though he believed he could control the future through sheer force of will, but Wayne had enough operational experience to know that fate always dealt a wildcard. For all their preparations, they could never truly control the outcome and when that card came, it could only be met by a calm head and years of experience. He was worried about Melody, and even more concerned that his growing feelings for her would compromise his judgment in that crucial moment.

Wayne checked his watch as they started up the west concrete ramp towards the stadium. It was approaching 7 p.m. and the match had approximately fifteen minutes left to run. He looked at the roof of the golden-yellow block of flats to his left. He knew Pearce would be up there, watching, but there was no sign of his well-concealed comrade.

They reached the top of the ramp and crossed the bridge before joining the curved pathway that led up to the entrance level. There was already a steady trickle of fans coming down the walkway, trying to beat the full-time rush, and their excited faces spoke of a good game.

A huge cheer signalled yet another goal, and Wayne saw disappointed looks on the faces of those coming towards him. A tiny woman elbowed her partner and told him off for insisting they leave early. A few fans had their phones out and were watching the action as they headed away. No one was paying any attention to the two people heading against the flow. It was as though they were invisible, which is exactly what Pearce had wanted. Somewhere incredibly public where they wouldn't be noticed.

They reached the top of the second ramp and turned right, walking towards the main entrance, which lay at the head of Olympic Way. The trickle of departing fans was turning into a stream, and there were now dozens of people around them. Wayne checked his watch: 7 p.m., the appointed hour.

'We're in position,' he said into his mic.

Wayne and Melody stood at the edge of the giant balcony, near the balustrade that overlooked Olympic Way. People were flooding out of the stadium now, desperate to get to the tube station before the massive crowds that would emerge after the final whistle. Wayne scanned hundreds of faces. He saw nothing familiar and no one held his gaze. They were all too engrossed in talking about the game, which sounded like a stormer: England were winning three–nil. Police officers in high-vis fluorescent yellow vests dotted the crowd, walking in slow circles, watching for trouble.

Wayne and Melody stood on the balcony, the only static figures in a swelling tide of people. As the minutes passed and the crowd grew larger, Wayne started to worry that something was wrong, that they were being set up.

'They're late,' he said.

Melody looked at him nervously.

'We should go,' Wayne said. 'We need to get out of here.'

'*Stay where you are,*' Pearce hissed into his ear. '*They're coming.*'

Then, between the passing faces, Wayne saw the man whose terrible scarring matched the stills Leila had produced from the footage transmitted by Pearce's surveillance glasses. It was the man who'd run over Pearce and tortured him. He wore trainers, jeans and his half-melted face was concealed beneath a black hoodie. His companion, the larger man with 'Salvation' tattooed on his forehead, walked a few paces behind in jeans and an England shirt.

Wayne desperately hoped that Pearce's memories of his horrific experience at the hands of these two wouldn't lead him to do anything stupid.

'*I've got them on camera,*' Leila said.

Wayne looked at Melody and felt his nerves rise. He took a couple of steps to her right, standing between her and the tall buildings that ringed the stadium.

'*What the fuck are you doing?*' Pearce asked.

'We're not good,' Wayne replied. 'I don't like it.'

'*Get the fuck out of the way,*' Pearce commanded. '*You're going to get her killed.*'

'What's going on?' Melody asked Wayne. She didn't have an earpiece.

'*You need to move, Wayne,*' Leila told him, but it was too late; the enemy was here.

'Melody Gold,' the Scarred Man sneered. 'We've been look-ing for you.'

'Where's my mum?' Melody demanded.

The Scarred Man glanced over his shoulder and nodded towards figures that were intermittently obscured by the pass-ing crowd. Wayne caught a glimpse of a woman who looked remarkably like Melody. Her auburn hair was broken by a shock of silver, her slight frame was carrying a little more weight and her pale skin was marked with the lines of age. She looked terrified, but she broke into a tearful smile when she saw Melody. Wayne recognized the two men who stood either side of Melody's mother. Robert Kemp and Steve Dunbar were the guys who'd been arrested at Heathrow and who'd attacked Pearce at Nathan Foster's flat. Kemp was a huge bull-necked old man in his late forties and Dunbar had the lean, muscular athleticism of a seasoned fighter. Lurking behind them was Brigitte Attali, the woman Pearce believed was working for French Intelligence. Her brilliant white hair stood out against the passing crowd and her sharp blue eyes were locked on Melody as she held a phone to her ear.

'One for the other,' Wayne said to the Scarred Man.

'*What are you doing?*' Pearce said angrily.

'*Move,*' Leila added.

Wayne ignored the words in his ear and kept to Melody's right, his height and huge frame shielding her.

'One for the other. Deals, deals, grubby little deals,' the Scarred Man sneered, but he nodded at his companion, who stepped away and spoke into his phone. Across the wide balcony, Brigitte signalled Kemp and Dunbar, who released Melody's mother, Bella. She stumbled forward and looked back at her captors uncertainly, before hurrying on, pushing through the sea of people, desperate to be reunited with her daughter.

The Scarred Man took hold of Melody's arm. 'Come on.'

He tried to pull her forward, but she resisted. 'I want to speak to my mum. And then you've got to take me somewhere safe,' she said. 'The client knows I'm a risk to his identity. He's going to try to have me killed.'

'*You've got to move,*' Pearce told Wayne urgently.

Wayne hesitated, wondering whether he could drop Salvation and the Scarred Man before the others took him out.

'*She's dead if you don't,*' Pearce said softly.

'Fuck this,' the Scarred Man said, yanking Melody towards him.

'Play nice,' Wayne advised, reaching for the gun holstered behind his back.

The gesture had the desired effect and the Scarred Man smiled darkly and released Melody's arm.

They waited for Bella to reach them, and Melody and her mum embraced, both with tears in their eyes.

'They wouldn't tell me anything,' Bella said. 'What's going on?'

'It's going to be OK,' Melody responded. 'You're safe now.'

The Scarred Man took her arm and pulled her towards him.

'No!' Bella yelled, but her voice was lost beneath the loud cheer that came from inside the stadium, signalling the end of the match.

The cheer died away to be replaced by the rising hubbub of the departing fans.

'It's OK,' Melody told her mum as she was pulled back.

Wayne grabbed her wrist and held her fast, earning a scowl and a 'What the fuck?' from the Scarred Man.

'*Don't do this,*' Pearce told Wayne. '*Move out of the way.*'

'*You can't save her like this,*' Leila added.

'Let go,' the Scarred Man said, rounding on Wayne menacingly.

'*Let her go!*' Pearce ordered.

'No!' Bella screamed and ran at the Scarred Man, her tiny fists raised.

Wayne instinctively reached for her, grabbing her by the shoulders. Freed of Wayne's grip, Melody was pulled clear of him by the Scarred Man.

Wayne felt Bella twitch with shock the moment she heard the loud crack of the high-calibre gunshot. It came from behind them and echoed along Olympic Way before bouncing off the stadium. Bella sank to her knees when she realized what the bullet had hit. Melody was still standing, but her eyes were lifeless and a perfect round hole had been drilled into her forehead, blood already oozing from the fatal wound.

A few people scattered as they saw her body fall, and their screams started a stampede that spread through the crowd. Bullets peppered the ground around Melody's body, throwing up fragments of concrete and clouds of dust.

The Scarred Man reacted angrily, his face twisted in a furious scowl as he gazed towards the source of the gunfire, a masked figure lying prone at the edge of the roof of a nearby block of flats, a bipod-mounted AS50 firing off regular shots. The Scarred Man avoided the barrage, took a couple of steps forward and produced a pistol. Wayne responded, producing his own gun, but the Scarred Man was quicker and fired two shots that hit Wayne in the chest, knocking him back.

'Fuck!' Wayne cried as he tumbled to the ground. He turned just in time to see the Scarred Man fire twice into

Melody's chest before running off with his huge companion. He guessed their logic was that if they couldn't have her, they wanted to be sure no one could.

The shooting further panicked the crowd, which went wild. People screamed and barged over each other, doubtless fearing a terror attack. Police were moving towards the trouble, and Wayne was surprised to hear the familiar sound of a chopper. They'd already managed to get rotors in the air, which meant the rapid response armed unit would be on the scene within the next couple of minutes.

Bella was on her knees, sobbing wildly. Ignoring the pain that came from beneath his protective vest, Wayne got to his feet and hauled her up.

'*Get her out of there,*' Pearce instructed.

'We can't be here,' Wayne said to Bella, pulling her towards the ramp. 'We've got to go.'

Bella looked up at him, her eyes robbed of anything but grief.

'We've got to go,' he told her, pulling her through the fleeing crowd.

Chapter 39

Leila's body ached as she crossed the otherwise deserted car park. The warm evening had given way to a mild night and she could see a few stars in the clear sky, faint pinpricks forcing their way through London's hazy ambient light. She'd picked up Wayne and Melody's grief-stricken mother and had spent two hours in gridlocked traffic before they were able to get clear of Wembley. They'd found a quiet side street and Leila had monitored police frequencies until, shortly after midnight, she'd heard the transmission she'd been waiting for.

She shuffled between two parked cars, heading for the low buildings at the very edge of the hospital complex. Northwick Park was located in north-west London, near Harrow. The main buildings were a pair of charmless concrete monoliths that could have passed as government offices in almost any country in the world. Spread out around them like ugly offspring was an unruly collection of two- and three-storey structures, spawned at odd angles, creating alleyways and little cubbies that were full of skips and box cages. As she walked on, Leila glanced over her shoulder at the Caravelle, which was parked in a space a few rows back, and wondered how Bella felt. She and Wayne were in the MPV and the big bodyguard was trying his best to calm and console her. Not that there could ever be any true consolation for such loss. The death of a loved one was so profound that it often veered into the surreal.

Sometimes Leila would have dreams so vivid that she truly believed her bereavements and her life of misery had been illusions. For a brief while, her subconscious would transport her to her parents' apartment, where she and her brothers and sister would gather around the dining table for one of her mother's famous feasts. The conversation, laughter and love would last until she woke, and the sweetness of her dreams would only make the sudden rush of lonely reality all the more painful.

Leila crossed a narrow road that ran round the edge of the site and headed for a two-storey glass and concrete building. The interior was concealed by thick blinds. She climbed the steps that led to the entrance and pressed the intercom button.

'Yes?' a voice said after a short wait.

'Detective Sergeant Amina Soubry,' Leila said. 'I have to take some prints.'

A buzzer sounded and Leila pulled the door. She walked down a short corridor to a reception area. A uniformed security guard emerged from a side door. Carrying a little too much weight, he lumbered through the room with the dejected air of a man who hated his job.

'Yeah?' he asked.

'You just had a delivery. There was some mess-up with the prints taken at the scene. They've asked me to redo them,' Leila said, flashing a fake warrant card.

'This way,' the man said, leading her towards a set of interior doors.

Leila followed the guard along a windowless corridor, trying not to look at the yellow perspiration rings that marred his white shirt. She could hear him breathing laboriously as they neared solid double doors. Beyond them lay the mortuary, a large space with two stainless steel tables set slightly off-centre. A long run of sinks and counters clung to one wall, and a neat row of white refrigerator doors filled the one opposite.

'Woman from Wembley?' the guard asked.

'That's her,' Leila responded.

'I was watching the match. Saw what happened on TV.' The guard walked to the furthest door and popped the handle before pulling it open. Inside were four shelves.

'Second one,' he said, standing back.

'Could you get me a glass of water?' Leila asked. 'They always make me feel queasy.' She signalled the bodies that lay on the shelves, concealed in zipped bags.

The guard sighed and lumbered off. When he was gone, Leila pulled out the shelf and unzipped the body bag. She looked down at Melody's perfectly still face.

Leila couldn't help but be startled when Melody's eyes opened and she sat up.

'Oh, that was horrible!' Melody exclaimed. 'And the drugs are wearing off. My chest is killing me.' She'd taken a high dose of painkillers in preparation for the pain of being hit.

Leila had marvelled at Melody's bravery. Pearce's plan worked on very simple logic. He believed that if their enemies saw a head shot they were more likely to tap her in the chest in the event they wanted to make sure she was dead. They'd created the illusion of a headshot with a squib placed beneath a layer of false skin. Melody had staked her life on Pearce's hunch, but she'd told them she was prepared to do so if it meant she and her mother might be safe.

'The balls worked,' Melody told Leila.

She dropped two rubber balls on the floor and they bounced beneath the fridge. Placed in her armpits, she could squeeze them to cut off the blood supply to her wrists and convince interested parties that she had no pulse.

Melody rolled her legs off the shelf and slid onto the floor. She shuffled out of the bag, and Leila was relieved to see that she still wore the clothes in which she'd been shot. Normal procedure wouldn't see them removed until the post-mortem. If they'd stripped her to run early tests on her clothing, the protective vest would have been found and the ruse exposed.

'Take off the jacket,' Leila instructed, pointing at the two bullet holes. 'And the vest.'

Melody complied and Leila crouched to untie the tag that was bound to Melody's ankle. She pulled out the shelf above Melody's and unzipped the body bag to reveal a man's corpse. She restored it to its former position and tried the other shelves before moving onto the neighbouring fridges. She finally found the body of a woman who bore a passing resemblance to Melody and removed her tag, before replacing it with Melody's. The deception would cause confusion and help sell the idea that there had been an administrative mix-up, a theory that would be advanced once Leila had altered certain hospital and police records.

'How's Mum?' Melody asked.

'Grieving, but OK,' Leila replied.

'Grieving?'

'We didn't want to get her hopes up in case . . .' Leila didn't need to finish the sentence.

'So she still thinks I'm dead?'

Leila nodded.

'Poor Mum,' Melody said. 'Come on. Let's go.'

Leila had just closed both refrigerator doors when the security guard returned, glass of water in hand. He stopped and eyeballed Melody, who had the Kevlar vest slung over her arm, the jacket on top of it.

'My partner,' Leila told him. 'DC Samantha Hendricks. I let her in.'

The security guard nodded. 'Your water,' he said, placing the tumbler on one of the stainless steel counters. Leila hated to think what might have rested there previously, but she took the glass and drank.

'Thanks,' she said. 'We're done here.'

'I'll let you out,' the guard said.

Leila saw what it was like for someone to return from the dead when Melody stepped inside the Caravelle. Bella shot across the cabin and hugged her daughter, clinging to her fiercely as though she was afraid she might slip away. Both mother and daughter were crying, and Wayne was grinning fiercely as he drove them out of the hospital car park. Leila couldn't suppress the vicarious tears of joy that sprang in her own eyes.

'What's going on?' Bella asked, when she finally recovered the ability to talk. She sat next to Melody, the two of them squeezed on the back seat.

Leila slid into one of the captain's chairs. 'She can't tell you that, I'm afraid, Ms Adler. All I can say is that you're both safe as long as the people who took you think Melody is dead.'

Bella gave her daughter a pleading look.

'She's right,' Melody said. 'I can't tell you anything except that I'm going to have to play dead for a while.'

'What? Why?' Bella asked.

'It's safer if you don't know,' Melody replied.

'What have you got yourself into?' Bella pressed.

It was a very good question, and Leila still didn't have a clear answer, but she hoped that somewhere across London, Pearce was going to get them closer to the truth.

Chapter 40

After slipping away from Wembley on a bicycle, Pearce had returned to the safe house on Vyner Road, where he'd changed his bandages and got ready for the night's business. He'd 'shot' Melody with a blank and she'd triggered a squib that was concealed beneath a layer of fake skin on her forehead. The tiny charge had burst a blood capsule and created the bullet hole. It was the sort of tech Hollywood used to sell its big-moment gunshot wounds. Pearce had switched to live rounds and carefully targeted the area around Melody's body with 50-calibre bullets to sell the illusion that she'd been assassinated. Pearce's worst moment had come when the Scarred Man had produced a pistol and shot Melody. Pearce's gamble had paid off and the bullets had struck her in the chest, where, Pearce hoped, they'd been stopped by her protective vest.

Pearce had watched the Scarred Man and Salvation flee south, round the stadium. He'd tracked them through the scope of the rifle and had thought about pulling the trigger. He'd pictured splitting their heads wide open from the moment he'd seen them, but had resisted his desire for revenge. Melody's safety depended on convincing the Scarred Man and whoever he was working for that Melody was dead, her killing ordered by a client determined to conceal his or her identity. Like the very public, notorious staged death of the Russian journalist Arkady Babchenko, Melody's life depended on people believing in her murder.

Pearce had been troubled by Wayne's behaviour and sudden change of heart. They'd spent days going over the plan, rehearsing it until it was second nature, but confronted by reality, Wayne had baulked. Pearce wondered whether anything was going on between Melody and Wayne. His last-minute deviation had put his and Melody's lives at risk, and Pearce couldn't have that sort of volatility in future.

He put on a pair of loose black cargo trousers, a long-sleeve black top, a neck-warmer that could be pulled over his face to form a mask, and light boots with steel toecaps. He necked some painkillers, strapped a set of small shinguards to his forearms to protect his wounds, and picked up a brand-new backpack, which was full of weapons and gear. Kitted out, Pearce mounted a ten-year-old CBR 600 he'd bought for cash earlier in the week. His arms burned as he operated the clutch and throttle, but it was the quickest way across London. After taking instructions from Wollerton via his Ghostlink, he set off for Newington Green.

Pearce turned into Beresford Road, a broad, tree-lined street, shortly before midnight. Tall Victorian terraces lined both sides of the road. Lacking ostentation, they were tidy, spacious and simple, but there was evidence of an influx of money everywhere, from the polished cars that gleamed under the bright street lights, to the pristine buildings and well-tended gardens. A couple of hundred yards from the junction with Newington Green Road, Pearce turned right and rode into a narrow alleyway that ran beside a small block of flats. Wollerton stepped from the shadows, and Pearce stopped and removed his helmet.

'You OK?' Wollerton asked.

Pearce nodded as he dismounted.

'Leila and Wayne have got Melody,' Wollerton advised, brandishing his Ghostlink.

Tension poured out of Pearce's body and he breathed a heavy sigh of relief.

'I know,' Wollerton said. 'I had my doubts. Especially when Wayne started playing up. I thought she might have copped one.'

'And the Evil?' Pearce asked.

Wollerton shifted uneasily, before handing over a small padded pack. 'Here.' He hesitated. 'You sure you want to do this?'

'You said yourself, business as usual won't work.' Pearce stashed the pack in his front pocket. 'Who's inside?' he asked, moving towards the mouth of the alleyway.

They stopped at the edge of the shadow cast by the block of flats and hugged the wall. Wollerton gestured across the wide street to a terraced house that was partially concealed by a mature beech tree. Broad leaves obscured the windows of the top three floors. Only the basement window was visible, but most of it was shielded by a low brick wall at the edge of the small front garden. The front door lay beneath a painted white portico that stood atop three steps.

'Kemp, Dunbar and Attali,' Wollerton replied. 'No sign of the other two.'

Pearce was disappointed that the Scarred Man and Salvation weren't in the building, but comforted himself with the thought that their time would come. He was just glad that

Wollerton had been able to pick up and follow one of their targets in all the confusion at Wembley.

'What's the plan?' Wollerton asked.

'No plan,' Pearce replied. 'Just go in there and get what I want.'

He headed into the street.

'Hey,' Wollerton said, grabbing his arm. 'I said you needed to break the rules, not go completely haywire. You can't just barge in there.'

Pearce felt a sudden rush of fury. These people had tried to kill him.

'I can,' he told Wollerton, freeing himself from the man's grip and striding into the light.

Pearce took off his backpack as he crossed the street, and reached inside for a Glock 19.

'I can't let you be a damned fool on your own,' the veteran spy said as he followed. 'You got anything in there for me?'

Pearce scoffed and produced a second pistol, two fifteen-round magazines and a balaclava. 'Try not to shoot yourself.'

Wollerton scowled and pulled on the balaclava as they started up the path towards the house. When they reached the entrance, Pearce took a roll of Primacord from his bag, unwound it and pressed it into the space where door met frame. He connected a small timer blasting cap to the cord and took a step back.

'Ten seconds,' he told Wollerton, and the two of them hurried out of the front garden and crouched behind the wall.

'I still feel that old magic,' Wollerton observed, his eyes alive with anticipation.

Pearce tensed, waiting for the explosion that would herald mayhem. His arms were trussed up with some protection, but he still wouldn't be any use at hand-to-hand. The gun would have to compensate.

The Primacord detonated with a bang no louder than a gate being slammed. The noise echoed along the street as the door blew open. Leaving his backpack by the wall, Pearce ran through the cloud of dust to find himself in the long hallway of the four-storey house. Pistol out in front of him, Pearce signalled to Wollerton to take the ground floor and basement.

Pearce bounded up the first flight of stairs, but as he crossed the landing, bullets thudded into the wooden floor and Pearce saw Kemp, the bull-necked man, standing at the top of the next flight, firing a suppressed pistol. Pearce responded with a single shot that caught Kemp in the thigh, and the big man fell forward, dropping his gun as he tumbled down the stairs. Kemp was reaching for the fallen pistol when Pearce brought his own down. It connected with the top of Kemp's head, the impact making a wet crunching sound, and Kemp fell forward with a groan.

'Not bad. A little slow,' Wollerton observed as he climbed back up the stairs from the basement level. 'Dunbar is in the kitchen, resting.'

'Tie them up,' Pearce said, before hurrying up to the second floor.

He came to a landing and found the woman he knew as Brigitte Attali waiting for him.

'You can take the mask off,' she said, gesturing with the pistol she held. She was wearing a pair of dark trousers and a matching T-shirt, but her feet were bare and her trouser buttons undone. She had dressed in a hurry. 'I know who you are, Mr Pearce.'

She let the words sink in, and the gun stayed exactly where it was, trained on his chest.

'And you knew they were going to try to kill me,' Pearce said, lowering his mask.

'I didn't know for certain,' she said. 'But even if I had . . .' she hesitated. '*Tu connais le jeu*. You know the game.' Her rolling, languid French delivery did little to soften her meaning. She would not have broken cover to save his life.

'And now you know that if I am to maintain my legend, I must kill you,' Brigitte said. 'Or you can escape. I assume from the noises I hear that you have a companion. And that mine are incapacitated?'

Pearce didn't answer. He stepped forward and leaned against the bannister, watching her coolly. 'I know the rules of the game,' he said at last. 'But it's your game, not mine. The game I play has no rules. I'm a dead man. I have nothing. I have no one. Take my life,' he challenged.

Brigitte smiled cynically, her bright blue eyes studying him intently.

'What about Nathan Foster? Did you know he was going to die?' Pearce asked. 'Could you have stopped it?'

'No,' she said, sadly.

'And Gabriel Walker?' Pearce pressed.

Brigitte looked troubled. 'He wasn't . . . I was there. We were supposed to question him. They want the name of his client. I had no idea he'd . . .' she tailed off.

'It's the game, right?' Pearce sneered. 'Except he wasn't a player. He was a civilian. Just like Melody Gold.'

'They think her client killed her to keep her quiet,' Brigitte said. 'Is that the way it went down?'

Pearce ignored her question, but saw her finger tighten on

the trigger. 'Know that if I die, my associates will inform the leaders of Progress Britain that you are a spy who is working for French Intelligence,' he said.

'Blackmail,' Brigitte countered accusingly.

'No,' Pearce responded. He lunged suddenly, stepped beyond the barrel of her gun and whipped round before she could react. He brought his arm up and pressed the muzzle of his pistol against her temple. 'Drop it.'

Brigitte shook her head slowly, before letting her gun fall into Pearce's waiting hand. He slipped the weapon into his waistband.

'This is blackmail,' he said, reaching into his pocket for the pack Wollerton had given him. He took a couple of steps back and unzipped the padded flap to reveal eight syringes. 'I call it Evil. Your friends inspired me when they dosed me.'

'They're not my friends,' Brigitte protested.

'This stuff is my own recipe,' Pearce continued. 'It'll make what your friends gave me look like a vitamin shot. Tell me what I want to know now, or feel the Evil and beg to tell me everything.'

Brigitte's eyes burned as she looked from Pearce to the row of syringes.

'We're playing by my rules now,' he told her.

He saw her weighing the prospects of getting his gun. He was ready to shoot if she made the wrong move. Perhaps she sensed his resolve, because after a short pause, Pearce felt hers crumble.

'Tell me what you know and then you can leave,' he said.

'You're burning a multimillion-euro operation,' Brigitte tried.

'Governments can always find more money.'

'I'll be dismissed.'

'Someone with your skills can always find a job,' Pearce observed.

Brigitte sighed. 'Two years ago, I infiltrated *Croix-de-Feu*, the Fire Cross, a paramilitary group. They were being directed to agitate in certain cities in France. Cities with high immigrant populations. I got to the heart of the group to discover the identity of their leader, but I couldn't find one. Only lieutenants who took orders from someone in the UK. I followed the chain of command to Progress Britain. These people – Dunbar, Kemp, the man on the motorbike who died, Benjamin Mitchell – they are C-Brigade, the paramilitary wing of Progress Britain. They recruit from within the ranks of the organization, seeking out ex-police, ex-army, people who have skills they can use.'

'And the others, the one with the tattoo on his face, the man with the scars?' Pearce asked.

'They're something else. I don't know their names,' Brigitte replied. 'The one with the scars leads something called Black 13. It's an elite unit picked from C-Brigade. If C-Brigade is Progress Britain's army, then Black 13 is its SAS. Men and women who've proved themselves.'

'Proved themselves how?'

'The same way you've proved yourself. With blood.'

'Why didn't you blow the whistle? Tell the Box or Six?' Pearce suggested.

'Because one of the first things I heard when I arrived was that the group is protected,' Brigitte replied. 'I tested it, feeding some details of a false French Intelligence operation to the big man, Kemp. Within weeks, the DGSE learned that the information was circulating MI6.'

Pearce was disappointed, but not surprised. He resisted the urge to press Brigitte for details of the DGSE's sources within Six – that wasn't his problem any more.

'What was the name of the false operation you used to expose the leak?' he asked.

'Faucon. Operation Faucon,' she replied.

'Why doesn't the DGSE just finish Progress Britain?' he remarked.

'A large-scale French operation on British territory? Even my presence here has been controversial. Anyway, I couldn't. Progress Britain is planning something. Something big,' she responded. 'I don't know what. Only those in Black 13 know. I would have found out. They were going to take me into the unit.'

Pearce sensed the hesitancy in her clipped sentences. 'And the price of your initiation?'

Brigitte took a deep. 'I was to torture the lawyer. I was to torture her, learn the name of her client and then I was to kill her. It's the game,' she said with a detached honesty. 'It asks a lot of all of us. One life to save many. Do you suffer the small pain? Or the big one? I don't know if I could have done it.'

'And you never will,' Pearce responded. 'It's good I came when I did. That's a line no one should have to cross.'

They stood in silence for a moment, and finally Brigitte nodded slowly. 'I don't remember what I wanted to be,' she said, 'but it wasn't this.'

'It's an ugly journey. It's easy to lose yourself along the way,' Pearce replied.

'We don't know what's going to happen,' she said. 'But we know when. They've been preparing. Whatever it is, it will happen in six days' time. On Friday.'

'Then I have work to do,' Pearce responded flatly. 'You'd better go.'

'I can help,' Brigitte offered.

'Would you trust me if the tables were turned?' Pearce asked.

Brigitte shook her head.

'Go home,' he told her.

She moved towards one of the doorways that led off the landing and Pearce brandished his gun menacingly.

'My shoes,' she explained, leaning into the room and grabbing a pair of trainers that lay by the door. 'What will you do with these men?' she asked, heading for the stairs.

Pearce lowered his weapon. Her cover was blown, her mission no longer secret. She posed no more risk.

'I'm going to make them famous,' he said.

Chapter 41

'My name is Robert Kemp. I was with the Metropolitan Police for twenty years. Most of it spent working the East End. I've seen some fucking things, let me tell you. I've seen the city I loved become a cesspit of crime and violence. I'm not talking about the stuff we used to see, I'm talking about fucking savagery. Pregnant women getting beat up for the shrapnel in their purse, kids hacking at each other with machetes, girls being taken off by gangs. Groomed and raped. Destroyed.

' "Racist!" That's what they said. The gobbling crows with their fucking careers and mortgages and shit. Got them saying yes, sir, no, sir, three bags fucking full, sir. What's your position on this, Chief Inspector? I'll tell you the fucking position. He's going to bend over and take it. They all just take it while the country is being fucked. But not me. I spoke up. And they eased me out. Pension! Bollocks!

'My mouth didn't meet their identity politics checkbox. I ain't got nothing against the colour of a man's skin, but you come to my fucking country, you live by my rules. You know what I've heard people say? Out there on the fucking street? "We came to London because it's so much like Lahore." Lahore! Where the fuck even is Lahore? I want people coming to London because it's like Britain, because they love Britain, not because they're trying to build a little fucking island of Lahore in my fucking country.

'And I told them. The bosses. And I told all the munchers I worked with. "Don't get so worked-up, Kempy. Why are you so angry?" Because my grandfather and his family sacrificed to save this country. They fought up in the skies, on the water and on the ground to protect this country, and they've fucking given it away. It's not theirs to give. It belongs to the past. It belongs to the future. It belongs to us.

'So they let me go. Early retirement. Fuck them. But bad don't stop just because you won't look at it. It's still there. They took away my warrant, but they couldn't rob my conscience. I joined Progress Britain five years ago. Six months later, I was asked to start its paramilitary wing, C-Brigade. I've recruited police officers, soldiers, firemen, all sorts from all over the country. People like me. People who are sick of the gobbling crows talking shit and doing nothing. The street knows. You go out on any street in Britain and you'll hear the truth. The whites know they're being pushed back and the others, they know they're doing the pushing. How's that going to end if you just pretend there's nothing wrong?

'We've fucked people up. We've done operations. Violence. Crimes. I led a unit that set fire to that Labour constituency office during the last election. Loads of things. They didn't listen to me. They didn't listen. So they turned me into a fucking villain. But I don't mind. Tommy got a stretch for speaking out, and if he can do the right thing with a wife and kids, we all can. I'll hang for my country because I fucking love it. You hear that? I fucking love it. It's worth fighting for. Worth dying for.

'I hate them. Hate them all. Not the people who've come

here. No. They're just doing what they do. Bringing their ways and lives with them. No. I hate the people who've let it happen. The people who said it was OK. Told us we shouldn't care about our culture, our values. Fuck them. Traitors. Scum. When you watch this, you remember there are thousands of good patriots like me all over the country and we know what you've done. Sleep well in your beds, because one night . . . one night . . .

'I was given my orders by Dominic Strathairn, Deputy Chairman of Progress Britain, and by Annabelle Crawford, Head of Policy for Progress Britain. They lead the political wing of this organization. We are its army.

'Last week I was arrested outside Heathrow. I was tooled up for a kidnapping and got caught red-handed. But the law sprung me. Someone high up pulled strings, made calls and the gobbling crows nodded and danced and let us all go. We have friends, see. Friends in places you can't even begin to imagine. So sleep well. Rest easy. Until the night you wake up in your bed with one of us standing at your throat.'

'That's the one we go with,' Pearce said, leaning over the monitor. 'It's stronger than Dunbar's.'

'Really?' Leila asked. 'I don't like the preamble.'

'Most people don't know what Progress Britain is. The introduction establishes Kemp as a far-right paramilitary and links him directly to Crawford and Strathairn. The racial stuff gives them nowhere to hide and he's very specific about someone pulling the strings to get the charges dropped. It's sinister. It'll stir things up,' Pearce replied.

Leila gave a half-hearted nod. He could tell she wasn't convinced. Or maybe it was the circumstances of Kemp's confession that bothered her. After Brigitte left, he and Wollerton had locked up the house and taken the two men into separate bedrooms where he'd administered the Evil. Suffering, their tongues loosened by pain and mind-altering narcotics, they'd each confessed on camera, their minds broken by what Pearce had given them. It was the sort of thing that would have once got him censured, but now, outside the service, it was the most effective way of getting what he wanted.

Part of him cringed at the ugliness he'd perpetrated, wondering if he could still consider himself a good guy. He was operating outside the law and torturing people. He tried to comfort himself with the thought that his actions reached back to an ancient directive: an eye for an eye. He was only doing to these people what they'd done to him.

After they'd got the confessions, Pearce and Wollerton had bound Kemp and Dunbar, found their weapons and some Progress Britain literature and left it all on display for the police. They'd taken the men's mobile phones and an iPad, and, once they were a safe distance from the house, had called the police claiming to have heard gunshots. Kemp and Dunbar would almost certainly be arrested, but even if they were sprung from custody again, a second intervention would leave another trail in the chain of command and once the confessions were made public, create an even bigger scandal.

Wollerton and Pearce had arrived at the safe house together, and Leila, Wayne and Melody had recounted Melody's extraction from the morgue and reunion with Bella. Melody's mother had been sent home to live a lie. She had to pretend to Melody's friends, her distant relatives, police and the press that her daughter was dead. Knowing that Melody's life, as well as her own, depended on the deception, Bella had left them, swearing she would deliver a convincing performance.

Wayne had driven Bella home, and when he'd returned, he'd found Pearce and pulled him aside.

'I'm sorry, boss,' he'd said. 'For going off-piste. I lost perspective. It won't happen again.'

Pearce had eyed Wayne carefully. He'd seemed contrite and genuine. 'OK.'

They'd returned to the kitchen, where Melody, Wollerton and Leila waited. Pearce had noticed Wayne avoiding Melody's gaze, and when their eyes had finally met, he'd given her the cold look of a stranger. Something was going on between them, but there was no point in recriminations. Wayne would either stick to his word, or he wouldn't. If he didn't, it would be the last time Pearce would ever work with him.

After sharing what had happened in Newington Green, Pearce had suggested they all got some rest. He'd lain in the front room, listening to the non-stop sounds of the city, watching shadows dance across the ceiling. He'd struggled to let go, instead obsessing over the past and running permutations of the future. He'd puzzled over Black 13. Brigitte had described it as Progress Britain's SAS. Few outside the SAS knew it had a Group 13, a shadowy, elite unit that was tasked with missions that were too ugly even for his old, battle-hardened outfit, the Increment. Was Black 13 Progress Britain's answer to Group 13? If so, what would their ugly mission be? Puzzling over such questions in the early hours, Pearce had finally fallen asleep, his nightmares plagued by the cries of the men he'd tortured that night.

Sunday morning, they had breakfast and watched Leila edit the videos. She'd brought some of the computers and screens in from the Caravelle and had established a workstation at the head of the table. She cut Dunbar and Kemp's confessions, and as snippets of their hateful words filled the room, Pearce thought back to the Progress Britain meeting. Dunbar and Kemp represented the end point of a journey that had probably begun at a similar gathering, the rational, high-minded ideology of the speeches Pearce had heard transformed into blind hatred by a careful process of indoctrination.

Now that the decision had been made to release Kemp's confession, their minds turned to what they would do next. Pearce wanted to go for Mark Sutton and give him the same treatment he'd given Kemp and Dunbar, but Leila surprised him by disagreeing.

'We can be subtler,' she said. 'Those men you questioned last night are going to be ostracized by Progress Britain. Once the confessions are public, the group will try to put as much distance between it and Kemp as possible. But if you don't expose Sutton, you can manipulate him. We could use the confessions to rattle him. Start upsetting him and making him suspicious of whoever he works for. I can pose as a journalist. He's holding a ministerial briefing tomorrow afternoon.'

'You're not a field operative,' Pearce objected.

'Really?' Leila countered. 'Exactly what skills do you think I'm lacking?' Her tone was acidic.

'He might recognize you,' Pearce suggested. 'If he ever saw you at Six.'

'I was a contractor,' Leila said. 'And he's a junior minister. I doubt he's ever been near Vauxhall. Don't give me any bullshit,' she warned Pearce. 'I'm not made of glass.'

'OK,' he said at last. 'But if you get a bad vibe, you—'

'Yeah, yeah,' Leila said dismissively.

'And you take Wayne with you,' Pearce told her. 'For credibility. He can be your photographer.'

Leila smiled. 'OK, but only because it helps sell the cover.'

'How are we going to release the confessions?' Wayne asked.

'Can you access any Box social media accounts?' Wollerton chipped in.

Leila nodded. 'Shouldn't be a problem. Most of them have got at least a few mainstream media followers. Definitely alt-right and hard left.'

Melody looked puzzled.

'MI5 runs numerous social media accounts on Twitter and Facebook. They're used to disseminate information that needs to look like it came from unofficial sources. Conspiracy nuts, alternative news providers, private citizens with high connections – a variety of profiles, but they're all under the control of the government,' Leila explained.

'You're kidding me. How would I know I was following one?' Melody asked.

'You wouldn't. Never believe anything you see or hear, even if it's come from someone you trust. They might have got it from someone you can't trust,' Leila said. 'You don't seriously believe the Russians are the only ones manipulating what we think?'

Pearce found Melody's naiveté endearing. She seemed genuinely shocked by the revelation.

'OK, if you're going to reel in Sutton, I want you to show Kyle and Melody how to release the confessions,' Pearce told Leila. 'We need to get them trending.'

'Shouldn't take much,' Leila responded. 'The media hates

Progress Britain. Something as damaging as this will be a gift.'

'And while you're at it, give Kyle everything you've got so far,' Pearce turned to Wollerton. 'See if you can spot anything we've missed.'

Wollerton nodded. 'And you?'

'I'm going to see a woman about a hard drive,' Pearce replied.

Chapter 42

Pearce could sense power all around him. Places like this changed the world. Away from the Punch and Judy politics of Parliament, beyond the dry corridors of Whitehall and far out of the reach of the masses, it was here in these rich towers that the fate of the world was decided. A bank like Bayard Madison could buy and sell millions of lives. It could reshape the economic landscape and make or break entire industries. Places like this were only accountable to shareholders, and the biggest of those were often other similarly powerful financial institutions. But Bayard Madison didn't even have that measly check on its influence. It was run according to the whims and wishes of its largest single shareholder, Lancelot Bayard Oxnard-Clarke, eighteenth Viscount Purbeck.

Pearce shifted his weight from one foot to the other, and felt the tightness of the suit he'd collected from his Archway flat, tightness that was made worse by the padded bandages he wore to protect his wrists and forearms. Saturday night's action hadn't reopened the wounds, but it had left his arms feeling bruised and sore.

Pearce was standing in the plaza directly in front of the Leadenhall Building, pretending he was waiting for someone. Through his large, reflective sunglasses, beyond the ground-floor windows of the skyscraper, he could see the bench where he'd sat listening to the two old homeless guys when he'd staked out Artem Vasylyk almost two weeks ago.

Pearce had been in position for about twenty minutes when Vasylyk's bodyguard, Prop Forward, emerged from the main entrance and walked towards the bench. When Prop Forward reached the pot plants that lined the bend in the road, he stopped. As before, Pearce saw the same woman – mid-twenties, long black hair, tanned – leave 1 Undershaft. She wore a pink and purple floral dress and set her vape to her plump lips the moment she stepped outside. This time, standing directly in front of her, Pearce got a good look at her face. She wasn't on her guard and her eyes seemed to twinkle with mischief. Pearce doubted she was a professional spy and wondered if she even knew what she was carrying. He'd analysed the footage he'd shot with the surveillance glasses, and knew Prop Forward had given her a USB drive.

The woman stepped out of the warm sunshine into the shade between the buildings and walked up to Prop Forward. Once again, Vasylyk's bodyguard handed her something and they chatted for a brief moment before he returned to his building. The woman watched him go, and when she started back, Pearce moved, closing on her. She stepped through the glass doors of 1 Undershaft, and Pearce followed and caught up with her as she crossed the lobby.

'Excuse me,' he said, touching her arm. 'My name is Detective Inspector Ben Mitchell.'

The woman's face turned red and she glanced round nervously. No one else in the busy lobby noticed anything untoward.

'What's your name?' Pearce asked.

He got no reply.

'We can do this here,' Pearce suggested, 'or I can arrest you and we can finish this at the station.'

'Judy Sykes,' she replied, flushing an even angrier shade of red.

'OK, Judy,' Pearce said. 'I'd like to see what's in your hand.'

Judy opened her fist to reveal her vape.

'The other one.'

Judy stared with fierce resentment. 'It's just administration files,' she said, holding up a USB drive.

'Is that what they told you to say?' Pearce asked, as he produced a tiny Gemini computer from his inside pocket. He took the USB drive and plugged it in.

'What are you doing?' Judy asked nervously.

'Copying the files.'

'You can't do that.'

'I can get a warrant if you like. Take this higher up,' Pearce suggested. 'Or we can both pretend this never happened. You can get on with your life and I can get on with mine.'

He watched a progress bar cycle up to 100 per cent.

'It's done,' he said, removing the USB drive and returning it to Judy. 'Thank you for your help.'

The dazed woman took the tiny device and Pearce turned to leave.

He tried not to betray any surprise as Lancelot Bayard Oxnard-Clarke, eighteenth Viscount Purbeck, came striding through the doors, heading directly towards him. The tall, thin man wore a beautifully tailored grey Prince of Wales check and a blue woven-silk tie. The tips of his shoes shone like polished gemstones. Oxnard-Clarke was accompanied by two men who had the sycophantic air of courtiers.

'Judy,' he remarked as though greeting an old friend. 'Is everything all right?'

'Yes, yes, of course, yes, Lord . . .' she stammered.

'How many times?' he interrupted with a smile. 'It's Lancelot.' He didn't wait for a response, his eyes instead turning to Pearce, who hadn't removed his mirrored sunglasses. 'And this is?'

Pearce disliked the man instantly. There was no humility, no hesitation. He'd strutted into the place like a cock bird and barged into their conversation with the entitlement of someone who got everything he ever wanted. His deep voice was that of one used to issuing commands and his words were flavoured with the soft plumminess of an expensive education.

Judy hesitated and Pearce stepped into the gap.

'It was a case of mistaken identity,' he said. 'I was passing and I saw Judy through the window. I thought she was an old friend.'

Oxnard-Clarke smiled but his eyes were joyless and he stared at Pearce intently. '*Verae amicitiae sempiternae sunt.*'

Pearce returned the unwavering stare. 'True friendships are eternal.'

'And enemies need but a moment,' Oxnard-Clarke responded without shedding his smile. 'Well, it was nice to meet you. Sorry to intrude,' he added breezily. 'Come, gentlemen,' he said to his two colleagues.

As he watched the three men pass through a security gate, Pearce leaned towards Judy. 'He'll ask you, and if you value your safety, you'll stick to the story. It was mistaken identity.'

Judy nodded uncertainly, took a deep breath and hurried through the security gates to the lifts. Oxnard-Clarke was holding one of the cars for her and smiled as she stepped inside. Pearce caught the man's eyes as the lift doors closed, and watched Oxnard-Clarke's smile fall.

Chapter 43

Wollerton studied the man's face and wondered who he was. The name on his Twitter profile said Savvy Nugent, but Wollerton suspected he didn't exist, or at least not in the form the account suggested. The photograph the laptop displayed was of a smiling black man with short hair, a winning smile and a broad, open face. He looked friendly and trustworthy, but Wollerton couldn't tell whether it was a photo of a real person taken from a stock library, or whether 'Savvy' was a synthetic person created using image blending software. Based on his recent research, Wollerton knew that the security services were using such technology for some of their social media accounts, but the ones he and Melody had accessed today were old, and had been lurking on Twitter and Facebook for many years.

Before leaving with Wayne, Leila had set them up with the accounts, using a back door to access the information unit of MI5, a team that was euphemistically called the 'Press Office'.

Sensing that social media presented unique opportunities, the Box had established hundreds of accounts with different affiliations that were designed to spread information, but also attract the disaffected and dangerous. MI5 ran fake accounts linked to Antifa, the far right, Islamic extremism, communism and just about every other extreme religious and political

persuasion imaginable. This bait had led directly to the identification of a number of individuals who were well on their
way to being radicalized, but they also provided a powerful
platform for the spread of unofficial information.

'Savvy Nugent' was a far-left account that had been used
to disseminate strident anti-fascist material during the US
presidential and UK general election campaigns. It was
followed by a number of alt-right and alt-left bloggers and
populist news sites. Wollerton estimated its total reach via
those intermediaries, some of whom were big hitters, at a
couple of hundred thousand people. Leila had set Wollerton
and Melody up on machines that were running through
proxy servers piggybacking a ghosting site to minimize the
risk of their interventions being traced. Wollerton copied the
YouTube link for Kemp's confession and pasted it into a tweet
box below a caption which read:

Britain's fascist army exposed #ProgressBritain #Fascists

'How are you getting on?' he asked, turning to Melody,
who was huddled over another laptop.

They sat in the kitchen, the back door open, warm air filling the room with the smell of the overgrown garden.

'It's already spreading,' Melody replied. 'People seem very
angry. I can't believe how easy this is.'

'What? Getting people angry? Or manipulating the agenda?'
Wollerton asked.

'Both,' Melody replied, checking her machine.

They'd chosen fifteen accounts, mainly left-wing, with
a couple of far-right accounts describing Kemp as a hero
thrown in for authenticity.

'We're getting a lot of responses,' Melody observed. 'Most hostile. Some attacking the accounts for spreading the material, some criticizing us for only sharing the edited highlights. Doesn't matter what you do online; someone always has a problem.'

Wollerton couldn't help but chuckle at this succinct explanation of the digital world. 'Amazes me that nobody ever questions it all,' he said. 'Like the Russians are the only ones who'd play these sort of games. I'm going to send this. It's the last one.'

Wollerton hit the 'tweet' button and 'Savvy Nugent' posted his first message in nearly two years.

'Far right are all over it.' Melody indicated a window that displayed the replies to one of the MI5 Facebook accounts. 'I never realized all this was out there. All these people. All these networks. Sharing, planning. It's terrifying.'

Dark and menacing profile pictures dotted their notifications, alongside hateful messages of support for Kemp and Progress Britain. Wollerton shook his head, questioning the years he'd spent risking his life to defend such idiots.

'They're a minority,' he said. 'It's not something I'll ever understand. I've worked all over the world and most people are decent. I just don't have that kind of hate in me.'

Melody nodded and the two of them watched the various posts being retweeted, shared and liked across different social media platforms.

'Looks like we've got full-on social media bingo,' Melody said. 'We've had "racist", "ignorant", "troll", "sock puppet", and we just got "false flag".'

'Sometimes I think all this stuff just feeds people's confirmation bias,' Wollerton observed, leaning forward to read the messages more closely. 'Apparently, Rod the Zod thinks the video is staged government propaganda. Well, he's a third right. It's not staged and it's not government, but it is propaganda. It's starting to get real traction. I'm going to let Leila know she's good to go.'

Wollerton took one of the pay-as-you go mobiles off the table and sent a single text to the phone Leila carried with her. Both would be disposed of later that day – their SIM cards destroyed and their bodies dumped far from anywhere that could hint at the team's location. For now, the phones acted as carriers of a single, simple message.

The story's broken.

Chapter 44

The late-afternoon sun lit the tops of the trees. Everything beneath the very highest leaves lay in the shade of the surrounding buildings. Leila had some niggling concerns as she and Wayne approached the main entrance to the Home Office. She'd dealt with the institution, first as an asylum seeker, and then as a contractor. It was an impersonal machine and anyone who fell on the wrong side of it got chewed up. She had downplayed the risks of being spotted to Pearce, but there was every chance the super-recognizer software installed in the building's video system would remember her.

'So, you and Melody?' she said in an attempt to distract herself from her worries.

Wayne was startled by the bold gambit.

'What? You don't mess around with a plan like that unless something's got you all confused. She's a good-looking woman,' Leila continued. 'My type, your type, everyone's type.'

'I don't want to talk about it,' Wayne said, recovering his composure. 'We're here on a mission.'

'A mission of love,' Leila teased as they walked on.

The Home Office was a modern, oblong building. Leila remembered it having seven or eight floors, but the patterned fascia that covered the exterior walls made it difficult to get any sense of the interior. Beyond the jagged irregular patterns of the fascia were glimpses of coloured windows. It could have been a normal office block, except it wasn't. It was the centre of order and security in Britain, and she was about to walk in using a false identity and try to snare a government minister.

'Do you think he's a racist?' Leila asked, indicating the white security guard who stood by the main doors. He wore heavy boots, black trousers, a black jacket and a high-vis vest. He was almost certainly armed.

'Excuse me?' Wayne replied. 'What the hell are you talking about?'

'Well, if he's racist, and they blow our cover, there's a good chance he'll shoot us.' Leila was gratified to see Wayne looking at her as though she was unhinged. She was half playing with him to assuage her nerves. 'What? You've never worried about it?'

'Not since I was a kid,' Wayne told her sombrely.

'Not even in the army?'

Wayne shook his head.

'Maybe that's because you're so . . .' she accentuated her search for the right word, '. . . formidable.'

Wayne shook his head derisively as they passed the guard.

'Me? I get it all the time. They see the cane, my fucked-up legs, the swarthy skin and they think, *What the hell, easy target*. I've never told anyone this, but when I first came to London, I was standing in line to use a cash machine. I felt a shadow on me and I looked up to see a guy standing over me. He was tall. Maybe taller than you. And his face was so full of hate. This man, this angry man, he put his thumb to his nostril and he blew his nose on me. A thick glob of snot hit me on the cheek. Some sprayed in my eye. "Go back to your own fucking country," he said. Then he walked off. No one in the queue said anything. I was too shocked. An old woman offered me a tissue and I wiped away the mess and we all pretended as though nothing had happened. That was very British of me, I suppose.'

'Shit,' Wayne said as they passed through the glass doors into the building.

'Now I carry a stun gun with me at all times.' Leila flashed a confident smile. 'Anyone gives me any shit, I stick them with fifty thousand volts.'

'All the time?' Wayne asked, suddenly worried.

Leila nodded. 'So,' she said loudly, as they approached the reception desk, 'do you think the country has lurched to the right? Is Britain more racist? Are we living in a fascist regime?'

Wayne grimaced and clutched the shoebox-sized camera case that hung by his side. He gave a conciliatory look to the receptionist, a young woman whose smile had hardly wavered when she'd heard Leila's booming question.

'We're here for the press conference with Mark Sutton,' Leila said blandly, flashing her fake press credentials.

'You need to go through security.' The receptionist waved them towards a checkpoint.

Liveried security guards searched their bags, and Wayne watched nervously to see if Leila had been telling the truth about the stun gun.

'Well, I don't always carry it,' she told him, as the guard finished with her bag.

She wasn't being cruel, she was simply being herself. In doing so she had provoked Wayne into a range of emotions that might be exhibited by a normal person. Anyone watching them would not have seen the determined intensity commonly associated with spies on screen, just a journalist and photographer bantering and bumbling their way through life. Wayne scowled, and Leila smiled and started repacking her things. She found a message on the burner, which simply said, 'The story's broken.'

The building was surprisingly light and airy – all open spaces, glass and pale wood panelling. When Leila presented their fake press credentials – she had put them on the Home Office approved list as foreign correspondents of *Il Giustizia*, a specialist Italian security journal – the liaison directed them to a fresh-faced man in a suit. Introducing himself as Alan, a graduate trainee, he led them through the building into the Home Office press briefing room. A dozen journalists were dotted around the space, occupying contoured wooden chairs. A few chatted, others made notes or checked their emails.

Thanking Alan, Leila led Wayne to the front row. She sensed grumbles from behind, so she took out her collapsible cane and turned as she flipped it to full extension. She saw confusion on the faces of the journalists, and their disapproval turned to shamefaced sympathy as she made a great play of hobbling to her seat.

She sensed Wayne shrinking away from her, but she didn't care. They weren't here to make friends. They took the two seats right in the middle of the front row, nearest the podium, and Leila pulled a pad from her bag. Wayne produced his camera from its case and started fiddling with the lenses.

'We should have gone to the back,' he whispered.

'Then I wouldn't have been able to see the whites of his eyes,' Leila replied.

The room wasn't as large as Leila had expected – perhaps

fifteen feet wide by thirty long. A large flatscreen TV was suspended behind a long wooden podium. To its left was a beige padded leather feature that clung to the wall, rising from floor to ceiling. Halfway up was a plaque that bore the insignia and logo of the Home Office. Six silver speakers hung from brackets above the podium, and a few of the white ceiling tiles had lights or fans set in them.

Leila grew impatient as the clock ticked on and tapped her pencil against the pad. She knew what was happening. In the minds of many politicians, the media were bottom feeders who deserved to be treated with disdain whenever possible. They'd be kept waiting until he was good and ready. Finally, almost ten minutes late, Mark Sutton strode into the room. His hair was a dirty blond, greyed at its outer limits, but his face was smooth and his skin plump and supple as a child's. As he moved quickly to his place at the podium, Leila was surprised to sense sadness radiating off the man. Another man, who looked older than Sutton, stood to the side of the podium. He was short with jet-black hair swept back either side of a widow's peak. He wore a slate-coloured suit and round glasses that made him look like Ebenezer Scrooge's banker.

Sutton cleared his throat and launched into an update on the latest measures the government was introducing to combat financial fraud. Leila grew dangerously bored. She continued to tap her pad, and fidgeted throughout Sutton's speech, drawing icy glares from Sutton and his stern minder. After thirty minutes or so, Sutton finished and opened the room to questions. A few were asked, and when Leila sensed things were wrapping up, she finally raised her arm.

'Yes, Ms . . . er . . .' Sutton said, glancing at the man in the black suit. 'You're new here.'

'Maria Grattan,' Leila said, 'Foreign Correspondent with *Il Giustizia*, we're an Italian publication specializing in security matters.'

'Italian?' Sutton smiled. 'And why does an Italian security magazine want to know about economic crime in Britain?'

'We believe our readers can learn a great deal from Britain. You are world leaders, after all.'

Sutton nodded. 'Go ahead, Ms Grattan.'

'Well,' Leila hesitated and felt every eye in the room on her. 'Did you give that speech in preparation for your promotion?'

'I'm not going to get drawn into speculation,' Sutton replied, his smile faltering. 'The Prime Minister will select the next Minister of State for Security and Economic Crime, not me. Thank you, everyone.' He moved towards the door.

'What can you tell me about Robert Kemp?' Leila yelled.

The words had the desired effect. Sutton instantly flashed an angry look at the pallbearer in the dark suit. The other journalists sensed something was up and froze. The pallbearer smiled coldly and stepped forward.

'My name is Phillip Swan,' he said. 'I'm Mr Sutton's special parliamentary adviser. I'd be happy to arrange a time for you to interview the minister.'

'How about now? I'm due to file my story tonight and wouldn't want there to be any inaccuracies.'

For a moment, Sutton and Swan looked like a pair of cornered animals, and Leila noted the puzzled expressions of the journalists around her as they wondered how the hell this newcomer had earned instant ministerial access.

'OK,' Swan conceded. 'I believe the minister can spare five minutes.'

*

Sutton and Swan led Leila and Wayne through a second security checkpoint, where their bags were searched again. Satisfied, two uniformed guards waved them through to the lifts, and they rode in silence up to the fourth floor. Wayne fiddled with his camera bag and dropped a lens cap as the elevator stopped. Swan held the doors open irritably and Sutton shook his head as Wayne fumbled with the cap and his case. Finally, with his gear slung over his shoulder, Wayne emerged from the lift and joined Leila and Sutton in a long corridor. Swan brought up the rear as Sutton led them along the broad thoroughfare, which was busy with Home Office staff going to and fro. After a while they reached a corner office, where a middle-aged woman sat on an orthopaedic stool. She wore headphones and was so focused on her computer she didn't notice Sutton until he was almost over her.

'Minister,' she bawled, removing the headphones. 'Sorry,' she added, realizing how loud her voice had been. 'You've had some messages.'

'Later, Annette,' Sutton said. 'We've got an impromptu press interview.'

'You wait out here,' Swan told Wayne, indicating a couple of seats beside Annette's desk.

'But I need—' Wayne began.

'No photographs inside ministers' offices,' Swan cut him off.

'It's OK,' Leila said. 'I'll draw a sketch. I might even draw him smiling,' she added, pointing at Swan.

The pallbearer ignored her, and Wayne sauntered over to the waiting area.

'Ms Grattan,' Sutton said, indicating the open office door.

Leila followed him inside.

She'd always imagined ministers lurking in dark, wood-panelled lairs, but Sutton's office was light and airy. It reminded her of a hotel lobby, with beech fixtures everywhere and stylish contemporary art positioned around a large, informal seating area. Sutton's desk lay in the corner of the room, near the windows, and the surface was scrupulously clean; not a single file or piece of paper cluttered the polished top.

When Swan closed the door behind them, the catch snapped like a bullet.

'Have a seat, Ms Grattan,' Sutton advised, gesturing towards the long, low grey couch opposite a trio of matching arm-chairs. He sat in one of the chairs, while Swan leaned against a console table. The atmosphere was frosty, but both men were keeping a lid on the full extent of their hostility.

Leila sat and put her bag and cane on the table in front of her.

'So what can I do for you?' Sutton asked.

'I'm investigating the case of Robert Kemp,' Leila said. 'He was arrested at Heathrow last week, possession of a firearm. The charges were dropped and he was released.'

'I see,' Sutton remarked, his tone one of ice-cold steel.

'It seems the order to free him came from your office,' Leila continued.

'This is a strange story for an Italian journal,' he observed with an arrogant smile.

'We're interested in the rise of the far right,' Leila responded. 'It's a problem Italy is also facing. And it personally bothers me. I've had some experience of extremism.'

'Far right?' Sutton sneered. 'It's a term that's bandied about with far too little care nowadays. If, and it's a big if, the order to release Kemp came from this office, it will be because our security vetting has cleared him.'

'I understand he's been taken into custody again,' Leila pressed. 'You wouldn't happen to know if he's still under arrest?'

Sutton shot Swan a brief glance, but Leila could read the sudden anxiety. He hadn't known Kemp had been arrested again.

'I'm not sure what any of this has to do with the minister,' Swan remarked acidly. He stepped forward until he was towering over Leila. 'I think you need to leave.'

Leila refused to allow herself to be intimidated by this undertaker, and she ignored him, instead casting her eyes at Sutton. 'I'd like to know what you think of Kemp's confession,' she paused, allowing her words to sink in. 'It's all over the web. Kemp was the head of Progress Britain's army. Some sort of direct action unit called C-Brigade.'

Sutton's eyes widened.

'I think it's going to be the lead story on tonight's news,' Leila said calmly. 'And if I can find the link between Kemp and your office, I'd imagine others will too. I thought you might like the opportunity to comment. To get ahead of the story.'

Sutton was as still as a corpse, but his eyes betrayed him. Leila could tell they were picturing years of wasted work, a career ruined, a life destroyed.

'You need to go now!' Swan yelled, his voice rising to a screech. He grabbed her, yanked her up, and in the ensuing tussle, Leila's bag spilled on its side.

'Get your hands off me,' she said, pulling herself free. She gathered her belongings and stuffed them back in the bag. 'I'm going. You'll be reading all about this.'

She brandished her cane as she stormed by Swan. He glowered like an angry god, but said nothing as she passed through the door and slammed it behind her.

'You did good,' Wayne said, as they rode the lift down.

'Of course,' Leila responded.

'Are you always this cocky?' Wayne asked.

'It's pronounced confident,' Leila said. 'Women can't be cocky. We lack the relevant equipment.'

Wayne rolled his eyes. 'Do you want to hear?' he asked, indicating a tiny flesh-coloured receiver that was embedded in his ear.

Leila nodded and he produced another from his pocket and handed it to her.

'I got two in their pockets when I pretended to drop the lens cap,' he said.

'I thought you were just being clumsy.' Leila smiled. 'I'm kidding. I also put one under the coffee table.' She'd planted a bug while recovering the items from her bag. 'Let's hear them,' she said, pressing the receiver into her ear.

'*You told me it was a respectable organization,*' Sutton was saying. He was angry. '*You told me they were our sort of people.*'

'*They are,*' Swan protested. '*They're exactly what this country needs.*'

'*You bloody fool,*' Sutton yelled. '*You've done us. We're finished!*'

'*No,*' Swan countered. '*It's not over. Let me make a call. Find out what's going on.*'

'*I don't want anything to do with—*' Sutton began.

'*It's too late for that now, Mark,*' Swan interrupted. '*We're in too deep. You've tied your colours to their mast. Our fate is sealed with theirs. We need to stand as friends, or we'll fall as enemies. And we don't want these people as our enemies.*'

Silence filled Leila's ear for a moment.

'*Make the call,*' Sutton said, his voice flat with resignation.

Chapter 45

'I'm going to play the rest of what we got,' Leila told them. 'It's not much.'

Pearce leaned against the kitchen wall. Melody and Wollerton were seated either side of Leila, near the workstation at the head of the table. Wayne stood behind them, by the door. They'd already heard enough to know that Sutton was linked to Progress Britain, but they needed to identify the person calling the shots. Before his job with Sutton, Phillip Swan had worked for Lexicon, the think tank financed by Oxnard-Clarke, and Pearce suspected Viscount Purbeck was behind it all.

Leila played an open media file on the central computer, and the speakers broadcast sounds of someone walking and ambient city noise.

'This is from the bug Wayne dropped in his jacket pocket. We get about twenty-five minutes of travel,' Leila said, 'suggesting Mr Swan walked somewhere between one and a half and two miles.' She scrubbed the cursor further along the media file. 'Then he makes a call.'

'*It's me.*' Swan's voice was clear and rose above the background sounds. '*Yes, I've seen. How damaging is it?*'

'My guess is they're talking about the news we broke,' Wollerton chipped in.

'*I just got out of a meeting with some journalist. She challenged Mark about his connections to the organization,*' Swan said. There was a brief pause. '*Three days ago. We do it twice a week. Oh shit.*'

'That's it,' Leila told them. 'After that, we get about ten minutes of background noise until all our devices go silent. My guess is whoever he was speaking to warned him he might be bugged.'

'We got confirmation that Sutton is tied to Progress Britain. It's a step forward,' Pearce observed. 'What about the USB?' He was asking about the drive he'd taken from Judy Sykes in the lobby of Bayard Madison.

'Seems to be a small data file,' Leila replied. 'But it's heavily encrypted. Without the key, I may not be able to crack it.'

'And I'm guessing the key would be located inside Bayard Madison?' Wollerton asked.

Leila nodded. 'It's probably in that server room. If I can just—'

'It's too dangerous,' Pearce said, cutting her off. For a moment he pictured Leila in Foster's place, falling from the high building, her spine shattering when she hit the concrete. 'We work the other angles.'

'I—' Leila began.

'We work the other angles,' he said emphatically. 'That's a last resort.'

Leila glared at him, but remained silent. Pearce hesitated, building up to the news he was about to share.

'We may have lost an advantage. Lancelot Oxnard-Clarke saw me in the lobby of the bank. If he's involved he'll have recognized me. They'll know I'm alive,' he admitted.

'We lose a slight advantage. Nothing more,' Wollerton

remarked. 'The story tying Kemp and Dunbar to Progress Britain is all over the news. It'll have their attention for a while.'

'Progress Britain is already denying all knowledge of Kemp,' Leila said. 'Their right-wing cheerleaders are claiming this is a mainstream attempt to discredit them.'

'When do we go public with Sutton's connection?' Wayne asked.

'I want to find out who's been pulling his strings before we burn him,' Pearce responded. 'If he's tarnished, they'll cut ties with him or maybe worse. We keep him in play until we've got what we need.'

Wollerton leaned towards the computers. 'Can we have a closer listen to that file? We might be able to do something to enhance the audio. Have you got ProTools or something like it?'

Leila nodded. 'You're pretty ambitious for an old dinosaur,' she said.

'Adapt or die,' Wollerton said. 'I thought about dying, but I'm not such a fan. Too much lying around. I'd get bored.'

'Do you know what you're doing?' Leila asked as she handed Wollerton a pair of headphones.

'That thing over there is called a mouse, right?' he asked sarcastically. He slipped the headphones on and plugged them in, before hunkering over the computer.

'What now?' Wayne asked.

'We keep the pressure up,' Pearce replied. 'Break the story about the sex ring.'

'But won't that put their families in danger?' Melody said.

Pearce saw Leila nodding.

'We tie them to Artem Vasylyk from the get-go,' Pearce

responded. 'Make it clear that if anything happens to them, Vasylyk is the first place the police should look. Blackmail only works as long as you're afraid of the threat. We go public and the threat no longer exists.'

'That's not our choice to make,' Leila said quietly. 'They're not our lives to play with.'

'Then we talk to them,' Pearce replied. 'We ask the men and women who are the victims here whether they'll give us their testimony. We offer them their freedom. Let them make the choice.'

'I'd like to do it,' Leila said. 'When you're . . . when you've been subjected to this kind of experience, it changes how you think. I want to make sure we don't exploit these people. No leading questions. No pressure. This really needs to be their decision.'

Wayne and Melody looked mystified. Pearce was the only one who knew the horrific experiences that had given Leila terrible authority in this matter.

'Fine,' Pearce replied. 'You play it how you want. Do what you think is right.'

'Scott,' Wollerton said. 'You need to hear this.'

He unplugged the headphones and the speakers came to life with a deep hum. 'I've muted Swan's voice, amplified the other side of the conversation and filtered out most of the background noise. It's rough and it doesn't make for pleasant listening, but there's something worth hearing.'

He adjusted the volume on the speakers and played a new media file. The room filled with a nasty, loud noise that sent a shudder down Pearce's spine. Like the muffled screams of a thousand devils, mingled with the sound of their claws being dragged across aluminium plate.

'*Hello?*' the voice that came through the speakers was mechanized and distorted. Deep and rumbling, Pearce could only guess at the processes that had been used to lift it from its previously inaudible form. Whatever Wollerton had done made the voice clear, but completely disguised the identity of the speaker.

'*Have you seen the stories?*' the roaring dark voice asked.

There was a pause during which Swan must have answered.

'*We should be able to contain it,*' the voice replied. Pearce guessed it was in response to Swan's question about how damaging Kemp's confession was. There was another pause during which they were assailed by the terrible background noise. This was where Sutton told the speaker about the visit from Leila.

'*A reporter? Asking about the story so soon after it broke?*' the voice roared. Even through the distortion, Pearce could hear the disdain. '*How do you know it was a real journalist? When did you last sweep for bugs?*'

The question explained Swan's reply and sudden silence.

'*Exactly. You've been played,*' the voice said. '*Get off the line and clean up your mess. Jesus.*'

The recording ended and the horrific background noise died away and was replaced by the soothing hum of the speakers.

Wollerton was smiling and Pearce was shaking his head in disbelief. Neither of them needed to hear the recording again. They both knew the identity of the speaker. It was the final word that had done it. Even through the distortion, the delivery was unmistakeable. Drawled out with an overemphasis of the vowels so the word sounded more like Jeezeus. Pearce had heard the word spoken like that many times before.

'We've got the next link in the chain,' Wollerton observed.

'What? How?' Melody asked.

'We recognize the speaker,' Pearce said, suspecting he now knew how details of a French operation had found their way from Progress Britain to MI6. 'It's Dominic McClusky, my former boss, the Director of Intelligence for MI6.'

Chapter 46

Routine made people feel safe. Pearce couldn't recall the last time he'd lived a routine life. He'd seen so many brothers struggle to adapt to civvy street that he hadn't even bothered trying to wedge himself into an ill-fitting existence, recognizing that his best hope for long-term sanity lay in staying as close as possible to the adrenalin rush. In truth, he'd not had much of a chance to consider other career options. His dismissal from MI6 had almost been a minor blip, a distraction that momentarily took his attention away from the investigation that had become his obsession. Pearce had simply picked up the threads of what had happened in Islamabad, following them to Thailand as a private citizen.

Dominic McClusky had ridiculed his suggestion that there had been other, as yet unidentified, conspirators involved in the attack on Islamabad, and had done everything in his power to block Pearce's requests for resources. Their animosity had grown and finally culminated in the public tirade that had earned Pearce his dismissal. So it was with a degree of pleasure that Pearce sat watching the live footage being broadcast by the camera Wollerton had placed across the road from McClusky's house. Rooting out a spy with divided loyalties was always rewarding, but Pearce's personal history with McClusky would make this particularly satisfying.

As Director of Intelligence, Dom McClusky was subject to round-the-clock protection. Pearce had toyed with the idea of some kind of revenge after he'd been ousted from the service, and had studied the man's security detail. At home, McClusky was watched by a rotating team of two officers from the Metropolitan Police's Protection Command. They were stationed outside the house and would stay to guard McClusky's wife, Annabelle, and their three-year-old son, Tobias, when McClusky wasn't with them. Pearce knew from his experience of working with Protection Command that their unmarked vehicle would contain at least two side arms, two assault rifles and various ancillary equipment such as body armour, a medical field kit and communications gear. In addition to the armed protection, local police would prioritize their response to any incident at McClusky's address, and neighbours would probably comment on how often they saw uniformed foot patrols and police cars in their street. Any attempt to snatch McClusky from home risked a noisy response.

The alternative was his office, overlooking the river on the fourth floor of the MI6 building in Vauxhall, one of the most heavily guarded, comprehensively monitored structures in London. Taking McClusky from there would require miracles beyond Pearce's limited resources.

The weakest link was McClusky's driver, a Protection Command officer who picked him up every morning and drove him to work. When Pearce had last examined McClusky's set-up, the car had been a BMW X5, which was bound to have police modifications, making pursuit and interception a challenge. However, their limited preparation time gave them little option but to try to grab McClusky in transit.

McClusky lived in a large detached post-war house on Rodenhurst Road in Clapham Park. The broad street was one of London's spawning grounds, a place where wealthy city dwellers went to raise families. The architecture was a mix of Victorian and mid-twentieth century, the post-war homes doubtless built on the ruins of some of the grand Victorian villas that had been bombed during the war. Most of the front gardens had been paved and turned into driveways and there were only a handful of trees standing at long intervals along the curved road. This was a low-maintenance, practical neighbourhood for people who had their hands full with demanding careers and children.

Wollerton had taken a stroll in the early hours and had stopped to tie his shoelaces by a house that stood opposite McClusky's. He'd placed a tiny, battery-operated, fish-eye camera on top of the garden wall, and the device broadcast a signal to an iPad, which gave Pearce a visual of McClusky's house and the unmarked BMW 4 Series that was parked in a bay directly opposite. Two men sat in the front, occasionally glancing in the direction of the house. Every thirty minutes, one of the officers got out of the car and patrolled the street.

Pearce was in a stolen Mercedes less than half a mile away from the camera and watched and waited. McClusky's driver always picked him up at 7.50 a.m., but it was now 7.51. Suddenly, a Land Rover Discovery Sport with blacked-out windows sped into the frame and stopped in the middle of the street, directly outside McClusky's house. Moments later, Dominic McClusky, the wiry Director of Intelligence, hurried down the drive and climbed in the back seat. Pearce felt a jolt of excitement at the sight of his prey.

'We're a go,' he said into his Ghostlink.

'*Copy that,*' Wollerton replied.

McClusky had changed cars since Pearce had last checked him out, but otherwise nothing about his security arrangements had altered. The Discovery would head north-east along Rodenhurst Road and would soon come to the T-junction with Park Hill, the quarter of a mile stretch of road where Pearce was parked. Park Hill joined Clarence Avenue, a main thoroughfare that led into Central London. One side of Park Hill was taken up by a primary school and Pearce had already seen a few members of staff pass through the security gate and go into the squat buildings. Low blocks of flats stood north and south of the junction with Rodenhurst Road, but very few of the windows overlooked Park Hill. The northern end of the road was blocked by traffic control bollards, meaning cars had only two ways off the street; back up Rodenhurst Road or on towards Clarence Avenue. It wasn't the perfect place for an ambush, but it was about as good as Pearce could have hoped for in London. Very little passing traffic and few prying eyes.

Pearce tapped the dashboard of the stolen Mercedes. An ancient 'R' registration, the C-Class was solid, easy to steal and mechanically bombproof. The last thing Pearce needed was for the engine to conk out. It ticked rhythmically, idling nicely at a thousand revs. Pearce fingered the ski mask in his lap as he glanced over his shoulder. Wollerton was about fifty yards behind, sitting in a Ford Mondeo on the other side of the Rodenhurst Road junction. He nodded at Pearce, signalling the approach of the target.

Pearce pulled on the ski mask and turned to see the Discovery come speeding round the corner. Pearce flung the Mercedes into gear and stepped on the accelerator. The old car

lurched into the middle of the road, blocking the Discovery's
path. Pearce had timed the move perfectly and McClusky's
driver had instinctively stepped on the brakes. He should
have mounted the pavement and forced his way past, but it
was too late for that. The Discovery was no more than two feet
from the Mercedes and didn't have the space to manoeuvre or
gather speed to ram its way through.

Pearce locked eyes with the driver. The man had registered
the threat. Pearce grabbed a five-pound sledgehammer as
he stepped from the car, and when he hurried forward, the
driver tried to throw the Discovery into reverse. But there was
nowhere for him to go. Wollerton had parked the Mondeo on
the Discovery's bumper and was climbing out of the old Ford,
mask on, carrying another heavy sledgehammer.

Trapped, the driver was fumbling at his chest, and Pearce
guessed he was going for a holstered pistol. Pearce gripped
the hammer tightly, and pain shot up his injured arms. He
sprinted towards the car, jumped on the bonnet and swung
the hammer directly at the driver. The windscreen shattered
and the heavy head of the sledgehammer went through, catching the man square in the chest. He buckled instantly, crying
out in pain. McClusky was on his phone in the back, shouting
hurried instructions. Wollerton's hammer smashed through
the back window, covering McClusky in glass. There were
sirens close by and Pearce guessed that McClusky's protection unit were on their way. He jumped off the bonnet
and ran to the rear of the car, where Wollerton was hauling
McClusky out. The small, thin man was surprisingly strong,
but a couple of punches to the head soon robbed him of any
fight, and Pearce and Wollerton dragged the dazed Director

of Intelligence towards the Mercedes. Pearce popped the boot and they tossed McClusky inside.

Wollerton jumped in the passenger seat and Pearce slid in beside him, immediately stepping on the pedal. The driver's door slammed shut as the car sped forward. Within seconds, they'd turned left onto Clarence Avenue. As they put the scene behind them, Pearce removed his mask and Wollerton did likewise, beaming like a thrill-seeking child who'd just stepped off a roller coaster.

They had what they came for.

Chapter 47

Wayne had come up with all sorts of excuses to stay out of the kitchen, but as the morning wore on, he felt increasingly foolish. Melody wasn't someone to be feared, and the looks she'd given him since the night they'd slept together suggested she felt just as awkward about the situation as he did. With Leila, Wollerton and Pearce out, this was their first chance to be alone together, and Wayne was wasting it, drifting about the safe house trying to avoid her. He gathered his resolve and went into the kitchen, where Melody sat absently watching something on one of the computers at the head of the table.

'Oh, hi,' she said, shifting uncomfortably.

'I just wanted to apologize,' Wayne said. 'I shouldn't have . . . when we . . . I'm supposed to protect you.'

'I'm just as much to blame as you,' she began.

Wayne's heart sank at the word blame. She obviously thought it had been a mistake.

She must have sensed his disappointment, because she shifted gears. 'Blame's the wrong word. We've complicated things and there was no need. We were both stressed, Scott was . . . well, we thought he was dead. We got carried away.'

Wayne nodded. 'Well, I just wanted you to know I'm sorry.'

'Let's forget about it,' Melody suggested. 'At least until this is all over. If we still . . . I mean, if we . . .'

Wayne smiled, and Melody blushed.

'What I'm trying to say,' she continued, 'is that if we still want to get to know each other, let's do it when we're not trying to deal with all this.' She gestured expansively.

'OK,' Wayne said, grinning. 'Sounds good to me.'

By the time she reached the tenth victim, Leila was struggling with the burden of human misery. She was all too familiar with the evil people could visit upon each other, but even she was finding it difficult to cope with the ugly stories she was hearing. Each tale tore into her and dredged up some raw memory of her own, but she kept a lid on her emotions and patiently listened to each of the men and women.

Posing as journalist Maria Grattan, Leila had spent the morning visiting people who lived in properties owned by Constellation, Vasylyk's Monaco company. Five of the women and two of the men had refused to even speak to her, but two women and one man had talked of their experiences, all three telling remarkably similar stories. They had been students at London universities when a man they'd met in a bar had invited them to a private members' club on Golden Square, offering them the opportunity to party with billionaires. Intrigued by an invitation they'd forever regret, they had gone, been drugged and awoken to find themselves trapped in sexual servitude, the threat of violence and death hanging over their families.

Leila had felt uncomfortable deceiving the victims into believing she was a journalist. It didn't fit with her aim of avoiding manipulation, but she couldn't see any other way.

She couldn't tell the truth and risk one of them informing their handlers. Leila forgave herself the deception, reasoning that she would only expose the ring if she could find someone willing to go on the record.

The man and women had refused to be recorded and weren't willing to allow Leila to use their names. They told her that she could quote them off the record and use their stories as background. One of the trio, a tall elfin man called Zhang Wei Tang who was originally from Hong Kong, asked whether Leila was going to see Emily Best. Zhang Wei thought Emily might be willing to be interviewed on camera.

Following Zhang Wei's suggestion, Leila pushed Emily Best up her list and headed straight for a ground-floor apartment on Holland Park Avenue.

She pressed the intercom button for flat one. There was a long pause, followed by a voice.

'*Hello?*'

'Ms Best?' Leila said.

Another pause, and then a hesitant, '*Yes?*'

'My name is Maria Grattan,' Leila said. 'I'm a reporter. I'd like to talk to you about the work you do.'

The intercom went dead. Then the buzzer sounded and the lock clicked open. Leila pushed the heavy black double door and stepped inside a small lobby. The wooden floor, Persian rug and Middle Eastern embellishments made Leila think of home. The place oozed money, from the gilt-framed artwork that adorned the common areas, to the long-stemmed flowers that stood in a cut-crystal vase.

Leila looked beyond the double staircase and saw a figure emerge from the adjacent apartment. Emily Best was pale, thin and had long, straw-coloured hair. She wore shorts, a

T-shirt and a loose-fitting, wafer-thin robe that did little to conceal her body. The only thing that prevented her from looking as though she'd just stepped off a *Vogue* beachwear shoot was the purple and green bruise that distorted her otherwise delicate features. Her right eye was almost sealed shut by its swollen lids and the colourful injury formed a semi-circle around the socket, covering the upper half of her cheek.

'Ms Best?' Leila said.

Emily nodded.

'I'm Maria Grattan. Can I come in?'

Emily nodded again, this time more slowly. She exuded sadness and Leila wanted to reach out and hug her. Instead, she followed Emily into a grand garden flat that was alive with potted plants and flowers.

'We're doing a story on—' Leila began.

'I know what you're here for,' Emily cut her off. She had a soft voice and an upper-class accent. 'Zhang Wei phoned me. They can't stop us talking. What would be the point? They've got us trussed-up tight, so what's the danger?'

She led Leila into a bright, vaulted living room full of tropical plants. A manicured, lush garden lay beyond the open French doors. 'It's my beautiful cage. Sometimes I can almost forget the ugliness I've seen.'

A lump filled Leila's throat. She could have said almost the same thing about her own beautiful home. In such surroundings, if Leila lied to herself hard enough, she could almost believe her horrors had happened to someone else. Almost, but not quite.

'Do you mind if I film you?' Leila asked, as Emily sat on a footstool in the centre of the room.

She looked towards the garden, but her eyes seemed to be

focused on something far beyond the ivy-covered wall. 'Go ahead,' she said at last, and Leila produced a small digital camera from her bag. She took a seat on the couch next to the stool.

'Are you sure you're OK with this?' she asked.

'Living in fear has got me nowhere. Something has to change,' Emily replied. 'I can't go on like this.' Her fingers touched the bruise that shadowed her face, and her eyes glistened. 'Sometimes you get so desperate, you'll do anything, right?'

Leila knew exactly where desperation could take a person.

Emily looked at her for the first time since they'd entered the room. 'I wanted to be a journalist. I was studying English Literature at King's. It seems like such a long time ago.'

She hesitated.

'You're going to name names, right?' she asked. 'It's the only way to keep my family safe. You're not going to bottle it because of libel or slander?'

'I promise you, there won't be anywhere for these people to hide,' Leila assured her. There was steel in her voice.

Emily nodded emphatically. 'Then I'm ready.'

Leila switched on the camera, focused and started recording.

'Emily, why don't you tell us your story?' she suggested. 'Start with your name.'

'My name is Emily Elizabeth Best. I'm twenty-two. I was born in Sussex and grew up in East Hoathly, not too far from Eastbourne. Two years ago, I was in my final year of English Literature at King's College. Some friends and I went out to celebrate the end of spring term. We wound up at this place in Soho called Bund. It's in Chinatown, on the main drag. We were all having a laugh. I'd had a couple of drinks, but

I wasn't drunk. Then this guy came on to us. He said his name was Paul, but you could tell straight away he was a liar. He was in one of those shiny, expensive suits with an open-neck shirt, showing off his chest hair. Lot of gold. Big watch, necklace, bracelets, all thick, heavy and brash. He said he wanted to take the four of us to a private club and introduce us to some of his rich friends. I didn't want to go, but my friend Willa suggested putting it to a vote and she, Steph and Rose all thought it would be a laugh. String the guy along for free drinks and giggles.'

Emily sighed at the memory.

'He kept talking the whole way across Soho and the little voice in my head was shouting at me to go home. We've all heard that voice and we've all ignored it. That's exactly what I did. I told myself I was being stupid, that I was out with three friends, that nothing bad could happen.'

She scoffed bitterly.

'We got inside the place and "Paul" took us into this crazy bar. It was all decked out in neon. Even the glasses were lit. He introduced us to these guys, and by now my inner voice was screaming at me to get out. You ever meet anyone who's made you afraid? Someone whose face just stirs evil thoughts? These men were like that. But I was worried about how it would look if I just left. Can you believe that? I was afraid of offending them. I was worried about ruining my friends' night. I put social nicety before my own safety. Never again.'

Emily's hands balled into fists and she sighed in frustration, exasperated at her former self.

'Never, ever ignore the warning signs. I've had a lot of time to read since that night, and one thing I've learned is that our instincts are a better judge of real danger. Instinct has evolved over millions of years to keep us safe. Never ignore it.'

She paused.

'One drink, that's all I had. When I woke up . . .' Tears formed in Emily's eyes, as words failed her.

Leila fought to keep the camera still as she trembled with anger. She knew exactly what this woman was going through and reached across to take her hand. Emily smiled sadly and wiped her eyes.

'When I came round, I was in this flat. One of the men was on me. Another two . . .' she sobbed again, before continuing. 'There were another two . . . waiting.'

Emily looked at the garden and took a moment to compose herself. 'The next evening, they showed me photographs of my mother and father tied to chairs in their home. They told me that as long as I continued to work for them, my family would be safe. But if I ever tried to run, or go to the police, or speak to anyone about what was happening, my parents would be killed. My mum and dad thought they were victims of a random home invasion. They still have no idea they were attacked because of me. I was forced into an invisible cage. I'm free to come and go as I please, as long as I'm available when they tell me. They've forced me to be with so many men. They've taken video, photos. I know because I've caught them changing the cards in the cameras hidden around the flat. The men . . .' Emily drifted away for a moment. 'Some of them have been so cruel. This is just the latest,' she signalled her ugly bruise.

'But a blackmailer only has power as long as you're afraid of their threats. And I'm not afraid any more. I can't live like this. Something has to give. I thought about suicide, but they told me they'd consider it running away and my parents would die. You wouldn't even let me die!' she yelled up at the ceiling. 'You wouldn't let me die, so this is what you get!'

Emily took a breath and calmed herself.

'When we're done, I'm going to call Mum and Dad and warn them to hide until this is over. Whatever happens to me is fine, but my parents never did anything wrong.'

'We can help protect you,' Leila said almost instinctively, her heart breaking for this strong woman. 'Can you tell us the names of any of the ring-leaders? People the police should look to if anything ever happened to you or your family?'

Leila's meaning wasn't lost on Emily. 'Artem Vasylyk,' she said. 'And Lancelot Bayard Oxnard-Clarke.'

Leila stifled a gasp. She hadn't expected the banker to be directly implicated in the sex ring.

'He's a peer of the realm and the chairman of a bank,' Emily remarked with disgust. 'And he knows exactly what's been going on. The two of them use us to run coded messages because they're afraid of being associated in public.'

Emily confirmed Pearce's assessment of what had been happening in the club on Golden Square.

'Do you know how many others they've done this to?' Leila asked.

'I've met about fifteen,' Emily replied. 'But I'm guessing there are more. All of us fit the same profile. We're educated, intelligent, from middle-class families. It took me a while to figure out why they'd targeted us. It's psychology 101 really. You go for intelligence because it usually correlates with empathy. Empathetic people have a hard time believing that people who lack empathy exist. They're always looking for the good in others and that makes them easy to manipulate. And you hunt the middle class because they've got a lot to lose. Hardship breeds strength and the poor don't tend to be as pliable as those with a lot to lose. Those who've only ever done what was expected of them, what they were told . . .'

Emily's quivering voice finally broke, and she choked back more sobs.

'There are more like me,' she said. 'Men and women, living terrible lives right here in London. This isn't about sex, this is about power. Male, female . . . doesn't matter. They're degrading all of us, turning us into objects they can use to satisfy their own needs. To pursue their own agenda.'

'What do your friends think happened to you?' Leila asked.

'After I dropped out of uni, they disowned me. They think I'm a gold digger, that I traded my body for a life of luxury, living as the mistress of some rich guy. They judged me for doing my best to cope with the mess they put me in. I couldn't tell them the truth, and nor would I want to. No real friend would ever cast someone aside so easily, and the fact they'd think I'd willingly sell myself shows how little they ever knew me. They have no idea how lucky they are that they weren't targeted that night.'

Emily's face flushed with anger, but she looked down and the heat of emotion passed. 'Do you have what you need?' she asked.

Leila nodded, her eyes brimming, her entire body bristling. 'I'm so sorry,' she said.

'Just make sure you get them,' Emily replied, her voice rigid with conviction. 'If the story is going public, I want everyone to hear it. I want the world to know what these bastards have done.'

Leila felt a hot flush of righteous fury, and the thought of what this woman had endured stoked memories of her own traumatic experiences.

'They're going to pay,' she said grimly. 'I'll make sure of that.'

Chapter 48

Pearce and Wollerton said nothing as they drove into Harwich. McClusky was in the boot, trapped and afraid. If he recognized their voices, he'd put the abduction into some sort of context, which might affect their ability to manipulate him later. They'd stopped at the NCP multi-storey car park on Cadogan Place, where they'd put on their ski masks, stripped McClusky, ditched all his possessions and forced him into a change of clothes. Satisfied the man could no longer be carrying a tracking device, they'd put him in the boot of a blue Toyota Avensis, also stolen, and driven north.

The journey to Harwich had taken a shade under three hours and it was shortly after 1 p.m. when they drove into the small seaside town. Pearce opened his window and the Avensis filled with the scent of the sea. The temperature was a degree or two cooler than London, and flags and bunting fluttered in a gentle breeze. Pearce made a right at a Celtic memorial cross, passing a parade of shops that looked as though they'd been frozen in time, relics from the latter half of the last century. A quarter of a mile further on, they turned sharply left, forced that way by the coastline. The sun glittered off the sea, creating a perfect day for the couples who shuffled along the promenade. Far in the distance, rising above the heat haze, stood the faint insectoid silhouettes of the giant cargo cranes of Felixstowe Port.

Pearce drove on, passing a coastal park where sun-seekers played and picnicked on mottled brown grass. The road curved away from the sea, and further inland the buildings thinned. Immediately beyond a community centre, which lay at the edge of the coastal park, Pearce finally saw what he was looking for: a tiny narrow track. He turned right and followed the rutted trail for half a mile or so. The landscape soon became wild and rugged, and they found themselves driving through tufted hillocks covered in wild grasses. They rounded a bend and stopped at a high gate which blocked the trail. Pearce reached behind his seat, grabbed a set of bolt cutters and jumped out. The chain-link fence was weathered and old and had been rusted by the sharp sting of the sea air. A faded sign informed anyone who fell this far off the beaten track that what lay behind the fence was the property of the Ministry of Defence, that there was a danger of death and that trespassers would be prosecuted.

Trespassing is the least of my worries, Pearce thought as he cut the thick chain which secured the gates. He opened them, ran back to the car and drove through. Beacon Hill Fort had once been a munitions testing facility. The buildings were severe concrete structures that had been designed to fool any passing spy plane or satellite into thinking they formed a small residential housing estate and water treatment plant. Up close, they were constructed of the rough grey-green re-inforced concrete common to hardened military structures. Beyond the main group of two- and three-storey buildings, a lone targeting tower protruded near the very edge of the high cliffs. A thicket of bushes formed a semi-circular barrier from the southernmost edge of the cliffs to the most norther-ly and behind that stood rank after rank of mature trees that obstructed all but the most determined eyes. A high fence acted as a final line of security, running beyond the wood, cut-ting the forty-acre plot off from the surrounding area. It was one of the most private and secure locations within easy reach of London, which is why it was sometimes used by Six opera-tives for combat training or interrogation. Not knowing how long they might have to hold McClusky, Pearce had opted for somewhere he could be kept indefinitely.

The crumbling structures on top of the cliff only told part of Beacon Hill's story. What lay beneath was far more interesting. Concealed within the high cliffs was a network of tunnels and chambers, some of which linked to the sea. The chambers had stored munitions and provided quarters for personnel, and the sea access tunnels had been used to get said people and supplies into the facility in a way that reduced the risk of the local population figuring out the true purpose of the base. Dwarfing the tunnels and chambers, on the lower levels of the facility were huge vaults that had been carved in the rock to create shooting ranges for a wide variety of battlefield weapons.

Pearce didn't intend to go to the ranges today, but the first layer of tunnels would provide a useful degree of privacy and there were rooms where McClusky could be locked up safely. Pearce drove the Avensis beneath a concrete canopy that had once been the first floor of an administration block. The outer wall had collapsed, enabling Pearce to park in what would have been an office. He nodded at Wollerton, and they put on their ski masks and got out of the car.

Pearce went to the boot and opened it to discover McClusky

in the foetal position. When they'd forced him to change, they'd blindfolded him and put him in a plain white T-shirt and shorts. It wasn't a flattering outfit. His wiry strength had been diminished by the mental ordeal of the abduction, and he now appeared every inch the pasty desk jockey – a house cat whose petty authority Pearce had always resented.

McClusky was silent as Pearce and Wollerton hauled him to his feet. He didn't resist as they pulled him across a scrappy, overgrown courtyard, steering him towards a turret that seemed to sprout from the ground. Pearce opened the rusty door to reveal a short corridor that led to a set of concrete steps. He produced a torch and lit their way.

The stairwell was dark and dank, the pool of light cast by the torch doing little to ward off the ominous shadows that danced all around them as they made their way down. They came to sublevel one and pulled McClusky through an open doorway, across a corridor and into an old munitions store. Rusty, tumbledown racks lined all four walls, and black mould clung to the ceiling.

Pearce fished in his pockets for the case that contained the syringes he had used on Kemp and Dunbar. The Evil. Wollerton removed McClusky's blindfold and he looked around blankly as his eyes adjusted to the dim light.

'We've got some questions,' Pearce said, disguising his voice as he opened the case to reveal the set of sharps.

McClusky's eyes widened at the sight of the needles. 'There's no need for that,' he responded eagerly. 'I'll tell you whatever you want to know.'

'How long has Mark Sutton answered to you?' Pearce asked.

'Sutton?' McClusky replied, his tone betraying surprise.

He didn't expect to be asked about Sutton, which suggested his most valuable secrets lay elsewhere. 'I recruited Sutton two years ago.'

'How?' Pearce quizzed.

'The same way I was brought in. Ideology and pleasure. Most of us believe in what we're doing. The girls and boys are just there as insurance,' McClusky revealed. 'It's not blackmail, just a little leverage. We're committed to the cause, but they help us keep the faith.'

Pearce was at a loss for a moment. Then a huge piece of the puzzle fell into place. He hadn't been able to fathom why men as powerful as Vasylyk and Lancelot Oxnard-Clarke would have anything to do with a tawdry sex ring. It was a honey trap, designed to snare powerful people like McClusky and Sutton: wayward politicians, civil servants and businessmen. Pearce had no doubt that if he searched the flats, there would be cameras in every single one and that the photos would be used to focus the minds of friends and enemies alike, guaranteeing loyalty and the granting of favours. The KGB had run a number of such establishments across Europe during the Cold War, and they were known to be simple but highly effective.

'Who do you take your orders from?' Pearce asked.

'Who are you?' McClusky countered. 'I recognize your voice.'

Pearce slapped him.

'Is this a test? Are you testing my loyalty?' McClusky replied.

Pearce hit him again, and he staggered back.

'Who in Progress Britain gives you your orders?' Pearce pressed, but he immediately saw that he'd made a mistake.

A faint smile flickered across McClusky's face. This wasn't about Progress Britain, and the question had told McClusky he was being interrogated by people who were out of their depth.

'Black 13,' Pearce said. 'What are they planning?'

'I recognize that voice,' McClusky scoffed. 'Scott Pearce, the hero of Islamabad.' His words dripped sarcasm. 'I'd heard you were dead. Opened up in some dark alleyway.'

Pearce punched him hard and felt the satisfying crunch of bone as the spymaster's nose cracked. McClusky buckled with a pained yelp and when he stood, blood covered his face.

'We're going to do this the hard way,' Pearce said as he opened the case of syringes.

'No. No. Don't do that,' McClusky pleaded. 'I don't know what they're planning. I report to Lancelot Oxnard-Clarke. He's my handler. He recruited me. I have no idea what Lancelot's private army are up to.'

'Then you're not much use, are you?' Pearce remarked.

'You don't have the balls to kill me,' McClusky scoffed, but his derision rang hollow.

'Why not? No one knows who took you. No one knows where you are. We'll just take you deeper underground and leave your body to rot that little bit closer to hell.'

McClusky smiled and cocked his head to one side. 'You hear that?'

Pearce became aware of a low vibration that rapidly grew louder.

'Choppers,' Wollerton said.

'Every year I go to Dr Azzam's very expensive clinic on Harley Street to replace the batteries in my signal locator.' McClusky pulled the neck of his T-shirt and exposed his collarbone. Just beneath it was a thin one-inch scar, and below that a small lump of raised skin.

Pearce couldn't believe Six had implemented security protocols he wasn't aware of. The locator must have summoned someone else: McClusky's true masters. 'Come on!' he yelled to Wollerton.

They grabbed McClusky, who now moved with the confident swagger of someone with the upper hand. They dragged him up the decaying concrete staircase to the short corridor in the turret. Pearce hurried ahead and listened at the door. The chopper engines were faint, as though the birds were some distance away. Pearce pushed the door open and realized he'd made a terrible mistake. The reason the engines sounded faint was because the choppers, a pair of Eurocopter EC 135s, were on the ground, their rotors slowing. Two squads of six men fanned out from each bird, but these weren't soldiers of any military unit Pearce recognized. They wore grey and black urban camouflage beneath their body armour, their faces were covered by a mix of bandanas and ski masks and they carried an odd assortment of weapons. Then Pearce noticed the rough badges on their epaulets and recognized the Black 13 insignia he'd seen on the card he'd found at Nathan Foster's flat.

'Over here!' McClusky yelled.

Pearce glanced over his shoulder to see Wollerton hitting their prisoner, but his effort to silence the man came too late. The noise and movement caught the attention of the two squads, and when Pearce turned back, he saw that one of the masked men had dropped to his knees and was sighting his Stealth Recon Scout sniper rifle. He was aiming directly at Pearce.

Pearce was trapped in the mouth of the corridor and knew he didn't have time to get clear, but before he could react, the gun spat twice, and to Pearce's amazement, the bullets whipped past him. It was only then that he realized who the shooter had been targeting. Behind him, McClusky screamed in agony. Both bullets had penetrated his gut and a bloody stain was spreading across his T-shirt.

Pearce jumped back and let the door slam as a volley of shots peppered the turret.

'Go!' he yelled at Wollerton, who started down the stairs.

Pearce sprinted along the corridor, grabbed McClusky and hustled the man down. The three men raced as fast as their tumbling legs would carry them.

'They shot me,' McClusky whined breathlessly. 'They fucking shot me.'

Bullets rained from above and the well exploded in clouds of dust, as dozens of thunderclaps cracked in their ears. Pearce felt McClusky grow heavier with each passing moment and was under no illusion: the man was dying.

'I – help me – please . . .' McClusky implored.

Pearce ignored his cries and shunted him past the first sublevel towards the gloom below. Above them, muzzle fire and torches lit the heavens, but the stairs between provided cover and soon the guns fell silent and were replaced by thunderous footsteps.

They passed the second and third sublevels and Pearce steered them deeper, where the air was cold and stale, the stairs were moist and crumbling, and the walls were ravaged by damp. They came to the fourth sublevel and Pearce hurried past Wollerton, crossing a wide corridor and forcing open a heavy door. Metal screeched against concrete as he pushed it wide. Pearce pulled McClusky through and the man stumbled further into the darkness. Wollerton followed and helped Pearce push the door closed as the sound of footsteps drew near. Pearce's torch illuminated the rusted green metal door and he saw a thick bolt lying in a housing halfway up. As Wollerton forced the door into its frame, Pearce grabbed the bolt. His arms stung painfully as he pulled, forcing the metal tube clear of the rust that held it. The bolt shot into its catch as the first bodies struck the other side of the door.

'It's locked,' a voice said.

'We're gonna need charges,' replied another.

'We don't have long,' Pearce whispered, as he turned from the door.

The torch illuminated McClusky, who'd collapsed a few feet away and was lying on his back, blood seeping from the huge stain that covered his T-shirt.

'Help me,' he begged, tears filling his eyes.

Pearce hurried over and crouched beside him. Wollerton stood nearby. Perhaps their expressions and lack of action told McClusky all he needed to know.

'I'm dying,' he said.

Pearce nodded.

'Fuck! The bug wasn't so they could save me,' he sobbed. 'It was so they could silence me.' He smiled darkly. 'Should have done a better job.'

'What are they planning?' Pearce asked.

McClusky coughed, rasping up a thick glob of blood. 'Said I didn't know what these fuckers were doing. Not true. I know. Ashamed. Sick. Evil. But when you're far in – no hope for redemption. Devil already owns you.'

'What is it?' Pearce asked.

The man didn't have long. His breathing had already changed, becoming rapid and shallow, the quick countdown to the last gasp.

'Darvaza is Hazelmere Darke. Suffer the innocents,' McClusky forced the words through his choking throat, before the convulsions started. After a moment of terrible agony, he fell still and his eyes glazed over.

Pearce shut them.

'We need to go,' he said, getting to his feet and sweeping the room with his torch. They were in one of the rifle ranges and if Pearce recalled correctly, there was a sea access tunnel at the far end.

'This way,' he said, leading Wollerton across the vast room.

When they reached the tunnel, Pearce heard the distant sound of waves crashing and caught the sharp smell of the sea. The metal hatch that capped the tunnel had fallen off its hinges and the walls and floor were sodden. The tunnel mouth had been eroded by saltwater and looked unstable. The outer hatch must have been breached by the sea, allowing the room to be flooded at high tide. There was no telling the state of the rest of the tunnel, but if the mouth was anything to go by, it was on the verge of collapse.

'We go through and there's a ladder at the other end. It leads down the cliff to a stone jetty,' Pearce said. 'It's safe water, about three hundred yards to the nearest beach.'

The room was rocked by an explosion and behind them a fireball blew the heavy door off its frame. The hellish noise made Pearce's head ring and the shockwave shook his bones. Concrete chunks fell away from the tunnel mouth and Pearce could see slabs of masonry tumbling from the ceiling further along.

'Go! Go! Go!' he yelled, and Wollerton ducked inside.

Pearce glanced behind him and saw shadows moving swiftly through the dust and smoke.

'Over there,' one of them yelled, the flashlight mounted on his rifle barrel pointed directly at the tunnel.

Pearce killed his torch and considered running, but hesitated. He'd been seen, and if he followed Wollerton, they'd both be caught on the cliffside. There was no way they'd have enough of a lead to get down the ladder to the pontoon in time. There was only one thing Pearce could do.

'Look for the signal,' he shouted up the tunnel, praying Wollerton heard him.

He picked up the heavy hatch. Forearms screaming, he swung it edge-first into the mouth of the tunnel. Three blows were all it took to bring the ceiling down and Pearce stepped back as the tunnel entrance collapsed. Taking advantage of the thick cloud of dust, he hurried into the darkness, carefully avoiding the torch beams of the men hunting him. He doubled back towards the door and raced to McClusky's body, its outline made faintly visible by the dull light from the corridor. Pearce reached into his pocket for a small knife and felt for the dead man's shoulder. He cut into the still-warm flesh.

'He's there,' a voice said, and Pearce suddenly found himself in a pool of light, as footsteps hurriedly converged on him.

He didn't have much time, and stuck his fingers in the wound he'd created. Someone grabbed his shoulders, but he resisted. Not yet. He didn't have what he needed. Someone hit him with a rifle stock, knocking him into McClusky. The hands took hold again, but as they pulled him back, Pearce felt what he'd been seeking, and his thumb and forefinger pinched the tiny metal tube that was embedded beneath McClusky's collarbone. He pulled it from McClusky's body as he was hauled away.

Pearce was forced to his feet and made to face the unit commander, a man in a grey ski mask emblazoned with a white skull. Pearce slipped the bloody tracking device beneath his own mask and put it in his mouth. The blood was cloying and warm, but he didn't care. The tiny beacon was his only hope, so he suppressed his disgust and swallowed.

'Who the fuck are you?' The commander asked, removing Pearce's mask.

He could sense their collective surprise, and took perverse pride in the fact that his face was known to them.

'I need to talk to your boss – Viscount Purbeck,' Pearce said. 'I have an offer he'll want to hear.'

The unit commander stared at Pearce before nodding at the man who'd hauled him up. Pearce felt the heavy blow of a rifle stock and everything went black.

Chapter 49

Leila stood near the old church. She still burned with the fury of her encounter with Emily and seethed with the desire for vengeance. Here, in the heart of London, was a brutal, wicked man she could reach out and touch. Pearce had instructed her not to go into Bayard Madison's server room, but he'd said nothing about Vasylyk's office.

She watched the big bodyguard give the dark-haired woman another USB drive. The woman scanned her surroundings furtively and didn't linger, instead hurrying back to the Bayard Madison building as soon as the exchange was complete. Her exposure the previous day would probably have shaken her, but she couldn't say anything to her employer or the stern-faced man who provided her with the drives. There was no telling what they might do if they found out she'd allowed Pearce to copy the data. Not that it was any use. As far as Leila could tell, the file Pearce had intercepted was encrypted using a 256-bit key and the data that lay within was likely to be coded. Even if she could break the encryption, there was no guarantee she'd be able to read the file. The only way to be sure was to obtain the encryption key. Like her, Nathan Foster had probably figured out the key was in the Bayard Madison server room, but Leila wondered whether he'd known that the source of the files was located in the neighbouring building.

A bank would be secure, a hard target to crack, and accessing the server room would, as Pearce had told her, be dangerous. But it had occurred to Leila that there was likely to be a copy of the encryption key in Artem Vasylyk's office, the source of the USB drives. All the more reason to pay the man a visit.

Tell yourself what you like, she thought. *You're not here for the investigation.*

Leila had lived and breathed death. It had taken her family and she'd been surrounded by it during her last few months in Raqqa, when executions, mutilations and massacres had become the norm. Existing in the shadow of such horror changed a person. It had given her a different attitude to risk and when death finally came for her, Leila Nahum would smile and hold out her hands, ready to feel the touch that had taken so many of her loved ones. They were all waiting for her. She knew her attitude could be mistaken for fatalism, but that's not what it was. She'd seen people fight, scream, cry, despair, haggle, beg and lose control of their bodily functions in the face of death. It had no pity and could not be reasoned with. Those who remained calm in the face of their end were the ones who had the best deaths. They made the final journey in a state of peace.

Once she'd reconciled herself to death, Leila's attitude to risk had changed and she'd found herself able to maintain her composure in situations others would consider stressful. In her private moments she wondered whether the change had been psychologically harmful, whether she'd rationalized the numbing of her soul, legitimized the cauterization of her senses in the face of the horrors she'd seen. She questioned whether her life had led her to become less than human. *Not less than*, she corrected herself, *just different. A difference that enables you to do things like this.* She felt nothing but controlled fury as she crossed the hot pavement into the shadow of the skyscraper that housed Vasylyk's office. The prospect of talking to the large man in the dark suit did not scare her in the slightest. She gave no hint of emotion as he turned to look at her, his face betraying puzzlement. Why was a sultry woman in a shabby T-shirt and jeans, leaning heavily on a cane, hobbling towards him?

'Hello,' Leila said when she was a few feet away. 'I believe you work for Artem Vasylyk.'

The man smiled in disbelief. His square jaw and lean face conveyed little joy in the expression. He looked like an eagle that had just spied prey far below on the valley floor.

'I'd like to speak to Mr Vasylyk,' Leila continued. 'I'd like to talk to him about the sex ring he's been running.'

'Really?' The man asked. His accent was Russian.

'Yes,' Leila replied. 'I also think he's been sending messages to Bayard Madison Bank, probably instructions of some kind, and I'd very much like to know what they say. You're going to take me to him because you want to know whether you should just kill me or interrogate me first and then kill me.'

The predator's smile widened.

'You are an intelligent woman,' he remarked. 'They say intelligence and insanity often share the same messy bed.' The cadence of the man's delivery anchored him to somewhere in the Moscow region.

'I'm not insane,' Leila assured him. 'Shall we go?'

The man scoffed and nodded. He followed Leila, who had already started towards the building.

*

After the heat of the plaza, the lift felt like the inside of a fridge, the cold air stroking Leila's skin, making her hairs stand on end. The bodyguard had taken her through building security, signing her in as a visitor.

'Make one up,' she'd told him, when he'd asked for her name, and her bluntness had earned another smile.

Behind the grin, he'd probably been picturing his hands around her neck, or a gun at her temple. She'd seen that look in the eyes of men who'd underestimated her before.

After building security, they'd stepped into one of four lifts. The plush interior was lined with thick carpet and covered on three sides by smoked mirrors. Her large companion admired himself in them before casting a critical eye at her. She could tell he saw only what she wanted him to see: a small, frail, disabled creature who was sufficiently unhinged to willingly walk into a nest of predators.

'*Ya prikhozhu c nezhelatel'num gostem,*' the man said into a lapel mic. '*Podgotov'te privetstviye.*'

Russia's longstanding commercial links with the country meant very few people spent any time in Syria without picking up at least a rudimentary understanding of Russian, and Leila had augmented her knowledge of the language when she'd found sanctuary in Britain. She smiled blankly, careful not to show that she'd understood his words. *I'm coming up with an uninvited guest. Prepare a welcome.* Even if he'd known, she suspected he wouldn't care. When he looked at her, he only saw weakness.

What he didn't see was the stun gun Leila slid from her bag. They were halfway through the twenty-two-storey climb when Leila thrust 50,000 volts into his neck. He gave a momentary look of disbelief before his eyes rolled back and he collapsed in a sprawled heap.

As the lift continued its climb, Leila leaned against the back mirror and eased herself onto the floor. She crawled forward and lay on top of the fallen bodyguard, putting her head on his back, and concealing the stun gun beneath his arm. As the elevator slowed to a halt, she closed her eyes.

The doors opened with a soft chime and she sensed movement nearby.

'Roman?' a man asked in a puzzled voice.

Leila felt the elevator bounce as someone stepped inside, and a moment later, a strong hand took hold of her arm and pulled her up. She swept round with the stun gun, her eyes snapping open to see the fat face of a huge man. She buried the prongs in the folds of his neck and pulled the trigger. He yelped as raw electricity shot into his body and shut down his central nervous system.

Leila rolled out of the way as he fell forward, landing on his colleague like a carcass thrown into a butcher's truck. Leila searched both men and took two wallets, a brace of phones and, from the fat man, a P-96 pistol that was holstered with two spare clips.

She used her cane for support and hauled herself up. She stepped through the lift doors, which had been prevented from closing by the giant man's legs. A large bouquet of flowers stood on an onyx plinth by a huge window that overlooked the Lloyd's building. Leila saw a fire escape to her left and a set of glass doors opposite it to her right. She went through the doors and found herself in a deserted corridor alongside a run of floor-to-ceiling windows. Dimly lit offices stood empty on the other side of the corridor. Leila hurried towards a solid wooden door at the far end and pressed her ear against it. She heard a strange rhythmic clicking, but nothing else. Leila checked the P-96 and stepped through.

Artem Vasylyk seemed genuinely shocked when Leila entered with her pistol trained on him. The Ukrainian was seated on a giant couch that lay at the far end of the huge corner office. The couch, the table football, the video games console, the pool table and the bar all made Leila think of some male fantasy bachelor pad. Everything was well worn, and only the large lacquered desk seemed unused; its leather-embossed top was devoid of any evidence of work and was the resting place of empty glasses, a half-full vodka bottle and a broken pool cue. When Leila looked beyond the desk at a compartment that would normally be concealed behind a section of false wall, she understood the reason for all the toys. Vasylyk and his men needed a way to kill time while they waited.

Standing in the secret section of the office was a machine that Leila had only seen in theoretical drawings. It was a ten feet high by twelve feet wide machine that looked as though it belonged in a NASA control centre. Over one hundred spherical vacuum chambers protruded from the machine and each housed a red laser that fired intermittently. The laser pulses were the source of the rhythmic clicking Leila had heard through the door. The untrained eye might have mistaken the machine for a supercomputer, but it was far more advanced than that. It was a particle communication system. For a moment, Leila's fury took second place to her astonishment. This machine wasn't supposed to exist.

Some years ago, scientists had discovered that photons that had become entangled could then be separated and any behaviour exerted on one would be manifest by the other, regardless of the distance of separation. One photon could be made to spin on Earth and the other entangled photon would spin even if it was on the other side of the universe. The possibilities for instantaneous, untraceable communication were recognized early on, but Leila had thought the science wasn't sufficiently advanced and that a working prototype was decades away. But one stood in front of her, invisible photons manipulated in vacuum chambers, their behaviour read by the lasers and translated into binary by the sensors that monitored them. Someone had built a working machine capable of delivering instant messages and the source would be impossible to trace.

'A photon communicator,' Leila observed.

'Who are you?' Vasylyk asked.

'Just a simple Syrian refugee trying to make a difference,' Leila replied. 'Why isn't it in the bank?'

Vasylyk glowered.

'You're sending messages to someone in the neighbouring building,' Leila said. 'Why not just install it there?'

Vasylyk didn't reply. He simply shifted awkwardly in his expensive sky blue suit.

'You're a hub,' Leila surmised. 'The bank isn't the only place you're giving instructions to.'

Vasylyk's expression betrayed the truth of Leila's theory. She'd hit home.

'I could threaten to kill you,' Leila said, 'if you don't give me the encryption code.'

Vasylyk's eyes darted over his shoulder and she followed them to see a laptop on a shelf beside the massive machine.

'But I don't really need to,' Leila said, shuffling towards

the secret chamber. She kept her eyes and gun on Vasylyk, who glared at her. 'Where are the messages coming from?' she asked.

'You're a dead woman,' he said.

'You would not believe how many men have said that to me,' she replied. 'I'd assumed you were calling the shots, but you're just a messenger boy. Who's at the other end of this machine?'

Leila sensed Vasylyk tensing. 'Don't do it,' she said. 'I know what you've done to those men and women. I'm finding it hard enough to not pull this trigger. Don't give me another reason to shoot you.'

'You don't have the guts,' Vasylyk responded.

Leila was surprised when Vasylyk made his move. He reached beneath his jacket and she caught a flash of leather: a holster. He must have really wanted to stop her getting the key. It was the only way to explain such suicidal desperation. There was no way he could hope to draw faster than she could shoot, unless he really was counting on her not to have the guts to pull the trigger. He didn't know she'd spent the morning with his victims.

She fired twice. The bullets struck him in the centre of his chest, and his body bucked into the soft sofa cushions. Startled and horrified, he looked down at the blood spreading across his shirt and a wet, choking rattle came from deep inside him. He glanced up at Leila, full of hate, and then his eyes went blank.

Leila felt a certain satisfaction at the sight of his lifeless body, but she knew she'd just killed one of their lines of inquiry and needed something to show for it. She turned to the secret room and took the laptop, an unremarkable Dell machine. She would have loved to examine the photon communicator, but doing so with a corpse in the room would have been reckless, so she felt around the frame of the retracted false wall until she found a concealed button that closed it. As the wall slid back into position, hiding the huge, state-of-the-art machine, Leila tucked the laptop into her bag and walked out. She shuffled along the corridor, returned to the small lobby where Vasylyk's now redundant bodyguards lay as they'd been left, piled in the elevator. Seizing the opportunity to complicate matters for the two men, Leila wiped the P-96 pistol on her T-shirt and placed it in the hand of the huge man.

With Vasylyk's laptop in her bag, Leila hurried into the fire escape and walked down three flights of stairs at what seemed like an agonizingly slow pace before she went through a stairwell door into the wood-panelled lobby of an accounting firm. There was no one else around and one of the three remaining lifts came shortly after she called it. As she rode down, she used her pay-as-you-go burner to phone the police and inform them that she'd heard gunshots coming from the twenty-second floor of the building. When she reached the ground floor, Leila hobbled across the lobby, her cane keeping a steady beat against the cool, shiny floor. As she looked at her reflection in the large tinted glass doors, she considered the ease with which she'd killed another man and how little it bothered her. Was she really just 'different'?

If anything, she felt good at having brought his victims a small measure of justice.

Chapter 50

Wollerton emerged from the water and ignored the bemused looks he drew from the holidaymakers who were startled to see a fully clothed man step from the sea. He was halfway across the beach when he heard the choppy thrum of rotors approaching. He ran across the dry sand and reached the cover of a pavilion as the two helicopters flew overhead. The birds split. One tracked the beach, while the other flew a line the other side of the old fort. After a short while, the choppers climbed and headed inland. They'd given up the search.

Wollerton couldn't believe what Pearce had done. Having made the climb down the rusty, broken ladder that clung to the cliffside with little more than habit and history holding it in place, Wollerton knew the two of them would have been easy targets for the Black 13 unit. Pearce had sacrificed himself so that Wollerton could escape. But he had no intention of letting sacrifice become martyrdom.

Wollerton broke cover and set off through the coastal park. As he ran with the hot sun beating down on him, he was grateful for his wet clothes. He reached the far corner of the park and hurdled the low perimeter rail. He turned down Barrack Lane and ran right, along the narrow track that led to the fort. Sprinting through the gates, he raced into the complex and reached the Avensis.

He got to the car and was about to jump in when he stopped short, recalling his hostile-environment training. He dropped to the rubble-covered ground and leaned down to peer beneath the car. His heart rattled off a couple of misfires when he saw a grenade lying between two big stones, an almost invisible strand of fishing line connecting the pin to a loop that had been fed around the bottom corner of the car door. Wollerton unhooked the loop and reached beneath the car. He took a deep breath and stood up, brandishing the hand grenade.

Dirty bastards, Wollerton thought. The door could have been opened by a kid hoping for a joyride. He circled the car, stopping every so often to check the underside. Finding nothing else, he got in the car and opened the glove compartment. He stashed the grenade and took out the Ghostlink.

'*Go ahead,*' Leila's voice came from the speaker.

'We ran into some trouble,' Wollerton told her. 'Pearce has been taken. You need to go to Harley Street. Find a Dr Azzam. He put a beacon in McClusky and we need the signal identifier to find him.'

'*I'm on it,*' Leila replied, before disconnecting.

Wollerton reached for the keys, still in the ignition where Pearce had left them. He pinched the key and made a half turn. The dashboard lights illuminated, but he was suddenly struck by a crackling wave of hot nerves. He froze, sitting absolutely still. Then he popped the bonnet and climbed out. He lifted the hot sheet of metal and scanned the tidy engine. Another stuttering misfire of the heart came when he saw a tiny, thin pin poking out from behind the cylinder head. He reached round and carefully removed the grenade, breaking the line that was attached to some unseen part of the engine.

Wollerton took a deep breath, slammed the bonnet shut and climbed into the driver's seat.

He stashed the second grenade in the glove compartment with the first. He hadn't been to church for years, but he found himself praying to God as though he was a familiar friend. He took a deep breath and turned the key.

The ignition housing moved round, and the engine came to life, purring smoothly.

Relieved, Wollerton put the car in reverse and backed out of the wrecked building. He turned in the courtyard and the wheels churned up dusty earth as he stepped on the accelerator.

Leila was in the back of a taxi on her way to the safe house when Wollerton called to tell her that Pearce had been taken. She gave the taxi driver new instructions and within moments they were heading east along Bayswater Road, back into Central London. She was reeling from the news and tried not to go to dark places. She forced herself to calm down. Wollerton wouldn't be sending her on this errand if there wasn't a chance of recovering Pearce alive.

Twenty-five minutes later, the taxi pulled to a halt outside an immaculately presented terrace on Harley Street. Like so many of the medical offices on the street, the clinic's name was publicized only by a discreet brass plaque beside a door that lay at the top of some steps. Leila paid the driver and leaned against her cane as she climbed up to the front door. She clasped her bag. Emily Best's recorded testimony now had Vasylyk's stolen laptop to keep it company along with the SD cards from four cameras she'd found hidden around Emily's flat.

Inside the clinic, piped music filled the grand reception area. A young, overly groomed, plastic woman sat behind a large desk and looked up as Leila approached. Her smile hardly wavered, but Leila noted the woman's eyes change as she clocked someone who didn't belong within the clinic's discerning walls.

'Good afternoon, madam,' the receptionist said. 'How can I help?'

'I work for a government agency,' Leila replied with an equally false smile. 'One of our operatives is missing and we believe Dr Azzam can help us find him.'

The receptionist's smile fell and she nodded. 'If you'd like to wait, Dr Azzam is just finishing with a patient.'

Leila moved to the waiting area and lowered herself into one of the soft leather seats, relieved to be off her pained legs. Ten minutes later, an elderly couple shuffled into the reception and made a follow-up appointment before leaving. A tall, gaunt man, with greying hair and a close beard, came into the room soon afterwards. His beautifully tailored suit clung to his slight frame, and his slender fingers danced on the desktop as he and the receptionist spoke in hushed whispers. When he looked at Leila, his warm, intelligent eyes clouded with suspicion.

'Hello,' he said, walking over. 'I'm Doctor Karim Azzam. How can I help?'

'I'm looking for a patient of yours: Dominic McClusky,' Leila replied, heaving herself up.

'I'm not sure I know the gentleman.'

'Just give me the signal identifier and I'll do the rest,' Leila told him.

Azzam looked at her uncertainly and then glanced over his

shoulder at the receptionist too nervously for a man who was doing anything legitimate. 'Who are you?' he asked.

'We're going to play a game,' Leila said, ignoring the question. 'It's called "pick a card". I want you to imagine I'm holding a single playing card. I'm going to turn it over. If it's red, I incapacitate you and your employee, I invade your office and cause as much damage as possible before I find McClusky's records.' Leila watched the stunned man's eyes grow wider with each word. 'In the process, I release every single one of your patient files online and I let it be known that you gave up the signal identifier of one of your clients. Your business is ruined and the people who've trusted you to be discreet about your little sideline – well, who knows how upset they'll be?'

Azzam's frightened expression suggested he knew exactly how upset they'd be. The colour drained from his face and he stared at her like a man who'd been shown his own bitter end. 'And if it's a black card?' he asked hesitantly.

'You give me McClusky's identifier, I walk out of here and forget we've ever met,' Leila replied.

Azzam's loyalty to McClusky lasted less than ten seconds. 'I'd like to pick the black card,' he said hopefully.

'*Ya gedaa*,' Leila exclaimed, startling the fearful man. 'Good choice. Shall we go?'

She gestured, making a point of letting the doctor see the stun gun she'd slipped into her hand. His eyes popped wide, and she slid the device back into her bag.

'This way,' he squawked, his quivering voice betraying his fear.

Fifty minutes later, Leila was sitting at her workstation accessing SatSys, a privately owned company that sold satellite location services. On screen, an hourglass twirled as the system searched for the locator details Dr Azzam had given her.

Melody and Wayne stood behind her, both still reeling from the twin revelations of Pearce's abduction and Vasylyk's death. The story had broken during Leila's cab ride from Harley Street, and she'd listened to the sombre announcement of his demise on the radio news bulletin. The report portrayed Vasylyk as a successful businessman and philanthropist and was utterly at odds with the reality Leila had spent the day hearing about. Early indications suggested Vasylyk's own bodyguard was the prime suspect in the murder, and Leila had spent the rest of the journey listening to so-called experts giving their opinions on the growing number of wealthy Eastern Europeans who'd met untimely ends in London.

When she'd arrived at the safe house, she'd raced to her computer and started the search for Pearce.

'*You got anything?*' Wollerton's voice came through the loudspeaker of Leila's Ghostlink. He was on his way back to London.

'It's processing,' Leila told him.

'I guess Vasylyk's death changes everything,' Melody said. 'We can't do anything with the sex trafficking story now. Especially not without Scott. There's no leverage to protect those poor people.'

'They all named Lancelot Oxnard-Clarke as the other ring-leader,' Leila said. 'He's not an unwitting participant.'

'*Really?*' Wollerton asked.

Wayne and Melody were just as stunned by the revelation.

'One of them does it on camera,' Leila told them. 'He's a pillar of society. He'll have even more interest in ensuring the women and their families stay healthy. Whatever happens, we do exactly what Scott said: run the story and tell the police to start with Oxnard-Clarke if anything happens to anyone.'

Her suggestion was met with silence.

'I'm not leaving those people,' Leila said. 'I promised to help them.'

'*OK*,' Wollerton said. '*Once we know where Pearce is.*'

Leila was relieved. She was glad she hadn't been forced to make a choice between this unconventional team and Emily Best and the other victims she'd given her word to.

Her display changed to a beacon flashing in a patch of green.

'There,' she said as she zoomed out and activated a satellite overlay, which showed the locator somewhere near Bath. Leila applied labels to the image.

'The signal is coming from Purbeck House,' Leila told them. 'The ancestral home of Lancelot Bayard Oxnard-Clarke, the eighteenth Viscount Purbeck.'

Chapter 51

Somewhere in the distance, a clock rang, its chimes resonant. Pearce heard them as raindrops in a dream and counted three falling into a black puddle before bridging the space between unconsciousness and waking. He heard another five chimes, and, as the rest of his senses kicked in, the next thing that hit him was the smell of lavender. Every breath was steeped in it and when he shifted his head, Pearce realized the scent was rising from the crisply starched cases that covered the soft pillows beneath him. He sat up, rubbing the back of his head, which was tender and sore. He was in a king-size bed in a large bedroom, surrounded by fine furniture and grand oil paintings. Soft evening light came through high windows and fell on the only other person in the room: Alexis Tippett-Jones.

'How are you feeling?' she asked.

'Where am I?' Pearce replied.

'Purbeck House,' Alexis said.

Pearce heard the hollow crack of gunfire coming from outside, the twin report of a shotgun.

'What are you doing here?' he asked.

'I go where they tell me,' Alexis responded sadly. 'I do what they tell me. They told me to watch you and bring you downstairs when you woke.'

'And the club?' Pearce asked. 'Did you know who I was? Did they send you to compromise me?'

Alexis shook her head. 'I saw you watching us. You've got a kind face. I thought you might be able to help me. I'm so sorry about all this.'

Pearce got to his feet. His filthy shoes and trousers had stained the bed.

'There's a change of clothes in the wardrobe,' Alexis said, crossing the room. She opened the closet to reveal an array of suits.

'I'm fine as I am,' Pearce told her. He wasn't getting dressed up so an aristocrat could kill him.

He went to the window and gazed out to see miles of parkland. Ancient trees stood here and there, with arching branches that reached over the long grass. In the distance, a herd of deer grazed beneath a giant oak, and beyond it lay fields that were home to cattle and sheep. The low sun painted the scant clouds pink and tinted the landscape a rose gold.

'We can escape,' Pearce said.

Alexis shook her head. 'There are men outside the room and more patrolling the grounds. You might be able to fight. I can't.'

Pearce rubbed his wrists, which were still raw and painful, and nodded. 'Take me where I'm supposed to go then.'

When Alexis opened the door, he saw the men she'd spoken of: two butcher's dogs, fit lean men with hungry eyes. They wore dark suits, sported matching crew cuts and fell in behind Pearce and Alexis wordlessly. She led the way round a huge galleried landing to one of two curved staircases which dropped into a grand marble hallway. A single glance over his shoulder was all it took for Pearce to know that both men were armed. The bulge of their holsters broke the cut of their jackets with every other step.

Pearce followed Alexis across the hallway into a huge library that was crammed with leather-bound books. Beyond it, they came to a drawing room that looked like the type of place used to entertain royalty. Pearce struggled to take it all in, almost unable to believe that this sort of old money still existed in the twenty-first century. Inherited wealth magnified by contemporary plutocratic greed.

They stepped through French doors onto a wide grey-slab terrace. The smell of freshly cut grass mixed with the aroma of the flowers that flourished in the beds edging the stones. Beyond it, standing on the close-clipped lawn, was the source of the gunfire. Lancelot Oxnard-Clarke sighted a shotgun.

'Pull!' he yelled.

Another man in a suit pressed a button on a remote, and distant traps, concealed in patches of long grass that lay beneath two oak trees, flung a pair of clays into the air. The first of the simultaneous pair was a whippet-fast battue that flew through the sky edge-on, smiling briefly as it showed its face. Oxnard-Clarke shattered it with his first shot, before moving swiftly to the second target, a high looper that was plummeting towards the earth. He broke it just as cleanly as the first.

'Your Lordship,' Alexis said.

Oxnard-Clarke turned and took the plugs out of his ears.

'Mr Pearce,' he said, pocketing the spent cartridges that were ejected as he opened his gun. 'I hear you have a proposal for me.'

He looked every inch the titled peer. From his easy swagger

and confident smile to the tailored shooting tweeds that hung perfectly from his lean frame. Pearce longed to take the man's gun and . . . but there was no point fantasizing. Even if he could scavenge shells, the two-cartridge limit of the over-and-under shotgun wouldn't be enough to take care of Viscount Purbeck and the three bodyguards. It would be a suicidal move and Pearce wasn't ready to die just yet.

'Thank you, Alexis,' Oxnard-Clarke said.

Alexis gave a wan smile and returned to the house.

Oxnard-Clarke studied Pearce, who glowered back.

'I don't know what you have in mind,' the viscount said finally. 'But I'd like to make you an offer. I want you to join our family.'

'I'm a little too brown for your gang,' Pearce smiled.

'True, your mixed heritage isn't ideal, but if you think this is about the colour of a person's skin, you misunderstand us entirely,' Oxnard-Clarke explained. 'This is about trust, Mr Pearce. Look at what the world has become. Chaos reigns. No one can be sure of anything. Why? Because the old structures have been torn down. The pillars that kept society standing have been dishonoured and destroyed. Family, religion, class,' his rant gathered pace, 'teachers, priests, royalty, politicians, journalists, bankers, all discredited. All ruined. Where do we turn for heroes?' He took a breath and settled himself. 'Are you a loyal man?'

Pearce said nothing.

The slightest flicker of a sneer crossed Oxnard-Clarke's face. 'You might think you are, but what exactly are you loyal to? Let's say a socialist government came to power and instituted labour camps along the communist model. Would you be loyal to such a government?'

Pearce wasn't interested in playing the man's games, but Oxnard-Clarke continued regardless. 'Of course you wouldn't. Because you're not loyal to a government. You're loyal to Britain, to an idea that goes beyond any fallible human being. We come and go like dust on the wind, but there are things that are not, and must never be, regarded as transient.'

He gestured theatrically. 'We hold these truths to be self-evident. That's what the Americans say, isn't it? A truth that needs no further explanation. Loyalty, tradition, security, freedom. And how far must we go to defend these self-evident truths? Well, sometimes even patriots must engage in treason. We each have to make our own decision about when such steps are necessary. I see what's happening around me and I say such steps are needed now. This country has been taken over by people who are interested in nothing but satisfying their own greed. They don't value any of the things that make Britain great.'

Pearce smiled wryly. Hearing a man who lived in such luxury decrying the greed of others was nothing short of absurd. 'You seem to have enough money of your own. If this is about ideology, why do you need Vasylyk's?'

'He's a traditionalist, like me. Why wouldn't his money and connections be welcome?'

'Because he's a criminal, a killer.'

'And what would your enemies say of you, Mr Pearce? You of all people should know that good and bad are narrative constructs. There is no morality. Only necessity. My people are loyalists, Mr Pearce. My family has helped protect and shape this country for hundreds of years. I am the land. I am this nation. It dwells in me. I represent order. I come from the old world, from a system you can trust. One that made society stable and safe. This is about tradition. I will do whatever it takes.'

'Even if it involves spreading hate,' Pearce remarked. 'Even if you have to kill.'

'We'll both do that if we need to. But you're wrong about hate. Race doesn't come into it.'

'Until you need it to,' Pearce countered. 'This game has been played before. You don't see people, you see labels. You're the acceptable face of hate. You start talking about tradition, honour and patriotism, but before long your followers are rounding up those with the the "wrong" labels and putting them in camps. Subversive, radical, Jew, Muslim, brown, black, and on and on, until the only ones left are those who look and think like you.'

'Unfounded assumptions, Mr Pearce,' Oxnard-Clarke responded. 'And to prove how unfounded they are, I'm extending you an invitation. I don't care about the colour of your skin, or who sired you. I'm interested in what's in your heart. We could use a man of your talents.'

'Is that why you tried to have me killed?'

'You were a threat. You would have done the same.' Oxnard-Clarke smiled. '*Audentis Fortuna iuvat.*'

'Fortune favours the bold,' Pearce sneered. 'You're not bold.'

'You're a surprising man, for one of such humble beginnings. Where did you learn Latin?'

Pearce refused to rise to the bait.

'Did you teach yourself? Well done. I can't remember when I learned Latin, or Greek for that matter,' Oxnard-Clarke said. 'Unlike you, I'm not pretending to be something I'm not. I didn't acquire these trappings, Mr Pearce, they are part of me. I am the standard to which men like you aspire.'

There was a kernel of truth in Oxnard-Clarke's words and Pearce hated him for it. He had taught himself Latin to read the original texts that were part of his philosophy degree. He could have relied on translations, but he wanted to prove to himself that he was the equal of people like Oxnard-Clarke, people who'd been handed the world. He burned with frustration and eyed the gun greedily.

'I can feel your eyes on my gun.' He held it out. 'Here. Take it. It's rather lovely.'

Pearce felt the three bodyguards stiffen as he took the empty shotgun. He closed the barrel and studied the intricate side engraving, which featured what he assumed was the Purbeck family crest: an eagle flying above a lion and unicorn.

'Boxall and Edmiston,' Oxnard-Clarke said. 'One of the finest gunmakers in the world. A blend of ancient craft and modern technology. The old and new brought together to create perfection. Much like us?'

'Don't kid yourself. You're just old. The world has been infected by your kind before, and it shrugged you off. It will do so again,' Pearce replied, returning the gun. 'Sutton is no use to you any more. With or without me, my people will release the information we have tying him to Progress Britain.'

'The news moves so fast these days,' Oxnard-Clarke remarked. 'Your interventions have forced a slight alteration to our schedule. By this time tomorrow, the world will have changed.'

He's bringing forward his plans, Pearce thought. *Whatever Black 13 has planned, it's happening in the next twenty-four hours.*

'How many innocent lives are you prepared to take?' Pearce asked, fishing blindly.

'Just what did McClusky tell you? Maybe something. Maybe

nothing.' Oxnard-Clarke hesitated before continuing. 'What matters isn't the number of people who die, but who they are and how they fall. The death of a single man started the First World War. Two thousand three hundred sailors were enough to bring America into the Second World War. Nineteen zealots, four planes and three thousand deaths were sufficient to change the world on September eleventh. We're not trying to do anything as bold as start a war, Mr Pearce. This is about moving pieces around the board. Creating the right conditions for me and my people to flourish. No chess game is ever won in a single move.'

'This is about Sutton. You want him promoted,' Pearce guessed.

'Imagine if someone in this country had the strength to stand up to all the foreign ideology we've been forced to accept over the years. A minister who would ban the preaching of foreign religions in British prisons, the dissemination of extremist literature, who wouldn't be afraid to recommend internment for those who weren't loyal,' Oxnard-Clarke said. 'You've served this country. You know boldness is what wins wars.'

'We're not at war,' Pearce objected.

'We are. You just don't realize it yet.'

They wanted Sutton to become Minister of State for Security and Economic Crime, that much was clear, but Pearce puzzled over what they could be planning that would put Oxnard-Clarke's ally in one of the country's most important law enforcement jobs. Something that would shift public opinion and make it impossible for the Prime Minister to appoint anyone other than a fierce law-and-order candidate. It had to be an attack of some kind. Something big enough to capture the country's attention. And as Oxnard-Clarke had suggested, if the attack was big enough the Progress Britain scandal would become background noise, getting drowned out by national grief and the clamour for revenge.

'What's it to be, Mr Pearce? Are you going to continue trying to fight the inevitable? Or are you going to do what's right for this country?'

'I've spent my life as an outsider,' Pearce said honestly. For most of his childhood he'd desperately longed to find somewhere to belong until he'd realized there was no tribe for him. He was destined never to fit in. 'Too brown, too white, too poor, too rich. The wrong school, the wrong background. Standing alone gives you a certain perspective. You can see people who join crowds being manipulated by arseholes like you. They get used and eventually they get betrayed.'

'I admire your honesty, Mr Pearce,' Oxnard-Clarke said. 'You do know it will cost you your life?'

Before Pearce could answer, a dark-haired paunchy man in a black suit approached subserviently.

'Excuse me, sir,' he said. 'There are some police officers here. They've asked to see you and a Mr Scott Pearce.'

Oxnard-Clarke gave Pearce a puzzled look. He handed his gun to the servant, who stepped aside.

'What have you done, Mr Pearce?' Oxnard-Clarke asked.

He signalled his bodyguards, who pushed Pearce inside. They walked through the grand house to the huge front doors. Oxnard-Clarke led them outside to the portico that stood at the top of a broad flight of steps. Three police cars were parked on the long sweeping driveway in front of the huge house, and six uniformed officers gathered in a small group at the foot of the steps. The most senior, a chief superintendent, started up towards the house the moment he saw Oxnard-Clarke.

'Lord Purbeck,' he said. 'I'm sorry to trouble you, but we need to ask you some questions.'

'What for? What's this about?' Oxnard-Clarke responded haughtily.

'Haven't you seen the news, Your Lordship?' the police officer asked. 'There's a story about a . . . well . . . a sex ring in London. You've been named as one of those involved, Your Lordship. The other man named is someone called Artem Vasylyk. He was found dead today, my Lord. Shot.'

Pearce was surprised by news of Vasylyk's death, but he would always remember the moment Oxnard-Clarke's confident veneer crumbled. The Viscount looked from the officer to Pearce, his fury building.

'And we've had a call, my Lord,' the officer added. 'It came when we were on our way out. Saying that a Mr Scott Pearce is being held at Purbeck House against his will. Would that be you, sir?'

The question was directed at Pearce.

He nodded. 'I'm Scott Pearce.'

Oxnard-Clarke laughed, but it was hollow. 'Mr Pearce is no prisoner.'

'If you'd like to leave, Mr Pearce, my officers can take you,' the chief said.

Pearce stared at Oxnard-Clarke. 'I'd like that very much. One of the women, one of the victims of the ring, is in the house,' he said. 'I'd like her to come with me.'

Oxnard-Clarke could hardly conceal his anger.

'If she'd like to go, I'm sure his Lordship wouldn't object,' the chief superintendent said.

Oxnard-Clarke closed in on Pearce. 'None of this will make the slightest bit of difference,' he growled. 'I will be out within the hour. You really think McClusky and Sutton are our only allies? All this will be lost in what follows. And then we'll find you.'

Pearce glared at the arrogant man, as two of the constables climbed the steps and gently ushered Oxnard-Clarke towards the waiting vehicles. The peer said nothing more as he was put in the back of one of the patrol cars, but he didn't need to; even at a distance Pearce could sense the man's ire radiating in angry pulses.

Pearce turned for the house, but saw that Alexis had already come to the door.

'These officers will give us a lift,' he said. 'You coming?'

Alexis nodded and hurried down the steps to join Pearce. The three bodyguards eyed each other uncertainly, but did nothing as Pearce took her to the nearest car.

Moments later, Pearce and Alexis sat looking through the rear window at the grand house shrinking into the distance.

Chapter 52

Purbeck House was twenty miles from Bristol, and when Pearce and Alexis made it clear they didn't want to press any charges or be interviewed about their experiences, the police dropped them off at Parkway Station. Pearce left Alexis on the platform and used a payphone and the proxy dialling system to call Leila. She was relieved to hear he was alive and free. He gave her the details of his train and she assured him someone would be there at the other end. Pearce returned to Alexis and they managed to catch the 21.50 to London Paddington. Alexis was silent, brooding, and Pearce could only imagine what she'd endured for fear that her mother might be tortured and killed.

'I want to destroy him,' she said at last. 'Now that everyone knows what he's been doing to us, I want him ruined.' She paused. 'I know things. Things I've heard from him. From the other men who assaulted me. I want to tell you. I can give you the names of his friends in government. The things he funds. The people who work for him. Politicians, business-men, police.'

Pearce recognized the fury of a victim out for revenge. She would almost certainly have valuable information, and she had the motive to share it. 'Let me think about it,' he said.

They sat in silence for a while. Two of the eight passengers in their carriage made trips to the toilet, but otherwise the late train was tranquil and calm, the only noise the rhythmic pulse of the wheels turning and the intermittent beat of them passing over the tiny gaps between each rail. Pearce weighed his options. He was almost out of time. Oxnard-Clarke had been clear: Black 13 would strike within the next twenty-four hours. Trusting Alexis was a risk, but he didn't have any other choice.

'Purbeck is planning something. Something very bad,' Pearce said at last. 'I can't figure out what it is. At least two people have been killed to cover it up.'

'I don't know anything about it,' Alexis said apologetically. 'But some of the people I can name might.'

'So tell me. Who are they?'

'Here?' she asked incredulously. 'I've been through enough. I don't need to take stupid risks. Get me somewhere safe and I'll tell you everything. I want to warn my mum too. Make sure she can take steps to protect herself before any of this breaks.'

'How do I know I can trust you?' Pearce asked.

'Because I'm trusting you,' Alexis replied. 'I'm putting my life in your hands. There's no one on this planet who hates that man more than me. The things he's made me do . . .' she tailed off.

'OK,' he said. 'I'll take you somewhere safe.'

When they arrived at Paddington, Pearce and Alexis found Wollerton waiting in the drop-off area in a silver Honda Civic.

'She's going to tell us everything she knows,' Pearce explained. 'We've got less than twenty-four hours to stop them.'

Wollerton nodded. 'Good to have you back. I owe you.'

'You'd have done the same,' Pearce told him.

'I'm not so sure. I think my hero days might be behind me.'

The two men grinned.

'Come on. We need to get moving,' Pearce said.

They reached Vyner Road soon after midnight and Wollerton parked near the house. He killed the engine and opened the glove compartment. Pearce was surprised to see two hand grenades.

'The bastards booby-trapped the car at the fort,' Wollerton explained as he grabbed them. 'I've been carrying them around since I stole this one.' He tapped the Civic's dashboard.

Pearce turned to see Alexis glancing nervously at the grenades. 'You're safe,' he assured her. 'Let's get inside.'

When they reached their base of operations, Wollerton knocked on the door and it was quickly opened by Wayne, who greeted Pearce warmly.

'Good to have you back,' Wayne said, patting him on the shoulder.

Wayne was puzzled to see Alexis follow Pearce and Wollerton inside. She kept her eyes down and sheepishly made her way into the kitchen.

As they entered, Melody approached. 'I'm so glad you're alive,' she told Pearce.

Wollerton removed the grenades from his pocket and placed them on the table.

'A present from the guys who took Scott,' he explained. 'They were stuck to the car. I almost didn't find the second one.'

Wayne shook his head and whistled softly. 'Close call.'

Leila was seated at her workstation. She didn't stand. 'Good to see you, *khawaga*,' she said. 'Bringing back strays?' she asked, indicating Alexis.

'This is Alexis Tippet-Jones. She's agreed to tell us what she knows about Viscount Purbeck's activities,' Pearce said. 'We need all the help we can get. Whatever they've got planned is happening in the next twenty-four hours.'

'I'm sorry for intruding,' Alexis added. 'But I want to stop him. And I want him to suffer.'

'We're going to debrief upstairs,' Pearce told Leila. 'See if Alexis knows anything that will put us on the right track.'

'What did you do with the locator beacon?' Leila asked.

'I ate it,' Pearce replied.

Leila grimaced. 'That's what I thought. I'm going to have to fry you.'

Pearce frowned quizzically.

'It's unlikely, but it might occur to them to look for the signal. We have to disable it, which means I've either got to cut you open to get it out, or use a high-voltage electrical pulse to disable it.'

'OK. I think I'd rather be fried than cut open. If it's all the same to you.' Pearce smiled. 'Grab me when you're ready.'

Chapter 53

Before Pearce started to debrief Alexis, Melody had suggested going to the police or security services, but Pearce shared what Oxnard-Clarke had said about having other powerful allies. They couldn't be sure who to trust. Wayne and Wollerton had agreed. At the very least Alexis might be able to give them a better idea who to avoid.

While Leila prepared to 'fry' him, Pearce and the others took Alexis upstairs and listened to her recount her experiences of abuse at the hands of powerful men. After twenty minutes, Leila leaned into the room and interrupted.

'I need to talk to you,' she said sombrely.

Pearce noticed she was pointedly avoiding making eye contact with Alexis.

'I'll be right back,' he told the others.

He followed Leila downstairs to the kitchen, and she led him to her computer.

'We've got a real problem,' she said. 'I ran a check on the SatSys interface to see if the locator you swallowed is still transmitting,' she gestured to a satellite image on her computer. It showed the house on Vyner Road, and to Pearce's dismay he saw that there were not one but two locator signals. 'You're not the only one who's bugged.'

Leila switched windows and brought up a scanned copy of an old document.

'When I found the signal, I ran a more detailed background check on Alexis,' she said. 'I found this. I'm kicking myself for not checking her out properly before, but there was so much to . . .'

'It's OK. You're doing your best,' Pearce assured her, but his eyes widened when he realized what he was looking at: a scanned copy of an old marriage certificate.

'Remember how Alexis's birth certificate was blank?' Leila asked. 'It didn't give a father's name? Her mother is now married to Philippe Durand, a French industrialist who likes to claim he's descended from aristocracy, but before that, she was married to Lancelot Bayard Oxnard-Clarke, Viscount Purbeck, Lord of the Manor and King of the Racists.'

Pearce struggled to take in the news.

'Look at the dates,' Leila continued. 'The ceremony was three months before Alexis was born.'

'Fuck!' Pearce said, his mind racing. Why would Oxnard-Clarke pimp his own daughter? The answer hit him instantly. It was the perfect cover. Hide a loyalist in a group of sexual abuse victims and she'd be a valuable operative. Most people, Pearce included, would only see her as a victim. They'd be disarmed by her suffering, and caught off-guard – she'd be able to get them to trust her.

He bolted from the kitchen and ran up the narrow staircase, barrelling into the front bedroom, where he found Alexis talking to Melody, Wayne and Wollerton. She hesitated when Pearce strode across the room, and retreated as he bore down on her. She cried out when he reached for her dress.

'Scott!' Melody yelled. 'What are you doing?'

Pearce didn't respond. He tore the collar of Alexis's dress and felt deflated when he saw nothing but unblemished flesh.

'What's the matter with you?' Alexis cried.

'Where is it?' Pearce demanded. 'Where?'

'Where's what?' Alexis replied. 'You're scaring me.'

'What the hell's going on?' Wollerton asked.

Leila entered, her face stony, her eyes burning. She held a radio frequency reader and pointed it at Alexis. 'There's a second signal,' she told the others.

Alexis was mystified. 'What signal? What are you talking about?'

Leila moved the handheld device, which beeped with increasing intensity as she brought it close to Alexis's left shoulder. Leila pulled at her dress, and Pearce was horrified to see a small lump embedded in Alexis's back, where the shoulder connects to the arm.

'What have you done?' he demanded to know.

'*Ya bent il kalb!*' Leila yelled, and Pearce grabbed her as she lunged for Alexis. Her eyes blazed with pure hatred and she hurled a stream of invective at Alexis as he held her.

'What?' Alexis said, backing away. 'What are you talking about?' She craned to see what everyone was looking at, but it was tucked out of sight. 'What is it?' she asked.

Was it possible she didn't know? Even if they could have implanted it without her knowledge, surely she would have felt the lump?

'Take her,' he said to Wayne and Wollerton, and as they clasped Leila's shoulders, Pearce bounded to the window and peered behind the curtain.

'What's going on?' Alexis cried. 'I don't understand what I've done.'

Pearce's heart thumped when he saw two dark vans mount the pavement outside. The rear doors swung open and two squads of Black 13 mercenaries streamed out. Whether Alexis had been a witting or unwitting party, she'd led death to their door. These men where here to neutralize them all.

'We've got to go now!' he yelled.

Ignoring Alexis, he pushed the others out of the room and barrelled across the landing towards the back bedroom.

'Don't leave me! Please!' Alexis implored. 'They're going to kill me.'

Victim or not, the tracking device meant they couldn't take her with them, and when Alexis realized she was being abandoned, she fell to her knees sobbing.

Pearce hesitated when he saw Leila and Wayne heading downstairs.

'I can't leave Vasylyk's laptop,' Leila insisted.

It took a moment for Pearce to register the significance of what she'd just said. Leila had Vasylyk's laptop. The man who'd been killed earlier that day.

'We need weapons,' Wayne added.

He was right. Pearce had seen what was coming at them from the front, but had no idea what lay in the alley at the end of the garden. He nodded and Leila and Wayne raced downstairs.

'Come on,' he said to Melody and Wollerton, leading them across the landing.

The sound of a large crash from below set his heart thundering.

Leila shuffled down the stairs as quickly as she could, totally confused by Alexis's denials. Leila's instincts were normally razor sharp and they told her that Alexis's shock was genuine. She didn't know about the tracker, which made their abandonment of her all the more brutal. But if they escaped the house alive, they couldn't risk bringing a tracking device with them. Wayne pushed past Leila and raced across the hall into the kitchen as the front door was blown off its hinges. She turned to see masked men in camouflage gear and body armour storm the house. The man on point raised his rifle and took aim at her. She braced for the shot, but a report sounded nearby and the gunman fell back with a hole drilled in his head. Leila looked behind her to see Wayne standing in the kitchen doorway, pistol in hand.

'Come on!' he yelled, firing at the others streaming in.

Leila moved as fast as she could, tumbling towards Wayne, as gunfire bit into the walls around her. The air clouded with dust and acrid gunsmoke. Wayne grabbed her and thrust her behind him, his gun spitting loudly. She fell into the safety of the kitchen.

There was a thud and a groan and Leila turned to see Wayne peering down at a hole in his chest. He grinned like a fool as he registered the horror on Leila's face. They both knew the gushing wound was fatal. Wayne dropped his gun and reached his hands into his pockets, producing the two grenades Wollerton had placed on the kitchen table.

'No!' Leila cried.

Wayne nodded, his face somehow no longer human, more plastic, like a doll's. Leila had seen the transformation before, on the faces of friends and family who knew death was imminent. Wayne disappeared through the doorway, staggering into the hallway on his faltering legs, as his body gave its last to his desperate ploy. Gunfire crackled around the place, rattling off the walls like so many angry slaps.

Leila's eyes filled with tears. She picked up Vasylyk's laptop on her way across the room and shoved it into her bag along with the radio frequency reader. She slung her bag over her shoulder and shuffled through the back door into the overgrown garden just as the grenades exploded. Leila felt searing heat on the back of her neck as the shockwave picked her up and sent her hurtling into the weeds.

The explosion rocked the house, and behind them, Pearce saw the floorboards burst open and licks of flame burn through the ragged holes, as though hell was rising from below.

'We've got to go,' Wollerton said.

Pearce nodded and opened the bedroom window. He was immediately greeted by gunfire. A third van had crashed through the fence at the bottom of the garden. Three members of Black 13 were stationed around the vehicle, one in the garden, two behind the van in the alleyway, their guns trained on the window, their muzzles flashing with each shot. Just before he ducked, Pearce caught sight of Leila dazed on the ground outside the back door.

As bullets thudded into the brickwork, Pearce ran over the splintered gap in the floor to the mirror that hung behind the door and kicked it. The glass smashed and he picked up three large pieces.

'What are you doing?' Wollerton asked.

Pearce didn't waste time answering. He ran to the window, jumped on the sill and leaped into the garden as the gunfire resumed. Landing in spiky bramble, Pearce ignored the pain and sprang up immediately, hurling one of the shards of mirror at the nearest shooter. The projectile missed its mark, but the guy ducked to avoid it, and Pearce ran forward, dodging the other two shooters. He threw a second shard, and this one caught the man in the neck. He waved his gun wildly, clutching at his throat with his other hand, but Pearce was on him. He kicked the man in the stomach, dropped the third shard and grabbed the gun. Flipping it round, he fired two shots into the man's groin, below his body armour.

The two shooters behind the van took cover as Pearce opened up on them, but he played the angles, running to the rear of the van, a move that kept him out of sight of the man at the front, but gave him a clear line on the guy to the rear. Pearce took the shot the moment he caught a glimpse of uniform, and the man at the back of the van staggered away from the vehicle with a wounded shoulder. Pearce finished him off with a bullet to the head. He grabbed the man's pistol and turned it on the last Black 13 operative, who was positioned near the bonnet. They traded shots, both using the van for cover. Then the man's gun fell silent and Pearce heard a guttural cry. He stood up to see Wollerton burying a shard of mirror deep in the man's throat. Behind him, Melody jumped from the bedroom window into the garden.

'Where's Wayne?' Pearce asked, peering into the blazing kitchen. He could see torches shining through the smoke and flames.

'Come on! We've got to go!' Wollerton yelled, gesturing at the torchlight. He grabbed Pearce and pulled him towards the van.

Pearce glanced over his shoulder and saw Melody pick up a large handbag that lay beside Leila. She helped the Syrian to her feet. Wollerton bundled Pearce into the passenger seat and ran round the van as Melody dragged Leila over. Pearce sat, stunned, unable to take his eyes off the burning house. Wollerton jumped into the driver's seat and Melody pulled open the side door. She pushed Leila inside and rolled onto the flatbed, yelling, 'Go! Go! Go!'

Wollerton had already started the engine. He flung the van into gear and the vehicle surged forward, rocking wildly as it drove over the body of the Black 13 operative he'd stabbed. As the van raced forwards, bullets peppered the bodywork and Pearce saw a trio of mercenaries standing near the back door, targeting the vehicle. Within moments, the van turned a bend in the alleyway and was out of range, racing through the darkness.

Wayne hadn't made it. Pearce was crushed by grief, bewilderment and guilt, but then came a familiar sensation. It tore through him like a raging inferno. He was consumed by the furious desire for revenge.

Chapter 54

Leila could hardly see. Tears flooded her vision, distorting everything. Wayne had given his life for hers, and his sacrifice had broken her. She'd lived through horror and endured the loss of so many loved ones, but this terrible kindness was too much and she sobbed freely.

They'd ditched the van a couple of miles from the house. The sound of sirens had filled the night, and they'd passed police cars, fire engines and ambulances en route to the scene. Leila had sobbed uncontrollably as Pearce had hailed a black cab. She hadn't even registered where they were, just some busy thoroughfare that was lined with shops.

Now, sitting in the back of the taxi, which was making its way across North London, she realized she wasn't the only one weeping. Melody was also crying, her face ashen, her eyes fixed on some distant point. Wollerton's brow was furrowed, his face stony and, although he was the only one of the trio who met Leila's gaze, he couldn't hold it for long. Leila wiped her tears and looked at Pearce, who sat on one of the fold-down jump seats, his back to the driver, his head turned towards the window. His jaw was locked, set so tight she could see his muscles bulge as he clenched his teeth. His brimming eyes weren't distant or wistful, they blazed with anger. She could feel fury radiating off the man, his hunched form poised to wreak terrible vengeance, like some risen devil. He glared at her, his searing gaze so raw she couldn't hold it. She glanced down at the floor, and there, on the toe of Pearce's shoe, she saw a dirty splatter of blood. Leila shuddered and her tears sprang afresh.

The cab deposited them in an eerie street in Archway. Leila could hear the distant sounds of the city, but the street itself was quiet, its residents hidden in the dark flats and houses that lined either side. Pearce led them into a terraced house halfway along the street and then took them inside the flat which occupied the bottom two storeys of the building. Leila's tears had subsided and been replaced by shuddering sobs that came and went like the tide. No one had said anything during the journey and still the silence continued. Melody followed Leila and Wollerton into a living room, but Pearce disappeared along a hallway and went downstairs into the basement.

Wollerton closed a pair of old curtains and switched on a ceramic table lamp. The room smelled of musty neglect. The furniture was a motley collection of items that looked as though they'd been discarded from a charity shop, the sort of tatty things that were beyond sale. Wollerton looked around and left the room. Moments later, Leila followed.

'You can't do this,' she heard Wollerton say, his voice rising from somewhere below. 'You're not thinking straight.' He sounded exasperated.

Leila followed his voice into the hallway, past a bathroom that was shrouded in darkness and down a flight of creaking stairs.

'Now isn't the time to indulge yourself, Scott,' Wollerton said. 'We've got a job to do.'

Leila reached the basement corridor and went into a bedroom that lay directly opposite the stairs. She found Pearce loading a holdall with weapons and equipment taken from a large metal locker he'd deposited on the bed. Wollerton stood at his shoulder, his disapproval obvious. Leila sat on the edge of the bed.

'You're angry,' she said. 'We all are. But we can't afford a vendetta. We need to find out what they're planning and we have to stop it.'

'You stop it,' Pearce responded coldly. 'I'm going to find Purbeck and make him answer for Wayne and Fozz. There's a debt to be paid.'

'The debt can wait,' Wollerton protested. 'Whatever they've got planned, if they pull it off, they win. We can't let that happen.'

'I'll make him tell me,' Pearce countered.

'And if he doesn't?' Leila asked.

Pearce wavered. 'I need you to fry me. Kill the tracer,' he said at last.

Leila sighed.

'Do it,' he said, 'or I'll do it myself.'

Leila reached into her bag for her stun gun and the radio frequency reader. She adjusted the settings on the former to reduce the voltage. Pearce came close and lifted his top to reveal his toned abdomen.

'Do it,' he told her.

Leila shook her head at the stubborn man and then hit him with 10,000 volts. The shock sent him staggering back, but he remained conscious. 'Shit,' he snarled. 'Check it.'

Leila switched on the radio frequency reader, which came up blank as she waved it over him.

'Good,' Pearce said.

'Scott,' Wollerton began.

'I'm doing this,' Pearce cut him off.

'What did McClusky tell you?' Leila asked, and she was gratified to see Pearce pause.

' "Darvaza is Hazelmere Darke",' he replied, and resumed what he was doing.

Leila could see body armour, magazines of ammunition, guns and scopes filling the holdall.

'Hazelmere Darke is a town in Derbyshire. It was a plague centre during the Black Death,' Wollerton said. 'Winston, my son, did a school project on it. He was fascinated by the gore. We heard all about the gruesome things that happened there. You know how kids are.'

Pearce continued packing, until Wollerton took his arm and held him fast. 'I know you're in pain, Scott. I know exactly how much it hurts, but you can't do this. You can't let Wayne die for nothing. You can't let the bastards win. We have to stop them. Whatever it is they're planning, we've got to stop them.'

Pearce glared at Wollerton with an intensity that made Leila worry he was beyond conventional concepts of friend and foe. She looked nervously at the weapons in the bag beside him.

'Don't do it like this,' Wollerton pleaded. 'Let's win. Then you can do whatever needs to be done to Purbeck.'

The weight of the moment seemed to press the air from the room. The walls closed in, and Leila found herself holding her breath.

Finally, very slowly and very deliberately, Pearce nodded.

'We should go to Hazelmere Darke,' Wollerton said.

'You think something that is going to reshape Britain will take place in a town in Derbyshire?' Pearce challenged.

'It's the best we've got,' Wollerton replied. 'McClusky was trying to tell you something.'

Pearce considered the point. 'McClusky was a traitor and a liar.'

'You were there. You can tell whether he was trying to make good,' Wollerton countered. 'I think he was.'

Pearce thought for a while. 'OK,' he said at last. 'I'm going alone . . .' he held up his hand to silence Wollerton's protest. 'I want you and Leila to work on Vasylyk's laptop.'

'I'm no technician,' Wollerton remarked. 'I'm a field operative.'

'Retired,' Pearce responded flatly, and Wollerton shifted angrily. 'You're a strategist and we need brains thrown at this. And what if you're wrong? What if it isn't Hazelmere Darke? What if it's another target? What if it's London or somewhere else? You have weapons,' he indicated the locker, which was still stuffed with gear, 'and you can deploy from here to the city much faster than I'll be able to get back from Derbyshire.'

Wollerton thought for a moment before nodding.

'The Ghostlinks, all our gear was in the kitchen. It's gone. We're going to have to use phones to communicate,' Leila said.

'Here,' he said, pulling a couple of old mobiles from the locker. He tossed one to Leila. 'They only have each other's number in their memories.'

Pearce pocketed the other phone, slung the holdall over his shoulder and turned for the door.

'*Khawaga*,' Leila said, 'whatever you find, be careful.'

'*Liqutil wahash, anta tursil al shaytan,*' Pearce replied, before leaving the room.

Leila heard him run upstairs and, moments later, the front door slammed. She looked at Wollerton. 'You know what he said?' she asked.

He nodded. 'If you want to kill a monster, you send the devil.'

Chapter 55

The curtain muted the sunshine, keeping the world at bay. Leila rose from her spot on the cracked leather sofa to stretch her legs and ease the pain. She peered beyond the veil and saw local residents making their way along the street, heading towards the tube as the working day began. She envied the simplicity of their lives.

Leila returned to her seat. Wollerton sat next to her. They'd been working for hours. Melody was asleep on a chair by the archway that led to the small kitchen. Leila had suggested one of the beds downstairs, but the lawyer had been in a terrible state and obviously preferred the presence of others. Wayne's death had hit Melody hardest. She hadn't said anything, but the hollowness of grief was there for all to see. Leila didn't know exactly what had happened between them, but it was clear from Melody's anguish that the brave man had meant something to her. Whatever possibilities had stood before them would forever lie unfulfilled.

Even as she thought of him, fresh tears formed in Leila's eyes and she envied Melody the release of sleep. She couldn't afford the luxury and had been hunched over Vasylyk's laptop since soon after Pearce had gone. Wollerton had spent the early hours on an ancient machine he'd found in Pearce's bedroom. Both machines were connected to the web by 4G dongles, which was a desperate move on Leila's part. The devices were as easily traceable as the mobile phone Pearce had given her, but they were up against it and had to take risks. If they did nothing, failure was certain.

Leila hadn't intended to reveal that the laptop was Vasylyk's, but there had been no other way to justify risking her life to retrieve the machine from the safe house kitchen. So far no one had questioned the circumstances in which it had come into her possession and she hadn't decided whether she would tell the truth if she was ever challenged. She would be confessing to a killing, which at best was self-defence, but in the eyes of the wrong judge, might be seen as premeditated murder. There was no need to share information that might one day be used against her.

Leila had managed to unlock Vasylyk's machine and had discovered thousands of files within, all coded transaction records. Wollerton was running a decryption program on Pearce's old computer, using a selection of Vasylyk's files to look for common features that might give a clue to the code that had been used to encrypt them. While he tweaked the program parameters, Leila searched Vasylyk's laptop for the encryption key. She'd been looking for hours. If she could just find it . . .

She came to the photos folder, which contained only a single image: a picture of Oxnard-Clarke and Vasylyk standing with their arms around each other's shoulders, beside a neon-lit bar. Leila was about to move on, when she noticed a tiny distorted section of the image, a perfect square in the bottom right corner, no more than a few pixels wide. Leila opened the image code and scrolled through the reams of data that told the computer how to display the photograph, and there, halfway into the file, she saw a section that immediately stood out. It wasn't a run of JFIF code, which is how a JPEG file is typically created, it was something else: an encryption sequence. More than that, it was a key. Leila could see a long series of letters and numbers, and then the binary code identifier of every symbol on a computer keyboard.

'I've found it,' she said.

Leila selected the encryption key and copied it into a DOS window she'd prepared. She hit return and the simple program she'd created came to life. A solitary search bar opened in a browser window and she typed Progress Britain into it. The search immediately rewarded her with hundreds of hits. She opened one file and then another.

. 'These are bank transfers,' she said, looking at the IBAN, or international transfer numbers. 'Vasylyk was giving Bayard Madison instructions to send money around the world.'

'Why the secrecy?' Wollerton asked.

'There are hundreds of payments to Progress Britain and its affiliates,' Leila replied, studying more records.

She typed in the words Hazelmere Darke, but the search request drew a blank.

A window flashed on the screen of Vasylyk's laptop. It was a message written in Cyrillic, with a data input field. The text read, *Enter Password Now.*

'Shit,' she said. 'It's activated something.' A clock appeared next to the window, counting down from sixty. 'It's a failsafe. We don't have long.'

'What about Darvaza?' Wollerton suggested.

Leila minimized the countdown and the Cyrillic message, and typed Darvaza into the search bar. She was relieved to see four results pop up and she opened them all. They showed large payments to a single account, totalling a combined three million dollars.

'Get the IBAN number,' Leila told Wollerton, who furiously typed the twenty-digit string into his aged laptop.

Leila opened the Cyrillic window and felt nothing but frustration as she looked at the password box. There was so much information on this machine. If she had more time, she could . . . the screen went black and the machine died. Whatever failsafe had been built into it had kicked in and Leila guessed that the hard drive had been wiped. Angry at her impotence, she put the machine on the floor. She would try to salvage what she could at a later date, but right now they had to find out what was special about Darvaza.

'Booby trap?' Wollerton asked.

Leila nodded. 'The moment anyone opens the files, the machine asks for another password. If it doesn't get it, it destroys the hard drive. Let's see what Darvaza is.' She held out her hands and Wollerton gave her the old laptop. She opened Google Chrome and typed the IBAN number into a branch identifier. It came back with a bank in Ashgabat, the capital of Turkmenistan. She found the bank, Turkmen Commercial and International, and ran a search for any customers who used the bank. She was rewarded with a number of hits, and as she scrolled down the search results, she saw a link to a pdf file, a terms-of-trade notice from Ashgabat Quality Building and Construction, and there in the small print were the company's bank account details. The IBAN number matched the one in Vasylyk's file.

'Why did Vasylyk send three million dollars to a construction company in Turkmenistan?' Leila asked.

She opened another Chrome window and entered an

address that would take her somewhere very dangerous indeed. 'Wake her up,' she said, indicating Melody. 'We're going to have to leave soon. I'm hacking into MI6's satellite surveillance archive. Without protection, they'll be alerted to the unauthorized access and be able to locate this machine within minutes.'

'Is there no other—' Wollerton began.

Leila cut him off. 'If they've been doing something in Turkmenistan, my guess is McClusky will have been watching. I'm going to access his search logs.'

Wollerton rose and gently roused Melody. Leila looked at the black window that was open on the laptop. It was an unbranded, blank screen save for a log-on form that didn't even mark whether the boxes were for usernames or passwords. She knew that the first box was for a numeric code, the second for a username and that there was a third, hidden input field further down the page for a password. Leila entered the log-on details of another analyst, an entitled shit who'd gone to work for the Box, Brian Kendall, and was relieved when the system accepted them. She was inside Six's satellite information system and she queried Dominic McClusky's search history. She got hundreds of hits, some of which related to Turkmenistan, and judging from the access history, McClusky had studied the Turkmen images dozens of times.

'Get your stuff ready,' Leila told Wollerton and Melody. 'It won't take long. They'll send the police first.'

She opened the satellite imagery McClusky had taken of Turkmenistan. The first pictures were high-altitude, low-resolution images of a desert. She opened more, and each image zoomed in, providing more detail of a smaller area. She clicked through until a small village appeared, a huge gas field beyond it, and to the south something else, a complex of some kind lying isolated in the desert, down a dusty trail, far away from the nearest road. She continued through the images, until she realized what she was looking at, and her heart stopped, the cold grip of horror squeezing it tight.

She understood why McClusky had looked at the pictures so many times. If he had any sort of conscience, they would have disturbed him as much as they did her. She imagined him sitting in his office, wrestling with his guilt, trying to convince himself he was still one of the good guys. The screen suddenly went blank as MI6's security protocols kicked in, but the image was seared in Leila's mind.

'They've cut me off,' Leila said, her words joined by the sound of distant sirens. 'We've got to go now.' She heaved herself up and removed the dongle before she handed the laptop to Wollerton. 'Get the other one too,' she said, and he grabbed Vasylyk's broken machine from the floor, took the dongle out, and they tossed the two small 4G devices on the sofa.

Leila felt sick inside, an ugly nausea that surprised her. Even after all the horrific things she'd experienced, it turned out she was still human. There were things that could shock her. The photographs of the complex in the Turkmen desert had done just that, and she shuddered as she led Wollerton and Melody from the room. Leila took the mobile phone from her pocket and made a call.

She was about to share the horror with Scott Pearce.

Chapter 56

Pearce was parked on a winding country lane that lay off the main ring road. He'd driven through the night to reach Hazelmere Darke by dawn, taking care not to push the stolen BMW 3 Series past the speed limit. The holdall in the boot was full of weapons, and he doubted the police would have understood any explanation he could have given them. He'd explored Hazelmere Darke, which, in addition to being famous for its plague-ridden history, was renowned as the home of Britain's best lemon drizzle cake. His search for sites of local interest yielded no obvious targets. There were no military installations, no government offices, no royal retreats. Hazelmere Darke was nothing more than a quiet, picturesque home to 15,000 souls. Surrounded by ruffled green countryside, it would have been an idyllic place to raise a family, but his fleeting, sentimental dream passed and was quickly replaced by the profound sense of self-loathing he'd had since the attack on the safe house. Wayne was dead. Another friend gone.

Pearce thumped the steering wheel in frustration. He was responsible for the loss. He'd brought his friend into this mess and hadn't protected him. His carelessness had drawn death to their door. Wayne was a better man than he, and had died protecting others. Pearce had simply bruised an ankle and aggravated the wounds in his wrist.

He was angry with himself. Furious beyond measure at what he'd done, at the friends he'd lost, and at the fact he was sitting in a stolen car many miles from the man he needed to kill. He wished he hadn't listened to Kyle, that he'd gone straight to Purbeck House and vented his rage.

Pearce hit the steering wheel again. When he looked up, he saw, reflected in the rear-view mirror, a weak man who had failed. He was reaching for the ignition when his phone rang.

'Yeah?' he answered, his voice throaty.

'*It's me,*' Leila replied. She sounded as though she was on the move. '*I know where they're going. I saw a satellite image of a training site they built in Turkmenistan. A replica they used to prepare. I saw –*' her voice broke – '*I saw a playground, Scott. I saw a climbing frame and a hopscotch grid. It's a school. Whatever they're planning, it's happening at a school.*'

Pearce put the phone on speaker. 'Describe it to me,' he said, bringing up Google Maps.

'*There's a rectangular playground, a hopscotch grid off to the left, the climbing frame in a fenced area to the right,*' Leila replied, as Pearce found Hazelmere Darke on his screen. '*And two buildings either side. One looks like a large hall.*'

Pearce zoomed in on the town and searched for schools. Six markers populated the map.

'*There was a small hut to the side of the playground between the two buildings. Looked like a little cabin or something.*'

'I've got it,' Pearce said, staring in disbelief at a primary school that matched Leila's description of the bird's eye view. 'Hill Manor Primary School, Leyland Road. Call the police now, Leila. Call them right now.'

Chapter 57

Esther Reed watched the steady stream of tiny tots pass the office window. The reception children had been weeding the raised flower beds in front of the school and their teacher was leading them back to their classroom through the main entrance. Their little faces were glowing with pride, because it was usually only grown-ups who got to use the front door. The children came to school through a side gate. Coming through the main entrance was a reward for doing something to help the school community.

'Don't daydream, Miss,' a little voice said.

Esther looked down to see Billy Pym marching through the inner security door. Miss Griffin, Hayley, his teacher, smiled and shook her head in disbelief. A little extra sass was to be expected at this time of year. Term ended on Friday and the children were all excited at the prospect of the summer holiday.

'That's me told,' Esther said to her.

'Any more confidence and he'd be running this place,' Hayley replied, as she followed Billy and the last of the reception children down the corridor to their classroom.

The door swung shut behind her and the magnetic lock clicked into place.

Esther backed away from the counter, rearranging her ivy

green tea dress so that it didn't cling to her quite as much. The office was already getting hot.

'Have you done the Parent Pay email yet?' Esther asked, turning to her assistant, Janice, who was sitting at her desk by the window. 'I was wondering if we should remind . . .'

Esther stopped talking the moment she saw Janice's face. Her eyes were wide, her skin was ashen and she seemed to be trembling. Esther followed her gaze and saw the reason for her terror. In the car park, just beyond the wide pavement that lay directly outside the main doors, were four men. They were dressed in matching uniforms which Esther had only ever seen on TV: the chilling black robes and hoods of ISIS fighters. All four men carried machine guns.

Gunfire came from somewhere further inside the building and Janice cried out as the first man stormed into the reception. Esther's hand, which had been reaching for the phone, froze.

'Do what I say and no one will get hurt,' the man commanded in a Brummie accent. 'Step away from the counter.'

Esther did as he instructed, not because she expected to live, but because she had to buy time. There was no way she was going to let this horror into her school.

Hill Manor was located on the southern edge of town. In normal conditions, the drive would have taken eight minutes, but Pearce made it in four, tearing through the peaceful streets like a lunatic, earning himself obscene gestures, shouts and hoots as he overtook everything and anything, mounting pavements, cutting corners and doing all he could to reach the school.

There was no sign of police when he approached, so he

turned through the main gates and sped into the car park. He didn't slow when he caught sight of what was happening in the main reception. Four men in ISIS black were holding two women at gunpoint. The women were separated from the men by a counter, which would protect them from the worst of what was about to happen. Pearce aimed straight for the main doors and threw the BMW into second gear as he stepped on the accelerator. The car shot forward, jumped the kerb and cut across a broad pavement. One of the men turned and opened fire with his Kalashnikov, but he was too late. His bullets made a wild pattern on the bonnet, but his aim was too hurried and reckless to put them anywhere near Pearce.

The car smashed through the double doors and the four men tried to jump clear, but there wasn't anywhere to go and they'd reacted too late. Pearce was doing around forty when he hit them. One caught a glancing blow and bounced off the bonnet. The other three were flung forward and crushed when the BMW slammed into the reception wall. The airbag burst and the engine over-revved wildly until Pearce cut the ignition. He pushed the airbag and caught a glimpse of movement out of the corner of his eye. The man he'd clipped was trying to get to his feet. Driven by a fury unlike any-thing he'd ever experienced, Pearce jumped out of the car and raced across the dusty, smoky lobby towards the rising man. He kicked the guy in the face, grabbed the barrel of the AK-47 and spun it towards the ceiling, which took the spray of bullets. One of the terrified women screamed and started sobbing. Pearce elbowed the gunman in the face, and he fell back, losing his grip on the machine gun. Pearce snatched the weapon, flipped it round and fired a single shot into the man's heart.

'You!' Pearce yelled at the older of the two women, as the gunman dropped dead. 'What's your name?'

'Esther,' she replied fearfully. 'I heard gunfire,' she gestured towards the interior of the building.

Pearce nodded. 'There will be more of them. Esther, I want you to take her and get out,' he signalled to her hysterical colleague. 'The police are on their way. I'm going to be sending kids out to you. Get them to safety.'

He pulled the mask off the man he'd just killed to reveal his pale complexion and blond hair.

'*Eagle Three, this is Eagle One,*' a voice came from somewhere in the folds of the man's uniform. '*What's happening? We heard a crash and gunfire.*'

Pearce ignored the transmission and moved to the boot of the BMW. He popped the lid.

'Shouldn't we wait for the police?' Esther asked as she led her crying colleague out of the office.

Her colleague looked at the dead men crumpled by the bonnet of the car and vomited.

'They've built a replica of the school to rehearse this attack. They're going to use the time to set up defensive positions, booby traps. Every moment that passes is to their advantage,' Pearce replied. He didn't have the heart to tell Esther a second, more troubling truth. Hazelmere Darke lay in one of the remote areas identified by the National Police Chief's Council as having a slow armed response time. Even when the local police arrived, they wouldn't be able to do much; the armed response team would be at least forty minutes away. 'I have to move fast.'

He opened the holdall and saw Esther's eyes widen as she registered the weapons inside. Somewhere in the distance, police sirens sang their ugly, unwelcome song, a sound no one wanted to hear heading for a school. They were still too far away and even when they arrived, what could they do against such heavily armed men?

'Go,' Pearce ordered, throwing on his body armour.

Esther pulled her colleague by the shoulders and led her towards the main entrance, while Pearce armed himself with two P226 Sig Sauer pistols and an AR-15 rifle mounted with a UTG 30mm scope. He slung an ammo bag over his shoulder. It contained six nine-round magazines for the Sigs, and twelve Lancer thirty-round mags for the AR-15. He slid a sheathed hunting knife into his waistband.

'Please don't let anything happen to the children,' Esther said, her brimming eyes overflowing.

Pearce nodded. 'I need the key.' He signalled the inner security door.

Esther pulled the lanyard from around her neck and handed it to him. She led her distraught colleague out and Pearce clambered onto the bonnet of the BMW to remove the hoods of the three dead men mangled between wall and bumper. They were all white males between twenty and forty, but Pearce did not recognize any of them. He jumped down and looked through the picture window set in one of the twin security doors. He saw nothing out of place, just an empty corridor, blue carpet and walls covered with brightly coloured children's artwork.

He swiped the key card and opened the door. His AR-15 mounted gunsight-ready, stock tight to his shoulder, Pearce stepped through and used his heel to control the swing of the door as it closed behind him. The door shut silently, but the loud click of the magnetic plate locking into place drew a black-clad figure through a doorway at the end of the corridor. The man opened fire, and Pearce side-stepped and dropped to one knee. Bullets whipped over his head and thudded into the door behind him, sending splinters of wood zipping through the air. Pearce scoped his target and fired a single shot directly into the man's skull.

A chorus of young screams came from the room beyond the open doorway, as the gunman slid down the wall, his wound leaving a thick trail of blood. Pearce ran towards the cacophony and stepped into a classroom in complete disarray. Tiny children were spread around the room, trying to huddle under tables, behind chairs, hugging each other, crying, screaming, shouting for their mummies and daddies. A woman, their teacher, was in the middle of a group who pawed at her motionless form. She'd fallen by her desk.

'Children!' Pearce yelled.

Some screamed when they registered his presence and saw his gun.

'I'm a friend,' he said, lowering the weapon. 'I'm here to get you out.'

He ran to the prone woman and checked her pulse. He was surprised to find a steady beat and rolled her over to discover a large bruise above her eye, the size and shape of a rifle stock. Pearce shook her.

'Hey!' he said, as she stirred. 'Come on. Wake up.'

All around him, young, terrified children, some little more than toddlers, cried, their angelic faces twisted ugly by the horror they'd seen.

'Come on,' Pearce said, lifting the woman as she came round. 'What's your name?'

She focused on him and her eyes widened with panic. She recoiled and tried to shuffle away.

'It's OK,' he assured her. 'I'm a friend. Can you stand on your own?'

The woman looked beyond him to the dead man in the corridor. 'Hayley,' she said. 'My name's Hayley.'

She brushed Pearce's hands away and took a couple of unsteady steps. She stopped when the sound of distant gun-fire and screams came up the corridor. Pearce burned with the need to move, to get to the source of the horrific sounds, but he had to make sure these little kids were safe. The woman swayed, but steadied herself against her desk.

'The police are on their way,' Pearce told her. 'Get the kids out front. It's safe and Esther and her colleague are there to help.'

The woman smiled with relief at the mention of Esther's name. 'Thank you,' she replied, her wild eyes wet and full. 'Children!' she yelled, trying to control the panic in her voice. 'Children! We're leaving. Remember your stranger-danger drill. Find your buddy and line up. We're evacuating.'

As the first children started to muster, Pearce saw a blur by the door, a black shape. He raised his gun instinctively and loosed a couple of shots before the man could reply. The guy took two bullets in the chest and fell onto his dead comrade. The children's screams started anew.

'Get them out!' Pearce told Hayley, whose horror was writ large on her face. 'Get them out now!' he commanded as he ran towards the corridor.

There, further along, by a set of double doors, was another assailant in the familiar black ISIS garb. The man opened fire, and his AK-47 sprayed the corridor with bullets. Pearce ducked behind the classroom wall and waited for the volley to stop. Yet again, he heard distant screams above rattling gunfire and the combination made Pearce think of a dark, twisted roller coaster. A wild bullet shattered one of the classroom windows, terrifying the children, who all cowered behind their teacher.

When the gunfire stopped, Pearce raised his rifle, leaned out and fired two shots. He was gratified to see them hit the man square in the face.

'It's clear,' Pearce told Hayley. 'Go!'

She gathered the children to her as Pearce stepped into the corridor. He removed the hoods from the two men who'd collapsed on top of each other. Both white, one had a neck tattoo of the Black 13 insignia, leaving Pearce in little doubt of their allegiance. The ISIS gear was a set-up designed to push Britain further right, to hand power to Mark Sutton and to harden public opinion in support of draconian domestic and foreign policies. In order for the deception to work, they'd have to protect their true identities, Pearce thought, which meant they either had a foolproof escape plan, or no one was ever supposed to leave this school. The murder of little children. This was pure evil. He had to move quickly.

He stepped further into the corridor, towards the man who'd fallen by the double doors. He turned and watched as the tiny children, their innocence forever lost, scurried to the security doors that led to the lobby. How could anyone ever explain the twisted nature of this attack to them? Nearly all of the kids were sobbing and whimpering, but they'd formed up in pairs and held hands, offering each other what support and comfort they could. Hayley hovered around the group protectively, and when she pressed the green button that opened the doors, Pearce nodded at her. She smiled gratefully, fresh tears of relief forming as she led the children towards the main entrance, past the wreckage of the car.

'Don't look, children,' she instructed, as she registered the carnage.

Screams from further inside the building got Pearce moving again, and he headed for the noise. When he reached the corpse by the double doors, he removed the man's hood. Another member of Black 13, but not one of the two men he was hoping to find – the Scarred Man and his large associate, Salvation, who had tortured and tried to kill him in Oxford.

The man at his feet was carrying a backpack, and when Pearce opened it, he was dismayed to discover motion sensors and demolition charges. Pearce took little comfort in knowing he was right: this guy was clearly meant to be setting booby traps. He wondered whether the man had managed to lay any charges, or whether he'd been killed before he'd had the opportunity.

Pearce looked through the inset window of one of the doors, into the corridor beyond. It was deserted and light spilled from classrooms on either side. At the very end, a glass fire door hung open and outside Pearce could see a crowd of children being herded across a tarmacked playground towards the large building that stood opposite.

Pearce pushed the door open and set off down the corridor. Each of the classrooms he passed was eerily empty and he checked every doorway for any sign of motion detectors, but found none. His intervention must have interrupted the saboteur before he could set any charges. The school Black 13 had chosen was perfect for their evil purpose. If he'd been an evil scumbag, this is exactly the sort of site Pearce would have picked. He guessed somewhere between two and three hundred children attended Hill Manor, a sufficiently large number of kids to grab headlines around the world. It lay well beyond the range of any rapid armed response unit and a small group of well-trained men could easily booby-trap and defend the location almost indefinitely. He had to take them out before they could dig in.

The first of the children in the playground had reached the other side and were being ushered through a double door by two gun-toting figures in black robes. Pearce accelerated. He had to stop the kids being taken inside that building. As he drew near the fire door, he got a better view of the playground and saw two frightened teachers being beaten and harried across the yard by two more Black 13 members in their ISIS uniforms. Another two were shouting at the children, most of whom were crying. It broke Pearce's heart to see such small children so afraid. Their young minds weren't ready for such horror, and their playground, a sanctuary of joy and fun, should never have borne witness to such terror. Pearce burned with murderous hatred of the men who'd done this.

The shadows cast in the playground told him that the morning sun was behind him. It was all the advantage he would need. He crouched in the doorway, dropping to one knee, bringing his rifle to the ready position, knowing that his silhouette would be difficult to spot in the shadow of the corridor. With the glare of the sun above him, he sighted all four men. They were moving away from him, but at a slight angle, making them almost down-the-line targets. He moved between them, noting his swing, position and angle of incidence. One, two, three, four. He rehearsed the slight, sharp movements. The children's cries spoke to some deep, primal part of him. No ordinary person could hear such distress and not be moved to alleviate the suffering. How had these men been brainwashed into thinking such horror was justified?

Pearce rehearsed one more time, then sighted the first target, the furthest man, aiming at his back. Pearce swung slightly left, anticipating where the target would be when the bullet struck. He squeezed the trigger and didn't wait to see the man fall, instantly swinging the barrel of his gun over the children's heads to the next furthest man, who'd frozen at the sound of the shot.

Another crack echoed off the walls and bounced around the playground. The bullet struck the man's head and the children's terror intensified. One of the other assailants made a lunge for a little girl with blonde braids, but there was no way Pearce was going to let him get a hostage. He fired three times, and the girl screamed as the rounds struck the man in the side. He wheeled round and went down, groaning. As he teetered on his knees, Pearce peered down the scope and finished him off with a single shot above the ear.

Bullets chewed chunks from the brickwork either side of the doorway. The last guy in the playground was firing wildly, as were the two men in the doorway of the building opposite.

'Get down!' Pearce yelled at the children.

The two teachers shouted, 'Lie down!' and 'Get down!', urging the kids onto their bellies. Pearce shot over them, taking out the nearest gunman with two in the chest. The moment the man fell, Pearce started running. He sprinted across the playground, firing a volley of shots at the doorway opposite. The two hooded men ducked inside and Pearce heard screams coming from within. He reached the first teacher, a short woman with a severe face, which was red, puffy and wet with tears.

'Get the children out,' he told her. 'Esther and Hayley are waiting in the car park. The police will be there. You'll be safe.'

'Children,' the woman said, grabbing a little boy and leading him by the hand. 'Come on! Hurry! Follow me!'

She led the boy towards the building Pearce had just left, and her colleague, a grey-bearded man with an earnest face and frightened eyes, followed her, rounding up all the sobbing, fearful children he could. As they followed their teachers, the kids parted round Pearce like waves rushing around the prow of a surging ship, giving him space to run towards the other building, a newly built, two-storey yellow brick structure. Pearce swapped out his AR-15 magazine for a fresh one, but when he was halfway across the playground, he saw something that stopped him in his tracks.

One of the hooded men had returned to the doorway with a small child, a little girl of about six, who had long dark hair, wide eyes and a sprinkling of freckles. She was crying and her bewilderment and terror could be felt at a distance.

'Stop!' the man yelled. He held a pistol against the girl's temple. His other hand had a tight grip on a clump of the girl's hair and he tugged her towards him. 'Every step you take, a child dies,' the man shouted. 'You have five seconds to turn around, or we start killing.'

Chapter 58

Pearce knew that if he left, every child in that building would die. These men, this horror, it was predicated on the world believing a lie. There could be no trace, nothing to contradict security camera footage that would identify them as Islamic terrorists. There could be no witnesses.

'Five . . .' the hooded man yelled.

He sized the guy up. Instead of crouching behind the child, the man was standing over her.

'. . . four . . .'

His torso was almost entirely exposed. At thirty yards it would be a challenging shot, but not impossible.

'. . . three . . .'

The little girl screamed. Pearce couldn't have her death on his conscience. He'd been lucky so far; no child casualties. He studied her little face.

'. . . two . . .'

Try as he might to suppress them, his mind was filled with imaginings of her mother and father, her aunts and uncles, friends and relatives, all of whom would suffer terribly and doubtless never recover from her loss.

'. . . one!' the hooded man cried.

Pearce turned around and took a step towards the other building, retreating the way he'd come. He knew what would happen next. It's what he would have done if he'd been in the coward's position. Pearce sidestepped as the man took a shot at him. He was too far away for his pistol to be an effective weapon and the small step had thrown the guy's aim off entirely. However, the attempt had taken the gun from the girl's head, giving Pearce a window.

He turned, brought the AR-15 up and targeted the hooded man through the scope. To his relief, the man kept shooting at Pearce, his bullets flying wildly through the air to his left. Pearce fired once and a single round hit the man in the heart. He dropped his gun and staggered back, clutching at his chest.

Suddenly free, the little girl screeched and ran towards Pearce. The hooded man collapsed to his knees and Pearce finished him with a shot that tore through his throat.

Pearce ran to meet the little girl. 'Go to the car park,' he told her. 'Do you know where it is?'

She was trembling and sobbing so much, he couldn't be sure she'd even heard him. A sound boomed across the playground, filling Pearce with dread. It was a gunshot and it came from the building opposite. They were making good on their threat.

'Go!' Pearce shouted at the girl, shoving her towards the building that lay behind him. She'd be safe, and his thoughts were now on the poor kids ahead of him.

The gunfire continued as he raced on, a steady rhythmic beat, and with each shot came horrified screams. The terrified cries mingled with the shots and echoed from building to building, terrible heralds marking the start of a family's misery.

Pearce sprinted, forcing his legs to move faster than they'd ever moved before, and as he neared the doorway he heard, amid the screams and cries, the shouts of two men.

Rifle raised, Pearce burst through the doorway into a huge gymnasium full of children and teachers. As his eyes grew accustomed to the light, he saw something that made his heart leap. Instead of the bodies of murdered children, he was greeted by two men struggling for control of a Kalashnikov. One of the men wore the dread black uniform of the others Pearce had killed. The man struggling with him was in jeans and a grey shirt. He was young and strong; a teacher or teaching assistant. As they fought, the gun discharged bullets into the ceiling, each shot renewing the children's screams. This is what Pearce had heard from the playground. No one had been executed. Not yet.

Beyond the two fighting men, a final black-clad figure crouched at the rear of the hall, his back to Pearce. There were two large flight cases either side of his hunched form, and the man had his head down and was concentrating on something.

Pearce tried to target the fighting men, but they kept twisting and tumbling about the place, and he couldn't be certain he wouldn't hit the teacher, so he ran through the crowd of cowering, crying children and closed the gap to the duo in moments. He slung his AR-15, drew his knife from its sheath, grabbed the hooded man, said a prayer of forgiveness for what the children were about to witness and pulled the man back. Momentum jerked the AK-47 free of the teacher's grasp, but before the Black 13 operative could turn it on him, Pearce stuck the eight-inch blade into the man's neck. He screamed a wet deathly cry, which was echoed by the children who witnessed the horror, and clutched at the wound, dropping the AK-47.

'Get the kids out of here!' Pearce shouted, grabbing his AR-15 and swinging it off his shoulder. He kicked the dying man, who collapsed, choking on his own blood.

The children erupted, jumping to their feet, and a few of them made it out before a spray of warning gunfire shocked everyone into silence. Pearce looked across the large space and saw the last of the men, the one who'd been hunched between the flight cases. He was standing with an AK-47 in one hand and some kind of device in the other. He shot another warning volley over their heads.

'Nobody move, or everyone dies,' he shouted. 'There's enough explosive in here –' he indicated the cases – 'to send us all to hell.'

More screams, cries and whimpers filled the room.

The man reached up with the hand that held the detonator and removed his hood to reveal an ugly, twisted, broad face that was marked with the word 'Salvation'. His tufts of black hair were slick with sweat. This was the huge guy who'd watched from the shadows as the Scarred Man had tortured Pearce.

Their plan hinged on the world believing this was an ISIS attack. It wouldn't simply pave the way for Sutton to introduce draconian measures in his new job, it would drive anti-immigrant and anti-Muslim sentiment and force the nation further to the right. Now they'd seen Salvation's face, Pearce knew that everyone in this building was destined to die.

'It's over,' Pearce yelled. 'Your explosives won't take out the whole school. They're going to find the others. They'll know who really did this. Your plan relied on all of you being burned beyond recognition, right? I don't care what you've got in those cases, you can't burn the bodies in the other building. Your plan isn't going to work now.'

'I've got one hundred and forty kilos of CL-20,' the man said, and Pearce's heart sank. That was enough to crater half the town.

'You can't be sure,' Pearce countered. 'I bet you were all supposed to be in here when the bomb went off. That's why no one's wearing protective vests. If just one of your men's bodies can be identified, they'll know the truth. The bodies are too spread out. You can't be sure they'll all burn . . . don't kill these kids for nothing.'

Pearce was gratified to see a flicker of uncertainty cross the man's face before it was replaced by renewed resolve.

'I have to do this,' he said. 'We have to do this, to save England. To save Britain. This is good,' he continued, as if trying to convince himself. 'This is good and it will be remembered as heroic. In years to come, they'll put up statues of me.'

'It will be remembered as murder and your name will be cursed,' Pearce responded. 'Look around you. They're just children. They are England. They are Britain. They're innocent.'

'They're not innocent! No one's innocent!' Salvation railed. 'We wouldn't have had to do this if people had protected us! If they'd stood up for us! But they didn't, and now we're here.'

Pearce could sense the man's turmoil as he looked around the hall at the innocent faces of those he was planning to kill. The sound of sirens added to the tension. They were very close, possibly already on site. He didn't have long. If the delicate stalemate was threatened by police arriving in numbers, Salvation would trigger the device.

'Let the kids go,' Pearce said. 'Keep me. I'm not innocent. I'm guilty. Just like you. Let them go and be a real hero. Ask yourself how you got here. You're being used by people who don't care about you. They're exploiting you. Don't let them. Don't hurt these kids.'

Salvation cast around desperately, torment written in his eyes as he took in the terrified children all around him. Pearce could see him trying to understand how life had led him to this point, where he now most definitely felt like the villain. Salvation looked away suddenly, as though the children's miserable gazes carried a deadly disease.

'I have to do this,' he muttered. 'I have to do this. There's no other way.'

Pearce recognized the signs of a zealot, a brainwashed drone chanting a mantra that had been drilled into him. This was not a person capable of critical, rational thought. The replica of the school would have offered these men the opportunity to hone their plan, but its real purpose would have been to drill out the human responses, to turn the attack into a process. Clear this room, lay the charge here, bring the hostages to this place. Automatic steps that didn't need thought, the victims dehumanized by a well-practised drill. Pearce knew from experience that it was better not to think about the humanity of the person on the receiving end of a bullet, and children . . . He wondered whether he could ever be drilled to accept that a child's life was meaningless. ISIS, Black 13, they were opposing sides of the same extremist coin, radicalizing followers into believing certain groups were less than human. ISIS used the bombing of innocents in the Middle East the same way Bastien Collet and his ilk exploited the existence of grooming gangs or terrorists. Terrible suffering used as an emotive tool to recruit angry, bewildered people and legitimize violence against an entire race or culture.

Pearce could see Salvation's natural instincts struggling against his training. He needed time to bring this guy back from the edge, but it was a luxury he didn't have. He could hear the tramp of boots crossing the playground and he saw that the bomber heard it too.

'Tell them to stay back,' he shouted. 'I'll do it! I'll send us all to hell!'

More screams as Salvation raised his hand and brandished the trigger.

Pearce knew it was as good an opportunity as he was going to get. He lifted the AR-15 and shot five times in quick succession, targeting the man's elevated wrist. Three bullets struck as intended, blowing an egg-sized hole in the guy's arm. The detonator fell to the floor and Salvation screamed and dropped the AK-47, clutching his bloody wrist with his other hand.

'Get out!' Pearce yelled, and the gym burst into wild pandemonium.

Children screamed and ran and their teachers fled with them, streaming through the double doors into the playground.

Across the hall, Salvation staggered towards the fallen detonator.

'Stop! Stand where you are!' Pearce shouted, but the man only turned and gave him a dark smile before reaching for the device.

Pearce ignored the sea of children churning around him and targeted Salvation's black hair. The shot rang out, prompting more screams and panic. Salvation toppled over with a hole in the side of his head and Pearce lowered his weapon, breathing heavily. Adrenalin burned in his veins, heightening every moment. The children were no longer in any danger, but Pearce could hear the approaching police officers shouting instructions across the playground. He couldn't afford to be caught. Not like this. Not with so many bodies added to his tally, no matter how much they might have deserved it.

'Thank you,' a voice said, and Pearce turned to see the man in the grey shirt, the one who'd been wrestling with the Black 13 operative he'd stabbed in the neck. 'Thank you,' he repeated, extending his hand, his voice crumbling like dry cake, his eyes brimming over.

'I'm not supposed to be here,' Pearce replied, without shaking the man's hand. 'Is there another way out?'

It took a moment for the man to register Pearce's question and when he did, his eyes clouded with suspicion.

'I'm not one of them,' Pearce said. 'But I'm not police either. I just need a way out.'

The man took in the dead terrorists, and the fleeing children, and then nodded. 'Through the cafeteria. Just in there.' He pointed to an interior door two-thirds of the way along the gym's inner wall. 'It'll take you onto the playing fields. There's a housing estate behind them.'

'Thanks,' Pearce replied, and he set off at a sprint.

As he ran past, he looked down at the detonator and Salvation's motionless fingers beside the device. These men had come within inches of perpetrating an atrocity on the most innocent of souls, and as he sprinted from the cavernous hall, Pearce vowed that the man behind it all would be forced to atone.

Such evil demanded a blood price.

Chapter 59

Pearce sprinted into a wide corridor that was lined with sports equipment. He found a large bag and emptied the footballs out of it, before stuffing his pistols, A R-15 and ammunition pouch inside and slinging it over his shoulder. As he ran on, he shed his body armour and put it into the bag. He could hear shouts coming from behind him as the police tried to get control of the situation, but hundreds of terrified children provided the best possible distraction, and he raced into a large, deserted cafeteria. He bounded across the room, leaping over tables and chairs until he reached the fire exit at the very rear of the building. He burst onto a large playing field and saw the outline of a housing estate clustered at its edge. To his left were three black vans, doubtless used to ferry the dead Black 13 operatives to the school. Pearce had no doubt the vehicles would be full of evidence implicating Islamic terrorists.

As he ran on, the clamour of children, school staff and police swirled around the building, and Pearce realized that no matter what traumatic memories they carried, those children would at least have other days to live.

'*You did good*,' Leila said.

Pearce had the phone on speaker and was steering a stolen Renault Clio south-west along the M5. He'd taken the car from one of the side streets on the housing estate, selecting something small and old.

'*It's all over the news,*' Wollerton added. '*No casualties. At least not among the children and staff. They're calling it a miracle.*'

'Use the social media accounts again. I want you to break the news about Sutton and Progress Britain. Hammer home his link to them,' Pearce responded. 'And connect them to today's attack.'

'*What about Viscount Purbeck?*' Melody asked.

'Keep him out of it for now,' Pearce replied.

'*Are you coming back?*' Leila asked. '*We had to move. We're—*'

'I'm not coming back,' Pearce said.

His answer was met with silence. They all knew where he was going.

'*I should come with you,*' Wollerton said at last, his tone grave.

'No. Spread the word. Finish these guys off,' Pearce told him. 'I'll handle everything else.'

'*Be careful,*' Leila counselled.

'You too,' Pearce replied, before hanging up.

Purbeck House lay at the bottom of a broad valley that had been hollowed out over aeons and robbed of any hard edges. Rolling hills lay either side, giving way to the valley floor so gently that anyone walking the landscape might not have noticed the change in elevation at all. A high brick wall marked the estate's perimeter, running along the far side of the hills to the south of the valley and following the summits of the ones to the north. To the south, the wall was about three miles from the house, to the north, four, and the eastern and western limits of the property lay some six miles from the grand old home. Beyond the wall, the hills were covered in ancient woodland that was damp and mossy even in the blistering heat. Further on, where the hills made their slow, gentle descent into the valley, lay the pastureland Pearce had seen from the house. A few ancient oaks peppered the fields and livestock grazed in their shadows. Then came the manicured gardens and the house itself.

Pearce spent the day exploring the perimeter, driving from one vantage point to the other, following public footpaths that skirted the property, trying to understand what he was up against. The wall was ten feet high. In places, the brickwork was rough and failing, but generally it was well-tended and in good condition. It was broken by two gatehouses, one to the north and the other to the south. The south gate was the grander of the two, and a high metal barrier stood between a pair of grey stone houses that were large enough to pass for family homes. When Pearce had driven by, he'd spied two men in suits, both with the grim look of members of Black 13. The news of their failure at Hill Manor had obviously hit hard, and Pearce got the sense that Oxnard-Clarke had tightened his security.

The north gate was more modest. Another high barrier linked the two ends of the wall. Behind it, set on a lawn, was another stone house, this one smaller than the pair to the south. Another duo of suited guards patrolled the space behind the gate.

As he'd hiked the paths around the estate, Pearce had spotted other men, these more roughly dressed, patrolling the grounds on quad bikes, and above them, machines that gave Pearce pause. Oxnard-Clarke had automated drones covering the area around his house. Pearce watched three of the machines fly a regular pattern, each sweeping a section of the gardens and pastureland, patrolling their allotted route with a camera that would doubtless relay live footage to a security control room. The flights lasted twenty-five minutes before the drones returned to docking stations on the roof of Purbeck House. As they descended onto their recharging docks, they were immediately replaced by three fresh drones. There were nine in total, operating in shifts to create a relentless twenty-four-hour surveillance system. Even with the benefit of his rifle scope, Pearce couldn't tell the manufacturer, but guessing by the recharge times and the look of the docking stations, Nightingale Security was the most likely candidate.

As afternoon gave way to evening and the sky grew dark with angry clouds, Pearce felt he had sufficient grasp of Oxnard-Clarke's security measures. He returned to the Clio, which was parked at the end of a track off the winding country road that ran to the east of the property, and opened the boot to check the contents of the sports bag. Ten magazines for the AR-15 and six for the Sigs. He wished he still had some of the gear he'd abandoned in the BMW at Hazelmere Darke, but he'd have to make do with what was at hand. He shut the boot and climbed in the passenger seat, which he fully reclined, and rolled down the windows. Setting the alarm on his phone, Pearce lay back and closed his eyes. As he settled into sleep, he rehearsed how he was going to reach the house and what he was going to do to Oxnard-Clarke when he got there.

He didn't dream and woke from a black void to the insistent sound of his phone alarm. It was dark outside and the moon and stars were lost behind swollen clouds. The air was soupy with the promise of rain. Pearce got out, walked along the bone-dry track to the boot and pulled his weapons and ammunition from the sports bag. Slinging the AR-15 over one shoulder and the ammunition pouch over the other, he set off into the dark forest.

A quarter of a mile in, the trees thinned and he came to a long narrow clearing that ran alongside the high wall. Pearce was on the valley floor, far from the house, but he believed there was less chance of him being spotted here than if he approached over the hills. And if the guards maintained their patrol pattern, this location would offer yet another advantage.

Pearce ran to the wall and leaped for the top. Pain shot along his arms as his fingers caught the upper edge, and he smeared his feet up the brickwork as quickly as possible. He made it to the top of the wall and saw another clearing and more woodland beyond it. He jumped down and ran into the trees, checking the time on his phone as he passed beneath the heavy boughs. It was 1.06 a.m. and he was just under a minute behind schedule.

Pearce picked up his pace, threading his way between the huge trees, nimbly avoiding the thick roots that reached into the moss-covered soil. Up ahead, he saw a break in the solid canopy, and the dark greys and blacks of the clouds hung in the gap. He was nearing the treeline and could hear a rattling engine approaching. The machine was close and it was slowing; he didn't have much time. He sprinted forward, but his haste was a mistake. The sound of the engine suddenly died.

'Stop where you are!' a voice yelled as Pearce came to the edge of the forest.

Ahead of him, standing over the seat of his quad bike, was a tall man, his features lost in shadow, his long rifle aimed directly at Pearce. He must have seen the movement in the trees, and rather than Pearce arriving in time to lie in wait for the guard, the man now had the jump on him.

'Stop!' he repeated.

Pearce ignored him, slung the AR-15 off his shoulder and moved it to the ready position in a single fluid motion. He shot before the other man had the chance to pull the trigger. He jerked back and fell off the machine. Pearce ran towards him to find a hole between his eyes.

Minutes later, Pearce had stripped the dead man of his jeans and black T-shirt and was wearing them as he steered the quad bike across open country. In the distance, on one of the northern hills, he saw the silhouette of another guard. The figure was black against the smoky sky, and if he noticed Pearce, he offered no reaction.

Pearce motored through a copse of trees and when he crested a low rise, he saw the grand house in the distance, perhaps a mile beyond the pastures which spread out directly ahead of him. He accelerated down the gentle slope, scattering a herd of deer that had been resting beneath a nearby tree. As he crossed the fields, the roar of the quad's engine filling his ears, Pearce heard another sound, and a dark insect-like shape buzzed overhead. One of the drones conducting a sweep. The machine flew on, but as he glanced over his shoulder, he saw it make a wide arc and retrace its path. Pearce kept his head down and steered the quad over thick tufted grass. He hoped that the rudimentary disguise he'd stolen from the dead guard would convince the casual observer that he was meant to be here.

The drone came in close, tracking Pearce's trajectory. It was no longer on automatic and was clearly being piloted by some unseen hand. Pearce pushed on, the night air gusting at him, the dark shapes of cows and sheep racing by as he neared the garden.

'*Stop!*' a voice came from the drone, which was now only a few metres above him, its four rotors whirring loudly. '*Identify yourself!*'

Pearce accelerated. He was less than a quarter of a mile from the house and could see sprinklers dousing the lawn with a fine mist.

'*Stop!*' the voice repeated.

Pearce glanced up and saw the drone's camera directed at him, and next to it a pair of loudspeakers. The machine rose suddenly and banked away, and the quad bucked as it jumped a shallow ditch and sped onto the lawn.

Night became something brighter than day and Pearce was dazzled as the garden was illuminated by powerful security lights mounted on a ledge that ran along the first floor of the house. The gunfire started immediately, and as Pearce acclimatized to the glare, he saw two shooters on the patio by the French doors that led to the sitting room. Bullets chewed the lawn all around him, throwing up clumps of sod. Pearce swerved, steering away from the men towards the giant oak that stood directly in front of the house. The quad was chased by a spray of bullets that thumped into the ground behind him.

Pearce squeezed the brake and stopped behind the wide trunk, and the gunfire ceased. He jumped off the quad and broke cover to scope the house. He was rewarded with an instant hail of bullets from the two men, who had split up and were now jogging towards him, one on either side of the tree. Pearce ran back to the quad and noticed a clay pigeon trap in the long grass at the foot of the tree. Next to it stood the device's power source: a car battery.

Pearce took his AR-15 off his shoulder and leaned round

the thick trunk of the great oak, firing a couple of shots at the approaching men. He hit the one on the left, catching him in the leg. His companion immediately responded to his pained cries and ran to him, shooting carelessly as he crossed the lawn. Pearce punished him with a shot to the body that spun him round and put him flat on his back.

Four more guards, drawn by the gunfire and the sound of their comrades' cries, came running round the east side of the house, all wearing the urban camouflage uniforms and insignia of Black 13. Pearce slowed them down with a spray of bullets, before ducking behind the tree, which protected him from their response.

He set to work quickly, realizing that numbers would eventually get the better of him. He opened the quad bike's fuel tank and ripped the car battery's wires from the clay trap. He lifted the heavy battery onto the quad, ignoring the thunderous gunfire that gnawed at the huge oak. Taking care not to let the battery wires anywhere near the fuel tank, Pearce slung his rifle and mounted the vehicle, which roared and spat up turf as he accelerated. The gunfire followed him as he broke cover, but he replied by pulling one of the Sigs from his waistband and emptying a magazine at the four shooters. As they dived for cover behind large stone pots that stood at the edge of the patio, Pearce aimed the quad bike directly at them, dropped the positive and negative battery wires into the fuel tank and jumped clear.

The raw power source ignited the petrol in the tank and the quad caught fire and then exploded when it collided with one of the large pots. Pearce was blown back by the force of the blast, and large chunks of stone flew everywhere, landing heavily on the lawn all around him. His head ringing, his heart thumping, Pearce rolled to his feet and saw three bodies splayed on the patio, their limbs contorted in unnatural shapes. The fourth man was dragging himself along the rough slabs on his belly. Pearce strode towards him, his mind full of memories of Fozz and Wayne. They'd survived the battlefield only to be killed in peacetime by these scum. The faces of his comrades mingled with the hundreds of children at Hill Manor. He reloaded his Sig and shot once, sending the wounded paramilitary on his way.

Pearce ran to the patio doors, but they were locked. He took a step back and shot, but the bullets didn't penetrate and instead lodged in the pane at the heart of small webs of shattered glass. Bulletproof. Pearce kicked the door, but the frame was reinforced. He heard the deep hum of engines behind him and saw three quads crest the low rise, heading directly for him.

Shouts came from somewhere nearby and Pearce heard the thump of boots on stone. He didn't have much time. He glanced up and saw an open window on the second floor, three or four rooms east of his position. He sprinted and leaped up to grab the ledge that ran around the first floor. His wrists screeched painful disapproval, but he pulled himself up and took hold of a gargoyle that sprouted from a column. He hauled himself over the ledge and stood on it, catching his breath for a moment and resting his pained arms, before setting off again. He clambered up deep grooves etched in either side of the column. Now above the security lights, Pearce was cloaked in shadow, and the men approaching on their roaring quads couldn't see him. Others ran round the house and joined them, equally blind to his location.

Leaning back, Pearce grabbed the windowsill and carefully

and quietly climbed up and over, dropping silently into the dark room on the other side. He swung the windows shut, locked the latch and pulled the curtains, as the men below conferred and started searching for him. As he crossed the room, Pearce's eyes grew accustomed to the dim light and among the shapes and shadows of bedroom furniture, he saw movement.

'Who's there?' a woman's voice asked, as a bedside light illuminated the room.

Pearce froze, his anger rising as he realized the figure sitting up in bed was Alexis. He pulled his rifle from his shoulder and aimed it directly at her.

'I'm sorry,' she said. 'I'm so sorry. I really am.' She slid out of bed slowly. She was in her underwear and there was a bandage over her shoulder. 'I cut it out. As soon as I got my hands on a knife, I found it and I cut it out.' She was referring to the tracking device. 'I didn't know. I swear. They must have drugged me when they put it in. I'm so sorry.'

Pearce wavered. If she was lying, she was one of the most convincing actors he'd ever encountered.

'I was telling the truth,' she continued, moving to pick up a dress that was slung over the back of a chair. 'Purbeck threatened to kill my mother if I didn't do what he said. I should have told you he was my father. But I'm so ashamed. He's ruined my life. He's been using me and now he's made me an accomplice to murder. I can't live with this.' She started crying as she slipped the pale green dress over her head. 'I never wanted anyone to get hurt.'

'You're a good liar,' Pearce responded coldly.

'I'm telling the truth,' Alexis protested. 'I've spent half my life wishing I'd never been born and the other half wishing he was dead.'

'I can fix that,' Pearce replied, his finger tightening around the trigger.

'Please,' Alexis implored. 'You have to believe me. I'm a victim in all this.'

'Where is he?' Pearce asked.

'He has a panic room off his study. I'll show you,' Alexis said, moving towards the door.

'Slowly,' Pearce instructed.

She nodded as she opened the door cautiously.

They stepped into an empty corridor and crept silently along a deep-pile carpet until they reached a staircase that wound down to the floor below. All around, portraits of Oxnard-Clarke's ancestors frowned at them. The whole time, Pearce found himself questioning why Alexis's window had been the only open one, and why she'd been asleep despite the gunfire and commotion outside. He couldn't help but feel he'd been meant to find her and that he was being manipulated. Was she really a victim or a conspirator? Finally, they reached the vast galleried landing that formed a horseshoe around the huge entrance hall.

'Stop,' he told Alexis. 'I'm going on alone. Where is he?'

'Please,' she responded. 'I know you can't ever trust me again, but I'm not safe here. I need your help. I need you to kill my father. It's the only way I'll ever be free. The only way my mother will ever be free.'

'Where is the panic room?' Pearce pressed.

Alexis's face fell. 'The study is two doors along from the sitting room. The panic room is concealed behind the bookcase to the left of the window and the keypad is under the desk. Four, six, two, nine opens it.'

Pearce approached Alexis. He wanted to kill her, but if she

was genuine, she was as much a victim as everyone else. He'd get to the truth later.

'Please,' she pleaded with tears in her eyes.

Pearce raised his rifle high above his head and drove the stock into her face, knocking her cold. As her eyes rolled back and she fell to the floor, Pearce sensed movement to his right and turned to see the Scarred Man barrel through an open doorway, his partially melted face contorted in rage.

Pearce tried to get the muzzle down, but he was too slow and the Scarred Man swept the gun aside as he charged. Pearce had no time to brace and was startled to find himself thrown, the momentum hurling him against the balustrade. With an almighty push, the Scarred Man forced Pearce over, and he dropped the AR-15 on the balcony. He heard it clatter against the hardwood floor as he fell towards the marble slabs sixteen feet below. He tried to turn, but it had happened so fast, and all he could take in was the contorted face of the Scarred Man scowling down triumphantly as he hit the cold, hard floor.

Chapter 60

'He's very protective of Alexis,' Oxnard-Clarke said. 'And he's upset you killed his comrades.'

Badly winded and dazed, Pearce lifted his head and saw the viscount emerge from a doorway two along from the grand sitting room. He carried his shotgun and Pearce saw the brass caps of two shells shining in the open barrel. 'Hector was once a soldier like you. He has a very strong sense of honour.'

As his senses returned, Pearce became aware of movement around him and turned to see three suited men, fit as butcher's dogs, lurking in nearby doorways, pistols drawn. Behind him, four Black 13 mercenaries in camo gear came running through the front door.

Pearce needed to be sharp. He rolled onto his belly and slapped his hand against the chill stone floor, sending an electrifying jolt of pain up his arm. As he pushed himself onto one knee, there was movement above him. The Scarred Man, Hector, jumped onto the balustrade and then leaped down, landing near Pearce with the grace of a large cat. He certainly had the eyes of a predator and stared at Pearce with all the hate the world had to offer.

'Hector served in some of the same places as you. His face was a gift from some Iraqis. It changed the way he saw the world,' Oxnard-Clarke said, as Hector circled Pearce. 'You should have joined us, Mr Pearce. You have the necessary credentials. You've doubtless heard of Group 13, Special Air Service. Black 13 is our own bulwark. We step in when no one else can. We are the honour guard, this country's last line of defence.'

'Men like you use honour to cloak all kinds of evil. You're not defenders. You're not soldiers. You're nothing. Sutton's finished. You're finished,' Pearce responded, rising to his feet. The floor seemed to shift beneath him and he tried to recall whether he'd hit his head when he landed. His situation was dire enough without the added complication of concussion. 'Your plan failed. Even if I die, you'll be unmasked as the mastermind.'

'Mastermind!' Oxnard-Clarke sneered. 'People like you never see the bigger picture. Do you have any idea the trouble you've caused? You've set us back years!'

Pearce looked from the arrogant peer to Hector, who was prowling the room like a fierce beast restrained by an unseen leash. Pearce's only consolation was that he still had his pistols hidden in his waistband.

'They were children,' Pearce said. 'Fucking kids. How twisted can you get?'

'Children of weak spineless people unwilling to defend their country,' Oxnard-Clarke responded angrily. 'Their parents, the whole country, would have finally woken up. They would have been galvanized to action. Their sacrifice would have given us strength. True soldiers do whatever is necessary.'

If nothing else, he would kill this hateful man. Pearce reached behind him, but was horrified to feel strong hands grab him. His senses were still dull and he'd been so focused on Oxnard-Clarke that he hadn't noticed two of the Black

Thirteen operatives close on him. They lifted his T-shirt and removed the pistols, and Pearce realized from the look in Hector's eyes that the man had something personal planned.

'You're going to have to do better than that to get to me,' Oxnard-Clarke scoffed.

Hector was about the same height as Pearce, but was carrying more weight, probably an extra twenty kilos of muscle. Pearce turned to assume a fighting stance, but was acutely aware of how tender and sore his arms still were beneath the bandages. Added to that was a pain in his back and tightness in his chest, more recent consequences of the fall from the balcony. His head was fuzzy, his senses dull and his reactions slow.

As if to prove a point, Hector stepped to him and feigned with his left before snapping out a powerful right cross that caught Pearce on the cheek. Flashes of light flared at the edges of his vision and he fell to his knees, the world swimming around him.

'You're going to go out the same way Nathan Foster did, lying at my feet, helpless and pathetic,' Hector said, and Pearce realized that this hideous man was one of the two figures that had watched Fozz die. 'He put up more of a fight than you.'

'Hector is angry that so many of our friends and comrades died for nothing,' Pearce heard Oxnard-Clarke say, but he had no idea which of the careening, shimmering shapes was the source of the plummy voice.

A sudden blur and Pearce was hit by another heavy blow to the top of his head. He went down hard, catching his chin on the marble floor. His teeth clattered painfully and darkness vied with light at the encroaching limits of his vision.

Pearce suddenly found himself back on the sheer cliff face, high above the bright blue sea off the Thai coast. He was hanging a few feet from the summit of Kok Arai, his hand in the beautiful, wide horizontal crack. Then he was falling, tumbling down towards darkness, but something stopped him and he looked up to see a pair of hands holding each wrist. Above him, smiling down, were the faces of Nathan Foster and Wayne Nelson. Good men. Brave men. His friends. His brothers-in-arms.

Then they were gone and Pearce found himself rising. He felt rather than saw another attack. His vision was badly blurred, but he hurried back, stepping clear of a combination of kicks and punches. He heard Hector exhale loudly with each missed effort, and sensed the man's powerful limbs around him. Pearce kept moving until the attack ended. A large shape stopped a few feet away and shifted slightly.

Pearce's eyes kicked back in and his vision crystallized the sharp edges of the world. The indistinct lump he'd assumed was Hector became clear and Pearce saw surprise on the big man's face as he squared up across the marble floor. Hector had thought the fight won and his enemy vanquished.

Pearce raised his hands and tucked his chin into his chest. He wasn't going down again. Hector came at him with a couple of rapid jabs, which Pearce ducked. A right hook caught Pearce's left arm, electrifying him with pain. He stepped inside the blow and stamped on Hector's left foot, but the guy was wearing steel toe caps and felt nothing. He launched a vicious headbutt, which Pearce saw coming. He stepped back and swung his fist into Hector's nose, landing an uppercut that would have put most people on the deck.

Hector staggered away as Pearce tried to shake off the pain

in his wrist. His arms were in no state for such punishment, but seeing his opponent dazed, Pearce changed tack and launched himself at Hector, lashing out with a side kick that caught the muscular man in the kidney. He followed up with a high kick to the chin and saw Hector's eyes lose focus for a moment. A roundhouse to the side of Hector's head was partially blocked by the man's raised elbows, but enough of it connected to knock him off-balance, and Pearce ran at the man, punching him in the kidneys. Each punch hurt Pearce terribly, but he could feel his opponent being worn down. Hector tried to fight back, but his efforts were ineffectual and Pearce grabbed him and delivered a knee to the groin. He went for another, but Hector caught him with a punch to the larynx and Pearce staggered back, choking.

He felt the men around the vast room closing in, but Hector, who was hunched double, waved them back. Pearce could tell that this contest had become a point of honour for the Scarred Man. He also knew that his opponent would have been better off letting these men kill him. There was no way he was losing this fight. There was too much at stake. Men like this must never win.

Pearce sucked in a deep breath and stepped forward. Hector managed to get himself partially upright and stepped back warily. Pearce moved quickly and landed a front kick on Hector's left knee, knocking him off-balance. He followed with a side kick to Hector's other leg, catching him just behind the right knee. As Hector went down, Pearce leaped forward and delivered a storm of jabs and hooks that left his adversary reeling. Hector's arms flailed wildly, but he was punch drunk and running on automatic. Alive with adrenalin and the scent of victory, Pearce clapped Hector's ears between his palms and then made a long fist and drove the heel of his right hand into the man's nose, shattering it and sending shards of bone into Hector's brain, killing him instantly.

There were sharp intakes of breath around the room, and Oxnard-Clarke made a choking sound. None of them had expected the fight to turn so quickly. Pearce stepped back, his arms screaming pain. Shocked silence surrounded him as Hector fell forward and blood oozed from his nose and mouth and spread across the veined marble.

Pearce heard a loud snap and wheeled round to see Oxnard-Clarke raise his shotgun. The man's face glowed with fury and his eyes betrayed murderous hatred. He opened his mouth a couple of times, but whatever words were on his mind stayed trapped there. He could only look from Pearce to Hector's corpse with a growing sense of rage.

The other men in the room all had their weapons trained on Pearce.

'You . . .' Oxnard-Clarke managed at last, and Pearce found himself staring down the twin barrels of the viscount's shotgun. 'I'm going to—'

'No,' another voice cut him off.

It was Alexis. Pearce looked up to see her coming down the stairs, holding his AR-15. She waved the gun around the room and finally settled on Pearce.

'This is my mess,' she said. 'I'll clean it up. Go,' she gestured to the suited bodyguards and members of Black 13. 'Leave us.'

They looked at Oxnard-Clarke, who nodded.

As the men withdrew, Pearce stared at Alexis, holding her gaze as she kept the gun trained on him, her eyes meeting his over the AR-15's long barrel. Finally, when they were alone, Oxnard-Clarke lowered his weapon.

'Make him pay,' the aristocrat said. 'Do it, Alexis.'

Pearce watched Alexis tighten her grip on the trigger. One, two, three steps and he could maybe disarm Oxnard-Clarke, but the viscount had the benefit of fury on his side and Pearce was injured and exhausted. Besides, Alexis would probably kill him before he made it across the room. Still, some hope was better than none, and he couldn't go out without a fight. Pearce was about to make his move, when Alexis squeezed the trigger.

Pearce stiffened as the bullet hit its target.

To his complete shock, she'd shifted her aim and had shot her father, catching him in the gut. Tears rolled down her cheeks as the man collapsed, his shocked eyes never leaving her.

'Lexi,' he said in disbelief, raising his gun at her.

'I'm ...' she sobbed, 'I'm making it right. This is the only way.'

A flicker of something – resignation, perhaps – passed over Oxnard-Clarke's face and he lowered his weapon with a sense of acceptance.

A second shot echoed off the walls of the cavernous room as Alexis shot her father in the chest. The bullet tore through his ribcage and lodged itself somewhere deep inside, killing him instantly. He toppled forwards, falling a few feet from Hector.

The only sounds to be heard were Alexis's sobs and the heavy beat of an old grandfather clock.

Alexis looked at Pearce. 'I told you to trust me,' she said at last.

The woman had killed her father to save his life. He hobbled over to her and tried to take the gun, but she brushed
him away.

'No,' she told him. 'You have to go,' and she looked at him
with intense, almost crazed eyes. 'Hector takes the blame.' She
wiped the trigger guard and stock on her dress as she walked
to the fallen man. 'I had to do it,' she said, placing the weapon
in Hector's hand. 'I had to free my mother, free myself . . .'
she tailed off into more sobs.

'I'm sorry,' Pearce said, taking her in his arms. 'Thank you.'

She stepped away and pushed him towards the door. 'Go,'
she told him. 'His men will be back soon. I'll tell them you
overpowered me.'

Pearce hesitated, wondering what he could say to someone
who'd made such a sacrifice. The taking of a life was never
easy. Taking the life of a parent, no matter how twisted, must
have been terrible.

'Go,' she said.

He nodded and set off at a run. Before he left the building, Pearce glanced back and saw the beautiful, slight woman
standing between the two fallen bodies. He turned and
sprinted into the night.

Epilogue

What truth lies in our hearts?

Leila pondered the question as she watched hundreds of people mill around the lawn outside Purbeck House. The place looked like a magical wonderland. Paper lanterns were strung across the gardens, the soft light at their hearts glowing gently like hundreds of distant stars. Waiting staff wove around the glamorous guests, keeping them well supplied with drinks and food. Leila had been surprised to receive an invitation at her home address. It had been forwarded by Six, which meant someone had pulled some strings to get it to her, and curiosity had made her accept.

It had been ten weeks since Pearce had escaped from the house and in that time, Wayne had been buried. Still grieving, Melody had returned to Denton Fraser with a commendation from the Home Office for her role in bringing down Oxnard-Clarke. Used to operating in the shadows, Leila, Pearce and Wollerton were happy for Melody to take such credit as could be publicly given. The commendation had led to the Solicitors Regulatory Authority dropping its investigation into her conduct, and Denton Fraser had talked of making her junior partner. Instead, Melody had quit, taking great satisfaction in hand-delivering her resignation to her boss, Michael Norton. She'd told Leila that she was through being exploited by others. She and Gabriel Walker's wife, Jessica, were in the early stages of setting up a charity in Gabriel's name, dedicated to fighting extremism.

Melody wasn't the only one whose life was changing. Leila had put her house on the market. It didn't matter that Oxnard-Clarke and his cohorts were either dead or facing trial, her sanctuary had been violated and she needed to find somewhere new. Somewhere she could feel safe.

Leila leaned on her cane as she crossed the lawn, weaving around the guests in her long black halterneck dress. She caught snatches of conversation, all centred on the scandalous death of Oxnard-Clarke and the equally questionable circumstances of his previously unknown daughter's inheritance. The official story was that Oxnard-Clarke had become embroiled with right-wing extremists led by Hector Drake, a disillusioned former soldier. After Melody had used social media to expose Progress Britain, the viscount had tried to free himself from their grip, and had been murdered by Hector as punishment. Hector had been killed by one of the viscount's bodyguards after the shooting. Alexis, the grieving daughter and, as it transpired, the sole heir to Purbeck House and the entire Oxnard-Clarke fortune, said that on the night of the killings she'd been in her flat in Regent's Park.

Thanks to Pearce, Leila knew that Alexis's official statement was a lie, and she wondered how much of the rest of the official account was a work of fiction. Sutton and his funereal assistant, Swan, had been arrested and were currently facing multiple criminal charges. They claimed to have had no knowledge of the attack on the school, and said they'd been hoodwinked into believing Progress Britain was simply a think tank and pressure group.

Eager to draw a line under an ugly political scandal and the fallout from the attack on Hill Manor, the authorities had accepted the official account of Oxnard-Clarke and Hector Drake's deaths. But Leila knew there was something more.

She had subsequently returned to Vasylyk's office, but it had been gutted and the photon communicator was gone. She'd searched police and security service logs and discovered that it had been taken away by GCHQ for further study. Leila recalled the day she'd killed Vasylyk and couldn't help but feel there was a missing piece to the puzzle, that it wasn't quite as perfectly formed as everyone else believed. The machine had been receiving orders from someone who had not yet been identified, suggesting there were others behind Vasylyk. She hadn't shared her concerns with Pearce. She didn't want to admit her role in Vasylyk's death. Not yet. Not until she had something more than speculation. She would keep watch on GCHQ and see if its research into the machine led to who-ever was sending Vasylyk orders.

Leila drifted through the party, moving from the edge of one group to another, never fully engaging in conversation, always listening, soaking up the gossip of the great and the good. Finally, Leila found herself on the far side of the south lawn, where she saw a small group set apart from all the rest. The Honourable Alexis Tippet-Jones, now Viscountess Purbeck, was standing beneath a huge oak tree with three others. As she drew near, Leila realized she recognized all of Alexis's companions. There was her mother, Willow Tippett-Jones, a woman who looked as though she'd floated through a thousand such gatherings. Standing next to her was Philippe Durand, Willow's conceited second husband, and beside him was Evangeline Lewis, the new Minister of State for Security and Economic Crime.

'I was very sorry to hear what happened to your father,' Leila heard Evangeline say as she neared. 'It's far too easy for extremists to operate beneath the radar. And the hold they can have on people is quite disturbing.'

Leila hovered a short distance from the group.

'Thank you. It was terrible,' Alexis said. 'I feel as though it's cast a great cloud over the family name.' She caught Leila's eye and acknowledged her with a slight nod. 'Ms Nahum, do join us. I'd like to introduce you.'

Leila drew near and smiled and shook hands, as Alexis introduced her to the others as an old friend.

'We were just talking about my father,' Alexis explained.

'You shouldn't feel bad,' Evangeline said with a reassuring smile. 'Your father's crimes were nothing to do with you.'

'I appreciate your kind words, Minister, but I want to erase my father's mistakes,' Alexis said. 'If you ever have the time, I would love the opportunity to talk about how I can use my wealth to help. Any programmes you feel are important or social initiatives that need extra funding.'

Evangeline smiled. 'That's very generous. I'll be sure to make time.'

'Ms Lewis, I'd like to introduce you to a few more people before they've drunk too much champagne to remember their own names,' Willow said. 'Alexis, darling, do mingle. This is your party after all.'

'Of course, Mother,' Alexis replied. She kissed her mother and stepfather and shook Evangeline's hand.

The small group departed and Leila listened to Willow babble masterfully, talking to Evangeline about nothing and everything, dangling the keys to her social kingdom at this recently promoted newcomer.

'I'm so glad you could come,' the newly created Viscountess said. 'Where's Scott?'

'He sends his apologies,' Leila said, looking across the garden at the huge hall. Wealth billions of people could only ever dream of.

'Maybe another time,' Alexis said. 'I never got the chance to thank him properly.'

'He told me what you did,' Leila responded. 'It took courage. He owes you his life.'

'I'd like to think my father wasn't evil, that he was a good man who lost his way, but it's difficult. I lived with his cruelty for years. He wasn't pimping me out like the others, but he forced me to pretend to be a courtesan to keep an eye on them all. And he used me to spy on Vasylyk. He didn't trust anyone. He really did threaten to kill my mother if I didn't do exactly what he said at all times. He was a tyrant. I should have told Scott . . . someone . . . I should have told someone the truth, but I was so scared. I was so scared of him.'

'I'm sorry,' Leila said. 'I understand the horror of being forced to make the choice you made. No matter how evil they are, it stays with you. It stays with you because you're not like them.'

Alexis nodded. 'Thank you.' She took Leila's hand and held it. 'That means a lot to me.'

They shared a brief moment of reflection before Alexis stepped away.

'If you'll excuse me,' she said. 'I must circulate.'

She smiled graciously and turned towards the house. Leila watched for a while and then began the long walk back to her car.

*

Clad in black, with a ski mask pulled tight over his head, Pearce scaled the wall and dropped over the other side. He ran between the high palms and across the large lawn, heading for the sprawling house that lay at the heart of the vast Santa Barbara estate. Somewhere in the distance, the Pacific Ocean crashed against the California coastline.

He encountered the first body in the drive by the Maybach. Pearce crouched and checked the man's pulse: steady and strong. He hurried on, up the steps and through the front door, which was wide open. Two more bodies. Unconscious men in suits who'd been paid to protect the man who owned the house. They'd almost certainly lose their jobs, but Pearce found it hard to feel sorry for their failure.

He checked the huge living room. There, lying in front of the huge windows that overlooked the Pacific, was one of the drones Wollerton had remotely piloted into the property. The gas canisters beneath the tiny machine's fuselage had discharged their contents throughout the house. Kolokol-1 was a synthetic opioid, the fastest knockout drug in the world, with a reaction time of under five seconds. Pearce left the room and ran upstairs, passing another unconscious bodyguard on the landing. A second drone had fallen beside him and this one looked as though it had been shot down.

Pearce ran into the master bedroom and finally found the unconscious man he was looking for. Huxley Blaine Carter, one of the richest people in the world. Huxley wore a short-sleeve white linen shirt and tan chinos. A pistol lay on the ground a few inches from his motionless hand, and Pearce guessed he was the one who'd shot the drone.

A Silicon Valley billionaire, the creator of HBC, an online payment system, and an investor in a multitude of hugely

successful tech start-ups, Huxley had a personal fortune estimated by *Forbes* at thirty-five billion dollars. By all accounts, he
was an eccentric genius, and Pearce believed him to be Gabriel
Walker's mysterious client. He grabbed the unconscious billionaire, slung him over his shoulder and carried him out.

The warehouse was a twenty-minute drive inland, and Wollerton was ready to open the door when Pearce rolled up in
the Maybach. He steered the car to the centre of the vaulted
building as Wollerton slid the door closed behind him. Pearce
dragged Huxley off the back seat and pulled him over to a
chair he'd set up near a medical trolley. The syringe case
full of Evil lay on the stainless steel surface. Pearce propped
Huxley up and shook him.

'Wake up,' he said, as Wollerton wandered over. 'Wake up.'

Huxley stirred.

Wollerton put on a ski mask and joined Pearce, as their
prisoner opened his eyes.

'How did you know about the bank?' Pearce growled.

Huxley swayed and stuck his hands out unsteadily. Pearce
pushed him back into the chair.

'How did you know about the bank?' he repeated.

'Scott Pearce,' Huxley slurred, smiling like a drunk who'd
just found a fresh bottle of single malt. 'Is that you? How did
you find me?'

Pearce looked at Wollerton uncertainly and then removed
his ski mask. His former mentor did likewise.

'I didn't know what you looked like,' Huxley observed. 'But
I do now.'

'How did you know about the bank?' Pearce pressed.

'I know things. I hear things,' Huxley replied. 'Technology

gives up all our secrets. Is this about your friends? I'm sorry about what happened to them.'

'So you did know what was happening?' Pearce remarked. 'You put us in this mess, and you did nothing to help us.' He punched the man in the ribs.

Huxley cried out. 'How could I help? My life would have been at risk.'

'My friends lost theirs,' Pearce said fiercely, punching the man in the face. He'd promised himself he wouldn't lose his temper, but seeing this entitled fool and hearing his feeble excuses was too much to bear. He grabbed Huxley and shook him. 'My friends died.'

'I'll take care of their families,' Huxley offered.

'Money,' Pearce sneered. 'You think you can fix everything with money?'

Huxley groaned and nursed his bloody nose. 'I deserved that. I'm sorry about your friends, but I've gotta know, how did you find me?'

'The newspapers,' Wollerton replied. 'Gabriel Walker had copies of the *Santa Monica Daily Press* in both his houses. We thought it was strange for Walker to be so obsessed with his home-town newspaper, so we took a closer look.'

'It's a shame about Gabe. I never thought he'd . . .' Huxley began wistfully. His momentary sentimentality evaporated. 'He wasn't supposed to keep anything, but I suppose it was the lawyer in him. Got to have a paper trail somewhere.'

'You were using an old NSA cipher to send coded messages in the classifieds,' Pearce continued. 'When I found out that you and Gabriel had both been to Crossroads, the same school in Santa Monica, and that the *Daily Press* is owned by one of your holding companies, it seemed a good bet you were the elusive client who'd instructed him. Then I discovered that a former NSA director, Robert Clifton, sits on the board of three of your companies. Word to the wise: old NSA ciphers will get you found and killed. The world has moved on.'

'Indeed,' Huxley said. 'Are you going to kill me?'

'We're going to give you some medicine,' Pearce said, indicating the syringe case. 'Find out exactly who you are and what you know.'

'I wouldn't do that.'

A familiar voice came from the back of the warehouse and Pearce looked up to see the woman he knew as Brigitte Attali step from the shadows. She was holding a Heckler & Koch MP7 sub-machine gun.

'The DGSE fired me,' she said. 'But you were right. It was remarkably easy to get another job. Move back,' she commanded with a wave of the gun.

Pearce and Wollerton complied, and Huxley staggered to his feet.

'I keep tabs on people with certain backgrounds. I hired . . . I believe you know her as Ms Attali . . . to watch me because I knew that if you were half the man I hoped you were, you'd find me. I don't think either of us expected you to do it quite so quickly.' He paused. 'I really am sorry about your friends,' he said. 'And I am going to make it up to their families with money, because that's the only thing I can do.'

'And us?' Pearce asked.

'I'd like to make it up to you, too,' Huxley replied. 'When Ms Gold hired you, you were investigating a link between Islamabad and Thailand.'

'How do you know about that?'

'It's the reason you were fired from MI6,' Huxley told him. 'It's out there.' He raised his hands, and his fingers danced theatrically. 'It's in the ether. I'd like to pay you for your work, and your associates of course –' he nodded at Wollerton – 'and I'd like to hire you to continue your investigation. Find out what really happened in Islamabad. Find the people really pulling the strings.'

'Are you crazy?' Pearce said.

'That's between me and my therapist,' Huxley replied. 'Listen, if I wanted you dead, I'd have already asked Ms Attali to shoot you. You did a good thing at that school, and I'd like to pay you to do other good things.'

Pearce looked at Wollerton, who curled his lip and shrugged.

'Like you said, the world has moved on,' Huxley said. 'The Hyperloop, space exploration, vaccines, military contracts – grand public initiatives that were once the preserve of governments are now in private hands. What about espionage? Why can't we play the game free of bureaucracy? Free of political interference? With an unlimited budget?'

'I want to know who you are,' Pearce said. 'Who you really are.'

'There'll be time enough for that, but right now, I've got a crushing headache.' Huxley started walking towards his car.

'Don't move,' Pearce commanded.

'She'll shoot you,' Huxley said without looking back.

'I will,' Brigitte confirmed.

'I'll leave you three to get acquainted,' Huxley said.

'Excuse me?' Pearce responded.

'Ms Attali is a useful asset. You'll work well together,' Huxley replied. 'And don't worry, I'll drive myself home.'

Pearce searched his mentor's face for guidance.

'It beats going back to that empty house and listening to the sea,' Wollerton said.

Pearce wasn't so sure. He didn't like being played, particularly not by someone as entitled and arrogant as Huxley.

'Listen to your friend, Mr Pearce,' Huxley said as he opened the Maybach's door. 'After all, the game has only just begun.'

Author's Note

Unless you've been stuck in a cave, you're probably one of the many people who feels we're living in strange times. I've spent over two years researching this book, and there is much of that research I couldn't share in *Black 13* – suffice to say that while the book is entertainment, some of it is inspired by real events.

Social media has removed any barriers between us and those who would seek to manipulate us. We have all become pawns in a geopolitical game and our opinions and allegiances are being shaped by people who have their own agenda. *Black 13* focuses on the far right, but in the real world it is a long-established espionage tactic to fund both sides in any political conflict to sow dissent and create chaos. It also ensures an enemy will always have an ally, no matter which faction wins power.

No one on the extremes of the political spectrum is blameless and it is up to the majority to guard the middle ground. We need to start thinking the best of people, rather than letting division make us suspicious of one another. These divisions make easy work for those who would seek to undermine our way of life, and the threat they pose is very real. A classic technique of all extremists is to encourage their followers to think of their opponents as 'the other', to dehumanize them with labels. We see this dehumanization everywhere. Liberal. Conservative. Leaver. Remainer. These are just a few polite examples of words that are designed to divide communities and diminish those we disagree with. Such division and dehumanization is the first step towards an ugly world.

Words have power. I wrote this note a few days after pipe bombs were sent to Barack Obama, Hillary Clinton, CNN and many others. It is the day after the terrible attack on a Pittsburgh synagogue in which eleven people were killed. My condolences go out to the victims and their families.

Since I originally wrote this note, terrible tragedy has struck again, this time in Christchurch, New Zealand. Until extremism of all kinds is tackled, it is unlikely we'll see an end to such horrific violence any time soon. My sympathies and condolences go out to all those who've suffered the terrible consequences of hate.

These events haven't happened in a vacuum. In the UK, the rise of banned far-right group National Action has taken place against increasingly intolerant rhetoric about minority communities and the 'liberals' who supposedly enable them to undermine society. The people espousing such hateful views need to be aware that such rhetoric motivates a minority to take action.

While researching *Black 13*, in addition to talking to experts and members of far-right and far-left organizations, I undertook a live experiment, creating an anonymous social media account that posted on political issues. Within a week I had over 1,000 followers, including prominent journalists and politicians. Within ten days I had fed a story into a national broadsheet newspaper, which ran what I'd written almost word for word. I did this twice before shutting the account.

I have experienced exactly how easy it is to sway public opinion and my success scared me. I'm a private citizen, not a subversive organization or state actor, and I managed to influence the public with minimal effort and zero expenditure. We live in an era of preconception and belligerence and people are more interested in perspectives that validate their views than in engaging in genuine debate. This lack of open-mindedness makes us prone to manipulation, and even well-established news outlets aren't immune.

As a parent, the Hill Manor Primary School sequence was difficult to write, but I wanted to go to an uncomfortable place. Social media has placed civilians on the front line of espionage, making us all vulnerable to manipulation. In a similar way, we're now all on the front line of violence. Whether it's Islamic militants, far-right or far-left action groups, or state actors poisoning people with radiological or chemical weapons, the tools and techniques of the battlefield are increasingly finding their way onto our streets and into our places of work, worship and play. We need to be mindful that it isn't some distant enemy who will feel the consequences of hate. These ugly consequences will be felt by our neighbours and friends, by people who share the same simple desire to live a safe and happy life.

I've spoken to members of far-right and far-left organizations as part of my research for *Black 13*. Most of the people I've met are ordinary folk who feel pushed to extremes by a system they believe has failed them in some way. Some are not. Some are actively seeking to stir ideological and sectarian conflict. If recent history is anything to go by, unless we're careful and change the nature of political discourse, reclaim the middle ground and focus on what unites us, extremism and radicalization will become bigger problems across the political spectrum.

Acknowledgements

I'd like to thank my wife Amy and our three children Maya, Elliot and Thomas for their endless support.

My thanks also go to all the brave, dedicated people who contributed valuable insight to the book. You know who you are.

I'm extremely grateful to my magnificent editor, Vicki Mellor, for helping shape *Black 13*. I'd also like to thank my literary agent, Hannah Sheppard, whose guidance and wisdom are proving invaluable. Thanks also go to my screen agent, Christine Glover, who I consider a rock star in the film and TV world. I'm extremely grateful for all the hard work and support from the whole team at Pan Macmillan. Thanks to Fraser Crichton for being such a thorough copy editor.

I'd also like to express my thanks to Ruth Wollerton, who won a competition to name a character in this book. I'm honoured that she chose the name Kyle, in memory of her son, who sadly died of asthma aged nine. Ruth raises money for Asthma UK and has asked anyone so inclined to make a donation to support the good work done by the charity at www.asthma.org.uk.

I'd like to offer a big thanks to all my friends and family. You've been incredible. I'm also extremely grateful for all the kind words and help I've had from so many writers who've generously shared their advice and experiences. I'd also like to thank all the reviewers, booksellers, journalists and readers who have helped spread the word about my books. I've made so many wonderful friends in the book world and deeply appreciate all the support.

Finally, I'd like to thank you, the reader, for giving Scott Pearce, Leila Nahum and the team your attention. I hope you enjoyed the book and that you'll join us for another thrilling adventure.